Praise for Malka Adler

'There's so much I could say and even more I can't express . . . An emotional gut-punch . . . It clawed my heart but made me count my blessings . . . a must read'
Glynis Peters, *USA Today* bestselling author of *The Secret Orphan*

'Great courage is needed to write as Adler does – without softening, without beautifying'
Yehudit Rotem, *Haaretz*

'This is a book we are not allowed not to read'
Leah Roditi, *At Magazine*

Also by Malka Adler

The Brothers of Auschwitz

THE POLISH GIRL

MALKA ADLER

Translated by
NOEL CANIN

One More Chapter
a division of HarperCollins*Publishers* Ltd
1 London Bridge Street
London SE1 9GF
www.harpercollins.co.uk

HarperCollins*Publishers*
1st Floor, Watermarque Building, Ringsend Road
Dublin 4, Ireland

This hardback edition 2022
1
First published in Great Britain in ebook format
by HarperCollins*Publishers* 2022

A catalogue record of this book is available from the British Library

ISBN: 978-0-00-852530-9

This is a work of fiction based on personal memories. Every reasonable attempt to verify the facts against available documentation has been made.

Printed and bound in the UK using 100% Renewable Electricity
by CPI Group (UK) Ltd

This book is dedicated to my husband, Dror,
who is always there for me.

Prologue

Hardest of all was when the Russians entered Kraków.

It happened to us at the end of the war, after Dr. Helmutt Sopp left the house. He went to live where he worked, at the hospital in Kraków. Mama said it was in the professor's best interests, and that the Nazis' good old days were over, just like a bad movie. Mama made Helmutt Sopp a professor, but according to his degree he was only a doctor. A psychiatrist and a Nazi officer in Hitler's army, but not a professor. I saw it on the letters he sent Mama after the war, when we were living in Haifa. On the envelopes he sent was written:

DR. MED. HELMUTT SOPP

Apart from that, I heard people calling him "Herr Doktor" when we were still living with him. For us he was the great savior. He was the director and responsible for Mama in Kraków. For me, he was tall, handsome, and a good man.

Mama was housekeeper to the Sopp family for two years. They hired her with special papers organized by Lydia, her big sister. Mama kept the name Anna, only changing her family name to Kwiatkowski, a Polish name that could save Jews from death. Thanks to Lydia's papers and Mama's working for the Sopp family, we were given a small room where we could live without fear of the cruel fate that could befall us every day, every hour, year after year.

When we learned that the Russians really were approaching Kraków, new instructions began arriving at the Sopp family's home in the city. Toni, Helmutt's wife, and their sons, Peter and Ammon, left for Germany as instructed. We remained in the house with Helmutt Sopp for another week or two and then, because of the new situation, as Mama said, Helmutt also left the house and went to live at the hospital.

We were left alone in the large, luxurious house, without the usual parties and without the protection of Helmutt and Toni Sopp, and then it was announced over the radio that the war was over.

One day—it was the month of February—the Polish landlords arrived. It happened after liberation, when the Russians were already in the streets of Kraków, lying there drunk, or wildly dancing the *kazachok* like crazy people. The landlords told Mama it was their house, and there were papers. They allowed us to stay until Mama could make arrangements. Mama thanked them and signaled to us with her eyes to go into the room and be quiet. The new landlords, a man, his wife, and a daughter who was older than me, immediately went into the landlords' wing. Mama, me, and my brother, who was a year and a bit younger than me, we disappeared into the servants' room adjoining the kitchen.

I was eight, the height of the door handle, tall and thin. Yashu was about seven, and Mama was forty and as beautiful as ever.

One day I heard the Polish girl ask her father: "How do you write *German*, with a capital letter or a small letter?"

"We write the names of all the nations with a capital letter, my daughter," he said, "except for the Jews. Jew is written with a small letter."

"Thank you, Father," said the girl politely and continued to write in her notebook.

I remember realizing at that very moment that all nations, all of them, were my enemies, and it didn't matter that the war was over, as they were saying everywhere. I said to myself, well, Danusha, you're worthless once again.

I also realized there was a world of many nations, and I was on the other side, having to hide on my side. And most of all, I understood that my mama and I were written with a small letter, that we didn't count.

I felt bad about it. This time I felt unworthy on a universal level, and it stuffed up my nose and burned my throat. Not even the mirror I loved helped me feel better. I was a very quiet, polite child with blue eyes and bronze colored hair; *how lovely*, people would say appreciatively. I still felt bad next to the new girl in the house and it didn't help that at six, I could already read in two languages, and it didn't help that Frau von Dorf, the piano teacher in Bad Pyrmont, said I was very musical.

As I remember, everything began in our small family. Only Papa was glad when I was born, but he disappeared after I turned five and if Mama decided that a girl didn't count, then that's what mattered to us.

A good mother dreams of a son for her first-born, not a daughter. She believed she'd have a first-born son who'd look like a privileged Polish officer, like her family before the war. She told her sisters that her first-born son would be very tall and good-looking, not a *Hassid*, a scholar, like her grandfather. Mama wanted a son who rode a noble horse, like the one she'd seen in her dream, the one she whispered about with her four sisters in the living room. Aharon, their younger brother, disappeared in the war. But who was the stronger sex in those days, who? The men hid or disappeared into the smoke or the wind, and the women survived. Who defeated my mama? Nobody, and not her four sisters either, who were as strong as the Rock of Gibraltar.

I was the first-born of a father who was a merchant from East Galicia, not an advocate from Lodz like my Aunt Franca had married, and granddaughter to Grandma Rosa, who was far happier with the advocate from Lodz. Grandma Rosa wasn't really happy with me. That's how I felt when I visited her in Kraków and played with my cousins. I felt that they, the children of the advocate from Lodz, were the really successful ones.

When the Polish landlord told his daughter that only *żyd* was written with a small letter, and all the other nations received a beautiful capital letter, I immediately understood that for me the war wouldn't end when the Russians entered Kraków.

And that's what happened.

Not everything was bad in the war.

Maybe it was because I was small, just two, when everything started.

When I was three, and four, and five, and later on too, there were sweet moments. Mama used to sing arias and parts of operas from early morning, and I'd beg, please, more, more. I didn't want her to stop the melodies. We had trips from one town to another, we met good people, and there was also a Tyrolean garden drawn on the sofas in the middle of the living room of that monster, Josef Wirth.

There was the good-looking Helmutt Sopp, amusing Toni, clean dresses to wear with matching ribbons in my hair. In the Sopp family's large house there was good food, the smell of spices in the kitchen, and "Frau Anna, *es schmeckt gut*—it tastes good". There were the friendly boys, Peter and Ammon, and a record player in the drawing room, and a pile of records; there were fresh rolls, wonderful tort, and ice-cream just like the movies. There was the newspaper, *Die Zeitung*. I learned to read on my own and there were beautiful books and important guests at elegant tables. There were drinks and delicacies and a lot of laughter. There was also an unusual liqueur, Mama's specialty, and marvelous singing by the men, *Oh, Wisła, Wisła*. Mama's cheeks were red. "Did you know that the name Kwiatkowski means flowers in German?" they'd say, and she was proud of the new name.

In the small room adjacent to the kitchen was a window overlooking the courtyard and there was a lilac tree there with heavily flowering branches, and the scent would keep me at the window for a long time.

Chapter One

My first memory is more or less from the age of two, maybe three. I'm sitting on a bed and standing opposite me is a young woman, her mouth half-open with large, protruding teeth. The woman is tying my bow and teaching me to say words in Russian.

"Boot Gatob," she commands, her fat fingers tapping my face.

I looked at the nail near my eyes and saw that it was small, swollen, and red all around. Another glance and I saw that all her fingers were the same, and she commanded me to say *Vsegda Gatob. V-se-gda G-at-ob. Vse. Vse.* Danusha. *Vse. Gda. Gaaa-tob.* Got it?

It was hard for me to repeat the words in Russian, but she didn't give up. She kept me there on the bed until we were both tired, me and the dog barking outside. The woman got up, saying, "A break now," and a few minutes later she lifted me off the bed and sat me down on the kitchen table.

"Don't move," she said and fetched a large loaf of bread. She ripped off a piece, dipped it into a pot of milk she had there, cut a large piece, and began to chew. Some of it inside and some of it outside her mouth. I'd never seen Mama eat like that. And then the woman said, "*Nu*, again, say *Vse. Vse. Gda. Gaaa-tob*."

Finally, I managed to say her words and she clapped her hands, turning to the older woman with holes in her face who sat on one side. The old woman took several dresses from a full sack standing beside her, shook them out, and placed them on her knees, and was pleased. She smiled such a broad smile that her eyes closed. The thin man standing beside her opening carton boxes remained serious.

Mama stood near the wall holding the new baby.

"This is your brother." She'd tried again and again to explain the wonder to me, and I wanted to stick my fingers in his eyes to stop them moving from side to side.

Mama pushed me away, "You mustn't," she scolded me.

"Hee, hee," the old lady shrieked joyfully as she pulled a thick, colorful sweater out of the sack, waving it back and forth in Mama's direction. Mama looked straight at me, her face silent, then she looked at Papa who was standing near the door and he slightly shook his head. I saw Papa's eyes shifting to me and he made a small, barely visible wave goodbye with his hand, and left our house.

"Come on," said the young woman, and gathering me up from the kitchen table, she took me into the large room.

I immediately felt the start of a celebration. Strangers were already seated at the table and dipping their hands into large bowls with food and a smell that wasn't familiar to me. Every time they raised their glasses high, they belched and spoke to each other in words I didn't understand. From their faces, I knew they were happy.

And then the young woman sat down, put me on her lap, and said: "Shhhh. Shhhh."

All at once there was silence. A woman with large brown eyes approached me, touched my face with her finger, and cried: "*Boot Gatob!*"

And in a flash, I sat up and shouted: "*Vsegda Gatob,*" and all the people laughed and laughed and made lots of noise. They pinched my cheeks, and gave me a candy when I held my cheeks so they wouldn't hurt. Even the large woman with the holes in her face was laughing at the noise.

This woman sometimes said things to my mama and Mama would immediately look down at the floor as if darkness was coming. But after I shouted the words in Russian the woman gave me a candy and laughed. I held it very tight, and from that day on I began to say *Vsegda Gatob* in the morning, *Vsegda Gatob* in the afternoon and *Vsegda Gatob* in the evening, and many other similar *Vsegda Gatob*s, especially when I saw the old woman with the holes in her face approaching Mama's ear and Mama not moving.

When I was twelve or maybe thirteen, I first heard Mama telling neighbors and admirers who'd gathered in our living room in Haifa about the old Russian woman from Tarnopol. At once I realized she was talking about the large woman with the holes in her face.

Mama spoke about her on many occasions, for many years, and in several languages. She spoke in Yiddish, German, Polish, and Hebrew and she went from one language to another depending on the people in the living room and how she was feeling. Apart from all these languages, she'd add words in French and English. And all that time, I'd sit to one side, gazing at Mama.

Erect in her chair, she'd sit with folded hands, speaking like an important actress. Her hair was tied back, and she had a high forehead, blue eyes, and a perfect, straight nose. She wore a long blue gown that matched her eyes, and she was as beautiful as a painting. Mr. Bogusławski, a neighbor on our floor and an engineer with connections at the Municipality, was an important monarch in our living room. He said Mama was as beautiful as Marlene Dietrich. Our friend, Bernard Cohen, from the building next door, who worked for the Egged Cooperative, would say, *Nonsense, she's as beautiful as Audrey Hepburn,* and then Mama would ask for quiet, *We're starting.*

The only argument in the living room in Haifa was who was Mama as beautiful as, who? Apart from that no one really interrupted her stories. Not one of the neighbors or acquaintances Mama invited to the living room missed an invitation to visit. They'd gaze at her, swallowing every word that came out of her mouth—even if she took a break to blow her nose, they didn't lower their eyes to the refreshments table, but I did.

In our living room, places were usually fixed and mainly men came. Three of the men were regulars: Mr. Bogusławski, whose wife didn't come because she had a migraine problem, Bernard Cohen, and Yozek Meltzer, a rather young bachelor who admired Mama. He had black hair combed back and long fingers. "Like a pianist's, definitely a Bohemian appearance," said Mama, but I knew he didn't stand a chance because he was her height.

My fixed place was a wooden chair to one side near the hall and kitchen. My brother Yashu's place was outside with his friends or at their homes. Sometimes I'd sit on the floor for a change, and it never bothered me to hear the same story over and over. There were times Mama would tell a story at least twice because one of the guests had gone away to rest at a Histadrut Sanatorium, which happened with Bertha Ketzelboim and her husband Jacob, a former athlete. They talked about her, saying she had a problem with her nerves, that they'd suddenly get bad and she'd need rest. There were some who were ill and needed a bed in hospital, and Mama didn't give up, everyone heard the story again and again—me, too, since I wasn't invited out by my classmates. Yashu's friends invited him almost every day. Mama received invitations at least twice a week, as far as I know, but I'm sure she received more and didn't talk about it.

"Valya taught our Danusha to say '*Vsegda Gatob*'," said Mama and she told the story about the Russian woman from Tarnopol whose family had taken our home.

"Valya was eighteen years old and as far as beauty went… so-so," she said. At the time the neighbors didn't know that Mama came from a family where beauty was a serious, often decisive affair.

Mama said that Valya was enchanted by her little girl, taking me on her lap, giving her a little flag to hold, and repeating the slogan of the Communist Youth League, "*Boot Gatob,*" which means "live ready," and the *kind* had to reply, "*Vsegda Gatob*" which means "always ready".

She told how Valya was head of the local branch of the Komsomol, the Communist Youth League, and from that day on she'd press Mama to bring me to evening parties that her parents, Yevdutya and Sasha Tarasova, held in our living room in Tarnopol.

It was 1939 when the Red Army entered Poland. The Russian

authorities took over our apartment in Tarnopol, Eastern Galicia. It was a new three-story building in a desirable quarter of the city, said Mama, and living there were Grandma Leah on Papa's side, Papa's brother Gustav and his family, and my family. According to Mama we lacked for nothing and life was very good. Mama didn't say that Papa would go to his mother, Grandma Leah, to eat before coming home and she'd get mad—I heard all about it later on when Mama was talking to her sisters.

The guests heard from Mama in the living room in Haifa that our family had a large haberdashery store in Tarnopol—men's shirts, collars for men's shirts, and sewing supplies. Everyone knew the store. The Russians also took over the store at the beginning of the war, but Papa managed to save some of the stock and used it to barter for food supplies.

Yevdutya, Valya's mother, was active in the Communist Party. "She had a high rank—she was a Commissar," said Mama, "and the Russian military gave her our home in recognition. Yevdutya, with her daughter Valya and her husband Sasha, took over our apartment on the third floor. She took the large living room and adjacent room for herself, and we were left with a bedroom and a room for the children. The kitchen, bathroom and toilet were communal. Yes, that's what happened when the Russians entered Poland," said Mama in the living room in Haifa and, in a flash, pictures of the Russians on the first day came back to me:

It is a gray cloudy morning. Mama is at her pots in the kitchen. Papa leaves for the store in a suit. Baby Yashu is asleep in his cradle. I'm playing quietly on the carpet with a big doll and a few pans and spoons, trying to think what to cook that day. I tell the doll, *Open your mouth, eat, eat,* and she doesn't open her mouth and I can't push anything in. I push the spoon in again, and then I hear a loud knock at the door. Boom. Boom.

And from that moment on, strangers come to live in our home. They wander around our home all day, talking in loud voices; I don't understand anything they're saying. They come into the kitchen a lot and eat at our table. They sleep in our beds every night, and then other strangers come along, come in, go out, day and night, eating and drinking; they're happy, and they use our toilet a lot. All the time the door would open and close, open and close. Mama starts cleaning the toilet every time she or I want to sit.

"Danusha," she'd whisper to me, "Danusha," and she'd lift up the brush so I'd see what she was doing, "never sit down on the toilet without cleaning it with this brush, all right?"

At first, I was afraid of allowed-forbidden every moment in our house, but most of all I was afraid of the huge noise in the living room, and the people. Afterwards I got used to it. Papa and Mama didn't go and talk to the strangers; they stayed in the room with us.

In the meantime, I heard Mama telling stories in the living room, how Yevdutya, the woman with the scarred face, had apparently caught smallpox and probably scratched and scratched and ruined her face forever. This woman came and spoke to her about how our family's lives were in danger. She told her that the searches start at night, they take the boys and the men, it wasn't good for Papa to sleep at home, and he should leave and find himself a safe place. It's dangerous, she said to Mama, they do surprise searches for capitalists, too dangerous.

The guests in the living room laughed at how Mama imitated the voice of a Russian Commissar and moved in her chair like a huge, fat peasant. "Wait, wait," Mama asked the guests to be quiet, and added sadly that the Commissar told her, after a serious conversation with her skinny little husband Sasha: "You and your little ones should also leave the house," and the guests in the living room tensed.

Mama waved a hand and said, "The Commissar told me that in the meantime she'd be considerate. Only in the meantime, because it was winter and the children were small—Yashu was then just under a year old. At every opportunity, she'd remind me that capitalists like me and my husband, who lived at the expense of the citizens, should be deported to Siberia."

No one laughed anymore in the living room when Mama imitated the voice of the Commissar or her husband.

And this is what Mama told the guests:

"Sasha, Yevdutya's husband, who was several years younger and had sunken cheeks and black eyes that darted about in panic, would disappear at night and return in the morning laden with parcels of expensive groceries. Nobody saw things like that at the market—he brought real delicacies. One morning I was shocked, *Ich war Entsetzt*. Yes. Half a big pig lay in the middle of our kitchen table. Can you imagine what that was like for people who keep kosher? I asked him where he got the pig, and he told me that he and his friends from the Party do night searches in the homes of rich farmers in Tarnopol, the ones who'd got rich at the expense of the proletariat, and they empty their cellars."

Mama stopped and opened her fan. A flush appeared on her high cheeks.

People chuckled in the living room. Mr. Bernard Cohen, the war partisan, with fingers as fat as sausages, was angry with Sasha and his Party friends: "I know them," he said in a loud voice, "I know these communists very well. Thieves for the Proletariat, *Yobtbiomat*, damn them! I know them the best."

Klara Cohen, his wife, who sat nearby, said, "Enough, Bernard, enough. You're interrupting Anna."

"So why did he come?" whispered Bertha Ketzelboim, pinching her fingers.

"Because he can only talk about his life here at Anna's," said her husband Jacob, a certified electrician with the body of an athlete.

Mama smiled at Klara, as if she were allowing her husband his anger, and I was surprised that Klara didn't rub fish oil on the dry hair she had all over her head. Even at the Sopp house Mama would sprinkle a few drops of oil on her hair to make it shine.

In the meantime, I heard that Mama wasn't forgetting the infuriating Sasha. She said, "That Sasha, who took care of the Proletariat, wasn't too ashamed to wear my husband's elegant suit and go out into the street in the best fur coat he could find in our closet. Even his wife, the modest Commissar, fell in love with one of my evening gowns, a beautiful white silk gown, *nu*. She certainly didn't find a gown like that in the village she probably came from, not a chance. I saw her hands, hands that had picked many potatoes; she didn't stand a chance of even receiving or buying a gown.

"I'd bought the gown at the best store in Kraków and then suddenly I see her wandering around the house all day in my silk evening gown, as if she were waiting for a large party, *ein großer Ball*. It didn't stop her from approaching me and saying quietly, 'Get ready to leave, get ready. You're leaving in the spring.'"

Mama paused for a moment, deliberating whether or not to tell and placing her hand on her chest.

"Courage, Anna, courage." Mr. Bogusławski, our neighbor from the building, rose from his chair. "You have nothing to fear, Anna. Life moves, goes on, or however you say it," and he sat down again, the others seated there approving of his words.

Mama looked at him; like me, she probably saw that he suffered from a lot of red hair in his ears, "like a forest," I heard her once say to herself and I knew that she meant his ears, because he had almost nothing on his head.

"Courage, Anna, courage." He leaned towards her, and she didn't bat an eyelid. She said:

"It was winter outside then. Many days went by and I didn't do the white laundry. I put it off every day, afraid that the Commissar would covet it. I waited until the day she said, "I'm out all day, today." Only then did I take the laundry from its hiding place and, together with Stefa, my helper, we began to do the washing.

"And then the Commissar appeared, her hands on her hips. She stood beside the laundry tub making a black shadow on the whites. Quickly I stirred and rubbed the laundry as if I were washing it. In the meantime, I tried to hide the handkerchiefs and towels my mother had embroidered with the initials of our names at the bottom of the tub, as well as the tablecloths she'd embroidered in *petit point*, a particularly delicate form of embroidery, especially for my dowry. I took my time with the white laundry, the pajamas, robes, turning the sleeves inside out, rubbing, turning them back again, working down from collar to hem, turning them inside out and back again, while she? Not a word. She stood next to me with black eyes, moving her lips as if she were already dividing up the pile of whites—a lot for herself, a little for the others."

Mama was breathing heavily when she said in a low voice: "That night, it happened. All the beautiful white laundry that we'd hung up in the attic disappeared. Not even one embroidered handkerchief remained. The most painful thing was that not even one keepsake was left from Mama and Papa's home."

A bird flew past the shutters on the balcony, knocked into them, and the guests jumped. The sadness lingered, and they looked at the floor, ashamed of what had happened to Mama's white laundry. The cool air heralded the fall and Mama took an embroidered handkerchief out of her gown pocket, patted her neck gently, and then tucked the handkerchief into the palm of her hand.

And then she took a deep breath as if preparing to dive and said quietly, "Please, you're invited to have a glass of tea."

The guests got up to the refreshments table without their usual noise. There were plates of peanuts and pretzels and a tray of cocoa pastries. I didn't go up to the table.

I glanced at Mama. I saw she was very distant, like she was during the war.

Chapter Two

One morning, we left our home in Tarnopol. Papa and Stefa, the maid, went downstairs first with several suitcases. They returned to the apartment. Stefa picked up another suitcase, Papa lifted me high in the air, told me to hold on tight, picked up a suitcase, and I held him tight as he began to go down the stairs. Mama, with Yashu in her arms, went down slowly before us. The building was now empty. All Papa's family from the first and second floors had already left.

Stefa waited next to a horse and cart. Snow was melting in the streets as Mama arranged the suitcases in the cart. Papa gazed at the building, now empty of his entire family. I went to stand beside him as he gazed at each window in the building. He rubbed his eyes with his hand, each one in turn. I held onto the hem of his coat, waiting patiently like Mama for him to finish gazing at the windows.

Stefa wept into the sleeves of her coat. Wordlessly, Papa adjusted the arrangement of suitcases in the cart. Finally, he called us over; everything was ready for us to climb on. Mama got on first with baby Yashu. I followed. Stefa ran to Papa and sobbed on his wool coat. He patted her on the back and bit his lips. Mama watched, her back erect, her eyes distant. Then Papa gently pushed Stefa away, saying, "Look after yourself for better days, Stefa," and waved his hand.

It was crowded for the four of us in the cart even though baby Yashu was in Mama's arms. I asked to sit on Papa's lap, but he didn't hear me. He gazed at our house without taking his eyes off it even when the horse began to walk away. I turned round and waved my little flag at Stefa. When we left the street, Mama took the flag away from me and put it in her bag.

That afternoon we arrived at the home of a Polish family. We were given a large, new room. It was in Brzeżany. In the large room where I slept with Mama, Papa, and the baby, no one asked me to say new words like *Vsegda Gatob*, so I didn't say anything. There was a wide wooden desk, chairs, and a mirror on the wall. Two little birds that seemed like good friends looked out from the corners of the frame. I was afraid their chirping would wake Mama's baby, because she was always saying, "Be quiet, be quiet, can't you see that Yashu is sleeping?"

Fortunately, those birds never chirped once, even when I wanted them to and waited especially. I had plenty of time to wait for the chirping. I could wait whole days; outside was dangerous for children and our lives were only inside the house, only in the big room with the whole family, and with the mirror and the motionless birds in the corners of the mirror.

After a few days it got boring in the big room. I missed Valya and her teeth, and how she'd put me on her lap and teach me to say words in Russian. I didn't say I missed playing with Valya from Tarnopol; I didn't say anything, just waited for surprises that never came. Papa wasn't home and Mama's lap was filled with that baby who either cried or slept all the time. Sometimes, when Mama left the room, I'd go past him, passing my hand over his hair until I caught some in my fingers. He had very little hair but when he felt I'd grasped some he'd start screaming like mad. I'd leave immediately and walk away from him. When Mama came running into the room, I wasn't anywhere near him.

"What's wrong, what's wrong, my boy," she'd ask the screaming baby and I'd stand far away from them, enjoying the birds in the mirror. Sometimes I'd try and think of a quick question to ask her so she'd stay in the room, but she left the minute the baby stopped crying, and anyway, I could never think of questions quickly enough.

Once, when she left the room, I got up on the table, stretched out my hand and stroked the little birds. Their bodies were cold as ice and it was then I discovered a big face in the mirror.

I turned around. Nobody was there. I turned back to the mirror and saw big eyes, blue as Mama's, pink cheeks, and hair gathered up and tied with a broad ribbon like a butterfly on the head. Slowly I raised my hand and touched my head—was it mine? I put my fingers on the glass; it was as cold as the birds. I came back to the nose, the lips—could that be me?

I laughed quietly and raised my chin. The face moved backwards diagonally, and I thought it was lovely. And then I pressed chin to chest, slightly lifting my head, turned it to the right, the left, I looked at myself from the side until my neck hurt, and then I heard the baby gurgling in his cradle. I got down from the table and walked over to him. He looked and me and gurgled, "Gru, gru, grum." I touched his cheek with my finger, and he laughed at me, saying "Ba, ba, ba," holding out his hand to me. I said, "Ba, ba, ba," and went back to the mirror.

After that, whenever Mama left the room, I got up on the chair and then onto the table. I tilted my chin upwards and then glanced in the mirror, half smiling, like Mama. I immediately understood that it was special. I felt love for the face I saw. I'd already seen a similar face in all sorts of beautiful pictures of girls between forest and sky. I knew the girl in the mirror was me and wanted to know how I'd managed to get inside it. How did I manage to get from my place in the middle of the table to the mirror on the wall? I took two steps forwards and looked behind it. I didn't understand. Sometimes I'd gaze for half an hour, sometimes an hour, sometimes I'd only have a minute to look, but I didn't give up our meetings. It was my first and only friend. A good-hearted friend who was always there when I came and stayed until I left; she never went anywhere. We had a lot of time and were never disturbed. Papa left early in the morning, Mama went out to hang up the washing or to buy something, my brother Yashu was asleep, and the two of us played nicely together.

There were times I didn't want to go to the mirror.

Like the days Mama would come into the room. Maybe she'd come back from doing the laundry or some errand in town; sometimes it was at noon, or in the morning, we'd just woken up, my brother and I, and then she'd come into the room and go straight to Yashu's bed and stroke him, saying, "Good morning, my sweet boy, did you sleep well?"

At these moments I'd immediately approach Mama, hold onto her leg, and it didn't matter that she pushed me away. She'd rock Yashu in her arms and push me away. I didn't let go, until she'd say, "What's wrong with you? Leave me alone."

Papa would come in sometimes and Mama, who had Yashu in her arms most of the time, would say, "Papa Moshe, see what a big boy we have. Isn't he big?"

Yashu already understood a little and would bounce in her arms and call excitedly, *"Tata, Tata,"* and then Papa would put out his arms and take Yashu, kiss him on the cheek, and look at me. He'd quickly pull a chair towards me with his foot, sit on it with Yashu on his lap, and put his arm tightly around me. I wanted to stay like that till tomorrow. But it was over very quickly. Papa would leave the house, followed by Mama. I'd stay in my chair, not feeling like getting onto the table and looking in the mirror.

Sometimes it would take me a whole day to feel like it, sometimes two days, even a week. For instance, if Mama had slapped my face, and I knew without looking in the mirror that I had a mark or swelling there, then I wanted to be alone, without my friend in the mirror. What I wanted most of all was to stand next to Mama's leg and hold onto her, so she wouldn't move away from me.

I remember once taking apart a large doll. I was curious about what was in the doll's body—maybe she had a boy baby in her belly? Or a girl baby? I opened up her belly and found straw. I took out the straw, and nothing, her belly was empty. I didn't know how to close up her belly.

Mama saw the broken doll and hit me. She hit my face, my arms and back, until her hand swelled up, and then she said to me, "You see, you made me hit you and now my hand hurts because of you."

I remember crying. I cried because my face hurt, my arms and back hurt, and because I made Mama hit me hard and it was my fault that her hand hurt.

When Mama went out to do the laundry, I went and sat down quietly on my chair and decided to be a good girl, the best in the world, who would never again make her mama hit her.

A few days later Mama came into the room holding a curtain. She climbed onto a chair to hang it over the window, and BOOM! A crash on the floor. Mama had fallen off the chair and broken her arm. Afraid, Papa rushed over to her, calling, "Anna, Anna, what happened?"

I had tears of worry and fear in my eyes. In the coming weeks Mama walked around with her hand tied in a sheet.

One day, I was four, maybe less, Mama was standing at the window, her hand tied to her chest. She was looking out as if thinking serious thoughts and I was fighting with Yashu over toys. Mama said, "Danusha, you're big, give in."

That's what I heard from her whenever I fought with my brother, even after he grew up and was stronger than me: "Danusha, you're big, give in, give in, give in."

I left my brother and went up to her. Her eyes were still on the window when I said to her, "How do I know that Mama is truly my mama?" From the day I began to speak I used the third person in Polish when speaking to Mama.

Mama was silent. She looked at me and then got up and went over to Yashu. He wasn't talking yet, and when he wanted something he'd scream like mad. Mama stroked him and kissed each cheek.

I went to sit in my chair and tried to know, how can a child be certain that the mama at home is really her true mama? Maybe the child needs to get a sign from her? But what sign, I had no idea.

The Poles had a home with a pig yard. Every time they slaughtered a pig, we'd hear terrible shrieks, and this was how I learned about dying. And there were mice that made a noise in the wall.

We often ate sour bread, and Mama used the oven to make the bread or bake potatoes. Mama, who knew how to manage in any situation, would make patties from coffee grounds and add an egg; sometimes I wanted to help her, but she wouldn't let me.

The two daughters of the Polish woman we lived with liked to play with Yashu. They'd say to him, "Yashu *yest chisti*," which means Yashu is clean, and they wanted him to repeat it after them. They chose hard words on purpose, repeating them again and again. Yashu couldn't say the words in Polish.

I knew how to say *Yashu yest chisti* and repeated it quietly to myself. The Polish woman's two daughters taught me that storks bring babies into the world. One day they said to me, "Why does the sun shine on a Saturday?" I didn't know.

"Because they washed Jesus's diapers on Saturday and hung them out to dry on the line in honor of Sunday, and since then the sun shines on a Saturday, get it?"

I didn't see any sun, not on a Saturday nor during the week. I saw gray, almost black skies.

Only in Haifa did I see huge skies like sea water, and that was on the way to our home. Sometimes I'd look out at the sea from the veranda and see how the water and the sky stuck together, clouds here and there like a pile of downy feathers. The clearest view was from my seat at the door to the living room. Mama left the veranda door open on summer evenings in honor of the guests who came specially to hear her stories about the war.

Mr. Bogusławski used to open the evening in his festive voice: "Today we leave Tarnopol," or "Today we will talk about Brzeżany, Anna, please," and he'd bow and sit down like an important official. There were times he didn't remember where we'd got to in the story and then, the moment he entered, he'd pause beside me, with a strong scent of perfume, and ask quietly, "Danusha, where did we get up to? Do you remember?"

"Start from the horse and cart," I'd respond quietly, "because that's at the end of Tarnopol."

Mr. Bogusławski began from the end but Mama said reflectively, "We left the new house on our exclusive street; we left three furnished stories, dishes, and sheets, tablecloths and a horse and cart." She spoke especially quietly and the guests were in shock. I saw it in their faces.

"And then it happened," added Mama. "It happened just after I heard the Commissar Yevdutya Tarasova screaming at her husband Sasha, 'You're not just Sasha, you're a Jew, *Żyd*. Isaac, *Żyd. Żyd'*. And Sasha the *Żyd* paled and was silent. He looked wordlessly at me and my children and I was so afraid.

"An hour went by, maybe a day, and Sasha took me aside and whispered that it would be better if we looked for another house, far away, maybe in a small village. He asked us to hurry before something terrible happened, and in fact my husband didn't wait. He went to Brzeżany and managed to find a large room on the ground floor of a devout Catholic family's house. He agreed the fee, always high, and we moved to the home of the Moskova family, parents and two big girls, and they made sausages and various meat products. My husband's brother Gustav and his family, together with my mother-in-law Leah, had also left Tarnopol for Brzeżany, and at the same time several other Jewish families were deported by the Russians, who then took their homes."

When Mama spoke about the Moskova family, I watched her telling what happened to our family in such a beautiful way. Quietly, without a sound, I ate fruit, noticing what a beautiful mother she was with that hair piled into a small bun closed on top with hair pins. With her erect back, her head held high, and her hands closed on her blue gown, she looked like a queen.

Mama told how we only spent a few days in that room; we hadn't even had time to open all the suitcases when they told her to come to the kitchen, look out of the window, and see for herself.

"What do you see?" asked Mrs. Moskova, and through the open window Mama saw German soldiers marching with rifles and opposite them, at a small distance, marched Soviet soldiers in rows, shouting, "Hurray! Hurray!" And bullets flew on all sides, and everywhere people were falling like flies.

Airplanes suddenly appeared and every few moments there were terrifying explosions. Many buildings collapsed. "The walls of the house we lived in were filled with holes, there was so much destruction," said Mama, and immediately added, almost inaudibly, "and then the Ukrainians began looking for Jews…"

When Mama said the word Ukrainians, I saw the guests start to shift in the Formica chairs which, by the end of the story, were shiny from being rubbed.

The red-haired Mr. Bogusławski shifted most of all in his chair. He kept calling out, "Courage, Anna, courage!"

Mama would make a small gesture in his direction, but he only lowered his voice, "Courage, dear Anna, courage!"

This Mr. Bogusławski was crazy about Mama's stories. His cheeks would go a red-purple color, as if he'd just eaten Shabbat *cholent*. This was how it was the first and second year of the stories. In the third year he sat in an ordinary way, but even in the following years when the guests began to change he didn't give up his usual chair at the window or his enthusiasm. "Courage, courage, Anna," he'd call out as if this was the first time he'd heard about the Polish house in Brzeżany, and I heard Mama's seamstress say: "Well, what can he do at home with a wife who has migraines? Of course he wants to come to Anna—she's beautiful, and the refreshments are good."

Mama told how the Polish landlords in Brzeżany helped us, saying that if there were a search, Papa could go up the ladder into the attic and hide there.

One day, Mrs. Žilinská, the landlady's younger sister, came in and told them that she'd wanted to see if the Jews they took to the woods at the edge of the city really were going to forced labor, as they were saying in town. She casually followed them, and when they entered the forest she hid at a distance behind the large trees and what did she see? Ah?

She saw the Jews digging deep holes, and they were told to jump into the holes and then there were shots, and quietly, quietly the Jews disappeared inside. A few minutes later, what did she see? She saw other Jews coming and filling the holes with soil, and she swore by everything sacred to her as a Catholic that when the Germans left, she returned and she saw what she saw, you already know.

Mama fell silent. Her fingers moved as if looking for something to hold onto.

Fat Bernard Cohen, who bit his nails from the moment he came into the living room, was stuck on his thumb nail. Three or four women were in the living room, most were men, and all the women were taking handkerchiefs out of their bags and wiping their eyes, and I was looking at Mama. Not a muscle moved in her face. She sat erect in her flattering blue gown. Mrs. Zelikowitz the seamstress had designed it especially for her. This Mrs. Zelikowitz often came to us, and she and Mama would talk a lot about women they'd known and met in life.

And then Mama said:

"One morning, very early, it was still dark, Mrs. Žilinská knocked at our window like a good angel and said to wake the children and run at once to the church for a few hours. She said that the Germans and Ukrainians were now chasing Jewish children, women, and men from the houses. She told my husband to hide in the attic. I immediately pulled Danusha and Yashu from their warm beds, managing only to put on their coats before swiftly running to the church.

"We sat quietly in a corner. The cold penetrated our bones. My whole body shook; the children pressed against me. People were gathering for morning prayers. Then the priest approached me, requesting I leave the church with the children. Yes, yes, he asked me to leave with the children, go out into the cold, to the Germans and Ukrainians who were knocking on doors and looking for Jews and he knew this—the whole town knew. News like that spread like fire through the streets. A great pain filled my heart. I took a deep breath, looked him straight in the eyes and said quietly: 'Why doesn't the priest pretend not to see me. After all, anyone can come into a church to pray. We too are

God's creatures.' And the priest went away and started the prayer ceremony."

Mama stopped and moistened her lips.

People looked at one another in amazement, and then, pouf, like a burst balloon, they began to clap and call out, "Did you hear, did you hear, she saved the children. Good for you, Anna, good for you."

"We need to pay tribute to the few who helped us when our lives weren't worth a garlic peel," said Bernard Cohen, "like that Mrs. Žilinská."

"Very true," said all the guests.

Mr. Bogusławski got up from his chair, smiled, and went to the toilet. On the way he looked at me and said, "A real heroine, your mama, nobody like her. You keep that in mind, yes?" And he disappeared behind the door.

I didn't remember the church or the priest but it was like Mama to talk like that to a priest. She wasn't afraid of anyone, not of the priest, or the Ukrainians or the Nazi officers. Only one thing frightened her more than anything: the pit under the Moskova family's kitchen. She was terrified of this pit, and I saw this fear when the landlord suggested Papa enlarge the pit in case any new danger came along. He already knew the Ukrainians and the Germans wouldn't leave us alone, and it was important that the four of us could go inside the pit and hide.

Papa was glad of the suggestion and dug and dug, and moved things from here to there, and lined the floor with blankets, and when everything was ready he called Mama, saying, "Come, Anna, come inside and check to make sure there is enough air to breathe."

Mama stood, leaning on a chair at the end of the kitchen. Her face was the color of a freshly painted wall. She shook her head from side to side, saying weakly, "I won't go in, no, no, there is no way I'll be buried alive," and she turned her back and vanished. I looked at Papa and he was very sorry. I approached him. He held out his hand and said, "Come on, Danusha sweetheart, come and see the pit."

I held Papa's hand and went into the pit. I wasn't afraid of anything. I sat on his lap and hummed our song.

Chapter Three

"Now you sing alone, Danusha, one, two, three." I didn't understand a word. I held onto the side of my skirt and sang, "How wonderful, how wonderful, that there are ights-ights like that," and Papa laughed and repeated the song he'd taught me in Hebrew: "How wonderful, how wonderful, that there are nights like that."

He sat at the table and I stood next to his knee. The birds on the mirror looked at us when Papa said, "Again, Danusha, both of us together," and he held my hands.

He had big, warm hands, and he'd dance our hands in tune on his knees, "How wonderful, how wonderful." We sang loudly. Papa's eyes never left me for a moment. He had eyes like the sky with sun and rain at the same time. Papa sometimes closed his eyes and after "how wonderful" a big crack would appear on his forehead, as if bad thoughts were digging a place for themselves. I didn't understand why he was frowning just when we were so happy. Mama would also interrupt and say something if she saw a frown on the forehead or worried eyes. Mama scolded about everything to do with appearance even if we had no guests at home. She'd say, "Sit straight, back erect. Straight neck. No frowning. Just a little laugh." I always obeyed her.

When Papa frowned, I'd try and sing as beautifully as I could, and he'd hug me and go off to the synagogue. Sometimes he'd come back with a guest for the Shabbat meal. Every time he'd bring someone else, even if there wasn't enough food for all of us.

I remember one guest, a dwarf, and when he climbed onto the chair, we were almost the same height. The guest looked at me and smiled, and I looked at Papa, who was saying grace. Mama also looked at Papa. That's how I knew that Mama loved Papa and Papa loved Mama, and I prayed in my heart that nothing bad would happen to us, even though we were far from our home in Tarnopol, even though the Poles' houses in Brzeżany were being bombed, like the day I went out with Papa for a walk in the Brzeżany fields. Everything before us was green and moving in the wind and Papa hummed a tune. The smell of green grass tickled my nose and moistened my eyes. I said in my heart, *Thank you God for being able to leave the big room, thank you God for getting us out of the darkness in the pit day and night. Thank you, God, for being able to walk with Papa in the fields. Thank you, God, for the birds' loud chirping, as if they were talking to each other.* One bird said, tsif, tsif, tsaaf, where have you been and what did you do; another bird answered, tsaf, tsaaf, tsaf, tsuf, tsif, I've been here and there, don't ask what happened to me, and things like that. The talking amused me. I looked at Papa and he pressed my hand and said, "Yes, of course, my girl, birds have a private language." I wanted to fly like a bird and raised my arms on either side of my body, and turned on the spot, and then I ran forward, Papa after me, not catching me once. I felt like thrusting my head into the wet grass and breathing in the sharp, unfamiliar smell, and then there was a strong blow in the middle of my back and Papa's hand threw me down, and there was the sound of an explosion in my ears, boom! Boom! Booom! And a huge fire poured from the sky, and bits of trees flew through the air and Papa yelled bomb, bomb, and covered me with his coat and lay on top of me.

The grass pricked my face and hands, but I wasn't afraid, not even when Papa's fingers constantly, restlessly trembled on my head. And then there was quiet. Loud, dangerous quiet. I was five years old and already knew that this loud quiet was dangerous. Mama also said this sentence and so did the uncles at Tarnopol. I raised my head; Papa's face was lined, even his big eyes. He got up at once, giving me his hand to help me get up.

"We'll go back now, Danusha. It's dangerous to wander about outside," he said, brushing the damp dirt off our clothes.

"But where are the birds? I can't hear the birds, Papa."

"They'll be back soon," he said quietly. "Let's go."

I heard no more birds until the end of the war, bombs yes, and on Yom Kippur I heard Papa whisper to Mama, "They're looking for Jewish men now. I have to find a safe place, I have to. The pit in the kitchen isn't enough. They're going from house to house, not leaving until they've been up in the attic and down to the cellar. I have to leave, Anna."

I wanted to say to Papa, "Mama mustn't go into the pit under the kitchen floor, she mustn't. It's dangerous for her to be closed up in the pit," but I didn't say a word. I remembered how fast she was breathing when Papa was satisfied with the protection of the pit and she didn't want to hear anything about it.

That Yom Kippur in Brzeżany I understood that it was dangerous to be a Jewish man.

I also understood that a Jewish man was a weak man. From the window in our room I saw men running away and they didn't return after the bombing or the search. I saw men doing their business at the river; it disgusted me when they pulled their trousers down a little and did it.

My Papa also went out and didn't come back. Before that he held my shoulders, bent down and said, "Soon you'll be going on a train with Mama and Yashu. You'll be going to another town, Danusha. I have to be somewhere else. Remember that you'll be safest with Mama."

I moved closer to him, "Will Papa come too?"

"Not now, Danusha. Papa is going to look for a place to hide. It's dangerous for me to travel by train. And it's dangerous for you to be with me."

I caught hold of Papa's leg, "When will Papa come?"

"Papa will come… in the meantime it's best Mama looks after you. Kiss?"

I turned away from him and went to sit in my chair.

I didn't move in the chair. I stayed there even when Papa and Mama left the room.

Then I went to sleep without dreaming about anyone.

The next day, I again sat in my chair, not moving from there even when Mama took Yashu in her arms, and Papa didn't come in. Finally, she went into the yard.

Till we left Brzeżany, I didn't climb onto the table and didn't want to see the birds or meet my friend in the mirror.

We left without Papa.

First, we were in the pit. Mrs. Moskova said, "Hurry, hurry, you must hide," and we went down into the pit in the kitchen. At first, I wasn't afraid. Nor was Yashu. But Mama stood at the stairs, hiding her face in her hands, her whole body shaking, tears leaking through her hands and wetting her blouse.

"Mama, Mama, Mama," we called her and she didn't hear. "Mama, Mama, Mama." I caught her by the hand and tried to pull her hand away, but her hand was rigid and I couldn't. I held Yashu's hand and we didn't stop crying until we left the pit.

Later, we left the Moskova family.

At the Brzeżany train station, I erased Papa from my mind. Didn't remember a thing. Not his laugh or the small smile he'd give me next to angry people. And not his hug. I no longer remembered the eyes that were like a warm blanket for me, or his large hands that held me when I wanted to cry. I erased every word from the song "How Wonderful, How Wonderful", but every word returned, to live in my head.

I told myself, who needs a Papa who disappears and leaves his little girl alone. I don't need a Papa like that, don't need him. Ever. Mama looks after me, Mama never leaves her children, you can see it in the photographs: Mama, Yashu, and me. No Papa, none. Yashu next to Mama. I'm standing next to them.

Mama talked about Papa in the living room, but not much. Nine or twelve words, and that's all. I looked at her beautiful lips; she had red lipstick and made small, gentle movements with her lips. I said to myself, I have to learn from her how to speak nicely, and I heard her say that her husband's family were *kaufmanishe familia*, a family of merchants, and they were wealthy. She spoke about her family most of all, saying all of them had received a good education. They'd all read the classics in several languages apart from Polish—in German, English, and French—and they also knew how to recite some of Heine's poems by heart. Only after many years did I find out that Papa wasn't just a wealthy merchant. It turned out that he was an educated man, knew languages at least as well as Mama's family, and he was a man of the world, about which Mama never spoke, not about that, nor about leaving Brzeżany. Not even after speaking about the war nine times or more in our living room did she ever mention how we got to Lwów, thanks to Bronka, her younger sister.

Her sister came especially from Kraków to help us travel to Lwów. That's what Mama's sisters decided—Lydia, Franca, and Bronka. The three of them lived together with Grandma Rosa in Kraków and talked to Mama through letters. Their sister Stella was in Berlin and they talked to her through letters as well, but less.

Bronka, Lydia, and Franca, who lived in Kraków, of course knew about the situation in Brzeżany. Why didn't Bronka take us to Kraków? Mama never said a word about this. Maybe the sisters thought and thought and decided that Lwów was the safest place for us, and why did Bronka come to fetch us? Mama never said a word about this either.

One morning she appeared at the home of the Moskova family. She wore a coat, hat, and gloves; she hugged us, saying, "Hurry, hurry, coats. Hat. Gloves." Even before we'd moved, she was holding a suitcase in each hand, and saying quietly, "We're leaving."

Mama took our hands and stood rooted to the spot. Mrs. Moskova looked at us. Bronka nodded at Yashu to follow her, said goodbye, and left. Yashu tugged at Mama's hand, Mama tugged at my hand, and we followed Bronka. We didn't stop to rest for a second in the snow, and only when we reached the train station did I hear Bronka speak, but Mama never said a word.

The station was empty. No one went out or came in. Aunt Bronka said, "We can sit here," on a wet bench outside the station.

We sat silently in the freezing cold that got inside hats and ears. Mama was silent without lines of worry on her face. I felt that if this loud silence didn't stop, some danger would come, I already knew that. I coughed, and the silence didn't stop. My feet, which were hanging in the air, grew very hot. I looked for Aunt Bronka, wanting her to say a few words to me, but she was busy with someone who happened to be passing by. She spoke with her mouth half-closed. Sometimes she glanced at Mama or around her. Even looked for someone behind her back, but no one approached the station.

In the meantime, my feet were on fire. I wanted to take my boots off but I felt it was dangerous to move on the bench, and there was nobody to talk to about it. Mama was present and not present—more accurately, it was as if she wasn't there.

Bronka approached us. She straightened Yashu's hat and coat collar, touched my cheek, and bent to say something in Mama's ear. Mama didn't move. Just looked at the snow as if it were perfectly all right for us to be sitting with wet noses on a bench outside the station where there were no people and no train. Yashu opened and closed his hand, not hearing when I whispered, "That's enough now."

I was thirsty and controlled myself. I didn't ask Bronka for water when she came back from a turn around the station, then set off again. Finally, she stood next to Yashu, said something to him, he answered her, and Mama shifted on the bench as if coming out of a dangerous dream. Then I heard people approaching and the frightening silence was over.

Mama didn't talk about or tell what had happened at the station, and I had almost forgotten that frightening bench until one day I found a reminder from Bronka, an old envelope and a sheet of paper written in Polish and this was what was written:

> *I arrived in Brzeżany, a small town, a three to four-hour journey from Lwów. At the station, I immediately asked where the Moskova family lived. I had to walk about two kilometers. I walked quietly through the village streets and fields until I reached a farmer's house.*
>
> *"You probably know who I am. I'd like to speak to Madame Anna," I said.*
>
> *Mrs. Moskova didn't bat an eyelash. I raised my voice—I thought maybe she was hard of hearing.*
>
> *No response! Finally, I sat down on a chair without an invitation. Again, I asked, "Does Anna still live with you?"*
>
> *Suddenly the woman bent down, opened a trapdoor and after a moment, there in the opening appeared my sister's pale and frightened face. Without any expression of happiness or relief she came slowly out of the cellar, followed at once by the children who climbed out into the room. They were very quiet; their eyes were swollen from crying and they looked as tense as their mother.*
>
> *Four-year-old Yashu listened intently to what I told them: "We're leaving now for the train station and there's no time to lose."*
>
> *Danusha, older by a year, began quietly, quietly to weep, sobbing inside herself—not a childish sobbing, but in the way only adults sob.*

We walked through the snow to the station. Before us stretched a snowy, quiet virgin landscape. We met no one on the way, but as we approached the village street, I suggested to Anna that she'd better not arouse suspicion at the train station with her puffy eyes and pinched face. I did everything to rouse her and tried to say it with humor:

"Just imagine, you're no longer Anna T. but Anna Kwiatkowski. This is the Polish name on the forged papers I've brought for you. Danusha and Yashu appear as Danuta and Yan."

She continued to look strangely at me, sad and tense, like someone who wasn't listening.

Suddenly, little Yashu caught hold of his sister's hand, saying: "Danusha, d'you hear? You mustn't cry anymore, or they'll recognize us." I smiled gratefully at him and said to Anna, "Look. Your son is more restrained than you are. Please calm down!"

But, completely withdrawn, she didn't respond. Fear and anxiety were still etched into her tear-stained face. I didn't know her, that beautiful, brave, aware woman, first lady of Tarnopol. The fear was too deep.

We reached the little train station. The sun shone, and the snow at the sides of the road sparkled as if threaded with thousands of diamonds. Calmly and slowly, I entered the small station building with its waiting room and benches and a door leading to the ticket counters.

The train was scheduled to arrive in ten minutes but there was no one at the station. I knocked at the ticket counters, no answer. I walked round the small building, not a person to be seen, and it was the middle of the day!

Anna and the children remained outside near the bench in front of the station building. I told them they should sit down; the train was apparently late.

But I gradually began to feel uneasy. My optimism and good mood with which I'd tried to encourage the children, and Anna in particular, who still looked frightened and distant, began to evaporate.

After half an hour we got up; it was too cold to sit. I didn't want to go into the waiting room because from there I wouldn't be able to see if anyone was approaching who might recognize my sister and the children. So we walked up and down, until I heard from a passing station employee that the train would be two hours late. Terrible news!

What should we do? Go back to the Moskova family? Impossible! Anna didn't respond at all—she remained apathetic. I started to feel frightened, thinking perhaps that she didn't understand the gravity of the situation. Maybe she was quietly praying to herself? Maybe she was sinking into a kind of silence, saying the Psalms to herself, unaware of reality?

I remembered that even during the good times, the normal times, she would take refuge in prayer. Nonetheless, I tried to explain to her that she now had Aryan papers and another name and that she had to focus on that, but my impression was that she didn't absorb anything.

Those poor, sweet children grasped it better than their mother.

I became nervous. A two-hour delay, that wasn't a good sign! The silence aroused my suspicion. In Słomniki, it happened before the aktion there would be that kind of silence. And recently, they'd rounded up Jews from nearby towns and loaded them onto trains intended for deportation.

I looked at the sad, pale faces of the children and said to Yashu, "Instead of standing here in the cold, maybe it would be better to return to the Moskovas'?"

He looked at me gravely: "But we're going to Aunt Palemira."

Anna suddenly woke from her reverie. Expressionless, unsmiling, she explained completely rationally what Aunt Palemira meant: "The moment Papa finishes his work at the town park, we're going to Palestine," that's what she'd told the children, and to prevent the name from sticking in their minds and being blurted out, thus giving themselves away, she'd invented Aunt Palemira.

In the meantime, people were beginning to arrive at the station with their baggage. Finally! The train would be there any minute! My sister appeared to have pulled herself together, speaking a few words. I was myself once more, my vitality and the belief we'd succeed in completing our task were restored.

Suddenly, a young woman approached us, perhaps thirty, thirty-five, saying: "Ah, Madame Anna, what is this? Are you leaving us?"

My sister again seemed to be surrounded by a wall. Mechanically, she put out her hand to the woman in greeting. I quickly joined them, introduced myself and said: "I've invited my friend and her children to Kraków to recover."

"But they're going to a large city, how will they recover in a city?" Asked the woman, looking me up and down, and then she complimented me on my hat that suited the coat so well, saying, "Real fur?"

I chatted to her about everything possible, about school, Kraków, and the woman listened, eyes fixed on the string of pearls I was wearing, which my mother had given me for the journey, although these were real freshwater pearls.

The strange woman and I walked up and down the platform. I wanted to distance her as much as possible from my sister because I was afraid she'd talk more than was necessary.

I understood she was Polish and married to a Ukrainian policeman.

The train didn't come. We were informed by the station employee that it would be another two hours late. Consequently, the woman walked decisively up to my sister to say goodbye. She no longer felt like waiting for the relatives she'd come to meet.

We parted and I was left aghast at having to wait so much longer for the train, I still hadn't grasped the danger we were in.

The Polish woman is married to a Ukrainian policeman! A Ukrainian!

I ran after her, calling: "Madame…" (I don't remember her name.) She hesitated but returned and we chatted a little more until she said, "But I really must get home—my husband will be home soon and I have to cook."

I felt an increasing sense that I should not let this woman go. With a sudden brainwave, I said to her that I was afraid she'd tell her husband that Madame T's Christian Polish friend, as I'd introduced myself, had come to take her and the children to Kraków.

She promised me: "No, you have nothing to worry about. I won't tell my husband anything. Apart from that, he may only come after four and by then you'll be far away from here."

She shifted her weight from one foot to another, occasionally giving my sister a piercing glance. Her admiring observation of my string of pearls did not escape my notice and, with a heavy heart, I decided to make a suggestion: "If you stay until the train comes, I will give you the pearls as a gift!"

Her face shone. I made a movement as if to remove the pearls on the spot, and she wanted to help me.

At that moment the train employee arrived on the platform and she took a step back. I hurried over to him, asking: "Will the train come on time after all?"

"No," he answered, "later!"

The woman waited for me in the same place. She'd heard what the man had told me and despite that she did not leave; she was waiting for the string of pearls.

"Really a beautiful string of pearls. You can see they're real," she said.

I thought to myself, interesting that a simple Polish woman, maybe a Ukrainian and married to a policeman, distinguishes between real and fake pearls.

I said to her, "Oh, you're a real expert," and we continued chatting about pearls and diamonds. I occasionally glanced over at my sister and the children sitting quietly on the bench. Those two little dears! They're worth giving the woman this valuable string of pearls from Mother, who loved jewelry above all. Even she had sold ring after ring when she had to pay the high rent or buy food.

The train finally approached! I took the string of pearls from my neck, holding it in my hand until the train stopped. I held out my hand with the pearls and she took them immediately in her hand, making a gesture as if to hug, and kissed me. Then she waved to us and I waved back, while putting my finger to my lips, reminding her to keep her mouth shut no matter what.

I found a relatively comfortable carriage and we sat down, exhausted by fear, very gradually calming down. Even Anna looked more peaceful. The children looked out of the window, staring out with sadness, with a seriousness that was so un-childlike! I tried to encourage them with some candies and sandwiches I'd brought from Kraków. The little ones looked at me with gratitude but the sorrow in Danusha's eyes, red with weeping, didn't leave her.

I cried quietly, quietly, not a childish sobbing, but how only adults wept, Bronka had written, and I wanted to know how adults weep. Maybe I looked out at the snow and swallowed my tears, as if drinking water, or swallowing a candy?

And later, I recollected the words Bronka had spoken to the Polish woman at the train station: "I've invited my friend and her children to Kraków to recover."

I was surprised; Aunt Bronka, a friend? And we're going to Kraków? Not Lwów? But I waited silently.

I sat quietly in the train, eating a sandwich and looking at the red fox-fur collar that Bronka had brought for the train journey to make her look like a real gentile. I remembered that Mama had a fur to put round her neck that fell to the shoulders. In the fox's mouth there was a flat clasp to close the coat. Her sisters also had whole fox furs with the head and the feet—everything in an elegant silvery color, as Grandma used to say, appreciating every coat the family bought.

I wanted to talk to Aunt Bronka. Tell her things about the pit in the Moskova family's house. I wanted to tell her that Mama should never have been put in the pit. She felt as if she were suffocating in the pit. That's what I heard from Mrs. Moskova too. Mama could have died in the pit, and Yashu and I were afraid of this and that Papa wouldn't come to save us. I was silent.

"Thank the Lord," said Bronka quietly.

"Thank the Lord," repeated Mama almost inaudibly, and I realized that we'd have been finished in that pit if Bronka hadn't come. Mama could no longer breathe in the pit.

Afterwards I heard Bronka whispering to Mama about the troubles they were having in Kraków. She told her that whole families, grandpa, grandma, father, mother, children, everyone was being deported from the city, whole streets were emptying and there wasn't a single safe place in Kraków, not one. Lydia and Bronka, Mama's sisters, were constantly looking for a new place to spend the night, for themselves, for the children, moving from here to there, and back again, it was very hard. Just as well we have the address in Lwów, just as well. "Stay there as long as possible, Anna, as long as you can."

And then I heard Mama telling how she'd cooked for the children and how the Moskova family liked to taste and eat the food; she was explaining exactly how to prepare patties out of coffee when I fell asleep.

When I woke up, I found that Mama and Yashu were sleeping and Bronka was reading a book. She looked up, opened her brown handbag, and took out a picture book. "D'you want to look at it?" she asked me, holding out the book. I opened it and looked at her, certain I wanted to be like her when I grew up.

Bronka smiled at me. She had a round face and good eyes. She looked at every new person who came into the carriage and her voice was clear when she spoke to the tall man in uniform who had a cap and tall boots. He listened to her intently, said, "Yes, yes, yes," nodding his head. I saw she wasn't afraid of anyone and didn't drop her eyes.

After an hour or two, Bronka woke Mama and Yashu and we got off the train. Bronka took a suitcase in one hand, holding Yashu with her other hand, Mama took the second suitcase and we followed them. I walked slightly in front of Mama, feeling that I was giving her the strength to go on. Then we reached a house with a yard and bushes full of snow and a fence made of planks. Some had fallen, some stood straight, and some were crooked. Bronka put the suitcase down next to the fence, bent down to me and Yashu and kissed us, hugged Mama, and whispered in her ear, "Goodbye, goodbye, look after yourselves," then she turned and was gone in a second.

Mama looked at Yashu, then at me, and said, "Now things will be good," and from this I understood that Mama was stronger, that I didn't need to be afraid for her, and I was right. I'd never seen Mama as silent as she was on the bench at the train station.

Chapter Four

"Don't speak to strangers, all right?" said Mama, stroking the red fur. She looked at us, arranged her hair, put a finger to her lips so we'd be quiet, and knocked on the scratched door. "Don't speak," she ordered in a whisper, and I replied, "All right, Mama."

"Shhhh… shh…" added Mama.

"Shhh… shh…" I whispered to Yashu, who had walked off and hadn't heard what Mama had whispered to us.

I gave him my hand and brought him close to Mama. In the meantime I went over what was forbidden in my mind: In Tarnopol, we were forbidden to sit on the toilet without cleaning it; in Brzeżany, we were forbidden to leave the room alone; in Lwów we were forbidden to speak to strangers.

"Understand, Yashu, forbidden to speak, forbidden," I told Yashu and he dropped my hand and drew back.

"He's not listening to us," I said, getting closer to Mama's leg, just as the door opened and a small, fat man smiled at us with yellow teeth. He wore a woolen hat that hid his forehead. I could barely see his face. Mama took a letter out of her bag, saying, "If you please, sir, this letter is from Mrs. Moskova in Brzeżany." The man took the letter, opened the door wide, and invited us inside.

Inside the house sat a woman with white hair. She kept getting up and sitting down, and getting up and sitting down, saying *"Bozhe moi, bozhe moi."* While she was getting up and sitting down, the little man finished reading the letter and gestured to her to show us a room. We didn't say a word.

There were also two big girls with braids down to their backsides. They'd pinch each other all the time, giggling, hee, hee, hee, and they taught me to say Christian prayers. They put a cross on a chain round my neck, and I learned all the prayers by heart and properly crossed myself whenever I passed the church. Mama saw and heard us, and didn't say a word.

Before the Christian holidays, Mama took us on a tram. I realized from the questions she was asking the man in uniform that Mama was asking about a particular street in Lwów.

We got off the tram. I held onto Yashu and Mama's hands and we began to cross the road.

Opposite stood a tall man in a hat and a long coat. We'd almost crossed the road when the man put out his arm and signaled to us with his finger to enter a yard behind an iron gate. Mama's fingers pressed my hand hard as we entered the yard. The tall man entered after us, closed the gate and stood in front of Mama. He said something in a language I didn't understand; his face was harsh. Mama spoke quietly to him and he nodded as if he understood and agreed with every word she spoke. And then he asked something, and Mama talked and talked, and in the meantime, my hand began to hurt from her pressure. I could feel how cold her hand was even through her glove. I was very frightened when the tall man fell silent and after a few seconds, he said, "Police." I understood that most of all.

Mama immediately let go of my hand and turned around. She opened up her coat, took out a paper package, and held it out to the man. He looked for a bird or an airplane in the sky while he thrust the package into his coat and smiled at me. And smiled at my brother. Said something to Mama, touched his hat, and walked off.

"Let's go back to the tram," whispered Mama and held out her hand. I put my hand in hers and felt the trembling of her fingers. I smiled at her but she didn't notice. Again, we crossed the road. A day or two later, we moved to a new house.

"We'll be gone before the holiday," Mama promised the old lady in her black scarf with the red flowers.

The old lady received us at the entrance to the house. In the yard a large fir tree lay ready on the ground. "Just a few days and we'll go back home," Mama repeated until we went inside and I already knew she didn't mean it. We had no home to go to after Tarnopol. Only in Tarnopol did we have a real home. Grandma Leah on Papa's side lived on the first floor, and Uncle Gustav, his wife Hilda, and their boy, Yechezkel, lived on the second floor. I heard Mama telling Bronka that they'd left for Brzeżany after us, she didn't know where, and we had the entire third floor, which came to an end when the Russians came and took our house for themselves along with my bed and the bright curtains and carpet. They even took the sideboard with the glass doors. How I'd loved looking at the delicate flowers painted on the cups and saucers standing in rows on the shelves of the sideboard. Mama used them when serving tea and nice cookies to guests, and all we had left were the clothes on our backs and two suitcases, which Mama reduced to one so she could give me one hand while I held Yashu's hand.

In the home of the old lady with the black scarf, we lived in a small room in the basement. There was one bed there, and high in the wall was a skylight. I'd climb onto a stool, peep out, and watch for Santa Klaus.

The girls who'd taught me Christian prayers told me that Santa Klaus comes to give out presents for the holiday. I didn't see Santa Klaus or receive any gifts. But I did get sick.

I lay on a narrow bed, my head and face burning with fever, my body heavy as stone. I knew what was happening around me, but I couldn't see well, as if a glass wall stood between me and Mama, Yashu, and the old lady in the scarf. *Is this what it's like to die?*

I didn't want to die.

I closed my eyes and started praying in Polish:

"Tyś powiedział że nie zostawisz nas na ziemi." You promised you wouldn't leave us alone on earth.

My mouth prayed by itself: *Tyś powiedział że nie… Tyś powiedział że nie…*

I prayed faster and faster when the old lady we were staying with came into our room and I saw Mama looking worriedly at her. The peasant shook her head from side to side and left the room. A few minutes later she came back with borsht and gave it to me to drink. I drank the borsht and saw Mama smiling at her. I wanted to sleep. I counted the carriages going past in the street, one, two, three, four, and fell asleep.

Three or four days went by before I was better and then Mama said we had to leave.

We put on our coats, gloves, and woolen hats. Mama picked up the suitcase and we left the house. "Don't talk to strangers. Smile if you have to," she said.

I knew we didn't have an address.

I remember my brother and me walking in the shining snow, snow that came up to our knees; we're cold, so cold that our eyes burn and our noses are wet. We don't say a word. Just walk and walk, looking at Mama or at the snow, not stopping. Even the stars in the sky tremble in the capricious wind blowing in the snow. After a long time, I'm already tired, no strength to walk after Mama. I want to sit down, but we walk, almost run to keep up with Mama, and the light outside is already dim. Darkness is falling and there are clouds. I cry quietly, "Stop, Mama, stop, I want to sit down," but she doesn't answer.

Suddenly a bright light. Like a train. We stop. Two soldiers are standing there, shining a large torch on us and my heart begins to beat in my ears: boom-boom, boom-boom, boom-boom.

The soldiers are wearing long coats, boots, and woolen hats. They speak quickly, gesturing with their hands, as if they can't understand a thing. Mama points at me, looking very worried. The two soldiers pick us up, and take us back to the house of the old lady who had given me borsht.

I remember the family around the table looking at the soldiers with big eyes, then at us, and then again at the soldiers. The soldiers talk fast, without stopping, as if they have music on their tongues.

The noise around the table makes the old lady happy and she invites us to come inside—everything is all right.

A few minutes later the soldiers go away and we go back to the room in the basement. The old lady helps me take off my shoes and wet clothes and put on my pajamas. I get into bed and finally warm up. I pray in my heart that we won't have to leave ever again.

The next morning Mama gave me a thick slice of bread spread with jam. I'd never eaten such good jam. She said the soldiers had brought it and that in the meantime we were staying. I saw that the suitcase remained packed. Mama washed the clothes we'd worn in the snow, dried them in front of the stove, and in the morning, we put them on again.

When guests came to our living room in Haifa, I sat on a chair, sometimes on the floor, where I saw dust, spider webs, a knitting needle, and a white sock. A sock I'd been looking for all week and more. Everything lay nicely under the sofa. From where I sat, I also saw that that Mr. Bogusławski didn't only suffer from dense hair in his ears, but he also had several thick hairs in his nose. They were the color of rust on the iron pipe behind the house. And he gave me two toffees every time he came in. I kept one for my brother.

From my place on the floor, I noticed a red rash on Klara Cohen's leg, Klara with the dry hair, and the place was swollen. I immediately checked the itch I had on the inside of my hand, and pulled down my sleeve.

Mama's fingers were also slender and seemed longer. She

closed them gently on her knees; her nails were cared for but not lacquered.

My hands resembled Mama's. When I cleaned the house, I didn't notice that my hands were swollen and red. I noticed that the slender fingers grew longer only when I grew up, and Mama also noticed: "What lovely hands you have, idle hands," she remarked when she noticed me holding a book.

"Huh?" I immediately closed the book, hid my fingers deep in my armpits, and gasped for air.

I had respiratory problems anyway, perhaps because of the sinusitis. I had to have inhalations occasionally to open up the passages.

"Before leaving Brzeżany," said Mama in her flattering blue gown, "I received a letter of recommendation from Mrs. Moskova for her sister in Lwów, in which she asked the lady to take us into her home on Bogdańska Street in exchange for a high monthly rent. Mrs. Yuzchynska, a fat, elderly peasant married to a Ukrainian, and her two high school age daughters, Stefa and Janka, agreed to take us in, despite the prohibition against giving asylum to Jews. I should mention that my sisters in Kraków provided us with forged papers and Polish names.

"The winter of 1942 was a hard one in Poland. The walls on the ground floor where we lived were covered in frost; we sat in our coats at home and shivered with cold. With great effort, I managed to buy a sack of coal and light the stove, and at last we were warm. But it was painful for me, a God-fearing Jewess, to give my children a Christian education. They learned Christian prayers and went to church."

"A Christian education for the children, how terrible," they said in the living room, looking at me, but it didn't bother me. I sat on the floor, the heel of one foot on the toes of the other foot, looking at the sock under the sofa.

"Ostensibly," called out Mr. Bogusławski, "don't forget, friends, *ostensibly* a Christian education. Anna, please go on."

Mama told how her *ausgeschprochen* Aryan appearance had helped her in a Polish environment, but she was frightened by the stories of the landlady's daughter, sadistic Stefa, about Jews who disguised themselves as Aryans and how the Gestapo hanged them in the streets. In a loud voice, she'd tell how in Lukitka Street, six Jews disguised as Aryans were hanged, and two more in a nearby street; they hang them all the time, all the time they drag more and more Jews out of their holes. Her sister, Janka, who saw my frightened face, called out, "How terrifying. You hold your tongue with all your horror stories."

This Stefa loved to guzzle food just like her mother, Mrs. Yuzchynska, who'd have guzzling attacks. She could fill her belly with bean soup, and roast with *kapusta,* cabbage, and the house would fill with unpleasant sounds and smells. Stefa would gobble and frighten everyone, telling them about a beautiful young woman who'd dyed her hair blonde, "That blonde could be seen from a distance, hanging from a rope," she said, chewing and chewing, terrifying us twice a day with a story about a Polish teacher—not just any teacher, but someone from the Gymnasium who had hidden a Jewish boy. They hanged him as well as the boy.

"*Nu,* stop that, do you hear?" the old landlord, Mr. Yuzchynska ordered his daughter. "They are very unfortunate people."

"Yes, I felt the landlord wanted to help me," said Mama, "and all in all you could say the whole family enjoyed the rent money I paid them for the room. But there was tension and that sadistic

Stefa would ask to see our papers at least once a week. I took them out of my bag and showed her, and Danusha would smile nicely at her. And the minute she left the room, the child asked, 'What does dead mean?' And she'd follow me, 'What does it mean? What is it?' What could I say?

"We stayed there for a few months until, one morning, the landlord came in and demanded we leave. The neighbors were beginning to suspect that we were Jews and he didn't want to end up hanging from a post in the street.

"The news fell like thunder on a clear day. What would happen? What would happen?"

"Oy, oy, oy, what will happen, what will happen," cried out Bertha Ketzelboim, who had transparent skin with a network of veins on her face. Her husband, Jacob, pressed his hand hard into her knee.

"What will happen, what will happen?" people echoed her, and Mr. Bogusławski raised his hands and waved them in the air, "Shhh, shhh, shhh."

"With no papers, only the forged ones that Bronka had brought us, and two small children, I was afraid to wander about the streets of the town but what choice did I have? I had to find a new roof over our heads at once. I asked Mrs. Yuzchynska if I could leave the two suitcases in their house for a day or two, and I left with the children and advertisements for rooms to let. It wasn't simple at all. I was asked for an ID card everywhere I went. I didn't have one. And then they started asking questions, 'Why don't you have any papers, and where is your home, and why do you need a room for a week, two weeks? More?' 'Madame, there's a war on, there's no place without identification papers, none.' I walked around the town and saw posters offering a prize of ten thousand gold coins for anyone who brought a Jew to the Gestapo offices and I got more and more worried by the day."

At this point someone would come out to smoke on the balcony, usually the silent Yozek Meltzer, who was a postal clerk, and Mama would stop to drink water from a glass. The others in the room also felt bad about our situation.

"What will happen, what will happen?" whispered Klara Cohen whenever there was a chance of danger or worry.

"Oy, oy, oy," sobbed Bertha Ketzelboim into her handkerchief.

"But you had sisters in Kraków, Anna. Why didn't you think of going to them?" asked Jacob Ketzelboim, putting his hand in his pocket as usual and jiggling coins.

"Generalgouvernement, Jacob, *Generalgouvernement,"* said Bernard Cohen, getting up from his chair.

"What do you mean?" asked Bertha Ketzelboim.

"*Nu,* in October, 1939, the Germans had already conquered Kraków and half of Poland as well," explained Bernard, returning to his seat, "and they decided that the capital of the occupied region, known as the *Generalgouvernement,* would be Kraków. Well, you can imagine what went on there. Thousands were expelled from the city, thousands, and there was a ghetto there, and they burned synagogues; it was very dangerous."

"Well, he was a partisan and he knows," said his wife, Klara, to the people in our living room.

"So, why is he sitting here?" whispered the new neighbor from the first floor, and Mr. Bogusławski smiled at Mama and said, "Because it's pleasant in her home and the stories are very good."

"Thank you," said Mama. "My sisters had to make special arrangements for us to get to Kraków; in the meantime, I decided to look for a relative I knew about who lived on Bernstein Street in Lwów. I believed he might be able to help in that difficult time. I took the children by tram to the Jewish Quarter, even though it wasn't safe to walk around there, but I had no choice. We got off the tram; I took the children's hands and approached a newspaper vendor standing there to ask him about Bernstein Street. A man in a hat who was standing there looked at me and said he would take us to Bernstein Street. I didn't like the man, but it was impossible to leave, I felt it inside. We followed him and he stood back and gestured to us to go in through the gate of a nearby house."

Mama stopped. The air was electric. People sat unmoving in their chairs. I didn't move either although my shoulders were hurting from sitting so straight.

"We went into the yard," said Mama as if she were back there now. "The man in the hat opened his lapel and showed me the Gestapo badge. I was very frightened, though naturally I looked at him as if I didn't understand why he'd stopped me. He asked for my ID card. I took out my papers. He looked at them and wanted to know what I was looking for, and if I knew the people on Bernstein Street, and their exact address. Obviously, I didn't give him any address. I said I was looking for acquaintances I'd known before the war. I didn't remember the address and they may have moved. The man returned my papers and said sharply, 'You're Jews, Jews, come with me to the police station.'"

Mama was silent, breathing deeply in and out.

The room was filled with suspense. Mr. Bogusławski slid to the edge of his chair and called out, "Courage, Anna, courage," and he passed a bottle of valerian to Jacob Ketzelboim who was sitting next to his wife, Bertha. She was waving her fan, almost breaking it, her head leaning against the wall.

Izzy Rappaport, Bernard Cohen's neighbor from the building

opposite, who was thin and wore round glasses, and who worked at the clinic and always had a bandage or two in his pocket, said, "In situations like that, always wise to be cool and collected, or we're done for."

Mama said quietly: "I felt as if my legs were weak, barely able to support me. I knew the Gestapo police would examine Yashu and discover that he was Jewish. In my winter coat were gold coins my husband had given me before we left for Brzeżany. I'd hidden a few hundred *złoty* in my bra. I took the money out of my bra, gave it to him, and begged him to let me go. He took the money and looked at the children. 'So Madame is Jewish. The children are very beautiful,' he said, putting the money in his pocket. 'Stay away from this place, Madame, it is dangerous,' and then he opened the gate and allowed us to go."

"The children are very beautiful," said Mama, and every time I heard her say that, even the tenth time, I'd get up from my chair, leave Mama and the guests in the living room, and go to the hall mirror next to the front door. I wanted to see for myself the face the German policeman saw.

At first, I saw a round, sun-burned face; sometimes the nose was peeling from the sun; the eyes were a little red, maybe from the water in the Bat Galim pool in Haifa where we'd go swimming. I also saw a broad forehead and short, puffy hair. After a year or two, the face lengthened, the hair too; there was acne on my cheeks, ugh, disgusting, and then it went away, leaving smooth skin.

I lingered over my mouth. I saw full lips, red as lipstick. I wanted to know what happened to that mouth next to the man in the hat. Had I smiled prettily so that he'd leave my mother in peace?

I wanted to find my brother's mouth and lips, to compete for the smile that would make the policeman leave us alone. But Yashu wasn't home much. He was almost never home. He played with the friends he'd find everywhere, rode his roller skates in the street. He'd stand on one, holding onto a bus that would pull him along the street, or so he told me one day.

"That is so dangerous, Yashu. What do you think you're doing?" I shouted at him, grabbing his hand.

"It's all right," he smiled at me, "don't worry and don't tell Mama, all right?"

"You must be careful. Promise me, Yashu, promise," I begged, not letting go of his hand until he promised me, and I gave him the candy I'd kept for him in my pocket.

Chapter Five

"Why are you here? Where is your husband? Where is your home? When will you go back?" In the living room, Mama repeated the questions she was asked every time she found a room. Every time, a member of the household or a relative would threaten us with unrelenting questions. Every night Mama would sigh, and I'd realize that in the morning she'd put on her peasant scarf, say, "Don't talk to strangers, smile nicely," and together we'd go out to look for another room. Mother first, holding my hand, while I held Yashu's hand, or Yashu would hold Mama's free hand. Each of us wore a hat and Mama wore a particular scarf to go looking. I understood that this was a special way of dressing to stop people from looking at us too closely, which gave us some security.

Interestingly, Mama would smile when the men in the living room jumped up, saying, "With or without a scarf you're beautiful, what does it matter, huh?"

When Mama talked about another room she'd rented in one

of the streets of Lwów, she stressed how popular her children were with the landlady. "They were so polite and quiet, they even touched the Gentiles' hard hearts," she said, smiling only at me. The guests also smiled only at me, and I stopped eating the apple or whatever I held in my hand while she spoke.

"But a few days later," she said to her guests, in a voice of impending tension like music in a movie, "just a few days later, a friend of the landlady grew curious, wanting to know who had rented the room, who these people were. That was that. I knew this was the moment to move somewhere else, before the questions started. I dressed the children in hats and coats, put a patterned scarf on my head, and out we went to look for a place," said Mama, half closing her eyes so she could still see her guests. I gave her a big smile, as I did back then when she'd glance at me with eyes half-closed to make sure I was all right if I was holding a suitcase or her coat.

"After walking for hours," said Mama, "I came to the Dumnievska family's house in the Kolprakov district and they immediately agreed to give us a place—maybe because I started with how much I was willing to pay. It was rather a dark basement, just one small window above the bed. The landlords, an elderly couple, wandered about nearby, looking hard at us, wanting to know how come I hadn't prepared for the holiday. I promised them that we'd leave before the holiday," said Mama, "but on the morning of the holiday, Danusha had a fever and she was burning like a thousand candles and vomiting all the time. I was mad with worry. That evening, I took her into my bed and held her. The fever didn't go down; her cheeks were like two burns. I put cold bandages on her head and repeated the Psalms. And then the little one repeated Christian prayers to me. My whole body trembled. Finally, she fell asleep, and I calmed down.

"In the morning, her fever rose and her body was red as fire. She was barely breathing."

Mama stopped, which evoked a heavy silence in the living room. Nobody moved or even opened a candy wrapping. Mama raised a delicate glass of tea, saying, "In the evening, the door opened and Mrs. Dumnievska entered the room, bearing *borscht* and Christmas cookies. She saw we had nothing in the room and realized we were Jews. She looked compassionately at the child, approached the bed, listened, and was astonished to find that the child was murmuring Christian prayers. It was a great shock to her but, nonetheless, she refused to call a doctor. She said it was dangerous to call a doctor, dangerous for us and for them, and on her way to the door she whispered that her son-in-law was complaining about her giving the basement to persecuted people like us. We had a difficult day and night and Danusha's fever dropped. Mrs. Dumnievska asked how she was, breathed a sigh of relief with me, but hinted gently that I should prepare to leave the room, yes. We could wait a few days until the child was better but we should prepare to leave. I wrote a letter with Mrs. Dumnievska's address to my sister Bronka in Kraków, asking her to help us leave Lwów. A day passed and I didn't wait for a reply. I packed one large suitcase and went out into the yard with the children. All these years I've remembered Mrs. Dumnievska's words: 'God's in heaven, and He isn't asleep.' That sentence accompanied me as we walked along the street. We just walked, I didn't know where. It snowed all the time."

Mama tapped her finger on her chin, as if preferring to postpone that story.

"Of course, Mrs. Dumnievska's God was sleeping," raged Bernard Cohen, the partisan.

"Like a bear, that's how her God slept," said Izzy Rappaport.

"Like the dead, would be more accurate," added Klara Cohen.

"All right, all right, we get it," soothed Mr. Bogusławski.

I saw that Bertha Ketzelboim had almost fainted, breathing from the valerian bottle, but Mama replaced her glass on the table, and related: "We came to a field at the edge of the city, in the Kolprakov district. It was afternoon. I knew we had to find shelter before dark. The suitcase I was holding was heavy. The children held hands and we sank into the snow. It was hard to progress. I felt with every minute how hard it was for the children and it broke my heart. The snowflakes covered our coats and hats; the children's eyelashes were white, and it drove me crazy. The girl suddenly fell onto the snow—she was weak and pale from her illness. 'You rest a while and we'll go on, all right?' whispered my little son to Danusha. 'I'm ready, we can go on,' wept the little girl, getting up and giving me her hand, and on we went."

"Courage, Anna, courage," gasped Mr. Bogusławski, as if hearing the story for the first time, but no less moved than the new guests.

Very tired, Mama closed her eyes and I felt in my heart that I could replace Mama until she was stronger, and tell the guests about the two children in the snow. I could actually see before my very eyes the white picture of never-ending snow. But I sat on the side like a little mouse, feeling as if Mama was talking about other children, not about me or Yashu, and why was the blacksmith, Efraim Sonnenfeld, whom the neighbors in the building called Monny or Bonny, constantly drawing a figure eight on the leg of the chair? And why did he run to the bathroom when things got very tense?

"Gustav, my husband's brother who lived with us in Tarnopol, used to say that he wouldn't resist the Nazis. He'd say that he was willing to share the fate of all the Jews. I refused to give up, no, no, I continued walking. I saw a row of houses. I approached one and knocked at the door. 'Maybe you have a room for rent?' There was none. I knocked on several other doors, nothing. I said I was willing to pay a lot, and they didn't even look at us. We went back to the field where there were some stones, and I sat down even though they were covered in snow. If there'd been sparrows in the sky, they'd have wept with cold. Little Yashu rested his head on me and immediately fell asleep. Danusha's beautiful blue eyes expressed sorrow and sensitivity. I took her head between my hands to hide my tears and whispered a prayer to the Almighty."

Mama fell silent. And I couldn't believe it. Sorrow and sensitivity? Which child was she talking about? I didn't know her, and then I wanted her to stop. I wanted them to get up, *Thank you Anna, it was good to be with you, blessings and good health to us all*. At least once a year I wanted to stop these meetings with guests in our living room. It happened when Mama told about the snow and when she told about Yashu who wasn't living with us, and it happened when Mama told about the convalescent home where we were left alone.

"Why are you angry?" she'd ask, and I was silent. I didn't want any more people or stories in the living room like a movie, without paying for a ticket, but there'd be refreshments. I was tired of Danusha being ill again. Danusha crying and falling again, Yashu being a hero again, neither falling nor ill, what a good boy. I wanted peace and quiet.

Peace and quiet. Go home, enough, I've had enough, don't want to see people's sad faces in our living room anymore, don't want to hear their *oy, oy, oy,* hear Mr. Bogusławski's *Courage, Anna,* don't want to hear Mama's thrilling stories, can't you understand that?

I wanted to hear stories in our home like the ones I heard from my classmates. I liked life in our living room with tea and refreshments, but without stories about snow and lives in danger. The story about the officer's jeep was much better, Gideon's father or Yael's. What's wrong with traveling in Israel? And if it's not about a father with an army jeep then at least we could have a dress store in downtown Hadar, like we used to, and Papa would work there, and I wouldn't be alone.

And Klara would say, "You know, Anna, they've opened a good fabric store in Tel Aviv. Maybe it would be a good idea to go and take a look?"

And also, "Listen, friends, listen," Bertha Ketzelboim would add, she who has a haberdashery and wool store. "I saw hats from Paris in a magazine… mmm. None like that in Haifa, none."

Could I have such thoughts? In my dreams! Maybe if I'd been born in the promised land and named Ruthi or Michal, and had a father who never left, a father who was at home beside me, or if I'd been born in Tarnopol after at least five sons, and Mama would look at me with joyful eyes and cry out, *Oh, what a delightful baby girl we have, how I've waited for a little girl like this,* and she'd hold me tight and not put me down even if Yashu came up, and Papa would call me "my princess" and take me in his arms to a special carriage harnessed to two horses with a saddle and beads and bells on their necks.

Is it possible? "In a night dream, when the stars are out", like the song children sing at summer camp, but that's another story, and now I'm escaping to the toilet, locking the door, sitting down on the lid of the toilet with a book in my hand. Jules Verne. I love reading Jules Verne, and the guests can't come in. I don't care. How strange that Mama hasn't scolded me about it.

I wasn't angry for very long. Not even an hour, according to the clock in the hall. And then I returned to the living room after or during the refreshment break, and listened to Mama without the anger I'd felt before.

"And then came the great miracle," said Mama. "Two soldiers approached us in the snow, gesturing with their hands, pointing at the children and speaking rapidly in Italian. I don't understand Italian, tried speaking English, they didn't understand, French helped. They asked what I was doing in the snow with the children, gesturing with a finger that I was mad, and where was my home, what, I'd gotten lost? They were right, of course, those Italians. Who goes out in the snow at night with two small children? We could have turned to ice; that sort of cold doesn't exist in Israel, nothing like it. So, I told the soldiers that I'd come from the village because my daughter is sick and I have to find a doctor, but at the Dumnievskas', my acquaintances, the house is too crowded, they have no room for us, and I was looking for a room for the night.

"The soldiers looked at each other and said *impossibile, impossibile*. I realized they wanted to take us back to the Dumnievska family. One soldier picked up the sleeping Yashu, the other carried Danusha and the suitcase. We returned to the Dumnievska family.

"It was Sunday, and the family was eating dinner. They were

astounded to see us in the company of two Italian soldiers, who asked them with large gestures to find room in their home for us, promising loudly and clearly, *Mangia! Mangia!* that they'd bring food for everyone in a while, repeating this at least three times before the whole family understood and nodded yes, yes, yes.

"Mrs. Dumnievska stripped off the children's wet coats and hats, dressed them in warm pajamas, and put them to bed. They immediately fell asleep.

"Within half an hour the Italians returned in a car with big paper bags. They placed a large loaf of fresh bread on Mrs. Dumnievska's table, sausage, a jar of jam, a bottle of alcohol, delicacies that could only be dreamed of in those days. They poured the alcohol into glasses, clinked glasses with the family; the atmosphere warmed up, I felt good in the warm bed.

"Several days later, I got a letter from my sister Bronka. She wrote to say she'd soon be coming to take us to Kraków. Oh, how I missed Kraków, the city of my birth, where my sisters, Lydia, Franca, and Bronka lived and, of course, my beloved mother. I believed that a higher power was directing our lives, and said a prayer."

Mama paused.

While Mama was silent, I thought, illness saved us, with Mrs. Dumnievska, with the Italian soldiers, mmm. Illness can be helpful, so why do people keep saying, "Good health", "Good health"? What, don't they know?

"*Mangia! Mangia!*" muttered Bernard Cohen, looking at the refreshments table.

"Shhh," whispered his wife Klara, digging him in the ribs with her elbow.

I looked at Mama. What? She motioned with her head. I turned my head in the direction of the refreshments table. She followed my glance. *Now?* she asked with her eyes. *Yes,* I nodded.

"The delicacies the Italians brought the Dumnievska family make us want to eat something, ah?" asked Mama, smiling at her guests.

"One moment, Anna, one moment," called out Mr. Bogusławski, getting up from his chair, "I'll be back in a minute." He winked at Bernard Cohen and disappeared down the staircase.

"What's he on about?" asked Klara.

"Sounds like something good," said Bernard Cohen, rubbing his hands together.

"Shall we wait for him?" asked Henia Sonnenfeld, playing with a packet of cigarettes she'd taken out of her purse.

"We'll wait," said Mama.

Mr. Bogusławski stood huffing and puffing in the doorway waving a bottle. "Now we can also raise a glass, in honor of our Anna. What an extraordinary story we've heard, ah? Danusha, would you bring some glasses for the guests, please?"

"From the sideboard, the gold-edged ones," said Mama.

I took out the glasses and handed them out to the guests.

"Bravo, Bogusławski, what are we drinking?" asked Bernard Cohen.

"Slivovitz, for the women as well, please," he said, pouring the guests a drink. "Danusha, where is your glass, *nu*?"

My cheeks instantly flushed. I looked at Mama.

"She doesn't drink," said Mama.

"I don't drink," I said quietly.

"Yes, you do, just a little," said Mr. Bogusławski, giving me a glass. "Don't you realize that you and your brother gave your mother a reason to live?"

I looked at Mama. She covered her eyes with the palm of her hand. I saw her fingers trembling.

I wanted to approach her and give her a handkerchief, but Mr. Bogusławski was quicker. He stood beside Mama, gave her a handkerchief, and put a hand on her shoulder.

"Your health, dear Anna, the children's health," he cried, and raised his glass. "Your health, your health," responded the guests and drank their slivovitz, then got up and went to the refreshments table.

I stood at the side, looking at Mama. She wiped her tears with the handkerchief, smoothed her hair, stood up, straightened her gown, and joined the guests.

I went to the window in the hall and glanced out. The line from the song, "*How wonderful, how wonderful, that there are nights like that,*" played in my mind like a broken record. I pressed my fingers against my mouth, I couldn't stop yawning.

Two weeks went by and Mama said to the guests, "Bronka," and chewed her lips.

"Bronka came to take us from Lwów to Kraków. She came to the Dumnievska family home without warning. When the door opened we saw her, and she told us she wasn't able to let us know she was coming because she was dependent on the schedule of her old school-friend Sophie's German friend, who was about to travel to Lwów.

"'Jew-hunters hang about the train station,' Sophie told Bronka. 'Ukrainians, Poles, and *Volksdeutsche,* German Poles. The man is traveling to Lwów for work, better you go with him, and he's agreed.' Sophie had converted to Christianity before the war but had nonetheless stayed in touch with Bronka who, of course, had Polish papers.

"Bronka had told the German that she worked for a coffee importing company in Kraków and was traveling to Lwów on business. On the way back, she wanted to pick up a close friend and her two children and take them back to Kraków—all this in broken German, although, like her sisters, she spoke German well. Unlike the Poles, the Germans couldn't distinguish between a Jewish and a Polish woman. During the journey, men with hats walked through the carriages, examining people's faces and asking to see papers. Seated beside a German in uniform and talking pleasantly to him on the train helped her get through the journey.

"My sister arranged with the German," said Mama, waving a finger in the air, "that three days later, he'd come to the Dumnievska family home with an army car to take her and her friend to the train station. They planned to take the night-train to Kraków.

"When they reached the Lwów station, the German linked arms with my sister and together they walked along the platform. He gave her his telephone number in case of need, and when she got into the taxi, he bent and kissed her and, my friends, you will soon see how fateful that kiss was."

"Oy, oy, oy," cried Bertha Ketzelboim, "open a window please —my nerves can't stand this tension."

Jacob, her husband, the athlete, leapt up from his chair and opened the window.

"It's cold," shivered Klara Cohen.

"Air, air," moaned Bertha, patting her chest.

"Half-open is enough," stated Klara.

"No, it isn't enough," Bertha said, glaring, "dress warmly when you come here."

"Shhh, shhh," requested Mr. Bogusławski.

I got up from my chair and went into Mama's room. I took out a wool shawl and gave it to Klara. She didn't move.

"*Nu*, put it around you," said Henia Sonnenfeld, adding in a whisper, "you can see she's suffering."

Mama cleared her throat. The living room calmed down.

"I was so happy to see my sister," said Mama. "The children were also happy to see their aunt. But after the children had gone to bed, I heard about the tragedy that had befallen our family. We were five sisters: Lydia, Franca, me, Stella, and Bronka. Can you imagine the joy our youngest brother, Aharon, brought when he was born after five girls? Aharon was our genius. By the age of twenty-two, he'd graduated from law school. Aharon was attractive, tall, fair-haired, blue-eyed, and he spoke German well, becoming the liaison between the community leadership and the occupation authorities. He arranged travel papers for people who wished to reunite with their families, wrote applications for people, all this happened before the Kraków Jews were expelled to the ghetto and the Płaszów Camp. The Germans treated Aharon well, often saying, 'What a pity he's a Jew, such a pity'.

"One day a letter came for Aharon at my parents' house, ordering him to report to the head of the Gestapo. My father and mother begged him to run, hide. But my brother refused. He knew that if he were to run away, they'd arrest the entire family.

"Aharon went and didn't return. A few weeks later, my older sister Lydia was told that Aharon had been sent to the prison on Montelupich Street in Kraków, and from there to Auschwitz.

"Lydia decided to keep this information from my mother, and told her that Aharon had been sent overseas to work. My mother became ill with heart trouble and lay in hospital. My father sat for many hours with sacred books, asking for mercy for him and trying to take comfort.

"One day, my father received a message from the Gestapo that all Jewish community heads and employees had died in Auschwitz. Shortly afterwards, my father had a heart attack and died."

Mama stopped. She put out a trembling hand for a glass of water and slowly drank.

Women in the living room wept into their handkerchiefs. Some of the men leaned forwards towards the floor.

"*Yobtbiomat,* damn the Nazis," said Bernard Cohen, striking his knee with his fist, then checking to see if he could slip in something that had happened to him. Bernard would use opportunities to talk about his life in the forest. Now, too, he said aloud, "In the forest, we—"

"May they go to hell," Efraim Sonnenfeld cut in, and Mr. Bogusławski cried out, "Courage, Anna, courage."

I stuck to the chair, staring at Bernard Cohen's hurt face.

I looked for my brother but, as usual, he wasn't home. I wanted him to sit next to me. I wanted to hold hands with him, like we used to when walking with Mama, when I held her hand and his.

"My sister Bronka told me that Lydia decided to go on protecting Mama who, in the meantime, had left hospital. Even more so after Papa died. She decided to forge Aharon's handwriting and began bringing her letters as if they were from him. In the letters, she wrote that he was in a camp in Germany, that he was fine, and after the war, he'd return home. Lydia made sure to bring Mama a similar letter every few weeks. And then Bronka embraced me and asked me to overcome my dreadful sorrow at my brother and father's deaths, to be strong for my children and my mother.

"Three days later, I parted from the Dumnievska family who had helped us. We blessed each other with great emotion and they wished us a safe journey to Kraków.

"The German was waiting for us at the appointed time. Bronka introduced me to him and we traveled in his army car to the train station. He parted from us and we walked along the platform in the direction of the train carriage. Bronka carried our suitcase, the children and me following her.

"'That woman looks like a Jew,' I heard one of the porters say to his friend in a loud voice. They stood next to the train carriage and looked at us. My heart started a mad pounding.

"'No, no,' responded the porter next to him, 'I saw her at the station three days ago. She came with a German soldier. Maybe she's his fiancée—he kissed her when they parted.'

"We boarded the train. I looked back. The porters weren't following us. Nonetheless, my heart almost jumped out of my body. The heavy pounding continued for several long minutes. I was afraid of every passenger who got into the carriage. I hid my terrible fear from Bronka and the children, praying we'd arrive safely.

"We traveled all night. Even when we got off the train in Kraków I was afraid, praying I wouldn't meet one of my old Polish classmates. I didn't know if I could trust my classmates in these troubled times of war."

Now of all times, I half close my eyes and look at the guests. In the meantime, I thought, Bronka put herself at risk again and again for us, oh, beloved *Ciocia*—Aunt Bronka, may she have a long life, I prayed.

Chapter Six

On the train from Lwów, Mama promised me it would be good to be near our family, that it was important to be nearby. When we arrived in Kraków, I saw that her eyes were darting from side to side, and things were falling out of her hands. Bronka hugged her, whispering things into her ear that I also wanted to know: Who exactly was waiting for us? How many people? How many children? What were their names? I started asking a lot of questions very fast, which tired Mama. Bronka said, "Leave Mama alone, sweetheart, it will be all right," and, in the end, what I most wanted to forget about Kraków was our first day in the city with the family.

Bronka took us from the train station to Franca's apartment. She was Mama's older sister and Grandma Rosa also lived with her. I remember seeing a distant hill on the way, and a large palace and another castle with a wall around it, and it was cold.

First, we arrived at Franca's apartment on Kremlicka Street. Mama said, "Here we are, Danusha and Yashu, and here are our cousins, that's Yehoshua, this is Bella, and that's Abraham." We laughed to each other and jumped up and down.

"And this is your grandmother, who is my mother. Please say hello to Grandma Rosa," said Mama.

We kissed Grandma Rosa's cheek; Mama wept on her shoulder. Grandma Rosa gently patted Mama's back and held a handkerchief to her nose. And then Mama said, "And this is Aunt Franca, and this is Aunt Lydia, my older sister," and again we kissed and hugged, and the sisters quietly wept, and Aunt Lydia said, "Welcome to Kraków", and gave us a candy.

I jumped again and Grandma looked at me and said, "Why are you jumping?"

And later on, "Why are you sneezing so much?"

And later on, "Wait, why are you getting up? Leave Mama alone now. Let her rest, sit quietly. Why are you touching Yashu, leave him alone," and she looked at me with eyes as hard as hard-boiled eggs.

Franca lived with her children in a two-roomed apartment. Yehoshua, five years older than me, was hidden by Bronka with a family in the city and occasionally came to visit. His sister, Bella, was a year older than me, and Abraham was six months younger than me. We were alike as siblings, that's what Mama said. And all of us had blue eyes, blond hair and fake papers with Polish names.

Franca's husband, the advocate, didn't live with them but was in hiding in the city. Every day or two he'd move to another room in exchange for a lot of money, because he was so afraid someone would inform on him.

"Danusha and Yashu, play nicely with your cousins," said Bronka, and Bella and Abraham looked curiously at us.

"You can play together," said Aunt Franca, hugging us.

I stood next to Mama and felt as if I were traveling on a train; my heart pounded, tuk-tuk, tuk-tuk, as if it were on a track. At last I'd found real friends I could play with, and not only that girl in the mirror who was me. At last I was allowed to talk and not fear the wicked eyes of strangers. And, more than anything, I knew that in the house in Kraków, even if my fever went up and my tonsils hurt, I wouldn't have to say the Christian prayers which had so saddened Mama.

Franca gave us lemonade to drink, and we ate sandwiches. I heard Grandma Rosa say, "Stella", and again, "Stella", and Lydia said, "It's all right, look, I've brought you a letter from Aharon. With God's help we'll all meet again after the war", and then Bella explained to us how to play Blind Cow We tie a scarf round the eyes of one of the children, everyone runs away, and the child who can't see has to catch a child who will take his place as Blind Cow.

Bella tied the scarf round her eyes, put out her hands and walked towards me. I stayed close to the table in the living room and began to run round it like Abraham; Yashu joined in, laughing. We ran round several times and then Bella suddenly stopped. She turned and ran towards us in the other direction. Oh, how excited I felt, but I managed to turn around and escape her. In the end, she caught me and we both laughed so much I think I peed a bit from laughing. My whole body tickled. It was like the feeling you get when soaping your foot; even my hair stood up from the tickling, aah, it was so good.

And then I saw Grandma Rosa's face.

She sat on the sofa, her chin pinched and her lips turned

down, looking down her nose as if she could smell something rotten, or something bad. Her eyes were on me gravely, coldly. As if she were superior and I inferior, and I had better keep my distance.

"The girl has a Galician temperament," said Grandma Rosa, and the saliva I swallowed got stuck in my throat. A Galician temperament? What's that? She was looking at me, yes. Not at Bella, only at me. She said "the girl has", not "the boy", which means that only I have the temperament problem, and that must be something very bad because Grandma Rosa looks harshly only at me. When Bella jumps and laughs, and then Abraham, Grandma Rosa smiles, holds out her arms to embrace them, Yashu too. What have I done? What?

I went to sit in an upholstered wooden chair as far away as possible from Grandma Rosa's eyes. In my mind I heard the sound of a bomb like the one I heard in Brzeżany, whoosh, whoosh, whoosh… I said to myself, my cousins' temperament is probably all right, what's wrong with me? What's a Galician temperament? Maybe it's dangerous? But I decided to be quiet, not even to ask one word about it.

Bella approached me. She wanted to tie a scarf round my eyes. I didn't want to play Blind Cow. I was cold, I wanted to sleep, as far away as possible from Grandma Rosa.

We stayed with Franca for several days. Bronka and Lydia left toward evening, and I realized that they each lived in another house. Mama said she'd have to find a room for us as soon as possible, and I couldn't stop thinking about what Grandma Rosa had said about me. What should I do? What should I do?

The more I thought about it, I realized it had something to do with wildness, God forbid, as Mama liked to say. And this made me realize that maybe Grandma Rosa was hinting that I came from a bad place. I understood from Mama that Eastern Galicia was considered inferior to Lodz, where our cousins Yehoshua, Bella, and Abraham came from. Mama also preferred Kraków to Tarnopol. In Kraków there were theaters, concert halls, interesting lectures to be heard, I heard Mama say so, whereas Tarnopol, in Eastern Galicia, was close to the Russian border and had less of everything, mainly culture, mainly music. Even Mama's sisters said that after the wedding she wasn't happy about going to Tarnopol but she had no choice; they found her a good match and she was relatively old, over thirty.

Clearly it was time she got married, apart from which she had two young sisters, Stella and Bronka, who also had to marry.

Was Galicia the reason for my being considered wild?

One night, in my bed in the dark—I don't remember where I slept—I came to a decision: I'd prove to Grandma Rosa and Mama that I was a good girl. Even if I did have a Galician temperament—which wasn't certain—like in Tarnopol. On second thought, and third thought, I decided I'd close up my heart under lock and key, and make sure day and night that I wouldn't want anything, not the smallest thing, God forbid—let's say wanting to be happy, to sing, or talk loudly. I prepared a list in my mind of the things I must never forget:

In a good family one never raises one's voice.

One never, ever talks with one's hands but keeps them close to one's body.

It isn't proper to run or jump up and down.

It isn't proper to laugh with one's mouth open; one must smile with one's mouth half closed, that's it.

I already knew that one should cry quietly, so that the Poles, the Germans, and the Ukrainians wouldn't hear and see.

On my first visit to Grandma Rosa I understood that it was most important that I learn to hide myself even from myself.

Ah, and in my closet I had rather a lot of wide-brimmed hats that were most comfortable to wear in the street.

It turned out that Mama told her guests the story of the day we arrived in Kraków on one of the days during Hanukah. It was after we'd celebrated Mother's Day in Haifa.

I brought Mama a bouquet of red roses I'd bought her with my weekly pocket money, and a special card we prepared in class with large letters:

TO DEAR MAMA, FROM YOUR LOVING DAUGHTER.

I decorated the card with flowers and butterflies, and Mama leant it against the vase of roses standing on the round table in the living room.

It didn't stop raining. There was lightning and thunder, but the guests still came, putting their wet umbrellas into a bucket in the entrance before coming into our living room. While they were taking off their coats and looking round the living room, each one remarked on the red roses and the card I'd prepared. I enjoyed it.

"Today I want to talk about my mother," said Mama, crossing her legs close to her body. She was wearing black nylon stockings with a delicate floral design and the women in the room looked at her legs and stockings with curiosity.

"I wonder where you can get stockings like those. They must be expensive," said Klara Cohen.

"Anna's worth it," said Mr. Bogusławski.

In the meantime, Mama spoke in a quiet voice no school teacher could match.

"When we arrived in Kraków, *ich war im zivten Himmel,* I was in seventh heaven. It's hard to describe the enormous joy that filled my heart when my mother embraced us, and all this in the middle of the war.

"Who could believe that all the trains in Europe were traveling like crazy, while we felt safe next to my mother? I felt relieved of the great responsibility of looking after my children. The children were filled with happiness at being with their beloved grandmother."

I looked at Mama. Happiness? Is she talking about Grandma Rosa who labeled me with a Galician temperament, which caused me so many problems?

I didn't say a word.

"Mayor Abba Hushi didn't just establish Mother's Day in Haifa, he even established a Mother's Garden," said Henia Sonnenfeld cheerfully.

"He was a mischief-maker, the one who took care of all the mothers," I heard Bernard Cohen chuckle to Mr. Bogusławski.

"Shhh, *nu,* be quiet," requested Klara, glaring at him, but he responded, "Look at you, dropping all the crumbs from those cookies like that. Why don't you pay attention?"

"Don't interfere, and move your foot," she commanded in a whisper.

"What for?" he asked.

"To pick up your crumbs."

People sometimes got irritable in the living room, but this

never got to Mama's armchair. The guests whispered to each other almost inaudibly. Their faces told me they were annoyed.

Sometimes Bernard Cohen got angry with Mr. Bogusławski because of the places that were occupied by the Germans, and who got to these occupied places first, Russians or Americans, and the story about Russian officers dressing up as Polish soldiers because Stalin wanted to create a Polish army that was loyal to Russians, right or wrong? Tell me! Right or wrong?

Mr. Meltzer was the only one who didn't participate in the talking. He observed Mama patiently even when he was drinking tea and eating biscuits.

"My sister Franca worked in a German government office in Kraków and at first she was given a tiny cubicle like a storeroom, and a room to live in on the ground floor of the office. Her employer, Dr. Kranz, allowed her to bring her small son and daughter to the room. One day, Dr. Kranz informed her that she could move into a small, pleasant apartment on Kremlitzka Street, which was of course a welcome change because my dear mother could also move in with them.

"Franca was very worried about her husband Chaim. He was in hiding and moving from one wretched room to another because of the informers. The constant tension, day and night, increased and became unbearable for some of the persecuted Jews. And, indeed, one day Franca's husband had had enough. He decided to turn himself in to the Płaszów labor camp in Kraków. There were groups of Jews in the camp who went out to hard labor every day; although the food was poor, they got somewhere to sleep and safety from informers. One day, he saw a group of Jews on their way back to the camp from work. He joined them unobserved and thus gained entrance to Płaszów.

"My sister Lydia and his wife Franca occasionally managed to send him parcels of food, but he warned them not to do it. He was afraid that someone from the family would be caught and, God forbid, tortured into betraying the rest of the family."

Mama stopped, looking at the guests and at me. I had nothing to tell her through my eyes and she knew how to read the expression on my face.

"Your sisters are better than husbands," said Klara Cohen.

"Braver, not better," said her husband.

"Better," argued his wife.

"Real heroes," said Bernard Cohen.

"Both better and braver," said Mr. Bogusławski, with a clap of his hands to end the discussion and called out, "Courage, Anna, courage."

While they were arguing, Yashu quietly entered the house. He took off his shoes at the door so they wouldn't hear him and summon him to the living room. He winked at me and disappeared into his room. I also wanted to disappear and close a door behind me but the only door I saw in front of me was the front door.

"Yes," said Mama, "we helped as much as we could, but Franca's small apartment wasn't big enough for all of us so we had to wander the city again. Bronka found us our first room in the city, in the home of the widow of a doctor, Professor Boyak, a noble woman. She received us well, but early one morning, Mrs. Boyak came into the room in alarm, whispering that two Gestapo men were looking for someone in the attic. Our suitcase hadn't been unpacked. I took out clothing for that day, washing the dirty clothes by hand, drying them in the room, and then we put them on again. With the help of Mrs. Boyak, I quickly dressed the children in coats and we escaped the minute she signaled to us to go. Naturally we went to

Franca's apartment. And then I found another room on the ground floor of a small hotel that rented rooms for just one week. I took the children to the room and put them to bed. I myself couldn't fall asleep for worry. I was quietly praying Shema Israel, when I suddenly heard knocking and screams in German: 'Open the door, German police, night check. Open up'. The noise came from a door nearby. By the noise, they'd ripped out the door and entered the room, screaming like maniacs.

"I felt my heart pounding. I immediately woke the children, helped them to dress, and we escaped by a side door directly into the yard, and from there into a dark and empty street.

"I couldn't go to Franca in the middle of the night. It was cold, and we walked straight along the streets until I saw a small opening in a wall. Inside were steps leading to an old furniture warehouse. There was no choice. We huddled in a corner of the warehouse, covering ourselves with our coats, and the children immediately fell asleep. I couldn't sleep. I heard mice and rats scampering about on the furniture. A rat came close to me; I saw scary teeth. Only the next morning did we return to Franca's apartment, where we met Lydia, who was angry with me for not discussing it with her beforehand. 'The Germans', she told me, 'carry out surprise checks looking for Jews especially in small hotels and hostels, yes. You have to be very careful, Anna.' She promised to help me find a better place, if possible, yes, in Kraków, during the war.

"'You have no idea what it's like sitting in a warehouse at night', I told Franca that night, 'every rat jumping on you and baring its teeth, or roaring, tsss, tsss. You don't know what it's like walking in the street at night. Every tree looks like a monster, and I was afraid evil dogs would jump out at us from the yards. I was afraid the earth would open up and swallow us, and maybe it would be good, the nightmare would end.'

"Franca held me, 'Shhh. You're safe here, Anna. It will be all right.'"

I remember wondering how safe we felt at Franca's, with Lydia and Bronka who came to visit. But as soon as we crossed the street and entered another room, huge fear would come up with Mama's instructions: "Careful not to break the vase, careful not to spill water on the carpet, careful not to talk; smile."

Yashu and I say "Yes, yes, yes," and she goes on, "Walk quietly in the room, don't make a noise, don't go out, stay away from the window, don't go out on the balcony," and Mama isn't at all quiet. I see she's focused. The slightest sound and she'll have her ear to the door, or switch off the light and cautiously peep out the window. The suitcase isn't unpacked, at night we sleep in our clothes and suddenly—shouting at the entrance to the building and we are into our coats and gloves, escaping in the middle of the night, feeling lost in the Kraków streets, looking for a place to hide. And as soon as morning comes, we feel safe again with Franca, and go out the next day to a new apartment. One day, two days, maybe a week, and then I see the questions on the landlords' faces, even though we look like Gentiles.

Mama of course smiles at them, speaks pleasantly about the weather. I also smile politely, my brother is quiet, and we open the suitcase, take out clean socks, good night, good night, and then, boom, "Get up, get up children, quickly, quickly, put on your coats, shoes, quickly, Danusha, leave the cushion, go out quietly, careful, steps, a corner, another three steps, now walk as usual, slowly, everything's all right, here, a streetlamp, we'll stop in a while and tie your shoelace."

Hot. Cold. Hot. Cold. Hot. Hot. Hot. Coooooold. My belly

hurt with all the jumping about. I wanted to sleep in the same bed like Bella and Abraham. I scratched my hand until it bled, don't cry, don't cry, smile, will it be all right?

Mama told the visitors in the living room that Lydia was married to a clever scholar, that he also had a broad general education. Grandpa and Grandma liked and respected their son-in-law, Israel. Why? He was an honest man, very likeable, and took pains with his appearance. She remembers how her younger sisters would laugh at Israel, who judiciously brushed his teeth after every meal. And his teeth really were beautiful and white.

During the first deportation of Jews from Kraków, Lydia, her husband, and children managed to reach Tarnów.

One day, Israel received an order to report on a certain day and hour for work in the town of Jonska, near Tarnów. Relatives advised him not to report. He didn't listen to them, and never returned. Lydia found work with a German family in Kraków for her fourteen-year-old daughter Katie; she herself and her seventeen-year-old son, Adam, wandered from place to place, with fake papers of course, according to the employment she found for them.

Lydia, who had arranged our Aryan papers under the name of Kwiatkowski, told Mama we had to be very careful when entering and leaving Franca's apartment. The instructions were clear. She'd look down at me and Yashu to make sure everything was clear.

"Don't dawdle near strangers."

"Don't talk, don't look people in the eye."

"Don't stop even for a second near the concierge who lives on the ground floor. She is curious and follows everyone who comes here, and she informs."

"You have to watch out for informers. They hang about everywhere in the city, trying to catch Jews."

Mama of course warned us to be quiet and polite, as if we knew anything else.

She particularly made sure to remind us about the probing eyes of the concierge, who had a wart under her chin. This concierge wanted to know things, "Where are you from? Where is your father?" Things like that.

Mama asked us and warned us not to tire Grandma Rosa, and to play nicely with our cousins. She'd say, "Goodbye, goodbye, children", and go off to look for a room for the night.

I don't know what I did beside Grandma Rosa when Mama went out. Maybe I observed Bella and Abraham too closely, to learn how to behave with a temperament from Lodz? Maybe I tried to talk like them, or laugh soundlessly? And maybe I sat quietly for too long on the wooden chair with the floral upholstery, and refused to play Blind Cow, so I wouldn't suddenly burst out into Galician laughter. Grandma would look at me, saying, "Why are you putting the serviette on the table, put it in the garbage," or "Why do you look at me all the time, *nu,* play with Bella and Abraham, see how nicely Yashu is playing."

When I was near Grandma Rosa, I needed the security of Mama.

In the living room, Mama told how she'd had to rush around for days to find an empty room, even though Lydia and Bronka helped her look. Sometimes they both said to her, rest, Anna, rest. We'll find an apartment for you. On those days, Mama said, she'd prepare a packet of sandwiches every morning, slices of bread and butter and some fruit, and she'd take us out to Dietlowska Avenue that crossed the city center.

Along the avenue were long benches. There were mothers there, or country nursemaids. She'd cover her head with a shawl like the country women and rest on the bench for a few hours. We played beside her and walked from here to there and back again.

Mama found another solution for the noon hours. She'd take us into the Raduta Cinema on Lowitch Street, close to the train station. They showed films there round the clock. She'd sit us down at the side, feed us, and then we'd fall asleep. This brought her some relief. The usher who'd accompany people to their seats sometimes managed to frighten her. He'd pass her and shine a torch on her. So, to be careful, every time the usher was busy with the doors to the hall, she'd wake us up and we'd go from one side of the hall to the other.

I hear Mama and, in an instant, I see rows and rows of chairs, and lots of people, and darkness in the hall. And I look at the screen without understanding anything, and fall asleep. Mama wakes me and Yashu up, whispering, *We're moving*. Moving. We hold hands and walk after her in the darkness, sit down again. I close my eyes, hear people speaking in a language I don't understand, a woman laughs, there are sounds of dishes and a piano playing. I enjoy hearing these sounds; gradually I fall asleep and then again, we're moving, moving.

At night, in my bed in Haifa, I'd often think back, wondering what films we'd seen at the Raduta Cinema in Kraków. For while we were hiding in all sorts of holes in Poland, the Americans were making romantic films like *Wuthering Heights*.

Maybe we saw a love story like the film *Casablanca,* which I saw several times at the Armon Cinema in Haifa, but didn't understand the content at the time, or we saw a children's film, maybe the *Bambi* cartoon that they made in America?

If in those days I'd seen the film, Bambi, who lost his mother and was raised by good animals in the forest, I'd immediately have covered my face with my hands and sobbed. Cried quietly, quietly, because crying was also a threat to our lives from the usher who thrust his torch into peoples' faces.

The thought of being in the world without Mama was disastrous for me, only next to Mama did I believe that things would be all right.

It didn't matter that there were Germans and Ukrainians, it didn't matter that there were Poles who looked for us with wicked eyes, there were also those who helped us. It wasn't important that Grandma Rosa had a problem with me, I always knew that Mama would take care of me, and that's what happened.

Mama and her sisters called Grandma *holy mother*. Maybe my mother was the same?

Chapter Seven

It was at Josef Wirt's house on Piłsudski Street in Kraków that I learned how to be afraid without escaping to another room. Mama found work as his housekeeper and we arrived without Yashu because during the war, everyone was looking for boys who were circumcised. If they'd discovered his circumcision, we'd all have been in great danger.

"You mustn't talk about our family, Danusha, not one word," ordered Mama, lengthening her strides.

I immediately fell behind. "Did you hear me? You mustn't talk—"

"Yashu?" I asked aloud and there was nobody beside me. I remembered that my little brother Yashu was no longer with us; he'd stayed behind to live with a Polish family who had a harsh landlord.

"Better for him, better for us," said Mama, putting her handkerchief to her nose every time we left Yashu, who cried and cried. He'd cry and she'd say mechanically: "Not a word about the family. There's no family, do you hear me?"

Josef Wirt lived alone in a large house with a spacious living room and a dining room furnished in pale blue with flowers. "Tyrolean style," said Mama, and to me it looked beautiful, like a picture in a magazine. Josef Wirt suffered from dark spots under the eyes and a grooved lower lip because he was used to tightening it as if constantly biting the place.

Ever since, I've learned that dark spots under the eyes and a chewed lower lip could be a sign of trouble.

I slept with Mama in a small room, and during the day I sat on a little chair in the kitchen. Mama cooked meals for the master and I watched her. Even when she looked at me and was upset about Yashu, I didn't look away and I didn't know what to say.

Sometimes, I stood at the window and peeped out. I saw a house and next to it another house, and after that another and another, and all the houses were empty. Each house had a fence and a dog kennel without a dog. We also ran away at night, leaving an empty building behind us. Afterwards, we moved from one small room to another and another, and in the meantime, Yashu was no longer with us and his place in Mama's bed remained empty.

After the first day in Josef Wirt's house, Mama said, "We're staying here, and remember, Danusha, not a word about the family, not one. There's no Grandma Rosa, no Lydia, Franca, and Bronka, no cousins, none, and most important of all, Yashu. There's no Yashu… no Yashu…"

I nodded quietly after each word Mama spoke. Returning to my chair, I looked at her. She straightened up when she heard the sound of boots, smoothed a finger under her eye, smoothed down her apron, and looked unblinkingly at the door.

We both heard Josef Wirt's boots as he walked about the house. The krrrch, krrrch, krrrch, krrrch sounded like a giant, endlessly opening zipper.

Josef Wirt had boots of all colors, black, light brown, dark brown, brown and cream, wine and gray, and probably many more whose colors I forget. He had many pairs of boots, and each one had its own creak, sometimes sounding like a bird cheeping, sometimes like a frog; the one I remember most is the heavy krrrch-krrrch-krrrch of the black boots with a buckle. He'd walk from one room to another then, a few seconds later, he'd return. Sometimes he'd pause, or stop in the corridor. Sometimes he'd advance to his Tyrolean sofas in the living room, the ones with the flowers. I learned the direction of his walking according to the step in the living room. The first stride after the step sounded a little different: short, heavy, like a fall, krrr. That's all. Sometimes after taking several steps he'd drag a chair, tak-tak and again, tak-tak. That was a sign he'd sat down at his writing desk and was relatively far from me and Mama.

When the heavy footsteps approached the kitchen, I felt as if there were cold pins and needles in my back, although it was hot in the kitchen. I immediately bent my head and started silently counting: "One, two, three, four…" By ten he would usually come in. I counted faster, "One, two, three…"

By the middle of the third time I'd counted from one to ten, Josef still hadn't said a word. I peeped at him. He was looking at Mama, thinking, and thinking. She tucked her chin into her chest and folded her arms on her apron. And then he'd speak. At the time I didn't understand a word of German. He had a whispery voice, psh, psh, psh, psh. He'd sometimes stop to cough briefly.

The fifth time I counted from one to ten, Mama answered

something. And then he talked and talked, and Mama spoke two or three words to him in German, no more—and silence.

During this time, my eyes burned and my hands itched, but I didn't move. I just counted faster and faster and faster in my heart, maybe ten times from one to ten, and only then did he leave.

Mama wiped her neck and forehead with a cloth, straightened her apron, picked up a wooden spoon, and went back to stirring the pots. I leaned against the wall and wordlessly scratched my hands.

"You can go and play in the room with Tushya," she said, after several long minutes of silence.

I scratched my hands and didn't get up.

"It's evening already. You can go and play with her for a while."

I nodded but didn't get up to play with Tushya, the maid. I missed Yashu. We visited him at the Polish family's house on a Sunday, which was Mama's day off.

Tushya was responsible for cleaning the rooms. She was shorter and thinner than Mama, and she had darting brown eyes. Tushya would stroke my hair and let me play with an old doll she took out of the suitcase. A doll that had no clothes, no hair, and only one leg. I loved playing with the doll. I rocked her in my arms, singing, na-na-na, but when Josef Wirt shouted "Tushya!" from his room, she'd jump and tense, and then I'd also jump. We were both alarmed, putting our hands on our hearts to stop them falling out. Tushya's face was as white as the wall, as for mine—I don't know. But I'd immediately throw down the doll and run to Mama, who also paled when he shouted at Tushya, and when she saw me, she signaled me to sit in my usual chair and keep my mouth closed.

I closed my lips tightly until they were warm and then she signaled me to relax them and smile if he appeared at the door.

He never shouted at Mama. Only at Tushya.

That's the life I remember from Josef Wirt's house in Kraków, apart from the Tyrolean sofas. If Josef Wirt wasn't home, I could spend hours gazing uninterruptedly at the blue flowers; I never tired of the blue flowers, or of going with Mama to visit Grandma Rosa in Franca's apartment. It gave me a good feeling on the one hand, but not so good on the other. Next to Grandma Rosa, Mama would smile and, most important of all, she was content, though not necessarily when I recited in front of her. This happened every Sunday, when Mama asked me to stand on a chair and recite the poem "Echo of the Cradle" by the Polish poet Adam Asnyk in front of everyone. "Echo of the Cradle" has thirteen stanzas and I learned them all by heart.

Today I remember the first, second, and last stanzas, as well as the refrain. I translated them from Polish into my arithmetic notebook when I didn't know how to do my homework:

When I was a little boy
Opening to the world
Hidden in a bud
My mother took me on her lap
When I was a little boy

To this day I recall
How she soothed tears and pain
humming a song of longing
And the voice borne on sweet waves
Reawakened the smile
And every word of the song

I remember to this day

My child, do not weep, no, no,
Brighten your face again
As long as you have a mother
No harm will come to you
Lay your head in my lap
I will protect you from all pain
No, my child, please do not weep, no, no.

Remember your mother
with wholesome love
Have no doubt
Bathe your soul in tears
Believe in the beauty of the enlightened soul
In love that is eternal
Remember your mother.

My child, do not weep, no, no,
Brighten your face again
As long as you have a mother
No harm will come to you
Lay your head in my lap
I will protect you from all pain
My child, please do not weep, no, no.

Whenever I recited, "As long as you have a mother / No harm will come to you", Mama would look at Grandma Rosa with moist eyes. Grandma sat erect, her eyes half-closed, her lower lip pressed against the upper lip, her nostrils widening. Not a single muscle moved in her face while she listened to me, but at the end she sighed, "Oy, Aharon, Aharon, oy, Stella, Stella." I naturally recited all the stanzas.

I really loathed it, but I loathed returning to Josef Wirt's house even more.

Mama told the guests in the living room that Lydia, her older sister, had found a notice in the newspaper from a German looking for a housekeeper who specialized in cooking and baking cakes. It was just after we arrived in Kraków.

Lydia called on the Nazi, whose name was Josef Sepp Wirt, presenting Mama to him as the wife of a Polish officer who fell in captivity, maybe in battle, no one knew. She emphasized that Mama knew German and cooked and baked well, and that she was clean and honest, but she had a little girl she couldn't part from.

"I had to part from my little son, Yashu," said Mama, pressing her fingers into the armchair until they were as white as the wall. "It was dangerous to bring a Jewish boy into the house of a Nazi, God forbid the secret got out, so I paid a large sum to a Polish family and my heart wept for my little boy."

"Intolerable," said Klara Cohen, plucking at the handle of the bag she held on her lap.

"But necessary, that's how come everyone is here together," responded Bernard, her husband, and looked at me. "Where's Yashu?"

"At a friend's house," I said quietly, looking at Mr. Bogusławski.

"And why are you—"

"Let's go on," interrupted Mr. Bogusławski, smiling at me.

"The German asked to interview me," said Mama.

"That very day, I presented myself at his house on Wolska Street; its name was changed before the war to Piłsudski Street, after the great leader of independent Poland, Marshal Józef Piłsudski. It was one of the most prestigious streets in Kraków. Before the war, the house belonged to a wealthy Jewish industrialist and after he escaped, they gave his house to Josef Wirt, who supplied goods to the German army and was important to them. He employed me at once.

"Also working in the house was Tushya, who was responsible for cleaning and order. She was eighteen years old; I was moved, actually shivered when I saw her. Tushya's eyes were Jewish eyes, sad and suspicious. The Polish Jewish poet Julian Tuwim managed to describe what I felt when I saw her for the first time," said Mama, gazing up at the sky she saw beyond the window, "do you know him? He wrote:

Eyes reflecting fear
Reflecting the heritage of generations
Boys scattered throughout the world
without a motherland
Wandering, anguished…"

Everyone in the living room followed her eyes to the sky, and only I looked at Mama.

She looked like an impressive stage actress, sitting on a chair mid-stage, gazing solemnly at the opposite window, as if at the horizon of the sea, waiting to receive Julian Tuwim in person.

"On my first day I set the table in the dining room," said

Mama. "The table was perfect. I cooked lunch and waited for my employer, Josef Wirt, to appear. The minute he saw the set table, he hurried to the kitchen to welcome me and asked to see my little girl. I called the little one, whom I'd told to play quietly in the small room adjacent to the kitchen, and he approached her, a huge smile spreading across his face. I stood behind him, making my face smile, and Danusha immediately smiled her charming smile…"

I smiled at Mama and she smiled back, demonstrating to our guests in the living room how our sign language worked, and naturally I let my head drop to my shoulder and broadened the smile.

"She's pretty as a painting, your Danusha," said Henia Sonnenfeld.

"She's prettier than a painting," said Mr. Bogusławski.

"Tfu tfu, enough of that." Bertha Ketzelboim was shocked.

"Tfu tfu," several said in unison.

Every time Mama asked me to participate in her stories, I'd get very nervous and immediately needed to go to the toilet. Sometimes I'd remember how I felt then in the war, which also got me up from my chair and straight to the toilet.

The first times Mama told the story about Josef Wirt, I'd go the toilet a lot. In time, I stopped. I wanted to hear her every word and see if we actually remembered the same thing from that hard and terrifying time. And I'd watch people. They changed over the years.

At first, neighbors were invited to our living room in Haifa, then acquaintances and colleagues. Later on, she met members of the General Zionist Party, followed by new guests from Tel Aviv. Only the regulars heard everything time after time.

Over the years, the economic situation improved and Mama's

refreshments, which began with a glass of tea, nuts and biscuits, occasionally yeast cookies, were replaced with lovely large fruit, good, home-made cookies that she baked, and cream cakes. I noticed that not only the refreshments changed but the stories did too, with added details she hadn't told before, and sometimes I'd remember them and sometimes I didn't.

"One day," related Mama, Josef Wirt informed her that he'd invited high-society guests and asked if she could prepare suitable refreshments. He meant lay a perfect table, just as it ought to be…

When Mama assured him that she could prepare the very best, different kinds of meat, cheese, smoked fish, and select delicacies were ordered from Wolka – the famous delicatessen in the main square of Kraków. Mama had to prepare salads, cakes, cookies, as well as an Austrian dessert known as *Nockerl* that was made of whipped eggs and a little flour.

Josef Wirt himself taught Mama to prepare the dessert, because he'd promised it to his guests. Most of the food remained, and Mama was uneasy when she brought half-full bowls back to the kitchen. "What, don't they like my food?"

"In summer," said Mama, "the table was elegantly set in the early evening: expensive porcelain dishes beside elegant vases of flowers, satin table cloths with lace serviettes, and dishes laden with delicacies brought from the Wolka store, as well as select drinks covered with ice."

In winter, after two springs, Mama added old silver cutlery to the story, and crystal goblets, truly *märchenhaft*, a fabulous sight, yes, yes, that's what Mama said.

Josef Wirt stood in the doorway of his living room while Mama finished setting the magnificent table and she never, ever forgot his face. He looked at the table in amazement and said, "Frau Anna, I imagine you come from a very elegant family. In any case, I have never seen a table set like this."

He was right. Mama had unbelievably superb taste and a highly developed aesthetic sense.

Neither will she forget, said Mama, that despite all the great compliments, she was afraid of Josef Wirt. He had a harsh face; even the guests entered cautiously, speaking quietly, like a collection of snakes. He spoke so quietly that they were required to lean towards him in order to hear him boast about the specially engraved silverware taken from the Jews sent to the Płaszów camp in Kraków. He'd brag, "I'd have to work for two hundred years to have the means to buy rows of boots or delicacies from Wolka, at least two hundred years."

People were also added to Mama's story.

When I was twelve, Mama told us that eight or ten guests were hosted by Josef Wirt, some of them very high-ranking officers who'd come with their wives.

When I was fourteen, Mama referred to many officers who came with their German aides, the entire street filling up with luxury cars.

I also remembered the events and was puzzled by the details added over time, but maybe I remembered less as time went by? And maybe details were added because what happened there could now be told?

The older I grew, the harder I listened to every word she said and didn't interrupt in any story she told.

She'd taught us from a very young age never to interrupt

when she was speaking, *never*, no matter what she said, and so, naturally, that's how we always behaved.

Mama related: "This Tyrolean German, Josef Wirt, son of a poor family as he himself said, stole an enormous amount of Jewish property, *Außer sich*, I was astounded to see his cupboards filled with elegant clothing. The finest Jewish tailors worked without pay in camp Płaszów near Kraków. They sewed suits from excellent cloth stolen from the Jews. Wirt was a military supplier and he himself did not wear a uniform, but jackets of high quality. He had an abundance of shoes: brown, white, black, white sports shoes, and riding boots, all the property of Jews. The shoes were arranged row upon row like soldiers on parade, *alles geraubt*, everything stolen from Jews who were sent to the crematorium."

Once, when Mama was talking about the excellent Jewish tailors of camp Płaszów, I noticed Efraim Sonnenfeld, whose face seemed to laugh and weep at the same time, tug nervously at his wedding ring. The ring had sunk into the flesh of his finger. He tugged and twisted it; I didn't understand what he was doing.

Mama looked at him and said quietly, "You need to use soap. Only then will you manage to get it off," and then she was silent.

A moment later, she said to the guests, "It reminds me of something terrible, maybe better not to say." And she sighed.

"You can say it," said Bernard Cohen.

"Everyone suffered in those days. Almost all of them probably died. How many are left?" asked Klara Cohen.

"Endless numbers of people died; they talked about it on the radio," said Bernard.

"Courage, Anna, courage, we're with you," urged Mr. Bogusławski, whose forehead had reached the crown of his head.

I moved to sit on the floor, and Mama said quietly: "One day,

Wirt brought a slab of soap weighing several kilos, noting that there was no need to save as he could get hold of as many kilograms as he needed. When I opened the package, I found small un-perfumed cubes I hadn't encountered before.

"I mentioned to the housekeeper, who used to complain about the small amount of soap, that my employer had brought home packages full of soap and did she want some?

"She looked at me with frightened eyes and said, 'Mrs. Kwiatkowski, haven't you heard about this special soap?'"

Mama took a deep breath; her breast rose slightly as she said quietly "And you already know…"

The guests sank into their chairs, saying nothing, but they looked strangely at one another. Clearly everyone knew about this soap but they were nonetheless shaken to hear that there were still more stories about it. Efraim Sonnenfeld stopped fiddling with his ring; his hand dropped and swung in the air.

"One day," Mama continued, her employer, Josef Wirt, informed her that he'd invited his German friend and her son to stay for several weeks. Her name was Erna. He instructed Tushya, the maid, to prepare the guest rooms.

Mama relied on Tushya and didn't check her cleaning of the guest rooms.

The evening before the guests arrived, Josef Wirt burst into the kitchen like a barbarian and immediately began to punch Tushya all over her body. The poor girl screamed with pain but he didn't stop even after blood was flowing from her nose, mouth, and neck; at least two teeth flew onto the floor and then, in an instant, she stopped screaming and lay like a rag on the carpet. Mama thought she was dead and stood trembling on the side. Josef Wirt then gave her the keys and demanded she go and see the rooms for herself, at once!

Mama apologized for not checking the rooms before.

The moment Josef Wirt left the house, Mama helped Tushya get up off the floor. She wanted to bandage her wounds but Tushya brushed her arm away and limped to her room. She quickly packed a small suitcase and left the house. Mama told Josef that when she returned from doing the shopping, she found that Tushya wasn't in her room. He became mad with rage, but didn't lay a hand on Mama. He rushed out to the concierge's apartment and punched her as well. She, too, was dripping with blood, all because she had no idea where Tushya was, but he nevertheless threatened to kill her.

On the following nights, Mama was unable to fall asleep. I heard her and my belly ached. I thought, how lucky that I didn't see or hear. Where was I? Maybe I'd gone out with Bronka to the Avenue?

The next day Josef Wirt's friend arrived with her son. She was gracious to Mama, enquiring what foods Josef particularly liked, and asked her to teach her how to prepare them.

A few days later, she informed Mama that from then on, she, Erna, would run the master's household so there was no need for her to remain in their house.

Mama said: "Thus, regretfully, full of confidence and unshakable faith in God, I once more set out into the unknown tomorrow. Now let's have a glass of tea. There are at least two kinds of cookies, one with chocolate and one with nuts and coconut."

People hurried to help themselves. What a surprise they had when, out of the kitchen, she also brought peanut cookies, salty sesame cookies and, of course, yeast cakes, chocolate rolls, and seasonal apples with sugar and cinnamon. I think that ours was the only home in the neighborhood where Mama, with barely any products, gave them a sense of confectionery. She had a special talent for this.

We left Josef Wirt's house and I wasn't sorry. We put our clothes into a suitcase, the same one we'd brought with us. Mama warned me not to take any of the little soaps in the bathroom.

We returned to Franca's apartment. Mama was worried; once again she had to go into the streets to look for a place for us, a roof over our heads. I was glad I'd no longer hear the house-owner's boots that made my back crawl. What frightened me most was the worry on Mama's face. I only regretted leaving the beautiful furniture with the pale-blue cover and blue flowers. For me they were like a little garden in the middle of the living room, a garden I visited every day, when the master left the house, a garden without scent, without bees, birds, or butterflies. Well, those sweet creatures had existed only in my mind for a long time.

I knew that Tyrolean-style flowers would also be with me when I wished to recall them if I felt like it, which is what happened.

Chapter Eight

What I remember best about Kraków is Helmutt and Toni Sopp's home on Siemiradzkiego Street. Mama found employment with them and I found a friend, Peter, and there was also Ammon, his little brother.

At the entrance to the big house, Mama looked at me, straightened my coat collar and said, "Don't talk about Yashu, don't talk about the family, that's all," and she removed the long blue scarf from around her head, winding it three times around her neck when we set out on our way, unwinding it three times when we came to the path.

We stepped on brownish-yellow snow. Empty bottles were arranged nearby—a lot of bottles—and it was cold waiting for the large door to open. I stood wordlessly behind Mama. I reached her hip, and peeped round at the woman who opened the door for us—a laughing woman with long brown hair and happy brown eyes that passed swiftly from Mama to me and back. She wore the suit of a lady, and said her name was Toni

Sopp. She shook my hand and spoke German, speaking as if I were an adult like Mama, "Glad to meet you, how are you?" And I understood that on my own.

The woman invited us inside. There was a passage, a hall, and a living room dimmed by heavy curtains. We stepped on thick carpets and it was pleasant and warm in the house. Mama helped me take off my coat and gloves and took off her own. Toni offered me some chocolate, but I was shy and looked down at the floor. I waited quietly until I heard her say something, which Mama translated: "Danusha, meet my children. This is Peter, he's six, like you. And this is Ammon, he's five."

I slowly raised my head. Peter was my height with light-colored hair and eyes the color of mine. He looked at me in such a way that I felt a lot of warmth in my cheeks. I turned to Ammon; he was Yashu's height—Yashu, whom we'd just left crying—and he had dark hair and eyes like Toni.

I shook hands with Peter and Ammon, took the chocolate Toni put into my hand, and we walked round the house. On one side was a living room with a balcony, a dining room and one or two bedrooms, which was the masters' area.

On the servants' side was a small room next to a large kitchen that opened onto a balcony. The small room was for us. I peeped inside the room. In it was a bed and a door that opened onto the kitchen. The bathroom was in the middle and was used by the masters and the servants.

"Take care not to break glasses or plates, take care, Danusha," said Mama quietly, glancing at the shelves in the kitchen.

And then I met Helmutt Sopp. He was very tall, and had blond hair with a side parting, and blue eyes like Peter. He shook my hand and I knew things would be good in this house. I immediately saw contentment in his face, and when he looked at

Mama, her color was good, as if we'd been walking along Dietlowska Avenue in Kraków.

On the very first evening, Mama unpacked our clothes from the suitcase and arranged them in the closet and I was certain this was a good sign for us.

On the very first day, Peter invited me to play with him, and he said everything in German—and I understood from his hands, that were also inviting me to come. I was shy at first. I didn't know any friends outside of the family, but Peter smiled at me, opened his fist, and showed me five stones he was holding, and signaled to me to follow him to the kitchen balcony. We sat on the floor and he taught me the game. I enjoyed it, and from that day on I repeated every word he spoke in German, he'd patiently correct me, and we both laughed.

I spent most of the day sitting on a chair next to Mama, watching her while she stirred the large pots. She wore a long white apron, and she had a scarf that she wound several times around her head.

In the kitchen there was a long wooden table adjacent to the wall leading to the balcony. On one side of the table was a tub in which Mama washed the dishes; on the other side Mama peeled and cut up vegetables from a full crate, which also had leaves that smelled good and that were unfamiliar to me. Village women would bring butter, cheese, and eggs to the house and receive alcohol from bottles Helmutt brought home from the hospital. Toni also shopped at the market. Farmers would bring vegetables and fruit at a good price. Mama said it was very hard to get hold of fresh food in the store—they were severely rationed then—but because of Helmutt's work and connections, we lacked for nothing. There was one village woman who came especially with chickens for the Sopp house. Mama would blow a long phooooo near their bottoms and scatter the feathers; that's how they saw if the bottom was fat or thin. Fat was considered good. After choosing one or two chickens, the village woman would put them in the sink, hold the neck, twist the head, kchakkk. That's all, and no need of a slaughterer.

I smiled at everyone who came into the kitchen. At the village woman, the man who brought the crates of vegetables and fruit, the handyman, as they came in I was already smiling, and Mama said that was very good.

Easiest of all was smiling at Helmutt when he came into the kitchen. His smile at me was like a blessing, and he immediately went back to Mama, looked at what she was stirring in the pots, good things, or not? I knew the answer by his eyes, if they were large, or narrow, as well as by his cheek, if something jumped there, or if it was normal. If he lingered, raised the lid of a pot, sniffed, maybe said *excellent, excellent,* this was a sign for us that he'd had a good day at work, and Mama would instantly blush.

We could tell by his body movements and smacks on his boots whether he was in a good mood or not. If he was silent and motionless, and his lips were like a line, I'd stand close to Mama's leg, holding on, almost without breathing when he'd start shouting at his children or at Toni.

Sometimes it was enough for me to see a small frown between his eyebrows the minute he glanced into the kitchen, in a hurry to leave, and I knew by myself that at the Sopp family lunch there'd be a heavy quiet like a mountain, and if I'd hear anything it would only be the sounds of cutlery. I could hear them from the small room next to the kitchen. I also found a crack in the door, and their dining table was opposite me on the other side of the door. Naturally I only clung to the door after Mama had gone to them with a large tray.

I was curious to know how Helmutt and Toni's faces looked after a large, noisy party and food and laughter. Was Toni angry about something? I guessed by the quickness of the voice rising and falling, and by the pace of the words, until the weeping started. From the way Helmutt would get up from the table and push back his chair I realized that he wanted peace and quiet, and if he didn't push back his chair and there was nonetheless quiet, I realized that he was looking into the distance, seeing nothing but the trays Mama brought in. Honestly? After a week I already knew by the faces of the family how they felt, and if we had to be very careful, or if we could talk ordinarily, at least for the moment. I was even excited to discover that Helmutt could laugh when he told Mama something to do with his work at the hospital, or about Jewish prisoners in jail, and Mama smiled more and more at him than at first.

Right from the beginning, Toni was kind to us. She'd stroke my hair and say, *How are you, sweetheart*, give me a candy, and look for Mama. She'd talk to Mama as if they were old friends. Whenever Toni went shopping at the market, she'd return with a large basket of vegetables and a large bag of white rolls. Their smell drove me mad.

From the moment I heard her come in that smell started tickling my nose, and I couldn't sit still. She'd spread butter on the rolls and give one to each child, and take one for herself and for Mama, who put it aside. I didn't even wait for a second, but immediately bent nicely over the plate and slowly, slowly ate my roll. First, I'd look at the color—it had a fine golden-brown crust and a maddening smell of warm bread—and then I'd take a small bite, roll it on my tongue and begin to chew: first on one side of my mouth, then on the other side, breathing quietly all the time, regretting the missing piece. I took another bite and saw that Peter ate his roll all at once. He took two or three large bites, barely chewed, before swallowing. Sometimes, he'd talk while he was eating, particularly if a friend or two had come over.

In the meantime, Mama and Toni talked between themselves. Toni played with her hair, throwing it back, and laughing until we could see all her teeth with bits of roll. It didn't bother her, but it bothered Mama.

She'd look away, and nothing would make her laugh like Toni, loudly, wildly, joyfully. After a few months at the Sopp family house, I decided that when I became a lady, I'd start laughing like Toni Sopp, exactly like her. And dress like Toni Sopp. But I only wanted to speak like my aunt Bronka.

Toni also brought *Schinken*, smoked ham, from the market, and fresh bread, and fresh vegetables and seasonal fruit, and gave Mama and me an apple and a pear. "Eat up, it's healthy," said Toni, "Eat up, it's healthy," repeated Mama and I saw her putting her apple into a bag wrapped up in newspaper.

Mama made sure I ate three full meals a day to make my body strong. I enjoyed eating, but I hated soup. This was because by the time I got to the soup, my belly was full. But she didn't give up, even though she was constantly busy in the kitchen and cleaning the rooms and barely saw me. Only if I left food on my plate did she get annoyed and sit opposite me. "Open your mouth, Danusha, open it," she'd say, telling me irritably what happened to a child who didn't eat, and how strong and heroic was the child who finished all the food on his plate. She'd tell the story very, very quickly and quietly and irritably and I actually enjoyed listening.

"Open your mouth, Danusha, *nu*, open it. You're pretending to be important and I don't have the time."

She'd also tell her sisters Lydia and Bronka what I didn't eat and the trouble she had with the child, taking an hour to eat a roll and not wanting her soup.

Food was an important issue for Mama. She was a *Feinschmecker* regarding food, sensitive to excellent tastes; she understood good food and ate slowly, but her cooking was fast. She taught me to eat with a knife and fork, and by the age of four I had table manners suitable for the Sopp household.

One day, Helmutt appeared in the kitchen holding a dead rabbit, and asked Mama to cook it in a pot. Mama didn't know how to cook rabbit. She thought it had to be cooked with its skin. She passed it from one hand to the other, wanting to pull out the hairs.

"What are you doing, Frau Anna?" Helmutt jumped up and took the rabbit.

Mama flushed red as a strawberry in the forest.

"You have to remove the skin, remember? Here, give it to me."

He hung the rabbit on a hook in the door-frame, cut wherever he cut, and ripped off the fur with all the skin. The moment I saw his hand approaching the rabbit's neck with a large knife, my eyes began to dart over objects in the kitchen, repeating the names in my mind: chair, table, bowl; one pot, second pot, third pot; plate; large knife, medium knife, small knife; forks; kettle; wooden spoon; rag; towel; broom; floor cloth; bucket; Mama; Helmutt. Poor rabbit, nothing left of it.

Where was I?

I was out of my mind.

My brother was out of my mind.

Papa was also out of my mind. Long out of my mind.

Helmutt took down what was left of the rabbit and held it out to Mama. Mama washed it really well and cooked it in a pot with sweet and sour seasoning. The family enjoyed rabbit meat; in general they enjoyed her cooking. Particularly Helmutt. He occasionally came to sniff the pots, especially taking an interest in the names of the new spices Mama used in the food. She let him taste the sauces she prepared; he'd bring the spoon to his mouth, fuuu, to cool it, suck once, twice, with his lips and then he'd nod, smile, and leave contentedly.

When we were alone in the house, Mama would sometimes sing in the kitchen, usually a beautiful aria from an opera. Oh, how I loved hearing her sing, I'd sing quietly with her.

During the first months we spent in the Sopp house, Mama didn't go with Toni to shop in the market. She was afraid of being out in the street and the market in case she was recognized by one of the goyim she'd known before the war. The fish vendor in the market, for instance, or the saleswoman in one of the dress stores, or a student from school. She was born in Kraków and had lived there until her marriage; then she left for Tarnopol in Eastern Galicia. Before I was born, she returned to Kraków to be near her sisters and mother for the birth.

Only after six months, maybe more, did Mama go to the market with Toni. This happened on days when important guests came for dinner and she had to choose special products in large quantities.

In winter, Mama wore a long coat, a hat and a scarf wound around her neck, which covered half her face. Under the wool, she wore the blue scarf wound three times around her neck. In summer, she wore a hat and the transparent scarf. Every time she left the house with all the scarves, she'd say to me, "You mustn't talk about the family, Danusha, you mustn't talk about Yashu, yes? Just smile if you see anyone."

It was my job to buy milk.

I was almost seven and I went to buy fresh milk at the dairy on Łobzowska Street. I remember a wall and walking next to the wall. I held the glass jar in my hands. Opposite me German soldiers passed; they had boots, a hat, and very serious faces. I wasn't afraid, even though Mama heard on Helmutt and Toni's radio that the German army was winning the war and occupying many countries adjacent to Poland. Every Sunday, I heard her telling her sisters the news. This was her day off, and on this day we visited Yashu at the Polish family's house and from there we went to visit Grandma at Franca's apartment, where Lydia and Bronka joined us.

Once, on my way with the jar, I knocked it against the wall by mistake, cracking it. The milk dripped onto the floor and at that moment I needed to pee. I hurried back to the house and just as I got to the door, all the pee came out. Dripping into my underwear, onto my legs, wetting my shoes and making a puddle in the entrance. I stood panting at the door and called Mama. She came and saw the crack in the jar and the puddle on the floor, and shouted at me, hitting me on the back, on the arms, saying: "You see, now my hand hurts because of you. You're no use at all."

I remember falling once and hitting my face, my top lip swelling up. Another time I swelled up from a bee sting and I shouted "Ouch, ouch, ouch… it hurts," and Mama jumped: "What are you yelling for? You gave me a fright."

I didn't mean to alarm Mama. I didn't understand why I couldn't stop the cries escaping from my mouth. I told myself, *You're no use at all, it's a fact. You write with your left hand, sleep with your mouth open, your tonsils swell up in your throat, and you shout for no reason and scare Mama so she has to hit you and hurt her hand, stupid girl.*

I liked wearing Mama's shoes. I wanted to feel big. I'd put on her black heeled shoes, a medium heel, plain colored, marching from the kitchen door to the wall and back, saying loudly:

"So good to have a mother
So good to be with Mama
So good that I'm a girl and not a boy
And I'm with my mother."

I enjoyed walking about in Mama's shoes, reciting all this goodness. Maybe I wanted to remember how good it was for me to be with Mama. Yashu wasn't with Mama, I was. And maybe I wanted her to hear me?

Chapter Nine

"It's freezing cooold," said the guests shivering at the entrance to our apartment in Haifa, and they removed their coats only after tea and cookies. Our "Fireside" paraffin heater barely heated even though it was turned to maximum. I sat on my chair, rubbing my hands together and couldn't believe it: Klara Cohen, standing with her bag next to the refreshments, stealing cookies? Not one, not two, five cookies were thrown into her bag, and then she poured herself some tea, took two more and went to sit down. I looked at Mama—did you see? She saw. She mouthed to me, *Take more cookies out of the tin.*

I went into the kitchen. Mr. Bogusławski followed me and poured himself a glass of water from the tap. "Where did we get to in Mama's story, do you remember?" he asked.

"We were in Kraków. Mama will probably start with the Sopp family," I responded, taking out date cookies.

He placed a hand on the red scarf he was wearing, arranged it properly on his chest and, following me into the living room, called out: "Today we're talking about Kraków. We're ready."

"Excellent cookies, Anna," said Bertha Ketzelboim from the haberdashery and wool store, cutting a cookie in half and smelling it. Then she dusted it, as if there could be any dust there.

"Really excellent," she said, still not tasting it.

She could move the cookie from her hand to her nose for a quarter of an hour without putting it in her mouth for fear of germs. Mama would tell her seamstress, Mrs. Zelikowitz, that Bertha would have no problem losing clients if she saw signs of dust in the thread drawers, and how could there be signs if she dusted every morning?

"You can only eat cookies like that in Vienna," said Henia Sonnenfeld.

"Who needs to travel to Vienna to smell cakes," retorted her husband, Efraim Sonnenfeld.

"No need," nodded Yozek Meltzer, Mama's admirer, "we have Vienna right here", and he gestured at the plate of cookies without saying another word.

"Nothing in Haifa or Hadar tastes like this," added Izzy Rappaport, bringing the cookie to his left eye. And then he lowered his glasses and gazed intently at it through the left lens.

"Nothing, nothing. Jacob, have you tasted it? *Nu,* at least smell it," suggested Bertha and he drew his head back, and she again wiped the cookie from front to back. "Is it cocoa, dates, almonds, and nutmeg, or cinnamon? Cinnamon, I knew it, so why don't mine come out like this?"

"There has to be sensitivity in the hands. A sense, Bertha. It's a sense," said Bernard Cohen.

"Sense nonsense," chuckled Mr. Bogusławski, "are we starting?"

"We're starting," said Mama, making herself comfortable.

"Lydia, my older sister who rushed around every day trying to organize fake documents and hiding places for the family, found a notice in the newspaper. A German doctor on Siemiradzkiego Street seeks a housekeeper for cleaning and cooking. This was in 1943. The cannons were firing, planes were bombing, packed trains were going wherever they were going. We didn't know where they were going, the rumors were frightening, and Lydia immediately sent me to the family.

"I went dressed like a servant, wrapped in a coat and colorful scarf. It was a particularly cold day; branches of trees were falling from the weight of the snow. The lady of the house, her name was Toni, a beautiful young woman in an elegant suit, shook my hand at the entrance and invited me inside. I introduced myself as the wife of a Polish officer who was missing in battle. Toni looked at me and said, 'Sad news, maybe he will return,' and took me on a tour of the large house. There were six rooms in the house; the Sopp family took up an entire floor.

"Her husband was a psychiatrist and a high-ranking officer, director, and chief doctor at a home for the mentally ill, as well as the chief doctor at the prison on Montelupich Street. They had two sons."

Mama stopped to take a breath.

"Jacob, I need some valerian," said Bertha Ketzelboim quietly.

Whenever Mama said "the prison on Montelupich Street", someone asked for valerian, or lemon, or air. "*Nu*, open a window, please." Even if it was winter outside, rain, a storm. Izzy Rappaport would say, "I have a bandage and an aspirin, anyone want one?" Every time it happened, Mr. Bogusławski would take a packet of mints out of his pocket. "Pass it around to the guests, please, pass it around, pass it around."

The packet went from hand to hand. I took two.

Mama didn't say that Helmutt Sopp was a Nazi but the guests all realized this and were alarmed for us.

Unalarmed, I peeled the cellophane from the mint, put it on my tongue, and sucked. I had several reasons not to worry:

1. Mama was the prettiest.
2. Mama knew how to cook really well.
3. Helmutt Sopp liked to eat. A lot.
4. Mama knew how to keep a secret. There were many secrets in Toni and Helmutt's home.
5. Mama was strong.
6. Creative.
7. Knew how to prepare a wonderful egg-liqueur.
8. I was a good, quiet child.
9. I smiled beautifully at the household and their guests.

Even if Mama had mentioned the word *Nazi*, I'd have stayed calm. I said to myself, *Don't worry, friends, while we're at the Sopps' we're completely safe*, and I was right.

Mama told the guests how Toni had explained to her that she was responsible for the house, the kitchen, for everything. She spoke graciously and respectfully to her. Maybe because she knew from Mama that she hadn't been a servant before the war. Toni took into consideration that Mama was the wife of a Polish officer lost in battle, respecting all the more her familiarity with housework and that she was willing to work in exchange for a modest wage if the lady agreed to take her with her little daughter.

"I'll have to ask my husband," said Toni, and asked her to return the following day.

The first time I heard Mama say, "if the lady would agree to take her with her little daughter", meaning me, I almost jumped out of the chair. And what would have happened if the lady had said no? What would have happened then?

Deep down in my heart, I felt… a little… but just a little… that maybe, if I were far from Mama, she wouldn't seek me out every Sunday like she did with Yashu. No, no, no, I mustn't think like that. I was angry with myself and pinched my knee. I thrust candies into my mouth, breaking them one by one with my teeth, and I heard Mama tell how the owner of the house, Professor Helmutt Sopp, received her the following day. He welcomed her at the door with a gracious smile, a distinctive man of about thirty. He was tall, impressive, and intelligent. She said she was tense before the meeting, fearing he'd interrogate her; he was, after all, a German military officer. In fact, after the smile, he invited her to come inside, sit down at the table, *Bitte*. He then asked to know everything: where she lived, where her husband was, how long they'd been married, and what experience she had in managing a household, did she have recommendations, and, most important of all, did she know how to cook well?

Mama looked directly at him and told him that her husband, the officer, was missing in battle, no one knew where. She knows how to cook very well, has experience, and she has a little girl she can't leave, and then she put her hand on her chest and lowered her eyes. At that very moment the Nazi professor stopped her, saying, "You've got the job. You can bring your little girl and start tomorrow."

Mama repeated the word "professor" and I knew that Helmutt Sopp was a doctor. I'd heard it with my own ears, "Herr Doktor," Mama called him in a polite voice. Even their guests called him Doktor Sopp. Only Mama called him "Professor" with every new group of visitors to our living room. "I thanked the Professor," "the Professor allowed me," "the Professor gave us great security." I thought Mama was confused. I didn't say a word, and this is what she said:

"I will never forget the first lunch I prepared in the Professor's home. Toni brought fresh vegetables, a dish of lentils, and pork fat from the market and asked me to make soup. I added fried onion, salt, and pepper to the vegetables and pork fat, cooked it well, then put it on the table in a soup tureen. I myself didn't taste it, of course, having sworn never to eat non-kosher food. After the meal, Helmutt came into the kitchen and said that he hadn't eaten such tasty soup in a long time. From that day on, the family trusted me to determine the menu in their home, even when important guests came. Toni took no interest in cooking and ate very little—she had the figure of a young girl, despite two births. Helmutt, on the other hand, understood good food, and appreciated my culinary knowledge."

"So do we, so do we," said Mr. Bogusławski, chuckling and looking at everyone.

"We've eaten the best *cremeschnitte* in the world in your house," observed Klara without enthusiasm.

"That's very true," Bernard called out happily, "the Garden of Eden," he added, winning applause from Meltzer.

"As you probably realize," Mama restored quiet in the living room, "only the great suffering of life without my husband and son remained like a shadow over my head. I worried and prayed to God to protect my two men, my husband and little Yashu, for whom I paid a great deal of money to the Poles who looked after him. My husband remained in Brzeżany, where he had a job with the district manager. In the meantime, all kinds of rumors about the bitter fate of the Jews reached us; we didn't want to believe stories that sounded crazy. Do you think we could believe that a hundred thousand children were being burnt in a week? A day? Who could believe a story like that? How could anyone imagine showers that emitted gas instead of water?"

I saw that Klara Cohen had held her bag on her lap the entire evening, even taking it with her to the restroom. Mama also saw and smiled with closed lips. And then she looked at me and understood.

"We'll continue in two weeks' time," she said. "Good night, friends."

The guests left the house.

Mama saw them to the door and returned to the living room. Her cheeks were particularly red. She looked at the refreshments table, and lay down on the sofa, drumming her hand on the upholstery, saying: "Come and sit down beside me, come, come. Did you see the fur coat Mrs. Sonnenfeld was wearing? Really special. Do you know where she bought it? In Tel Aviv, in Stefan Braun's store, yes. Stefan Braun is the name, on Allenby Street in Tel Aviv. She told me that only high society buy from him. They even come from America to buy from him, even film actresses come to him, yes. He's from Bratislava. You can see he's a real professional; I need to visit him. Do you remember Toni Sopp's beautiful fur coat?"

I didn't remember.

"Don't you remember?"

"No, no," I whispered, embarrassed.

Mama sighed. "She had the most elegant fur I'd ever seen and she wore it only for special events. She told me several times how everyone admired it and she didn't tell them she'd bought it at a bargain price, and she was right. She knew how to make a good impression, that's for sure. And do you know who Toni Sopp bought that very, very expensive fur coat from?"

"No, Mama."

"It was my sister Lydia's coat. Oh, dear Lydia, she sold the coat because she needed the money to secure all the family papers. I told Toni that the coat belonged to my friend; she didn't know I had sisters. Aaah, those were hard years, Danusha, very hard."

Mama nodded her head. "And what furs we had in Kraków, what furs. Shall we have another glass of tea now?"

I brought us tea and a plate of cookies. I took off my shoes and sat cross-legged like an actress next to Mama on the sofa.

"Do you remember, once Helmutt bought new shoes and brought them to the kitchen to put them in a pot full of water so they wouldn't squeak?" I asked Mama.

"Of course I remember," she said. "They were very good leather shoes. I put them into the water, dried them thoroughly, and the shoes didn't squeak."

"Why did he have to do it?"

"Well, he worked at the hospital, and there you had to be quiet. You couldn't make a noise around those poor patients, right?"

Mama looked at the clock. "I'm tired and that's it. Let's go to bed," and she got up and went to Yashu's room. From my chair in the living room I heard the sound of her ten kisses as he slept.

I went to bed and glanced at the window. Rain was knocking against the shutter. There was condensation on the glass. Putting out my hand, I wrote *Good night, sweet dreams* on the window with my finger.

Getting into bed, I pulled the blanket over me, hearing in my mind the voice of Helmutt Sopp, "Frau Anna, I'm here," the minute he entered the house, clinking the kitchen door keys. He was tall and wore an ironed uniform with important badges, and on his head, an officer's hat, so I heard Mama telling her sisters in a low voice, and I realized from her face just how lucky we were to be with that family.

Every Sunday, after we'd visited Yashu, we went to visit Franca, who was responsible for the incoming and outgoing post of a German governmental office. Every Sunday, the sisters met in her apartment to talk about their concerns.

"I only hope you'll stay with the child until everything is over," Lydia prayed.

"Don't worry, Anna, we'll help you with Yashu. We'll visit him, take him things, don't worry, it will be all right," promised Bronka.

"And you must also be careful. The most important thing is not to talk, not to stand out, do you hear, Danusha?" asked Bronka, her eyes strong. I smiled at her, and when I saw Grandma Rosa looking at me, I immediately closed my mouth and strode into the kitchen. I wanted some water. Grandma Rosa would sit for hours without getting up, and pray from morning till dark for her only son Aharon's safe return, and for Stella not to lose her hair, for the Lord to be of help; she barely rested from her prayers. Sometimes, the sisters would stroke her head, or take her hand to put cream on it.

What I also understood in Franca's living room was that her husband, Chaim, the son of wealthy people from Lodz, a lawyer, extremely religious, was at the Płaszów camp in Kraków, and he had to take great care not to get caught, because the Germans also interrogated people with papers, and entire families vanished from their homes, who knew where. What caused most pain for everyone was that Lydia's husband had reported for work when they called him and had since disappeared. Everyone wept about it together every Sunday and prayed that he, too, would return safely.

"Good morning, Herr Doktor," said Mama when she heard Helmutt Sopp at the kitchen door, and she'd arrange her hair, straighten her apron, and in her eyes there seemed to be a spark of light. In his eyes, too, something seemed to ignite.

Sometimes, she'd rub her eyes or nose, using her handkerchief, even if she didn't have a cold—maybe because of the steam and sharp smell of spices in the kitchen.

I sat aside on a chair watching Mama preparing an omelet for Helmutt out of fifteen eggs—fifteen!—and he finished everything on his plate. She also knew how to prepare a special egg-liqueur that Helmutt and Toni were crazy about, as well as their guests. She was expert at setting a table for the family: white table cloths, flowers, and beautiful dishes arranged in straight lines. Any table she arranged looked festive even on ordinary days. Helmutt would look at the table, his eyes would open wide as if in great surprise, and then he'd look at Mama, smile, and compliment her, mostly at the end of the meal. "The meat was excellent, Frau Anna, the cake... superb."

Mama would smile with closed lips and delicately nod her head.

Toni also loved Mama's expertise. Toni called Mama "Mrs. Kwiatkowski", the name her sister Lydia had arranged for on her papers. I was Danuta, according to the papers, the daughter of Mrs. Anna Kwiatkowski, and Yashu was Yan. No one used those names; everyone called me Danusha, Anna's daughter.

Toni was the happiest, most cheerful person in the Sopp family home. Nothing frightened or worried her. She'd come and go every hour or two; she'd leave happy and return happy, showing off a new dress, suit or scarf, saying that she'd bought it on sale in a corner shop near the market, shoes as well, and a bag, and whispered that this one or that one had given her a bracelet, laughing as if life was very good in Kraków and she didn't miss life in Germany at all.

Sometimes, I heard Mama advising Toni on the best place to buy, or sending her to a particularly well-regarded store. Even more so before dinner with important guests from Germany. Mama knew all the respected stores in Kraków and she had good taste in women's fashion. She even knew how to fold dresses and suits as they did in the store, and Toni, with her clutter everywhere, greatly appreciated Mama's order. She'd come to the kitchen, ask Mama to take a break from the pots and pans and come and help her pack a suitcase. Every month she'd go at least once or twice to visit friends and relatives.

Mama would leave the pots and pans, remove her rubber gloves, wash her hands with water and soap, smile nicely at Toni, and gesture to her that she was ready to pack.

"You see," Toni would say laughingly, "with your folding, Mrs. Kwiatkowski, there's no need to iron, no need to look, everything's in place," praising her before every trip, and Toni had many trips of this kind. Two to three days, sometimes five or six days before she'd return from Silesia with a healthy color in her face and shining eyes, and she'd laugh to herself, saying, "Danusha, how are you, sweetheart, how you've grown," and she'd give me a candy she'd kept from the journey, and say, "Mrs. Kwiatkowski, look what I was given," and she'd take a pretty box out of her bag, open it carefully, and show Mama a ring set with a shiny stone, or a gold chain she'd received as a gift, and from Mama's expression I realized that the relatives or friends had good taste. Mama would help Toni to put on her jewelry and say, "What a lovely jewel, it suits you, it really does." Toni would embrace Mama, humming a song as she went, leaving a trail of spicy perfume behind her.

She'd just have left the kitchen and Mama would already be muttering irritably, "Nobody is our friend, do you hear? You mustn't say anything, and not a word about Yashu."

Then she'd put on the gloves, or fold her arms across her chest, go to the window, and stand quietly, looking out silently for a long time, barely breathing. I was also like her then. I didn't move in my chair, didn't say a word, barely breathed, making sure that Mama had some quiet for her thoughts. Long minutes could go by until Mama returned to her work at the sink. In the meantime, I said to myself, when I'm a lady, I'll laugh and dress like Toni Sopp, and just like her I'll go on trips round the world, and return with beautiful jewelry, and not only that, I'll also have a tall, handsome husband like Helmutt, and I'll have two or three sons.

When Toni went away, she'd take the children, Peter and Ammon, with her. On those days, Helmutt would invite friends and have parties at home. Mama worked very hard before the parties, cooking large quantities of food that impressed everyone. Apart from everything she prepared, pastries I'd never seen before would arrive at the house, boxes of special cheeses, and bottles of alcohol in various colors. Mama transferred all the food to silver trays and arranged it on the table, Helmutt hanging around her, observing, not saying a word, occasionally jingling coins in his pocket.

Guests started arriving late in the evening when I was already in bed, watching Mama rushing between the kitchen and the living room, carrying loaded trays. Every time our door opened, I heard men and women laughing, and someone saying something, and again endless rolling laughter. In our living room in Haifa, I never heard that sort of loud laughter that went on for even longer than an hour.

The morning after the party Mama would clean the entire house. Sometimes she needed two days, one wasn't enough to restore everything to its place. If I left the kitchen and went out onto the balcony, I'd hear her say every time, "Keep your head down, Danusha, better to sit down."

There were times when Toni went away and no guests came, and then the house was very quiet. Helmutt barely spoke; he'd sometimes come back from work and go straight to the room, without coming out, and at night I'd hear Mama praying about Yashu into her pillow, *May God take care of him, may he be healthy with God's help*, and she'd sigh and pray and weep, and then I'd need a glass of water. My throat burned I was so thirsty, even a little slice of bread could help, and I didn't ask Mama, just bit my fingers.

And then, after a particularly quiet night an even quieter morning came to Helmutt's house. If I peeped through the crack in the door when he was eating breakfast, or, rather, drinking coffee, I'd see that he was barely eating; even at lunch he ate little and without enthusiasm, the same in the evening, and the following day too, that's how it was for several days. All this time Mama did her work almost soundlessly, and I spoke to her as if someone was sleeping. Mama barely spoke, and I didn't breathe well. I already knew that every time Helmutt's silences and lack of enthusiasm for anything began, Toni would pack her suitcases and go away with the children. Sometimes the silence would start before she went away and would continue even after she returned, but she paid less attention to that silence than Mama and me; she did laugh, but not loudly. And then, surprisingly, without warning, in an instant, the entrance door would open and Helmutt would call out, "Frau Anna, I'm home," and jingle his keys noisily, and Mama would smile, saying, "Herr Doktor," and he'd take an interest in the pots, sometimes telling Mama something funny about his crazy patients, and ask when dinner would be ready as usual. When he sat down at the table and talked as if he were content and life was good, I felt I could breathe better, and asked Mama what were crazy patients and she'd say, *not now*.

"Hans Frank, Governor-General of the occupied Polish territories, was a personal friend of Helmutt Sopp, yes, and he visited the Sopp family home," said Mama, observing the guests to see how impressed they were.

"He also hosted important guests from Germany, as well as doctors from the hospital where he worked. You could say that Helmutt Sopp loved the good life, and knew how to make and give a good life. The parties at his house were always grand and he never counted the number of bottles finished in one night, and it cost him a great deal of money, yes. He loved living well, and Hans Frank himself knew best of all how to live well."

"Hans Frank himself?" People in the living room were excited.

"Yes, Governor-General Hans Frank. Himself. And what did the Governor like drinking best of all? Egg-liqueur. From the moment he took the first sip he wanted all the details. Helmutt

Sopp pointed at me and said proudly: 'It's called Kwiat-cognac, after the respected Frau Anna Kwiat-kowski who works in our home and prepares it herself according to secrets passed down from her Polish family.'

"I was moved. One of the Polish doctors who worked under the Professor said in my presence that the meaning of the Polish word Kwiat is *blume*, flower in German. Naturally, he liked the meaning, and he looked at me and laughed, asking everyone to pour another shot of the flower lady's Kwiat-cognac.

"'Frau Anna', they said every minute in Helmutt Sopp's living room, 'Frau Anna, *es schmekt goed, ach wie machen Sie das?'* A few minutes later, I hurried to the kitchen to fetch more champagne or whiskey, and someone would stop me every second, saying, 'Frau Anna, this tastes good, how do you make it? Herr Professor, how?'

"I looked at Helmutt Sopp and we both smiled. It was clear that I'd keep the Kwiatkowski secret from them."

Mama stopped a moment, thinking. Every time she said Kwiatkowski she'd stop, even after telling the story ten times. The guests in the living room, especially the new ones, looked at each other with large eyes, wondering at the Jewish woman who won admiration and respect in the home of a Nazi officer; they'd never heard such a story.

Mama looked at me while gently touching her cheeks and forehead with an embroidered handkerchief. It was as if she were giving the guests time to adjust to an abnormal life. But actually, she needed that time for herself, or so I felt in my heart, and didn't understand why this was so whenever she said Kwiatkowski.

"One day, invitations to a Christmas feast at the house were sent out to high-society guests and very high-ranking officers.

Mr. Byzenz, who in partnership with his brother ran a prestigious café and restaurant at the corner of Kremlitzka, opposite the university buildings, was also invited. Before the war, his café was called 'Byzenz Esplanade' but everyone knew it by the owner's name, 'at Byzenz'. It was the meeting place for all the who's who in Kraków society—financiers, important government officials, and artists. Gentlemen and ladies would meet there for coffee and cake, and in Kraków it was considered bon ton.

"Mr. Byzenz, an older, respectable-looking man and a regular guest in Helmutt Sopp's home, sent several kilos of huge carp for the holiday; there aren't any carp like that in Haifa, none. Really big carp, and I prepared the fish from a recipe I learned from Mama, who learned it from her mother. Carp with plenty of onion, salt, and pepper.

"Helmutt Sopp's guests enjoyed the fish and at some point, Mr. Byzenz himself appeared in the kitchen. He looked at me, holding a glass of a drink I'd made, a rather full glass, and said, 'Frau Kwiatkowski, where did you learn to cook fish like the Jews?'

"I looked right at him and said without fear, 'I learned to cook carp, sir, from a woman who worked for us.'

"He nodded his head, turned, and left. There were always a few who came into the kitchen, tossing out a compliment, a word, asking something. Honestly? I was afraid of questions. Words didn't bother me, but questions? Questions were a hazard for me and Danusha."

"What else did they ask?" pressed Bernard Cohen.

"Interrogation questions. Like, where was your home before the war, or was your husband really a military man? And they'd look intently into my eyes and wait for the answer. Of course I answered them naturally, but I was very frightened."

"Shema Israel," said Bertha Ketzelboim.

"God help us," added Klara Cohen.

"Courage, Anna, courage," called out Mr. Bogusławski, and "You are courageous, good for you."

Mama thanked him with a small smile and told us about the festivities that went on into the small hours, especially when beautiful young Polish women also came to make merry.

"It took many hours to clean up after them," she said, as if it were really easy.

"There were occasions when evenings with the Polish girls were followed by evenings with married couples who would sit at the table with candles and wine, talking politely and respectfully. Not a single woman at that table could have guessed at the festivities that had taken place previously in Helmutt Sopp's living room, and just as well, too." Mama smiled with the small chuckle that was heard maybe two or three times during her story.

"Interestingly, it was then that Toni would appear in bright-colored dresses. She had a dress the color of wine with a really low neckline and a shining chain. I immediately saw Helmutt's glances. Oh, he'd be irritable all evening, and after the guests had left, he'd shout at her, 'What kind of dress is that to wear for a respectable dinner? Don't you see how married women come to visit us?' And Toni would shout back, 'Don't tell me how to behave,' and she'd weep, but then she'd instantly get over it. 'Come and see my new dress,' she'd call to me to come and see, even before the tears had dried.

"Toni was a good-hearted woman and she knew more than anyone what was good for her husband, what was difficult for him. She knew when the silences would come and she'd go away, and when he wanted a lot of people and good wine around him. I remember that at one of the merry parties she told a colleague of Helmutt's, an older psychiatrist, that it wasn't always that joyous around Helmutt, no, no, there were other times as well. That's what I heard from Toni when I offered more egg-cognac, and I also saw Helmutt's colleague shaking his head, yes-yes, yes-yes, finally hugging Toni like a good father, and she wiped something from her eye.

"I have to admit," said Mama, "I believed that if disaster struck, good Toni would help me and the child."

I heard every word Mama spoke and remembered nothing about all that, maybe because the parties were at night when I was asleep, but that Toni would save us, not Helmutt?

"Toni wasn't ashamed to admit that I was more educated than she was," continued Mama. "She told me that Helmutt fell in love with her while she was still in high school, that she was very beautiful and they married before she turned eighteen. In her family, they used to say that she was indeed beautiful, but nothing would come of her. How could someone who was to be a doctor ask for her hand? And for such a groom it was worth leaving school, they advised her, and that was the reason, or so she told me, that she didn't write well, but between us, no movie star knows how to write without mistakes. Whenever she sat down to write a letter, she'd ask me how to spell a word correctly in German; I willingly helped her, of course."

Ausgezeichnet, excellent, was a word Toni never remembered how to write. "Frau Kwiatkowski, how do you spell

Ausgezeichnet?" I heard her ask Mama, and every two or three days she'd write a letter and I'd hear how Mama dictated each letter to her, and Toni laughed at something nice she'd written about in her letter, and I didn't understand, when people are embarrassed do they laugh or are they sad? And maybe if they're sad they laugh? Or if they're afraid?

"And she had suitors," added Mama. "One of Toni's regular guests was an actor from the town theater who was caught by the Germans. His name was Dagobert von Carlblum, and he'd spend the morning in Toni's living room when Helmutt was at the hospital. Toni used to bring Dagobert von Carlblum to the kitchen and ask me to give him a taste of the dishes I'd prepared. He'd taste with pleasure, purr a bit, and then back they'd go to sit in the living room. But the closer it got to noon when Helmutt was supposed to return home, I'd get nervous. I'd raise the lids of pots, put them back noisily, opening-closing. Finally, I'd knock on the living room door, apologize, and invite Toni to come and taste—the meal was ready.

"And she'd come. And with a charming smile, she'd say, 'Mrs. Kwiatkowski, you're *eine Perle*, a pearl,' and she finally understood that the suitor had to go and we all breathed more easily."

The minute Mama said, "Dagobert von Carlblum", I remembered Mama's nervousness on the days he and Toni would burst out laughing in the living room. I heard them myself.

Mama would tap her hands on her apron, stop, look at the clock, tap again, loosen her hair and gather it up in a bun again, glance out of the window, at the clock, again at the door, look at the pots, then approach them. Picking up a large wooden spoon, she'd raise the lid of the pot with a towel, and boom, close it with a bang; with her other hand she'd bang the wooden spoon on the pot, sounding together like a drum and cymbals. A few minutes later she'd stand at the door, saying, sorry, *bitte*, did the lady hear or not?

"Clearly, no secret would get out of the Sopp family home," added Mama.

"Because of the danger," said Klara Cohen.

"Because a secret cannot go through a wall," said Mama, "neither morning secrets nor night secrets. That's just how it is. When Toni went away, Helmutt would invite friends over for wild parties."

When Mama talked about the theater actor who visited Toni, the men chuckled and said words in Yiddish I didn't understand. The women would look down, or say, "Shhh. Shhh. There's a child here," pointing at me.

It didn't bother me. Klara Cohen came over to me and said, "Don't you have anywhere to go? There are lots of children outside. Why don't you go with Yashu?"

"I don't go anywhere when it's dark," I answered, and tightened my hands on my neck.

When Mama looked at me and said, "Sit up straight, straighten your shoulders. Why don't you sit on the whole chair like Yashu, *nu*, sit up straight," I got up and went to the hall window to look at the moon. I found a damaged moon in the sky, like the poem they taught us in class. I opened the window and felt the wind bite. I closed the window and heard Mama say softly, "Please, please. Won't you have some tea and biscuits."

I went to have a look at Yashu's room. The door was closed. "Yashu?" I called quietly, "Are you there?"

"I'm here."

I went into the room and sat on his bed. He was sitting at the table doing homework.

"I thought you were outside. I didn't hear you come in."

"Tomorrow, I'll take a notebook from someone," he said, closing the notebook.

"I also want to see Haifa in the dark. Why only you? Why am I always with them?" I said, gesturing towards the living room.

"Anyone tell you not to go?" asked Yashu, putting everything into his bag.

Silently, I got up from the bed. I went back to the window, the moon, and the dark sky.

Chapter Ten

Mama told the guests that Helmutt, a friend of the influential Governor-General Frank, was frequently promoted. This is apparently how he gained the title of professor, thus achieving a higher military rank. Interestingly, he didn't ask his wife Toni to sew the rank badges onto the epaulets of his coat, which bore the insignia S.A. and not S.S., but approached Mama, requesting that she do it for him. And I remember that very well.

Mama would sit at the kitchen table, smoothing the sleeve of Helmutt's coat or shirt, straightening the badges, setting them in place, measuring and comparing the two sides and thus, slowly and very carefully, she would sew on the badges. She constantly checked to see it was straight, that the stitches were perfect, like a sewing machine.

After the story about the badges, Mama would stop to take a breath and her thoughts would travel far, far away, even beyond the Haifa Sea. All around her, the guests would send her loving looks, even though some of them had heard it more than ten times. And in my heart I saw how beautiful Mama was at these moments, her cheeks red, her eyes shining; did she perhaps miss sewing on the badges of important officers? Not Nazis of course, but other officers? Naturally I brushed aside such a thought at once—an unhealthy, bad thought, I told myself.

"You were very lucky, Anna," said Bernard Cohen and Mama raised blue frozen eyes to him, stiffening her neck, indicating she wasn't interested in an argument.

"Yes, yes, it's the luck of dreaming Jews, not Jews living at war," he said aloud, and for some reason, Mama didn't like hearing it.

"Don't forget that it was conditional luck. It could turn at any hour, did you think of that?" Izzy Rappaport rebuked him and Henia Sonnenfeld said, "An hour? It could turn in a minute!"

Mama leant towards her, nodding and smiling. "Soon, Henia, soon, we'll get to the part of luck," and she straightened up in her chair, folded her hands nicely in her lap and spoke as quietly as she could:

"One day, a Ukrainian guest came into the Sopp family kitchen, a Gestapo man called Ivan; Toni was standing next to me in the kitchen. She was pouring cognac into several glasses and I was arranging the glasses on a tray. Ivan addressed Toni, requesting a large glass of cognac, a double shot; he had to clear his head, yes. He'd returned from an *aktion*, and during the selection at the camp, while they were selecting Jewish women for labor, he went crazy at one Jewess. A young woman, even pretty, with long hair, who was holding her baby, holding him tightly, refusing to give him up, though she'd received a specific order to give the baby to one of the old women standing at the side, and she insistently refused.

"She was given another order, then another. And she refused.

The opposite, she held him even more tightly to her chest and wept quietly. He had no choice; he went up to her and shot them both. But the pleading eyes of that Jewess pursue him everywhere; he doesn't have a moment's peace because of that Jewess. Her baby also looked at him, an ordinary baby, in pajamas, and he, Ivan, can't bear the eyes of those two any longer. He must have cognac, maybe cognac will shift those eyes away from him and he'll get some peace and quiet after the day."

Mama sighed and crushed a handkerchief in the palm of her hand.

"Hrrrr," snorted Bernard Cohen, pressing a finger to his cheek until it left a mark.

"Toni looked at him," said Mama, "and didn't say a word. As if she hadn't heard what he'd told her. She poured cognac into a large glass, gave it to him, and left the kitchen. He followed her out. I got dizzy, feeling as if all the blood in my body had sunk into my legs. I continued arranging the glasses on the tray and thought about the *aktion*, about the endless convoys, about the thousands of Jewish children traveling by train for the first time, but where, where? And the world was silent. True, all sorts of rumors reached us about terrible things happening to Jews, even a few streets away from the Sopp family. We heard they were grabbing people by the hair, dragging them along, and beating them to death in the middle of the street for no reason. I couldn't believe it. I thought about that young woman who was given a chance to live and who refused to give up her baby; my heart broke. I went on serving drinks to guests. They enjoyed themselves and laughed until late at night and, drunk, they linked arms and swayed, singing aloud, *'Uns ist alles ganz egal wir sitzen jetzt in dem Weichsel-Tal'*, which means, nothing matters to us, as long as we're sitting in the Wisła Valley."

"Evil woman," said Klara Cohen.

"No," said Mama.

"Damn that Ukrainian," said Bernard Cohen.

"That, yes, but Toni treated me and Danusha well."

"She hated Jews," said Klara Cohen. "I feel it inside."

"Toni didn't hate anyone; she loved Toni," said Mama, uncrossing her legs and pressing her knees together as if seeking strength.

There was a slight tension in the living room. On the side, I heard teeth grinding or chattering, don't know, and I immediately closed the zipper on my sweater.

"A few days later, the same Ukrainian, Ivan from the Gestapo, came back. He was invited to a party at Helmutt's," said Mama.

"Toni and the children were away at the time for a weekend in Silesia. Helmutt invited his friends as well as lovely young Polish girls. Like Toni, he trusted me to keep a secret.

The festivities with the young girls went on all night. I heard drunken singing and wild laughter, I heard women chattering, shouting, coughing, the slamming of doors and the sound of cars. Only at dawn was there finally quiet.

"That morning, Helmutt left the house early and, contrary to his custom, said he'd eat breakfast outside.

"I went in to clean the rooms and found Ivan the Ukrainian lying in bed, half-clothed. His face was puffy with sleep and he had a huge belly. I jumped back."

Bertha Ketzelboim grabbed her sweater and put the edge in her mouth. Mr. Bogusławski bent down to her and said quietly, "Luck is unpredictable in war, Bertha. We said this before, unpredictable."

Bertha bit her sweater, vigorously moving her head from side to side.

Mr. Bogusławski took out a small box, opened it, and offered it to her. She took it, swallowing at once as if it were medication.

"Why did you swallow?" he asked, and offered the box to her again.

"I was alarmed," she said in embarrassment and he smiled gently at her.

Mama looked distant and I knew, he's nice. I didn't feel that Mama thought Bertha was nice. I saw how she looked at her and how she drew her eyes away and smiled at Yozek Meltzer. She drew her eyes away from me too when she didn't like me and then she'd smile at someone else as if I wasn't beside her.

"Did I say cruel Ivan? Maybe Ivan the terrible? Well, the Ukrainian asked me to enter the room and said that he'd lost his wallet, would I look for it for him?

"I started looking for it under the sofa and the armchairs. And then he laughed sadistically and said, 'No need to look, I've found it.' I quickly left the room. I hurried to make breakfast for him. I was afraid of that Nazi.

"A few minutes later he sat down at the table in the dining corner. I served him breakfast and wanted to leave but he quietly told me to sit down beside him."

Mama stopped. She looked at the wall opposite and moistened her lips. I also moistened my lips and in a second the picture came back to me.

Mama came into the kitchen in full swing as if a wild wind had blown her from the passage straight through the door; her face was red as a beet. And then she swiftly chopped vegetables, tak. Tak. Tak. Tak. Tak. Tak. And I was used to hearing taak. And taak. And taak. Like that. I immediately realized that something bad had happened. She made hot coffee, toast, and fried eggs so quickly that she burned her finger.

"Ouch," I heard her whisper, putting her finger in her mouth. While she was arranging the food on the large tray, she dropped a glass. Lying across the table she managed to catch it. Then she smoothed her hair with her hands, straightened her apron, put her hands to her face, and closed her eyes. She took a deep breath, signaling to me with her finger, mouth closed, not a word, took the tray, and left the kitchen.

I immediately attached myself to the crack in the door.

I saw a large, fat man with short black hair, sitting at the Sopp family dining table. He wore a short brown coat and dark pants, he had a huge head and neck, and his black or brown eyes looked puffy. He also had a thick, brush-like mustache sharpened at the tips. He looked at Mama with narrow eyes, not moving a millimeter, and by his face I knew that this was a dangerous moment for her.

He said a couple of words to her and gestured at the place next to him.

Mama sat down. Her face was calm. She put her hands under the table, on her knees, palms together, her fingers intertwined. Her eyes were on the vase of flowers on the table—a bouquet of red roses. She occasionally turned her gaze to the big man and returned to the roses.

The man took the coffee, sipped once or twice, put the cup down and began to butter a slice of toast. Slowly. Mama waited quietly. One of her fingers was jumping on her knee and my feet grew hot. The heat climbed to my ankles.

The fat man took a large bite of toast, chewed, and addressed Mama. She left the roses and looked at him. He stared at her with his narrow eyes and said something in German. And was silent. He continued to chew the bread, his evil eyes on her.

And then Mama spoke. Her head rose slightly, very slowly, a

movement that could hardly be seen. I didn't understand what she was saying but from where I stood, she looked as though she was tall and he was short, even more so when he bent over the plate, and shoveled almost half a fried egg into his mouth, and then she returned to the roses. He chewed and chewed, drank his coffee, put down the cup and again addressed a few words to her.

Mama's finger jumped faster under the table. My feet grew hotter. I pressed them hard into the floor and felt the smell of burnt food. I quickly turned round and remembered that it was early in the morning and Mama hadn't started cooking. I went back to the crack. In my heart, I prayed that this fat man would leave Mama alone, and what a pity I wasn't next to her; maybe if I could have smiled at him, that big man would have left us in peace and gone away.

The man's wicked eyes never left Mama. Never mind the cold egg, never mind the coffee, what did he want from her, what? My belly was churning.

And then Mama compressed her lips, held onto the edge of the table with both hands, got up from her chair, said several words to him, turned around, and came towards the kitchen.

I jumped back against the wall. My heart beat in my ribs. Boom. Boom. Boom. Mama came into the kitchen, caught hold of my hand, and pushed me onto the balcony, told me, *Don't leave, don't leave,* and she closed the door behind her.

My legs burned up to my groin.

Suddenly I heard the slam of a door; I knew it was the front door.

"You can come out," said Mama. "He's gone." Her voice was quiet, as if nothing had happened.

I came in. Mama was holding onto the sink with both hands;

she bent over and cleared her throat. She stayed bent over for a minute or two, it seemed like hours to me. And then she straightened up and slowly drank a glass of water, all of it. She smoothed her fingers over her hair, went over to the cupboard, took out a soup pot, and whispered, "Danusha, what soup shall we cook today?"

I said, *Doesn't matter, Mama, doesn't matter. Whatever you want, like yesterday or the day before, I'll finish everything on my plate*. I completely forgot I hated soup.

In the meantime, Mama told the guests that Ivan the Ukrainian had interrogated her about her husband. She told him that her husband served in the Polish army and was lost in battle.

Ivan the Ukrainian wanted to know his rank and the military unit he served in.

Mama didn't lose her head. She got up from her chair, apologized, and said she had to cook and clean the house because the mistress, Mrs. Sopp, was coming home today, and her husband, the respected doctor, wanted the house clean and tidy before she arrived, he'd said so specifically, and she apologized.

The Ukrainian looked at her and said: "You managed that well," and he left.

Mama fell silent. Her chest rose and fell as she breathed. Some people were pale. Nobody said a word. Everyone heard Mr. Meltzer, Mama's admirer, chewing his lips and wheezing.

Mama gently wiped her forehead and said that from that day on she was afraid the Ukrainian would come and knock at the door. Maybe Helmutt Sopp had left the house early without saying a word about the guest in the living room so the man from the Gestapo could quietly interrogate her without interference?

And maybe, despite Helmutt and Toni Sopp's graciousness,

some suspicion had arisen that she was a Jewess? She was wretched and soundlessly sipped water.

"A dangerous situation," said Henia Sonnenfeld, "it would have been best to run and have done with it."

"Run, run," said Bertha Ketzelboim.

"Run where?" asked Klara Cohen.

"Nonetheless, you were very lucky, Anna," said Bernard Cohen and went over to Mama. He bowed, pressed her hand and said in festive voice: "I was a partisan. I fought against the Germans in the forests. Your courage, Madame Anna, was extraordinary, but you also had great luck."

I knew he was right. Mama never lost her head in the most difficult situations. People couldn't see if she was alarmed; only I sensed it happening. When I saw her expression of fear, I was very frightened, and it seldom happened, like the day we waited with Bronka at the Brzeżany railway station, on our way to Lwów.

At the time, Bronka said to Yashu, "Oy vey, it's as if she's paralyzed," and stroked his cheek when he jumped on the bench. And to me she said, "Leave Mama alone," when she saw me trying to hold onto her coat, and she hugged me. And, actually, not a muscle moved in Mama's face, and she had a frozen, distant look, as if she'd stayed in the pit under Mrs. Moskova's kitchen floor. The pit held great terror for her, but that paralysis of hers was a rare event; she really was brave and we endured many dangers and also luck, as Bronka herself said several times.

I couldn't be as brave as Mama or Bronka. When I walked in the street, I always looked straight ahead so, God forbid, my eyes wouldn't meet those of passersby. If anyone looked at me, I didn't feel good, even worse if they turned to look at me. I'd at once start to check what was wrong, what they'd seen. What were my eyes like in the sun? What color was my hair? Was my skirt torn? Or my sock? Was my dress stained?

I looked at myself. I looked so sloppy. I'd worn a crumpled dress, short socks, and unpolished shoes. Even my schoolbag thrown down next to me looked bad.

I recalled what Mama had said to her sisters about Papa: "Remember, Anna, what is important in life is family. You can always trust your husband and children." That's what Mama said, and I knew Mama could be trusted.

But not with regard to order and organization of the home or closet. Mama was brave but she paid less attention to whether I had socks or underwear in the closet.

I, on the other hand, am a girl who's worth less. Why? Because there was always something wrong with me. I held my pencil in my left hand, not like Mama. And I slept with my mouth open. Because of this problem sleeping, when I was little, Mama decided to take me to a doctor who'd take out my tonsils.

I remember a doctor with thick glasses and a cleft in his chin. He dressed me in a long rubber apron, but first he tied me to the chair, and said: "Open your mouth wide, wide mouth, good. Stay, don't move." And then he took an enormous pair of metal pliers, put the plier in my mouth, caught hold of something, and pulled with force. Without an anesthetic. I remember screams, drumming of feet, and blood, a lot of blood on the apron. As if my tongue had been pulled out, taking with it my throat and a piece of my heart. Is that how you die?

The tonsils grew back, bringing laryngitis. Every year with its laryngitis. I especially enjoyed my laryngitis. It was like a sweet holiday for me. I stayed in bed from morning till night, the next day too, and the third day, sometimes a week, and if it got worse, I stayed with Mama, two weeks. I wasn't bored. I thought thoughts and watched her motions while she dressed and arranged her collar and very slowly brushed her hair. Or when she sat in a chair, with a straight back, of course, eating with her mouth closed, tiny, tiny movements, her cheeks not seeming part of the picture, her forehead smooth. How she laid the fork and knife at the sides of the plate, for instance, if she wanted to drink something and then she'd gently wipe her mouth on a serviette.

Chapter Eleven

"Today, we're talking about Yashu," reminded Mr. Bogusławski, which made me yawn. At first, one long yawn, and then one after the other until my jaw ached. Almost every year, when Mr. Bogusławski would remind us that this was the day to talk about Yashu, I'd fall half-asleep, even if the guests were sitting down at seven or eight o'clock in the evening and Yashu was still looking for things to do outside with his friends.

Mama's voice would fade away from me when I closed my eyes, as if it were going out into the third-floor corridor, descending the stairs to the second floor, the first floor, finally audible to me as if she were calling from Eilat—the southernmost town in Israel. After a few times, I knew how to say it just as she did, in her Polish accent, "How I suffered from worrying about my only boy, ayyy…"

I practiced the word *ayyy* for hours, the pause in her speech, that special, restrained, delicate movement of the shoulders. She'd almost fall forwards when she'd add, "That dear son, just a little boy, little, think about it… barely six years old and motherless from the age of four…" And that voice was so gentle and special it was hard to replicate with the movement in front of the mirror in the bedroom. When I grew taller, I knew this would be how I'd move my shoulders and exactly how I'd speak to the sweet baby girl I'd have. I even held a small cushion in my arms, na, na, na, I rocked her, my eyes closed.

"It's hard to describe in words," Mama would say, her head bowed, "hard to relate how I'd wait to meet my beautiful boy every Sunday afternoon. His blue eyes would shine with happiness when he saw me coming, but those eyes would go mad when the time came to leave. Ayyy… How he'd hug me, kiss my hand and sob, pleadingly, 'Mama take me, take me with you. I'm good, I'm a good boy, why just Danusha? Why not me?' And he'd lie on the floor and drum his feet… ayyy… and repeat, 'You're going and they hit me, and put me in the cellar.'

"And me? I'd be ill about it for half the week. My little boy ripped out my heart, ripped it to pieces. Even the man in that Polish family told me, 'When you go, the child cries. Better for him if you don't come, understand? Every time you leave, he cries non-stop and there are many neighbors who can get money from the police if they say a word about us or your boy. It's very dangerous, and we have to shut him in the cellar to keep him quiet, yes?' And I understood everything, I understood it was dangerous, and I realized that my child was shut in the cellar alone. Can you imagine the situation?"

Every time, Mama's voice would break at the same place, and the others had nothing to say, but everyone's eyes wept and wept, and in the quiet, birds, butterflies, and lilacs flew about in my head, like the ones I saw on the tree in Helmutt and Toni's garden, and I went on yawning, and I wanted all that air coming into my body to fly me out through the window like a balloon, so I wouldn't hear Mama speaking as if she were calling from Eilat.

"Well, it's understandable that such a little boy couldn't understand problems like circumcision and that if he came with us, we'd all be in danger—his life, and my daughter's life, as well as my own. We had Polish papers and Polish names and a little boy who was circumcised—how could this be?"

"Well, how?" agreed Bernard Cohen, and rolled his eyes upward.

"How indeed, how," mused Klara Cohen, and shook her head for a long time.

"Danger, no doubt about it," said Izzy Rappaport, removing his glasses to clean the lenses, to better hear what should be done.

"To the end of my days I won't forget how my darling boy pleaded, ayyy," Mama repeated to the guests, adding, "What did my boy want? He wanted to come, and he promised to sleep under my bed in two pairs of pajamas without crying even once. Well, how could I sleep at night after that? I couldn't..."

"Impossible," agreed Henia Sonnenfeld.

"I'd die on the spot, your child alone..." fretted Bertha Ketzelboim.

"Well of course, we aren't made of steel," declared Efraim Sonnenfeld.

"Heartbreaking," added Klara Cohen, who was sobbing aloud just from Yashu's story. With the same words and that embroidered handkerchief of hers every time, "Such great suffering, such suffering, the child must be returned home, he must be."

The guests in the living room agreed without argument, and I just tried to remember a special tune, which was also part of our lives, not just Yashu's, my poor poor brother, and I'd recall the "Queen of the Night" aria from Mozart's *The Magic Flute*—*Come, my love, don't let me wait any longer, come, my love*—and hum the tune in my mind.

"In the end, I brought Yashu home," said Mama, and the guests in the living room smiled lovingly. "There were no miracles, none, none. Not one miracle came down to us from the heavens. It was serious planning with a great deal of thought, and Helmutt helped, without a doubt," she said, gathering the strength to explain what happened with our little Yashu, who was raised by the Poles, maybe until he was six.

"One evening," said Mama, "it was in the winter of 1944. At the time, I heard from my sisters that the Germans were losing battles against the Russians, which of course encouraged us. We realized that Russia was taking the same action as during the war with Napoleon, and the harsh Russian winter helped them subdue the enemy… Well, that evening, Helmutt invited several men for a party in the large living room. A few days before the party, he said: '*Bitte*, Frau Anna, in two days' time, *Bitte*,' he asked me to prepare a gourmet meal. 'I rely on you. Buy whatever you need.'

"I understood from him that a friend of his, an important general, had arrived from Germany and it was important to make something special for him and for several other officer friends.

"And indeed, I cooked all manner of things, set the table, and served the food. All the men watched me serve, pour, clear, bring out more, arrange it like a meal in a great castle, and they appreciated it with gracious words. It's also important to say that when I was young, I was known to be a beautiful girl. My portrait, painted in oil by Ignacy Pieńkowski, a famous professor from the Academy of Fine Arts in Kraków, adorned my parents' house, and there wasn't a single person who didn't stop to admire that portrait."

"You're still beautiful today, Anna," said Mr. Bogusławski, loudly and seriously. "We have no complaints, very beautiful."

I got up from my chair and I felt Mama talking to my back without saying a word. I didn't care that my chair creaked a little when I got up. Mama looked but I went out into the hall where I slept; I didn't have my own room. I sat on my bed, opened a book, closed it, thrust a candy into my mouth and crushed it with my teeth, watered a small plant on my window ledge until it drowned in the plate, and returned to the living room in time to hear Henia Sonnenfeld saying, "No doubt about it, beautiful, beautiful, and that's the truth."

Yozek Meltzer straightened up, wordless and red-faced, nodding his head in agreement, yes, yes, yes. He finally drank a glass of water and swallowed noisily.

I thought, another professor, this artist, again only the best for Mama, but it's true she had a perfect face and skin as smooth as a mirror. I raised my head to look at her. She'd lifted her chin, her broad forehead seemed to stretch, and she smoothed a finger under her chin, and the light in the room seemed brighter.

"After the meal for the general and the officers," said Mama, "I went into my room and lay down quietly, but I couldn't sleep; I was very worried about my little boy. From the living room came sounds of song and wild laughter. And then I heard a loud knock at the door. I quickly put on a robe, tidied my hair and opened the door. A young officer of the highest rank I'd seen in the living room stood before me. I was very alarmed, but nonetheless looked him straight in the eye and asked him what he wanted. He smiled and I saw he was a little embarrassed, yes, I recall that very well, and then he asked if he could please go into the kitchen to make himself some coffee. That's how it was. The entrance into the kitchen was through our room; he had no other choice. I said politely that I myself would make the coffee and serve the guests. Suddenly, I saw Helmutt bursting with laughter in the corridor.

"'You've lost the bet,'" he called to the officer, who was as red as a beet, and they both turned and went back to the living room.

"The next day at breakfast, Helmutt apologized for his drunk friend's behavior. His friend took a bet with him that he could conquer any woman, and he, Helmutt, regretted not stopping him, 'The man had drunk too much cognac, do you understand, Frau Anna?'"

Mama coughed quietly. The guests looked at me and back at Mama, and again back and forth.

"Really and truly in the lion's den, really and truly. Ah…" said Efraim Sonnenfeld.

"Really and truly," said his wife, Henia.

"Good for you, Anna," said Mr. Bogusławski, and blew her a kiss.

I heard Bernard Cohen coughing as if he'd swallowed a nut, but he didn't give up; he insisted on speaking, insisted, but the cough prevented him and his wife hit him several times on the back, "Look up, look up, and stop talking," she scolded him.

"But between us," he didn't let Mama off the hook, "between us, what stopped that officer or Helmutt from touching… after all, those Nazis, damn them, had no scruples, did they?"

Meltzer jumped in his chair gesturing no, no, no, with his fingers.

"No, no, no, they didn't," said Mr. Bogusławski, instead of Meltzer who didn't like to speak in front of Mama. I think he was afraid of getting confused.

Bernard and his wife Klara moved close to Meltzer's ear. "What's wrong with that psychiatrist whose wife is always going away, eh?"

"Shhh. Shhh," said Henia Sonnenfeld.

"Enough," requested Mr. Bogusławski.

"Wait, wait, the real miracle hasn't yet occurred." Mama surprised them and put out a hand, bending her fingers and looking at the nails. She told them how Helmutt treated her most graciously after that night, how she felt he was looking for a way to make amends for the unpleasantness.

And so, one Sunday, while she was busy preparing supper, he came into the kitchen and began to compliment her. He was surprised that such a young, handsome woman was always so serious, and how few clothes she had; after all, every woman likes pretty clothes.

And then he took out his checkbook and said: "Frau Anna, you don't need to save so much on the shopping for the house. Please buy yourself a pretty dress."

Mama stopped and took a sip from the glass of water beside her.

"Excellent," called out Klara Cohen, "*nu*, and what did you say to him?"

"I must admit I was very surprised," said Mama. "I didn't know what to say. Helmutt also looked embarrassed and didn't say another word. When he returned his checkbook to his pocket, I wanted to believe that he didn't know anything about the Jews apart from what they thrust into his young head, and then I said, 'I'm not in a position to think about clothes, Herr Professor,' and he raised his head, frowned, his eyes bright and half-open. Finally, I said quietly, 'I am very worried and it's hard for me to sleep at night.'

"Helmutt frowned and said, 'Frau Anna, you, worried?'

"'Worried and anxious, sir.'

"'Would you tell me, please, what it's about?'

"I looked out through the window at the sky and asked if it was appropriate for me to talk about my suffering. And then I was filled with courage, I looked straight into his eyes, and said very quickly: 'Very great worry about my little boy gives me no rest. I once told you and Toni that my son is with relatives in the country.'

"Helmutt came closer. 'Can I help you?'

"'My relatives have asked me to take my boy. I don't know what to do.'

"He pursed his lips, paused and said: 'How old is the boy?'

"'He's the same age as your little boy, Ammon.'

"'Bring the boy here to us,' said Helmutt, without thinking twice, and my heart jumped for joy. I was sure that in the home of a Nazi officer, and with his mother, my dear son would be protected and safe."

The women in the living room clapped their hands. The men slapped their knees. "I must say a heavy burden fell from my shoulders. Nonetheless, I feared then that Helmutt's action wasn't only compassion for the boy; I feared he had other intentions, perhaps. However, I never forget that he related to me like *eine anständige dame*, a decent woman, yes, and, most important of all, the boy would finally be with his mother."

Mama said *decent woman, decent woman,* and every time I saw her wordlessly warning me to be modest.

"Now we must raise a glass," called out Mr. Bogusławski, "we'll drink lemonade, that's enough."

"We'll pretend it's Kwiat-cognac, ah?" said Bernard Cohen, with a broad smile.

"Oy, could I have the recipe, please?" said Klara Cohen, taking paper and pencil from her bag.

Mama nodded agreement.

"Yes, yes, note it down, note it down," said Bernard Cohen.

"Wait, I also want it," said Henia Sonnenfeld, looking in her bag.

"What about me?" said Jacob Ketzelboim, flexing his muscles, "*Nu*, Bertha, wake up."

"You," said Bertha, taking out a mirror from her bag. Passing her little finger under her eyes, and, wetting her finger with saliva, she straightened her eyebrows. Jacob looked at me. I tore out a page from my Hebrew notebook and gave it to him.

Mama looked at the guests and smiled, "To this day I remember the recipe: Whip the yolk of an egg in milk..."

"How much?" called out Klara Cohen.

"A little milk, you'll sense it," said Mama. "Add sugar and schnapps..."

"What did she say?" asked Jacob Ketzelboim quietly, and looked at me.

"Give it to me and I'll write it down," I suggested, and Jacob handed me the paper.

"Cook the mixture, cool, dilute with alcohol, an excellent drink, worth trying," concluded Mama. "Now let's drink tea."

"She doesn't give quantities on purpose," whispered Klara Cohen to her husband.

"*Nu*, so work out the quantities yourself. Do you want to be given everything on a plate?" responded Bernard Cohen, and received a pinch from his wife.

Finally, Yashu joined us. *Thank God he came*, Mama and I said several times a day.

When lying on my bed in the hall, I often remembered the dream Mama had when she was pregnant with me. She dreamed she'd have a son as handsome as a Polish officer, tall, beautiful uniform, mounted on a noble horse; that's exactly what she'd tell her sisters every time, from the beginning, not tiring of the good-looking Polish officer mounted on a good horse.

When I grew up a little, I realized that my brother Yashu fit in with Mama's dream, at least in appearance, but I happened to be born before him, and it was from him that she had to part, and maybe that's why in every picture we have together, my brother is always close to Mama. He's the one she's embracing tightly and closely, and I am standing next to her. Maybe she was afraid that one day an evil enemy would come along, God forbid, and take her child from her. And then what, she'd be left only with me?

When I grew up, I read what Bronka, Mama's younger sister, wrote about Yashu; at the time, she was an unmarried woman of twenty-eight or nine, and wasn't considered beautiful like her sisters. But, nonetheless, I liked to sit next to her, lean against her knee a little; maybe because she was born after four girls and they wanted a boy and another girl came along and she wasn't pretty. Interestingly, a family that so valued beauty had a fifth daughter who lacked the beauty talked about in Kraków.

And she was the most successful at her studies. Of all the sisters, only Bronka completed high school, received a certificate, and was considered educated.

And this is what Bronka wrote:

One day, in the afternoon, I was resting with Mama who at the time was hiding in my apartment. We had to move her from one place to another so as not to arouse suspicion. I got up and said, "I'm going to Yashu." At the time, Yashu was staying with a Polish family.

Mama looked at me in surprise and said, "No, no, no, don't go out."

I said, "I have to go." I dressed quickly and went out into the street, although it was very difficult for me not to obey Mama.

I arrived at the Polish woman's house; she came out to meet me. I said to her, "Where is Yashu? Where is he? I've come to take him for a walk."

Hearing my voice, Yashu ran to me, pleading: "Ciocia Bronka, take me with you, take me."

The Polish woman didn't want him to go for a walk with me; maybe she was afraid of the neighbors. I insisted, took him from the house, and we went for a walk along the avenue.

There was another Jewish child hiding in the Polish woman's house, for a large sum, of course.

I walked with Yashu and he cried: "Ciocia Bronka, I don't want to go back there, I don't want to. I cry and they hit me—please let me stay with you."

I took Yashu to my apartment and discussed what I should do with my mother. She said to take him to his mother.

I listened to her and brought Yashu to Anna, who was working in Helmutt Sopp's house.

A short time later, I heard that the Gestapo came to the Poles' house and took away the Jewish child who was in hiding with Yashu.

I read what Bronka wrote and wanted to believe that Yashu's crying was different that day, and that Bronka felt it was a special sign, that they had to do something. And maybe she brought Yashu to us and Mama hid him under the bed, and only then asked Helmutt for help. And maybe Mama doesn't remember right. I don't know.

What do I remember about my brother?

Not much.

I knew Yashu lived with a Polish family for two years, maybe more.

I don't know if I was sorry he didn't live with us. I asked Mama once, why Yashu wasn't with us.

Mama said, *Better he's in hiding, for his own good and for ours*. I accepted it.

The Polish woman was a teacher. Her husband worked for the railway—or he was a teacher and she worked for the railway, I don't really remember. They had two boys with epilepsy. Every Sunday I went with Mama to visit Yashu at the Poles' house. It was her day off and she'd take fruit she'd collected for him in a bag. I knew she didn't eat it, keeping it for him. I didn't say a word. I didn't tell Mama that I also hid candies that Toni gave me in my pocket, and I thought, I wonder if he'll remember that I gave him my candies.

Every time we went into their living room, we saw them sitting on an old sofa with shabby brown upholstery. They sat there, a man, a woman, and two boys, their features blurred. I felt we weren't wanted there. They looked at us with evil eyes, and I don't remember seeing Yashu there.

We visited Yashu on many occasions, but I don't remember seeing him. Even if I squeeze my eyes shut and make an effort to remember.

At the time, Yashu, like Papa, was erased from my mind.

Neither does my brother remember the period he lived alone with the Polish family who looked at him with evil eyes.

Only after many years did I understand what happened there. We come to visit Yashu, sit on the sofa in the living room. Mama talks to the owners of the house; I look at the boys. We take Yashu out for a walk, around the block once or twice, come back, two three hugs and kisses, and he cries, "Take me, Mama, take me." The man in the house gets angry with him and shouts, "Stop crying, stop it."

We walk away from the house and hear the crying, "Take me, Mama, take me," and thump. A blow on the head, and quiet. Complete quiet.

Where was the crying? Down in the cellar. The door was closed on him.

After an hour or two the crying stops. Yashu returns to the living room with the family that hides him.

For Mama the crying stayed in her head. Stayed for an hour, two hours, three hours, all night, another night, it stayed all week. Not for me. No wonder her heart broke.

I remember my brother from the time he came to be with us in the house of the Sopp family. He was small and thin. Maybe from sadness.

At first, Mama hid him under the bed. He stayed there a few days until one morning Mama said to Toni: "I've brought my son from the village. I had no choice; he has to stay."

It was the first and last time I heard Toni shouting: "What do you mean you've brought a child? You didn't say you had another child. Where does this child come from? I don't understand it." She screamed and screamed until finally she put on a hat and went out to do some shopping.

I don't remember what Mama said, but Yashu remained and slept with us.

Helmutt Sopp looked at my brother and asked, "Who's this?" And then he said casually, "What have you prepared for us today, Frau Anna? Mmmm. I smell something really good, excellent." And then I went out onto the balcony to play.

I remember my brother's first days with the Sopp family.

At first, he refused to get out of bed in our room. Peter and Ammon invited him to play with them, and he looked at them and was silent. If for some reason he remained alone in the room for a few minutes, we'd find him hiding under the bed. Even when Helmutt came into the kitchen he hid. Mama called to him to come out, held his hand, and said to him, "In this house there is no need to hide, Yashu, no need. Mama takes care of you. Look at Danusha; she's quiet, isn't she?"

Yashu nodded his head up and down; I noticed that his eyes didn't agree at all. They darted from side to side, and every time the front door opened, we'd find him under the bed. I called to him to come out; he didn't want to. Sometimes I lay next to him and told him a story, like Mama told me when I was eating soup, and I gave him a candy. Only after the story did he come out.

After two weeks, he agreed to come out of our little room and play silently in the kitchen or on the balcony. What he most enjoyed was looking out of the window. He'd lean against the glass and talk to himself. Did he have an imaginary friend, perhaps, and want to tell him things? But if a car door slammed in the street or there was a knock on the front door, I saw him immediately look for a place to hide, behind the curtain, or under the table, covered with a large cloth. Sometimes he stayed there, even when Mama called, "Yashu, Yashu, come to me sweetheart." Nothing helped.

After a month, Yashu began to play with Peter and Ammon on the kitchen balcony. They'd put their school bags on their chests and run towards him, pushing him. He didn't push back.

One day, Yashu told me that if Mama hadn't forbidden him to fight with them, he'd have pushed them back with the school bag, oh, how he'd have pushed back. But he listened to Mama. Both of us listened to Mama. Sometimes the tiniest movement of her head was enough for us to understand when to get up, when to sit, when not to move in the chair, when to pretend to be asleep. When it was allowed to take a candy, when to sleep, get up quietly—quietly, dress quickly, and run. When to take small steps. When to answer and when it was better to be silent. When it was finally permissible to cry, but without a word, and not to talk to strangers.

If someone asks a question, say you don't know, and Yashu, you may not bathe with Peter and Ammon, absolutely forbidden and that's all there is to it. You know that, yes? Do not forget. If the children invite you to take a bath, you tell them Mama needs you in the kitchen, yes?

We kept Mama's rules. It was like walking along a never-ending ruler. We didn't stir one millimeter away from it, not one millimeter. A straight line, always, and it was as natural to us as the night follows the day.

In the room adjoining the kitchen at Helmutt and Toni's, there was only one bed. My brother slept between me and Mama, both of us embracing him; we managed well.

When we went to bed, Mama would tell us about the house Papa bought before the war in Palestine. She said, "Children, a house is a most important thing. We have a house in Haifa, a city near the sea."

The stories about the house in Haifa were, for me, like a large candy before going to sleep. I imagined a room with pink walls, pink curtains, a pink blanket, and a pink embroidered pillow. And a wide bed just for me that was also pink. I imagined another room in the color blue for my brother. Next to mine.

The thoughts about the house in Palestine, which Mama called Ciocia Palemira, gave me hope that one day we'd reach the Promised Land. I didn't know what the Promised Land was, but from Mama's face I understood that it was a good place for Jews, they didn't have to fear anyone, and there were certainly no Nazis.

Chapter Twelve

We spent two years with Helmutt and Toni. For two years we didn't go out in the snow at night, or to warehouses, or to Polish families. For two years I sat almost without moving in the same chair in the kitchen, bathed in the same bath, and looked out of the same window at the lilac tree. For two years I listened to the same records on the Sopp family's record player in the living room—naturally when Mama and I were alone in the house. When the family returned home, they addressed me in German, and always politely.

Peter, Helmutt and Toni's eldest son, was two years older when we played on the balcony. We both grew taller and we had agreements that we kept. One of these agreements was that I'd teach him Polish and he'd teach me German. Peter didn't learn Polish but I learned to speak German; my brother also learned while playing with the two boys. They'd bounce a ball and counted who was better at it. Yashu was good with the ball. Peter taught me a song he liked:

Parade marsch
Parade marsch
Der Kommandant hat
Ein Loch in den Arsch

The parade marches
The parade marches
The commander
has a hole in his ass.

We walked in a line, Ammon and Yashu joining us, we waved our arms, sang "*Parade marsch*

Parade marsch," laughing aloud to each other.

Peter and Ammon went to school and they had satchels. I had neither a satchel nor school. I had Mama in the kitchen. She knew how to sing more beautifully than anyone I'd heard and it was from her I learned to sing arias from operas. Mama sang arias to us from when I was little, like mothers sing children's songs, she sang to us in German. Best of all I loved hearing the opera "Madame Butterfly" as well as "Samson and Delilah". I especially remember the last words Delilah sang to Samson:

Du bist mein ganzes Glück
Du bist mein leben
Samson ich liebe dich.

You are my happiness,
You are my life,
Samson, I love you…

Sometimes I added my voice to Mama's singing and she'd

smile if she noticed. Mostly, she'd sing to herself as if there were no kitchen, no Sopp family, and no war.

I also played with Yashu on the kitchen balcony. We looked at pictures in books and newspapers, and I tried to read words aloud in German; Yashu listened and repeated after me.

I remember the day I understood the difference between the Polish and German languages.

I was sitting on the toilet. On the floor was a newspaper in German. I understood I had to read the headline differently from *Zeitung* in Polish.

"How do I say *Tseitung* in German?" I asked Mama, and showed her the headline in the newspaper. "*Zeitung*. *Zeitung*", said Mama, and that's how I began learning to read by myself.

In the newspaper I looked for words like *ich liebe*, or *ganzes Glück*, like the opera "Samson and Delilah"; the words seemed beautiful to me, but I didn't find any. In the newspaper were words like *Panzer, Flugzeug, Armee*, which is a tank, a plane, an army.

I learned to read Polish with the help of my cousin, Adam, Lydia's son. Adam, who was of medium height with blue eyes, would come to visit us at the Sopps'—more often toward the end of the war, and mainly when we knew the Sopp family were out of the house. He'd bring pictures of planes bombing here, and here, and there. He also taught me and Yashu to look at the pictures and read the headlines about the end of the war. I invited him to the window, to the lilac tree, but he got bored after a minute.

In Helmutt Sopp's garden there was a lilac tree with branches full of tiny mauve flowers. For hours I'd look at the flowers, changing color according to the position of the sun in the sky and the weather, from a milky color to a darker one. The flowers had a pleasant scent that I liked to breathe in. Years later I smelled a similar scent in a French perfume. I also checked cars that passed in the street. Every time a car stopped at the house, Yashu would jump and immediately glance at Mama. Only after she nodded to him that everything was all right, everything was all right, did he stop jumping up and down, and calm down with a record on the record player in the living room. We both sat quietly, almost without moving, listening to music for a long time. Sometimes we drew or looked at pictures in Polish children's books. The Sopp family had records of classical music as well as songs in German. There was one song I particularly liked to listen to:

Hello, hello,
I'm looking for a tiny, sweet, pretty woman,
She must be pretty,
But smart, too, that's enough…

I'd sit on the sofa next to the record player and gaze at the center of the revolving record. It had a picture of a white dog with brown ears and a spotted collar around its neck. The dog leaned towards the large opening of a metal gramophone connected to a wooden box with a handle on the side. The dog and the record revolved opposite me: head down, head up; down, up. Sometimes I turned my head in tiny circles with the dog, singing, *Hello, hello, I'm looking for a pretty woman, mmm. Mmm. Mmm,* until I got dizzy. When the song ended, I took the record in my hands, stroked the dog with my thumb, as if we were old friends, and then again, from the beginning. *Hello, hello…*

It was much later that I understood the words on the record, "HIS MASTER'S VOICE."

One Sunday, Bronka joined us on our way to Franca's apartment. I noticed Mama humming, which had never happened before. I was used to silence and the sound of steps, that's all. I didn't dare hum beside her in the street. After all, there were Nazi soldiers who took whole families out of the houses.

"You remember that you aren't going back with Mama?" asked Bronka.

I didn't remember, and she rubbed lipstick on my cheeks right after we entered Franca's apartment.

"You do want to see where I live, don't you?"

"Is Yashu also coming with us?" I asked Bronka.

"Just you, sweetheart," said Bronka. "Grandma Rosa is also there, and tomorrow you'll go back to Mama," she promised.

I looked at Mama. She nodded in confirmation, and smiled at me.

I went out to the street hand in hand with Bronka.

"From now on, my name is Valeria," said Bronka, "Valeria. And not a word about our family. Don't forget, all right?"

"Yes, Bronka… Valeria."

"Valeria, a maid at a German lady's house, don't forget."

"And who am I?"

"You're a sweet smart girl called Danusha," she smiled at me, "and that's enough."

Bronka opened a brown door with a key she took out of her bag. She led me into a small room where there was a bed covered with a blanket, a tiny table, and a chair. I didn't see Grandma Rosa. I heard her quietly snoring.

"Get into bed," whispered Bronka even thought it was light outside.

"The mistress of the house is coming home, and we don't tell anyone that you and Grandma are here, all right?"

"All right," I said and sat on the bed.

"You don't need to undress, just take off your shoes and give them to me."

Grandma Rosa woke up, peeping out of the duvet and smiling at me. She raised the edge of the duvet and gestured to me to get into bed.

I remained standing as if no one had spoken to me. I wanted to return to Mama. Bronka smiled at me, stroked each cheek, and spoke soundlessly. Nonetheless, I understood every word: "The mistress of the house will be back any minute. I'm closing the door, and don't come out until I open it." She gave me a kiss and a caress, and left the room.

I lay on the edge of the bed without moving, without saying a word. I was afraid Grandma would speak to me again, say hurtful words, Galician temperament.

"Come on, I'll teach you the words of a song in German," said Grandma Rosa after the silence had lengthened and it was clear I was about to cry. Grandma sang:

Herr von Haagen
Darf ich wagen
sie zu fragen
Was sie tragen
Als sie lagen
Krank am magen

In der Hauptstadt Kopenhagen

Mr. von Haagen
May I ask you
What you wear
When you lie
With a stomach ache
In the capital, Copenhagen.

I found it easy, learning it quickly. And then we heard the slam of a door. Grandma signaled to me to be quiet; we immediately pulled the blanket over our heads.

I heard a woman's voice. I didn't understand what she was saying in German.

I heard Bronka answering her loudly, as if she were angry. I didn't understand a word but was alarmed by Bronka's loud, irritated voice. I'd never heard anyone speak to landlords like that. Mama spoke quietly, almost inaudibly, and she always nodded and agreed to everything.

I could hardly breathe. Grandma wasn't still. Every moment she piled more and more of the duvet on my head. I had no air.

Time went by, maybe a quarter of an hour, and again we heard the slam of the door, and a knock at the door. Bronka told us we could get out of bed; the lady had left the house.

"Thank God," said Grandma Rosa, "thank God."

"Speak quietly," beseeched Bronka, hugging Grandma.

Grandma put her fingers over her mouth and winked at me. Finally, I got my breath back. I drank a glass of water. Grandma also drank a glass of water, and asked me to recite the song about Mr. von Hagen to Bronka.

I remembered it all. Grandma was pleased and gave me a candy she took out of her pocket.

"How come you weren't afraid to shout at the German lady?" I asked Bronka. "How come you weren't afraid?"

"I don't give a damn about her," she said, looking at me.

Not give a damn about her? I didn't understand. Is it possible not to give a damn about Germans?

I could ask Mama if one day she wouldn't give a damn about Germans, but I didn't ask. Mama does care about important people, and, in her eyes, Germans were important after the war, too.

Years later, Bronka told me: "I decided during that terrible bloody war that no one would bring me to my knees, no one, ever, do you hear, Danusha?"

At once I wanted to be a heroine like Bronka and say loudly, pointing straight ahead: "No one, no one will bring me to my knees," but instead out came my usual smile—smile nicely and don't say a word—and for this I received a tight hug from Bronka and abundant kisses, but not from Mama.

When I got back to Mama, I asked Peter how to say *whistle* in German. He said *pfeifen*, and asked me if I wanted to learn to whistle with my lips, and he whistled. Phew. Phew. Phew.

Phew. Pheeeew. Pheeeeew. I didn't want to. Yashu did, and learned from Peter. I went to the mirror and smiled a big smile, tilting my head to the side so my hair would be puffier and longer.

One day, I recall, Franca's eldest son, Yehoshua, took me to the Germans to eat ice-cream. Yehoshua was twelve, maybe thirteen, and slept most of his time outside his mother's apartment because it was dangerous to be together. During the daytime he sold atlases in the street to make a little money. I didn't understand where he got the courage to wander the streets—after all, Jewish boys didn't wander the streets, girls yes, and even then, very seldom.

I remember a pleasant sun. Clouds like whipped egg whites traveled above Yehoshua's head. People strolled the sidewalk, talking among themselves, pushing baby carriages with pink babies. Some went into stores, others came out carrying parcels; I looked straight ahead, not daring to say a word.

We got to the ice-cream parlor. Yehoshua ordered two ice-creams from the German vendor, who was wearing a long white apron knotted over his large belly. He wore a funny white hat that stuck up like a tower.

Yehoshua took money out of his purse and paid for the ice-creams. I felt my heart leaping with excitement. Here it is, here it is, the vendor was filling a cone with ice-cream especially for me. Here I am, holding the ice-cream with both hands, *thank you, thank you, sir*.

I lick the wonderful ice-cream slowly, slowly, as slowly as I can, before it runs like milk. The ice-cream tastes like heaven. Much tastier than the fresh rolls I ate at Toni's house. I lick one side, second side, on top, all around, oh, I wish this ice-cream would never end. I lick and feel how wonderful it is, so wonderful it even presses on my belly. It's so wonderful that I, Danusha, can stroll around Kraków, looking ahead, to the sides—I didn't, but I could—and stop at the ice-cream parlor, and get an ice-cream from the Germans.

Yehoshua walks beside me, and I shorten my steps so that neither the way nor the ice-cream will end; no need to hurry to Grandma Rosa or to Helmutt's house with a jug of milk.

I felt I could lick that ice-cream for as long as I liked, and pass the man on the bench, who was reading a newspaper and holding the leash of a small dog.

I looked at Yehoshua and understood from him that I could stand next to the sweet dog and just look at it. I didn't, I walked on, and smiled at the ice-cream when Yehoshua wanted to buy me lemonade, and I refused because I didn't want to spoil the taste of heaven.

We walked along the road, me with the ice-cream in my hand like a torch and him looking at the stores with his quiet, handsome face, as if life was just fine. I was truly happy, almost cried. I wanted to hold his hand, and prayed to the Creator to grow up nicely and marry only Yehoshua. Quietly, I sang from "Samson and Delilah"—"*Samson ich liebe dich*; Samson I love you"—and Yehoshua looked at me with pleasure. I was sure he, too, wanted a wedding.

He finished licking his ice-cream, and then I did. I was afraid time would come to an end. I so wanted to continue strolling down the avenue of trees until the next day, the next week, but the trees in the avenue ended. We turned into a new, narrower street. I began to count steps: one two, three, four. I stopped. One two, three, four. Yehoshua gazed at the cars passing by. I gazed at him, and I saw by his face that he wasn't in a hurry, and that if another ice-cream parlor appeared in front of us, he would probably have offered me another one, *want one?*

I wouldn't have agreed because it wouldn't be polite.

I wiped my mouth with my palm and looked at my skirt and blouse; no stain, that's good. I looked ahead, growing sadder the closer we got to the Sopp house.

Chapter Thirteen

The taste of heaven hadn't left my tongue when again I heard Mama praying at night, "May God help him come back safely." She got into bed, groaned, prayed, and then sat up in bed for a few minutes, covered her face with her hands, and again, "May God help him come back," and lay down again. And got up. And again. I lay next to the wall, I faced Mama, and Mama faced the door, in case someone needed something. She was covered by a blanket. I was hot and thirsty, wanted a drink of water and was silent. I didn't know who should come back safely, and I didn't want to know who was in danger and needed such urgent help from heaven. Whenever I heard her groan at night, we'd fall asleep at dawn.

"May God help him come back safely," repeated Mama beseechingly when washing her face early in the morning. I saw she was in a hurry and I followed her immediately, dressing fast, brushing my hair fast, and washing my face even faster.

"I'm going with Toni to the market," said Mama and left.

I remained on the chair in the kitchen, and it took me time to realize that Mama was no longer there, nor was Toni, that the boys were studying and I'd forgotten Yashu—maybe he was at Grandma's. Finally, I went out onto the balcony, taking some magazines; maybe I'd find out how to say in German that whoever needs to will come back safely.

After an hour, maybe two, Toni and Mama returned with baskets from the market. I had just sat down again on the chair with the last magazine, and saw that Mama's face was a different color; it was grayish and her red lips were almost white. She signaled to me to come with her to our room.

"Put on your coat, Danusha. We're going out."

I put on my coat as I walked and hurried out after Mama.

I matched my steps to hers, quick steps, not letting go of her coat flap, listening to her heels, and trying to lower my foot when she lowered hers.

"Papa arrived in Kraków last night," she said. "It was planned. A Polish woman helped him get to Kraków. Understand?" She slowed her steps, wanting to see if I understood. I nodded without letting go of her coat flap. Again, she took my hand. "Listen to me. Papa is with the Polish woman now, waiting at her home for us to come and take him to a hiding place. Understand?"

"Yes," I said, my heart starting to tremble.

"We need to hurry, Danusha, the house is nearby."

I closed my mouth because I felt as if my throat was closing up with sand. Papa? Papa Moshe coming to us in Kraków? I'll see Papa, now, here, with us? I started coughing without stopping but I heard Mama's heels and put my foot down on the sidewalk when she did. I couldn't see the road even when I rubbed my eyes with my hands.

I knew about Papa from Mama and her sisters' whisperings on Sunday in Franca's kitchen. Every Sunday there'd be whisperings in the kitchen and plans for the week. Once I heard Mama say, "In his letter, he begs us to hurry with the papers."

Lydia nodded, *yes, yes, yes*.

Mama tugged at Lydia's hand without speaking.

"Yes, it's difficult," whispered Lydia.

Mama moved close to Lydia, "You must be quick."

Lydia nodded without a word.

"A friend from Tarnopol who works with him at the district office has disappeared," added Mama.

Lydia looked at Bronka.

I noticed that Bronka was angrier than the others and she made the decisions.

"Before him, two others disappeared." Mama repeated things she'd already said, and Bronka opened her eyes wide and turned her back, while saying words that weren't nice about the Nazis. Then she turned her head and looked straight at me and smiled a big smile, took a candy from her pocket, and gave it to me. "It will be all right, you'll see."

"My husband Moshe writes that no one knows what will happen tomorrow," sighed Mama. "What will happen, what will happen?"

Franca looked at the children in the living room. Bella and Yashu were amusing Grandma Rosa. She also looked at me, standing next to Mama and listening to the sisters.

Gradually, I realized that Lydia was responsible for getting Papa forged papers; she had contacts. Bronka was responsible for finding a hiding place for Papa's first days in Kraków. Franca explained where it was best to look for a room for Papa, where he'd be safe. She said she'd coordinate between Mama and Lydia, and the moment they were ready she'd make sure to get a message to Mama.

"Franca is very responsible," I heard Grandma Rosa say without rhyme or reason. She'd just hear the four sisters whispering and she'd say, "Franca is very responsible!"

All the whisperings would stop, Franca would signal to Grandma Rosa to close her mouth, and she'd immediately fall silent. And there were times when I'd hear Franca warn the sisters when she heard something really important at the government office where she worked. Franca mainly warned Bronka, who did things others would be afraid to think of doing.

"Be careful," they'd beg Bronka. "Everything is dangerous," they'd repeat worriedly, and she'd toss her hair and run off to do things for the family. The other sisters would also take on roles, like moving Grandma from Franca's apartment to another one, or finding a safer place for the older children in the family, or visiting my brother Yashu when he lived with the Polish family. They constantly checked to see what people needed. Not enough food? Not enough money? Did they have to sell jewelry? Pay someone to do something secret and give someone a chance to escape from one place to another?

Sometimes we'd come back from the sisters and Grandma, and I'd see Mama crying about Papa. She'd sit huddled on the edge of the bed in our small room, leaning against the wall, pressing Papa's letter to her heart, and wiping the tears. "What will be, what will be, I don't know what else we can do," wept Mama, looking at me and Yashu.

"Mama mustn't cry. Papa will come to us. It will be all right in the end," I told Mama as if I were Bronka, the bravest of the sisters. They were just words; I wanted her to stop crying.

She didn't stop. I noticed that as more time passed between the letters she told her sisters about, Mama spoke more quietly to us. Sometimes, I saw her looking ahead as if she were already far away.

"We're late, Danusha, hurry," begged Mama.

"Is he already waiting?" I asked and she didn't hear.

"Faster, Danusha."

I was no longer sure that Papa was waiting, and my heart hurt. Had he really come to us in Kraków or was Mama just saying that? She never just said things and I saw she was trembling when she looked at the house yard. There were people and a chicken there.

My heart began to beat faster. Tuk-tuk. Tuk-tuk. It was already hard to breathe.

When Mama stopped, I wanted to vomit.

"This is the place," she said, passing her bag from one hand to the other.

I was trying to moisten my tongue when a fat woman with a black scarf and a dark dress with white spots appeared. She had an evil face. But I still smiled a little.

"Jesus Maria, Jesus Maria, the Gestapo took him," she shrieked in Mama's face, throwing her hands in the air and stamping her feet.

"Shema Israel," whispered Mama, beating her chest with her hands, trying not to cry.

"They took him, they took him!" shouted the Polish woman,

extending her hands and pushing us out towards the gate. Mama stood still. She looked directly into her eyes.

"Let's go, come on, let's get out of here." I grab Mama's hand and pull her with all my strength, not letting go of her hand until Mama moves. We start to walk away.

We walk fast, not speaking a word. My heart presses against my ribs when I glance back. Is there anyone there? No one. We're alone in the street.

We entered Helmutt Sopp's house. The house was empty and dim. Going into the bathroom I washed my face. I returned to my chair in the kitchen and Mama was already standing at the tub and washing dishes. Tears slid down her cheeks and into the tub water. I didn't know what to say to her. I sat in silence and watched her.

The huge pile of dishes grew taller and still she wept, soundlessly. I felt heat on my neck and the soles of my feet, stood on one foot, the other in the air, and then I swapped feet, waiting for Mama to stop crying.

I didn't cry. I'd erased Papa at the train station in Brzeżany. I was sorry for Mama; she was the saddest mother I'd ever seen. At night she wept and wept, and the tears that fell onto the pillow reached my head, wetting it. I finally fell asleep and heard nothing more of what happened on her side.

The next day we left early, Mama wearing a large shawl over her head and a scarf wound three times round her neck, and I in a hat and my red hair on my shoulders. Mama took me with her to the Płaszów labor camp in Kraków. I think she wanted to find Papa, but she didn't say a word the whole way.

I recall a cloudy, almost black day, a long, gray wall with a fence and a smoking chimney. I wasn't afraid. I was never afraid when I was with Mama. But I could sense when danger was close.

The Płaszów camp gates were closed. Maybe she hoped to see Papa through the fence, someone who knew him? We couldn't see a thing. The wall hid the people and the noise if there was any.

We returned to the Sopp house. Mama was tired and very sad. I saw how grave she was and didn't disturb her. I did everything quietly so no sound would disturb her. Her eyes barely moved. And I already knew that was Mama's face when she was thinking, what's to be done? How to go about it? I saw that expression many times. That was the face after which we usually packed our bags and left. I thought, will we pack and go now too?

"Yashu had already returned to us. There remained the great anxiety about my husband," said Mama to the guests in the living room in Haifa, who had immediately settled into their places.

"After great effort, promises, and many disappointments, my sister Lydia managed to arrange forged Polish papers for my husband. I approached a Polish woman named Grochowska, who had experience transferring Jews from dangerous places to safer ones, and I asked her for help.

"When I went to meet Mrs. Grochowska, I observed her closely. She had a fat double chin and cold, narrow eyes, like a fish. Her appearance didn't make me feel confident, but I needed to trust my sisters who recommended her, naturally after making discreet enquiries. There was no choice.

"Mrs. Grochowska agreed to travel to Brzeżany and bring my husband back; I paid her the entire sum in advance. She traveled to him by train, and in her bag she had a railway employee's uniform for him. The plan was that my husband would wear the uniform and they'd return together on the night train to Kraków. Our agreement was that we'd meet at her house at eight o'clock in the morning. From there, the plan was to take him to Bronka's house; she'd found him a place to hide for a few days.

"My husband had a blue suitcase that he'd taken when he left our home in Tarnopol. In the blue suitcase we had jewelry that enabled us to pay to move from one place to another. In the last letter my husband wrote me, he said that his rich friends from Tarnopol, with whom he worked, gardening at the district officer's house, gave him jewelry and gold coins from home to take to their families, because their lives in Brzeżany were daily at risk. They didn't know whether their families were still alive, but they trusted my husband to look after their property and, if necessary, to send it after the war to addresses they gave him. My husband had all the jewelry and gold in the blue suitcase. He had no other suitcase."

"Oy, oy, oy, that means trouble for him," whispered Bernard Cohen, and crunched a candy between his teeth.

"Be quiet," commanded Klara.

"Don't interfere," he said and continued to crunch. "Lots of trouble, I know them."

"Shhhh, *nu*, shhhh," said Henia Sonnenfeld, taking a fan out of her bag and fanning her face; she was obviously hot.

"According to the plan, Mrs. Grochowska and my husband arrived in Kraków early in the morning," said Mama. "She apparently suggested my husband get some sleep until I came to take him at eight in the morning. But that very morning, Toni wanted me to go shopping with her in the market. The Governor-General of the conquered region of Poland, Hans Frank, with other dignitaries, was invited to their home that evening.

"Naturally I couldn't tell Toni that I had to be at Mrs. Grochowska's at eight in the morning, that my husband had arrived… I went with her to the market, *Ich war sehr ängstlich,* I was full of anxiety. My head was full of difficult thoughts: Had Mrs. Grochowska really found my husband at the place they'd agreed on in advance? Had my husband aroused suspicion on the train, and had they arrived safely in Kraków? Could this Mrs. Grochowska be trusted to keep her word and not inform on him to the authorities? What would be?

"I'd promised to come at eight, and I was delayed by Toni at the market with vegetables and fruit and smoked meat and even flowers… What would my husband think of this delay? Would he worry? Think that something terrible had happened to stop me from coming to get him? And what would Grochowska do when she realized that I was late? Would the neighbors be suspicious?

"Every second I tried to see the time on Toni's watch—what was the time? I had no watch of my own—was it eight thirty yet? A quarter to nine? Oy vey, my husband was probably really suffering—what was to be done?"

Mama was silent. She looked at her watch and moved the hand. The guests in the living room also looked at their watches, me too. Only Yozek Meltzer didn't take his eyes off Mama, but she didn't see him. What I understood from her face was that she was at the market in Kraków, and this part of life during the war was hard for her.

Yozek Meltzer felt her difficulty, and as he leaned forward, I realized that again he wanted to save Mama. Both the first and second time he visited our living room, I saw that he almost burst with worry—no less than Mama. I knew that he loved Mama, but he didn't stand a chance; he was her height, without heels, and without any serious lineage.

"Come, Anna, go on," begged Mr. Bogusławski.

Mama left her watch alone, rubbed her nails against her gown: "We wandered through the market. We chose vegetables and I quietly urged every vendor to hurry. It didn't help me. Toni stopped all the time, said, 'Hello, hello, how are you, what's new.' She met half the city at the stalls.

"In the meantime, I saw that it was a quarter past nine. We'd almost finished the shopping when Toni met a rather attractive German friend—I knew her from parties at the house—and they started chatting as if they were in a café.

"What can I tell you, dear friends, the tension began to affect my head. I got a migraine, afraid that my husband would decide of his own accord to leave Grochowska. Maybe he suspected that someone had informed on him, and if he left, where would he go? He did have Polish papers, but he didn't know the apartment we'd found for him; my sisters and I had invested a lot of thought in it, after all, we were born in Kraków—he wasn't. We made sure that the place was safe enough for at least the first few days.

"I was as tense as a spring but nothing showed.

"Toni finally parted from her friend; I was beside myself by the time we got home. And then I had to arrange our purchases. Things were falling out of my hands, I may even have been pale, I don't know. I felt a weakness in my feet, everything I picked up fell, I picked it up, it fell. Toni looked at me and said, 'What's wrong, Anna? Are you ill?'

"What could I say?

"After ten, I took Danusha with me and we finally went to my husband. We walked fast. I looked to the sides—was I attracting undue attention? Were people looking at me? We stopped to catch our breath and I glanced back—was I being followed?"

Mama glanced sideways as if she'd remained there and I followed suit, a habit that hadn't changed after all this time. The guests were motionless, barely breathing with tension. A tap was dripping in the kitchen; the drip sounded as if it were coming through a schoolyard loudspeaker on Independence Day.

Mr. Bogusławski applauded, as if wanting to say, *Strength. Strength, Anna.*

The guests' alarmed faces made me understand the great danger we were in during that war.

And then Mama said: "We approached the house. There were a lot of people in the street. *Not a good sign,* I said to myself. Saving my husband should have happened with great discretion; there were informers everywhere. I didn't know why people were gathered in the street, but I felt my body tremble; my hands were damp with perspiration. And I didn't stop.

"We went into the yard. Grochowska's husband came out of their ground-floor apartment just then and in his hand was a blue suitcase. I almost screamed, *That's ours, that's ours, what are you doing with my husband's suitcase?*

"Grochowska's husband saw me and hurried away from the house in the direction of the street. I burned on the spot but didn't say a word. Honestly? I didn't burn. I went mad.

"My legs trembling, I entered the apartment. Grochowska saw me.

"'Jesus, Maria, run, quickly, quickly, the Gestapo were just here and they took your husband, now, now, a few minutes ago!' she shouted, waving her hands to push me out.

"'What have you done, what have you done? Have you no fear of God?' I shouted back. A terrible pain sliced through my heart. 'Mama come, let's go, quickly, quickly.' My little daughter pulled my sleeve and dragged me out.

"'Get out of here, Jews, get out of here! You're endangering us all,' Grochowska continued to shriek, waving her fists in the air. Grochowska betrayed us," said Mama in a choked voice.

"Grochowska took the money from me, took my husband's blue suitcase with our jewelry and the jewelry of his friends who trusted him, and then she called the Gestapo. Grochowska must have suggested they wait until eight o'clock—the hour I was supposed to arrive—but because of the market and Toni's friends I arrived after ten. I heard from people in the street that the Gestapo had left the place just a few minutes before we arrived.

"We returned to the Sopps' house. *Ich war zerbréchen,* I was shattered and alone. That evening I had to finish preparing for the Governor-General and other dignitaries, prepare enough Kwiat-cognac, cook a gourmet meal, and set a table for kings, smile at the guests who came to the house, *Bitte, my lady, dankeschön, sir*.

"Only later did I believe that the hand of God had intervened, saving my life and the life of my little girl."

"*Nu,*" said Bernard Cohen in despair.

"*Nu,* what else is there to say? Nothing," said Mr. Bogusławski.

"Nothing. Life is something you don't even see in a film," added Bernard.

"How could they see? People didn't sleep at night because of the horrors there," said Klara Cohen, and her red eyes looked as though they were coming out of their sockets. Bertha Ketzelboim wept quietly into her handkerchief.

Her husband Jacob said, "Go out onto the veranda perhaps, get a breath of fresh air."

Efraim Sonnenfeld's arm lifted and stayed suspended in mid-air.

"Efraim, put your arm down, *nu*, put it down," said his wife Henia, and he stuck his hand in his armpit, apologized, and went to the toilet.

"Enough for today. Please have some tea," said Mama tiredly, leaning back against the armchair.

People began to rise quietly. I didn't get up. I looked at Mama.

"Sit properly. Why don't you take up the whole chair like your brother, *nu*, sit properly," said Mama, looking quietly at me.

I got up from my chair and went towards the door.

"Where are you going? Where are you going now?"

"Not going," I responded quietly. I raised my head and whispered, so no one would hear, "And why don't you ask Yashu where he's going?"

I slammed the door behind me, went out to the stairs, turned on the light, and went down. The street was dark. I looked up at the sky. Found the Big Dipper without a moon. My brother had taught me to find it among the stars. Honestly, it had always looked like a chariot to me and at that moment, all I wanted was to jump onto it and get away from there. My brother told me it revolves but always, always remains close to the North Star.

Chapter Fourteen

"The Gestapo took my husband to a prison on Montelupich Street," Mama told the guests in the living room, exhaling into the open part of her gown, "thus changing our fate in a second."

"Goodbye and don't come back, that's what happened. May their memory be damned," muttered Bernard Cohen.

"Goodbye and don't come back, that's what happened? Was it? Is that what you think?" his wife scolded him.

"May their memory be damned. That's what I think of them," he retorted.

Bertha Ketzelboim exhaled like Mama. For every long breath Mama took, she exhaled twice.

"In a situation like that we must ask heaven for pity," said her husband, Jacob.

"Shhh. *Nu*, shhh," snapped Mr. Meltzer.

"Courage, dear Anna. Go on, please." Mr. Bogusławski put an end to the small commotion in the living room.

"Lydia told me that my husband had been taken to a prison on Montelupich Street," said Mama. "At the time, Lydia was in hiding with a Polish woman. This woman knew one of the prison guards. She made discreet enquiries and was told that a Jewish man had been brought in that morning. A Polish family from central Kraków had called the Gestapo.

"Wanting to calm me, Lydia told me that her landlady went to visit my husband in prison and found him in reasonable condition. And I naively believed Lydia. I wasn't thinking logically; how could anyone visit a Jewish prisoner in the basements of the Gestapo?

"Only later on did I realize that my sisters invented the visit to the prison in order to calm me down, but I was still restless. I knew that Helmutt Sopp was chief doctor at that prison. His wife, Toni, had explicitly said so when I got to their house on the first day. I wasn't entirely sure I could turn to him, ask him for help—how could I? After all, I'd presented myself as the wife of a Polish officer who was lost in battle. How come the interest in the welfare of a Jewish prisoner? Since when do Poles take an interest in Jewish prisoners?

"But my husband was in the prison on Montelupich Street and Helmutt Sopp was chief doctor at the prison on Montelupich Street. And I knew him—was that not a sign from heaven that I had to intervene on my husband's behalf?

"Think of something, I said to myself, *nu, think.*

"I wandered about the house racking my brains. Even supposing I'd find a way to approach him, what would happen if Helmutt suspected me? We had a good relationship, but there was no knowing whether he wouldn't change his mind the moment he suspected me, and turn me over to the Gestapo, who are, after all, very cruel indeed. Would it be right to put the lives of Danusha and Yashu at risk, the lives of my sisters and their children, or my mother's life?

"I knew that the best thing to do would be to wait until Sunday for our meeting at Franca's. Instantly I decided that it was out of the question. My husband was in the hands of the Gestapo and they would want to know who paid that Grochowska woman to bring him to Kraków, and the Gestapo wouldn't wait for a sisters' meeting to extract information from him.

"I thought I'd go mad. I couldn't sleep at night. I tried to comfort myself. I told myself there was no chance my husband would talk, no chance at all. He always said that a husband, wife, and children could be trusted, and he was a tall, strong, and very handsome man. But I couldn't get rid of frightening thoughts—would the devilish cruelty of the Nazis bring about the end of us all?

"After very great distress, I decided I'd approach Helmutt Sopp before it was too late.

"I waited for an appropriate moment.

"That evening, I prepared an excellent meal. Toni and the children had gone to Silesia. I served the meal on beautiful dishes. I was polite as usual; he complimented me and smiled pleasantly.

"I waited patiently until he finished eating. Naturally I was very nervous, even though my face was serene.

"'May I ask Herr Doktor something?' I asked Helmutt when he finished eating.

"'Of course, Frau Anna, how can I help?' said Helmutt, looking at me gravely.

"'A good friend from school married a Jewish man who is at

the prison on Montelupich Street. Would Dr. Sopp be willing to take food and money to him for her?'

"'A Jewish man?'

"'Yes, they were married years ago.'

"'What is his name?'

"I gave Helmutt my husband's name.

"'I'll look into it,' Helmutt promised me, 'tomorrow I'll bring you an answer.'

"I thanked him of course. I felt greatly relieved but was still very tense, afraid that my action, without my sisters' advice, would bring disaster on us.

"I waited for morning. Helmutt left the house and I followed. I went to Franca's apartment. Lydia was there. I told her at once about approaching Helmutt Sopp.

"'Are you mad? Why didn't you discuss it with me first?!' cried Lydia in despair.

"'Have you forgotten that your husband has forged papers in his pocket with the same surname you have? He is now called Mechislav Kwiatkowski. Where will you run to now with two children?'"

The air in the living room was as thick as the morning fog over the sea of Haifa.

I crossed my legs and revolved on the chair like a spinning top.

"Enough," said Mama.

I revolved another turn and a half.

"She made a bad mistake," whispered Bernard Cohen.

"She was worried about him," sobbed Klara Cohen into her soft checked angora scarf.

"Enough," begged Mama.

I stopped annoying Mama by revolving and looked at her. She gave me a look that said *We'll discuss this later*, and raised a glass of water.

"A very dangerous mistake," declared Bernard firmly.

"Filled with anxiety, I returned to Helmutt and Toni's house," said Mama. "I was worried. How would Helmutt react the moment he saw my husband's papers? Kwiatkowski isn't an unusual name, but I sent Helmutt to him; it was me, me, and he's no fool. Would he throw us out into the street?"

"Enough. I can't bear this," said Bertha Ketzelboim, getting up from her chair and leaving the house.

"Sorry, Anna, sorry," said Jacob, following her out as if bearing a burden.

"Poor Bertha. She's suffered from weak nerves for a long time," explained Henia Sonnenfeld to her husband Efraim, who was frantically making figures of eight on the leg of his chair.

"Go on, Anna," begged Mr. Bogusławski, passing a packet of mints around the guests.

"I was afraid," said Mama in a heroic tone. "I was afraid he'd call on that Ukrainian, Ivan, who tried to interrogate me in the past. The thought that Helmutt would turn me and my young children over to the evil hands of that cruel Ukrainian caused me terrible suffering. I was sorry Toni and the children weren't at home. I trusted her. Toni and I were close, and she loved the children; Peter and Ammon also enjoyed playing with them. My heart told me that if Toni had been home, she'd help us in our trouble.

"I told the children not to leave the room and to be very, very quiet.

"I waited tensely for Helmutt to come.

"I heard his steps at the door.

"Heard the rattle of the keys.

"Clinging to the kitchen door I barely breathed.

"Helmutt entered and went straight to his room.

"He didn't call out *Frau Anna, ich bin da*; Frau Anna, I'm here. Didn't look into the kitchen.

"A bad sign, I said to myself, my belly churning. What should I do? Approach him, apologize, and tell the truth? Take the children and go at once, but where to? Wait for Toni?

"I walked about the kitchen, pressed my hands to my temples, feeling as if a great chasm was opening in the floor.

"I stopped. Took three deep breaths. I prayed quietly and decided to behave as if nothing had happened.

"At the usual hour Helmutt sat down at the table.

"I served him dinner. He was silent. I didn't say a word either. I looked at him. There was a distant expression on his face; he looked like a stranger. Was he dangerous? All his courtesy had vanished. As I was about to return to the kitchen, he gave me a cold look, as if to say, *We both know the truth, better to say nothing.*

"Naturally I didn't dare ask him about my husband.

"That night I couldn't sleep for bad thoughts filling my head. I prayed for my husband's safety and the safety of my children and trusted in God. And then came the dawn.

"Would Helmutt eat at home or go without a meal? I had no answer.

"I prepared his breakfast as usual. My hands were cold as I set the table. I waited tensely in the kitchen, telling the children to stay in the room. I knew the danger was alive and breathing.

"And then I heard him sit down at the table. He ate his breakfast; I came in to serve him hot coffee. We didn't exchange glances or say a word. I immediately returned to the kitchen. After a while he left the house and I went mad. Had he waited until morning to send me Gestapo interrogators? But he could have done so yesterday—had he decided not to turn us in after all?

"I took the children and hurried to Franca's apartment. I thought I'd go mad with worry about my husband."

Mama paused to drink some water.

I got down from my chair and went to the kitchen to fetch two small sugar cubes for her. I put them on a small serviette beside the water and returned to sit motionless on my chair. Mama picked up a cube and set it on her tongue. I knew she was already sucking on the cube and would then straighten up as if everything was all right.

"And then Lydia told me the worst possible news," said Mama in the weakest voice, but one that could be heard in every corner of the living room. "Lydia told me that my husband died while being horribly tortured in prison. The Gestapo people wanted to know the whereabouts of the relatives who had helped him obtain forged papers. He didn't talk before he died. That was hard for me. I burst into tears. God, what did they do to you, my dear husband, what did they do?

"'You have to leave the Sopp home as fast as you can,' said my mother, her hand on my shoulder. 'Leave the children here and look for another room.'

"I knew my mother was right. My brain told me to *run, run Anna*. But where would I go with the children? I couldn't go back to sleep at Franca's apartment; the concierge had become suspicious and a danger to us. And my dear son was with us. I knew I wouldn't agree to part from him, no, no. The thought of having to wander from house to house again was the most difficult of all for me.

"I looked at Lydia. Her face held no advice for me. I realized I'd have to decide on my own.

"My brain said run, but my heart said, don't be afraid, Anna, don't be afraid. Helmutt Sopp won't harm you. He respects and appreciates you. He likes the children, or so I wanted to believe.

"And there was another issue. At the time, there were strong rumors that the Germans were losing the war; that it was coming to an end. I realized this from London broadcasts I'd secretly listened to on the radio in Helmutt and Toni's house. The news was encouraging. I decided to remain, to return with the children, not to set out on dangerous wanderings."

During refreshments, I left the living room and went to the hall window above my bed and peeped outside. The moon was almost full. I gazed at it, fighting in my heart with everything to do with that war.

I heard Mama tell Helmutt Sopp that she had a friend who was married to a Jew, and this friend knew her husband was in the prison and was very worried. I heard her say that her friend had a diamond ring she was willing to give in exchange for information about her husband. Would Helmutt please find out what had happened to him?

Helmutt agreed. The next day he returned from the hospital and told Mama that there was indeed a Jewish prisoner at the prison on Montelupich Street who had been executed. He didn't say why they'd executed him; Mama of course didn't ask, and that was the end of the story. That's what I remember.

I continued to stand at the window until the residential block not far from us hid a piece of the moon. The air was pleasant. I continued standing there even when I heard Mama say that Toni had returned with the children and behaved as usual. From this Mama understood that Helmutt hadn't told her anything, and she calmed down a bit, even if he remained remote.

One day, Toni entered the kitchen, grabbed Mama's hand and said in a trembling voice that all the German women and children were leaving Poland and returning to Germany. Only the men were staying for the time being. Yes, Helmutt was staying, and she needed Mama's help packing the suitcases.

Mama was saddened by the news.

I went back to my chair in the living room.

"What will happen to us? Will we also have to leave?" Mama asked the guests, but they didn't answer the question.

"I was bothered by something else as well. I held Toni's hand and quietly asked, 'When will this take place?'

"'In the coming days,' said Toni, smiling sadly. 'Who knows, Mrs. Kwiatkowski, if one day I won't have to be a maid in a Polish household if we really lose the war.'"

Mama looked at me. I made a face indicating that everything was all right and she smiled at the guests. We both knew that Toni would need something from Mama in other times.

"Peter and Ammon are going to Germany with Toni," said Mama while I was reading to Yashu from a German newspaper that was open on the floor of the balcony. He was my good little brother, never bothering or insulting me; Mama did, from time to time. Peter and Ammon were also good to us. But when their friends came to the house, we knew we had to go back to the room or the balcony.

"Peter and Ammon are going to Germany, Yashu," I told my brother, and closed the newspaper.

I went up to Mama. "When will they be back?"

"They aren't coming back. They're staying in Germany."

"They aren't coming back," I told Yashu. "We'll play on our own."

"All right," said Yashu, "we'll play on our own."

I wanted to ask Mama when they'd be going, and why they weren't coming back, and would Toni be back? Would Helmutt also be going away?

I heard Mama praying quietly, sighing and praying with earnest intention. I knew this was a bad sign, and instantly wanted a slice of bread, but was silent. I heard her praying like that before Yashu came home and before we went to fetch Papa.

Two cars and a Nazi officer waited on the street at the entrance to the Sopp family home. I saw them from the kitchen window. The drivers of the car entered the house and took out six or seven huge suitcases. Mama had helped Toni pack the suitcases, and it had taken them several days to organize it all. I thought about our suitcase—we only had one, not a large one. I knew that if we had to leave, we could pack it in half an hour, that's all.

Toni came into the kitchen and called us to go with her. Mama, Yashu, and I followed her.

"Children, say goodbye to Danusha and Yashu," said Toni. "We're leaving now."

I shook hands with Peter and Ammon, the way we did on our

first day with them. I noticed that I was taller than Peter. When I said goodbye and wished them a safe journey to Germany, I saw they were sorry.

Yashu and I were also sorry. We were excited to receive from them colors, drawing paper, erasers and pencils, and Yashu received at least two cars, a red one with an open roof and a police car. Mama was sorrier than all of us; I saw her take a deep breath and exhale only a little.

Toni hugged us, weeping on Mama's shoulder. Mama gently patted her back, saying, "Maybe we'll meet again one day, maybe."

A great silence fell on the house in the coming evenings. The chairs made no sound in the living room. The children's rooms were dark. Helmutt barely spoke; most of the time he was busy in his room. Mama didn't sing any arias; she cooked food for Helmutt, tidied the house, and washed the kitchen floor again and again. I saw her going to the window every now and again and looking out. Her steps were soundless and her eyes pierced the floor.

I noticed that all our clothes were packed in the suitcase. Every day Mama washed the socks and underwear we changed and put them back in the suitcase.

"Are we going away?" I asked.

"No, no."

"Leaving here?"

"No, of course not!" She gave me a look to stop.

I stuck to Mama even more. I didn't feel like putting records on the record player or playing with my brother on the balcony.

Sometimes I'd walk around our suitcase and listen to the great silence. I missed Peter, missed playing with him on the balcony, learning words in German from him; I think my brother also missed playing ball and the bag game with them, watching them from the window when they brought a friend home and played in the yard. I saw Yashu looking for them in their room and coming out with a sour face.

One day, a few days after Toni left, I heard Mama coughing all the time. Helmutt was eating his breakfast.

"Are you feeling all right?" I asked.

"Of course," she responded and I sat down in the closest chair to her.

Mama rolled and unrolled her sleeves. She washed her hands with soap, dried them on a towel, went to the window, glanced out, and then she suddenly turned round as if she'd heard a knock at the door. The house was quiet. She took a deep breath, went to the door, listened, and again returned to the tap, opening and closing it and tugging at her apron. She smoothed her hands over her blouse, tapped her face with her hands, and took a jug of hot coffee out to Helmutt.

I clung to the crack in the kitchen door.

Mama approached Helmutt and poured him coffee. He looked at the coffee, and then at Mama, and again at the coffee.

"Frau Anna, I need to talk to you," said Helmutt.

Mama put the jug down on the table and waited quietly.

"Frau Anna, I must ask you to leave the house. You know that Toni and the children will not be returning. There is no longer any need for you to stay here. I can eat at the hospital.

You can stay for a day or two, until you've made arrangements to leave."

Mama's chin touched her chest as she rocked forward. She caught onto her dress, closed her fist and stood still.

Helmutt Sopp took a sip of his coffee. Mama didn't move, didn't say a word.

"Frau Anna?" asked Helmutt, as if he were playing the words.

Mama was silent, as if she were the oldest and sickest woman in the world.

And then, in a moment, I saw Mama at the train station in Brzeżany, on our way to Lwów. Bronka speaking to Mama who was silent. And her face the color of snow. I knew that this was the face of great fear.

The soles of my feet instantly grew hot. I felt fire behind my knees.

Helmutt looked unwaveringly at Mama. Raising her head, folding her arms on her chest, she looked directly at him and said: "*Bitte,* Herr Doktor, where will I go? May I stay here with the children in the small room? We're quiet, as the Doktor knows, and times are very hard, *bitte,* there is no need to buy anything special for us. We can manage, may we stay?"

Helmutt put his coffee down and pushed away his plate. Leaning one elbow on the table he covered his mouth with his fingers, tapped his lips, and rose without a word.

Now the fire had spread to my groin. I began to count in German: *Eins, Zwei, Drei, Vier.* I saw he was facing the window and drumming his fingers on the lintel, still looking at the floor, *Fünf, Sechs, Sieben, Acht*. He put one hand in his pocket, slightly moved his head, and was silent. Barely breathing, I whispered *Neun, Zehn,* and then he swiftly turned, approached the table with long strides, took another sip of his coffee and said: "Yes, Frau Anna, you can stay. I will stay at the hospital. I have a room there, but I will have to hand over the apartment to the German Office responsible for housing. Naturally I will have no objection if they allow you to stay."

Mama chewed her lips; I knew she was trying not to cry. She took a step towards him and he waved his hand as if to say, *No need, no need,* picked up his bag, and left.

"Thank you, Herr Doktor, thank you very much," she said, hurrying after him. "I don't have the words to thank you, sir, thank you very much."

Mama returned to the kitchen, leaned against the wall, and covered her face with her hands. I heard a sound like choked coughing. Yashu came in from the balcony and together we gazed quietly at her, and then she held out her arms to us. We drew near and she hugged us, whispering, "We're saved. We're staying."

The following day Helmutt told Mama we could keep all the food products Toni had left in the pantry. There were tins, packed parcels, as well as a supply of coal in the cellar.

Before he left, Helmutt brought us an almond sponge cake. It was a quarter of an almond sponge cake a patient had given him, he told Mama. He brought it to us to taste as if we were family. Mama put the sponge cake on the cupboard in the kitchen. Every time we wanted to taste it, we'd climb onto a chair and take a small piece so no one would notice.

That almond sponge cake and the white rolls Toni brought us from the market were the best foods I'd ever eaten. To this day, I can smell them, feel the delicate taste on my tongue.

And there was also the parting from Helmutt.

Helmutt entered the kitchen and stood still. Mama, who was

standing next to the table, put the knife down, wiped her hands on her apron, and looked up. I looked at them both from the side, as if I were in a film.

Helmutt gazed at Mama and she returned his gaze. And then I saw Helmutt's eyebrows rise slightly towards his forehead, as if questioningly, or as if to say, *That's that, it's over*, and he had furrows in his forehead. Mama looked down, and Helmutt didn't move his eyes from her. His eyebrows and forehead gradually settled; he took a deep breath, Mama did too, and the world seemed to stop.

Oh, what a beautiful moment that was. Helmutt, tall, fair-haired, carefully combed, and Mama with her delicate features and broad forehead—they were so handsome in that moment of parting. I could have cried if it weren't for the tension I was feeling in my body, just cried.

And then Helmutt strode towards Mama, held out his hand and pressed hers. He said a few words, but I'd moved away and didn't hear. I saw it was a moment for weeping.

When Helmutt went out, Mama accompanied him to the door. He threw a last glance at the house, shook her hand again, and left.

Did Helmutt Sopp love Mama? Did he really hope they'd meet one day?

I have no idea if he loved her, but they found each other after it was all over.

When Mama visited Grandma, she quietly told her sisters in the kitchen about the treasures she found in the pantry and cellar, and how moved she was by the doctor's gesture. Naturally she was uneasy about the people from the office responsible for housing in Kraków, who would come to the door to snoop around.

Franca said she'd ask in her office what it meant.

Lydia said she was also worried, particularly since she'd seen Yula in the street.

"Yula?" cried Bronka aloud. "Yula from our house? When?"

"Shhh," said Lydia, looking at Grandma, who was teaching Yashu, Bella, and Abraham the song about Copenhagen.

"Yes, Yula, the concierge's daughter. Anna, you remember the Christian family from the house we lived in before the war?" Mama remembered and immediately covered her face with her hands then dropped them, drew closer to Lydia, and touched her hand.

Lydia looked down. Mama, Bronka, and Franca drew near as she said, "I ran into her a few days ago. The moment she saw me she said with hatred, 'You're dressing up as a Christian and walking about the city, your children and sisters are probably in hiding, but I'll find them and tell the Gestapo if you don't bring me money tomorrow, a lot of money, do you hear?'"

"Oy vey, Yula knows all of us. What did you tell her?" asked Franca, tugging at her skirt again and again.

Lydia sat down on a chair and wiped her nose with a handkerchief. "Nothing. I got out of there immediately and went back to the Poles' house."

"Did Yula follow you?" asked Bronka, tapping her foot on the floor. "Lydia, did you notice if she followed you?"

Lydia shook her head from side to side, saying quietly, "From that moment till now I didn't leave the house. I was afraid to go outside; there are searches in the area."

"Be careful, Lydia, be careful," said Bronka, laying her hand on her sister's head.

"I'm afraid of Yula, but there are so many like her," said Lydia, getting up from her chair. "We have to hold on, for Mama, for the children."

That night I heard Mama praying, tossing and turning in bed and then praying again. I knew we were in very great danger.

A few days later, I hear Mama say to her sisters that Helmutt apparently hadn't informed the authorities that he'd left the house, for no one had come around or taken any interest.

Bronka said, "Yula?"

Lydia said, "I'm being careful. There was a lot of hatred in that woman," and she asked Mama to take Grandma Rosa with us for a night or two. There were rumors of searches in the area of Franca's apartment.

"We have to pay attention, particularly when coming in or going out of the house," said Franca. "The concierge also worries me," she murmured, and I felt that the family's days of safety had come to an end.

We set out with Grandma Rosa to the Sopp house.

A few days later, Lydia was caught by the Nazis. She was taken to the prison on Montelupich Street, so the Polish woman with whom Lydia had been in hiding told Bronka. Gestapo people tortured her, wanting her to inform on the family. Lydia said nothing.

Grandma Rosa, Lydia's children, Katie and Adam, Franca and her children, Yehoshua, Bella and Abraham, Bronka, Mama, Yashu and I all survived.

"Lydia, my dear, brave older sister, who always encouraged us, died in the torture rooms of the Gestapo. They didn't stop until she died."

So Mama told the guests in the living room, smoothing the nail of her little finger under her eye and placing her palm gently on her knee. The little finger trembled. And it seemed to me that dark shadows traveled the wall behind her, spreading up to the ceiling, every season with its shadow. Sometimes I saw the shadow of a large bird with outspread wings, sometimes the shadow of a heavy bear without a neck, sometimes the motion of leaves moving in the wind appeared on the wall, or a broken cloud. Sometimes thunder and lightning made the house walls tremble and then the shadows leaped in alarm. I shrank into my corner, thinking of my beloved Lydia. She had bright-blue eyes. Particularly big eyes. Lydia with lips painted in a fine line as if with an artist's brush; not even in the last days of the war would the Nazis give her up.

She kept us safe, in her last moments as well, and didn't live to see the day the Russians entered Kraków.

Chapter Fifteen

Six years after the Russians came to Tarnopol and took our home, they entered Kraków. Mama was happy. I was already eight and knew how to read Polish and German.

Cars with Nazi flags disappeared from the streets. Many people gathered on the sidewalks, threw their hats into the air, waved scarves, hugged, kissed, and called out excitedly: "The Germans have run away, no more Germans, none! Hitler *kaput*!"

"The war is over, thank God," the women said and crossed themselves over and over again.

The church bells rang out, blessing the Russians who had liberated the city, ding and dong, gling and glong, as if asking the black skies to open and draw us nearer to our Lord Jesus.

"Long live liberty, long live the Russians, hooray, hooray," announced loudspeakers, receiving applause from passersby.

"The Nazis have been arrested, may they burn in hell," people shouted, waving flags and wiping away tears as they advanced like an enormous flow of water in the direction of the city center. Whoo! Whoo! Whoohoo! The shouts of joy shook the stillness of the night, illuminating the darkness in people's hearts. Small fires shone on street corners, the entire air seemed to be on fire, *na zdorov'ye, lachayim,* to life, shouted Russian soldiers, to life, to life, to the Red Army, answered their comrades. I saw it all on the way to Grandma Rosa, where we found Franca and Bronka and the cousins. Mama was the first to enter, holding out her arms and calling, "Thank God, the nightmare is over."

Grandma Rosa wept in her armchair, "Lydia, oh Lydia," and her body trembled and her face was the saddest I'd ever seen. Mama, Franca, and Bronka clung to each other and hugged Grandma Rosa.

"They took you from me, my Lydia, my flower, my child, my love," wept Grandma in a crushed voice that broke into fragments of words and she moved constantly as if stabbed from within.

Bella, Abraham, Yashu, and I sat on the sofa in the living room and gazed tearfully at Grandma.

I said quietly, "What will happen now without Lydia?"

Bronka got up and came over to us. "You can go out and play, children, no more fear. You can go out with your heads held high, and you, Abraham, can say clearly, without fear, 'My name is Abraham, Abraham.' Do you understand?"

We stayed inside the house; only Yashu went out.

"Where is Stella? Where is our Stella?" wept Grandma, getting up from her chair and going to the door.

Mama, Bronka, and Franca returned Grandma to her chair and gave her a glass of tea and three sugar cubes. And then the three went into the kitchen and began whispering among themselves. I knew they were making new plans for us, now that peace had come.

Yehoshua, Franca's eldest son, came in with Yashu. He'd found Yashu outside, competing with himself in a race from here to there and from there back here again. Yehoshua promised him a candy and so he stopped running. He was wearing a peaked cap and looked tall. Franca gestured to him, and he turned to us and said, "Come on, children, put on your coats and hats and let's go outside. Come and see how many people there are in the street. Do you want to build a snowman?"

The noise in the street was particularly loud. Trucks with loudspeakers were driving along the streets, playing noisy rhythmic music. Terrum. Terrum, tam-tam, tam-tam. The glass in the windows shook. Franca's radio also played loud, though different, music, with the sound of drums. People around me were talking at the tops of their voices, crying and laughing even more loudly, or cursing the Nazis; some were dancing in a circle and shrieking we're saved, we're saved, hooray.

I wasn't so happy because of the Russians and the piano.

Russian soldiers lay drunk on the sidewalks, singing, laughing, hiccoughing, and holding out their arms to passersby. I was very much afraid of them. Earlier, several soldiers had appeared at the Sopp house—we were living there alone—and asked for *chasy, chasy*, watches. We had no watches to give them. And then they began to shout; Mama sent me and Yashu away and faced them, said something and they went off.

In the coming days, I saw them rolling about on the sidewalks, cursing each other, laughing wildly, waving bottles in the air, and boom, breaking them against the wall. Some asked for cigarettes, or threw up in the street.

As it turned out, I saw them mainly on the way to see Franca and Grandma. I ran as fast as I could. I was sure that some Russian would jump on me, grab me in both hands, and throw me against the wall like a bottle. On Radio Kraków in particular they blessed the Russian soldiers who saved us, and played Russian melodies for them to enjoy. Because of them, they stopped broadcasting the piano concertos. Every time there was a concerto like that, I saw how Mama stopped tidying things, dishes in the cupboard for example, looked at the radio, and her eyes would moisten.

One day a large motor car stopped at the house. Mama ran outside, Yashu backed away, I stayed at the window. I saw six people getting down from the car. I was alarmed—what had happened? What did they want? Mama spoke several words to them, and then they took an enormous package wrapped in blankets off the car, as if they didn't know that Helmutt and Toni had left.

The men dragged the huge package into the house, stopping from time to time, shouting at each other and gesticulating. One said like this, another said, not like that, just like this, another said, nonsense, like this and this. I saw Mama was worried about the package. She rushed about them, calling, careful, careful and, in the end, I saw she was directing them to our small room, adjacent to the kitchen.

They pushed and pulled in that small room, stepping on each other's feet, moving things from one side to the other, I heard Mama say, that over there, that over here, wait, wait, push up…

And then a small boom. The package received a knock, Mama shrieked, oy, oy, please, be careful, and then one of the men called out, good, enough, thank you very much, and then four people left our small room, the door slammed behind them, they said goodbye, goodbye, and went away. I remained alone. Yashu drew near me; we looked at each other. Finally, I said, they've brought us something, don't know what.

I heard noises from behind the door. I stepped up to the crack I'd found in the door, peeped inside; it was completely dark. I waited a few seconds, swapped eyes, and what did I see? A shiny black piano emerging from the blankets the man had removed. A piano? A piano in our room? Where would we step, now? Was there any room?

I stood up, rubbed my eyes, turned to the table; it was in its place. I bent down to the crack again; it was black in there, and then the door opened. I jumped back. The last two people left the room and the house, and a few minutes later, Mama called us in.

"Surprise," called out Mama, clapping her hands. Her face was red and her eyes especially shining. "*Nu*, what do you have to say?"

We said nothing.

"It's ours and it's a Bechstein. I bought it myself. Do you remember the piano we had in Tarnopol?"

We both shook our heads from right to left.

"It's a beautiful piano, isn't it?" said Mama, stroking the keys. "How I've dreamed of this."

"Yes, Mama," I said quietly. "Will the piano stay here?"

"Of course, Danusha, it's ours. Tomorrow you will begin to learn to play the piano."

"Ahhhhhh?"

"I've found an excellent teacher for you."

"Just me?"

"Yes, tomorrow."

I swallowed and looked at Yashu. His face was to the door; he pulled his pants higher and left the room.

I looked at the room. Mama had freed up an entire wall for the piano.

Our bed was pushed up against the wall, the table up against it, closing half of the closet door.

"No problem," said Mama and, approaching the closet, she half opened the door and peeped in, then thrust in her hand and pulled out a shirt. The way to the bed was also blocked.

"No problem," decided Mama, and that very night she showed us how to climb onto the bed from the narrow space at the head, without stepping on the pillow.

We had three chairs and Mama put one on top of the other. When we all wanted to sit down in the evening, we blocked the entrance door. Yashu jumped easily onto the chairs and showed me how to get out; in the meantime, he left the room and didn't return.

That night I couldn't fall asleep. Mama and Yashu slept quietly. I was worried about the excellent teacher who was to come to me the following day.

Madame Jenia arrived the next morning. Tall and very thin, with thin eyebrows drawn with a dark pencil, and a light mustache you could hardly see.

She put notes in front of me, played a few sounds, and asked me to repeat them. I repeated them without any problem. The teacher, Jenia, smiled at me, added some sounds; I also added them and I enjoyed it.

"Please, Madame Jenia, how long will it take the child to learn to play?" asked Mama.

"The child has a musical ear, but it depends."

"On what does it depend, Madame Jenia?"

"Oh, she needs to practice, yes, a lot of work, a lot of work."

"Oh, she'll practice as much as she needs to, trust me," said Mama.

Madame Jenia was satisfied. She smiled at me and Mama. "Shall we go on?"

I glanced at Mama. I saw she was excited and I understood: Soon I'd have to appear in front of the family in Franca's living room. What, hadn't she stood me on a chair in Franca's living room in order to recite Adam Asnyk for Grandma Rosa, the aunts, and the cousins? I thought, that piano with the excellent teacher must pass to my brother, Yashu, I'll stick with the reciting; that's what I said to myself and looked for Yashu. Where was he? Yashu wasn't home; maybe he'd found a friend to play with outside. Yashu managed very well without us; only I clung to Mama's skirts. No wonder she gave me all the tasks!

I hated the piano, hated it so much, but I could never oppose her.

Madame Jenia came every week. I learned to play with notes. She was very pleased with me, said I had a suitably musical ear, but when I practiced at home, I felt Mama's eyes boring into my back, as if she were saying, *Nu, nu, when can you perform?* Mama did everything fast and that's what she wanted from me and the piano. If I played a wrong note, I heard her gasp. Every mistake and her gasp. Sometimes there were two or three gasps in a row, and then I would immediately get a stiff neck, my fingers were like sticks on the keys, and I missed.

I didn't manage to progress much in the lessons, even though I enjoyed listening to the arias and operettas that Mama sang in the kitchen and the concerts I listened to on Helmutt's record player, and an excellent pianist called Szpilman, who played on

Radio Poland. Madame Jenia told me to listen carefully to Szpilman's playing, because that Jew was truly a virtuoso, nothing more to be said.

When Mama listened to classical music that she particularly loved, with a well-known pianist or violinist, I saw her face soften like butter in the sun. Her cheeks would moisten and she'd say: "*Von Gott begnadet,*" graced by God.

And I had another problem:

At the end of the war, Mama sent me to a Christian school in Kraków. I was eight years old and starting first grade. From the day I remember myself, I was free to wander about the house, sit on a chair in the kitchen and dream, look in the mirror, peep out of the window and gaze at passersby, at the flowering lilac tree in in the yard, or listen to a record, play with my brother on the balcony, watch Mama preparing food or a liqueur, and even teach myself to read. However, since the arrival of the piano I dreamed less and felt a lot of time was spent practicing piano, and Mama made sure I practiced every day, but sitting on a chair at a desk at school, sitting for hours, without getting up, made me nervous and very tired. Breaks were short and I was eaten up by loneliness. In the yard, many young girls went past me; there were also girls my age and they were cheerful and giggly. It surprised me to see so many girls together and I didn't have a single friend among them.

I was the tallest in the class and the girls didn't come near me. I also preferred to sit alone. It was at the Christian school in Kraków that I realized for the first time in my life that I was different from the other girls.

During prayer, for instance. All the girls prayed with great enthusiasm; I also knew how to pray to our Lord Jesus very enthusiastically, but I'd forgotten some of the words of the prayers. I pretended to say the words and saw that the teacher realized that I was just murmuring. She didn't say anything, but I was ashamed she could see the muddle of words on my lips.

The general studies were also problematic for me.

I knew how to read Polish and German from the age of six or seven—my cousin Adam taught me. And I also taught myself a great deal, but I pretended not to know. I didn't want to be different from the others. And so, while the teacher taught the Polish alphabet, I repeated it with everybody, but I got bored and sometimes fell asleep for a while.

I studied in first grade in Kraków for only a few months. It was enough for me to learn from the priest who taught religious studies that the Jews were evil—they killed our Lord Jesus. Jews? Jews. I was alarmed. I was a Jewess, my Mama was a Jewess, Grandma Rosa was a Jewess, and we were the ones who were cruel? This taught me that I wasn't the only one with problems; all Jews were bad and because of this they all deserve to be beaten. And then I remembered that Jew is written with a small j. That Polish professor who, after the war, returned with his family to his home, which I believed was Sopp's house, and allowed us to stay in the small room until we got organized, thought that something was wrong with the Jews. He told his daughter that all nations receive a capital letter but not the Jews—they have a small letter, yes? That's what I heard him explaining to his daughter who was doing her homework. What could I think?

I was self-absorbed until the end of the war. Only at the end of the war did I understand from the priest at the school that I belonged to a nation the entire world had to hate. And that made me very sad. The piano also made me sad. Every time I made a mistake in rhythm or tone, Mama would tightly shut her eyes;

she'd sometimes stand next to me, marking time with her head, one-two-three, one-two-three.

I saw that it was important to Mama that I play well, the best I could. She herself didn't know how to play. Honestly, I also wanted to play well, even hoped that if I succeeded, maybe Mama would love me more. I tried, tried so hard, until I had no air left. There were times I felt as if a heavy stone lay on my chest, I could hardly breathe. Sometimes I was so angry that my playing wasn't good enough that I fell off the chair. And one time, I got up from the piano to cut bread for supper. Without meaning to, I cut my finger. Mama shouted at me because of the bleeding. "Oy, oy, oy, what's wrong with you? Come, let's put a bandage on the cut. Tomorrow, Danusha, you won't be able to play, only in two days' time, when Madame Jenia comes."

On the following two days I breathed easily. Mama took off the bandage and I continued practicing.

But a week or two later, the toilet door closed by mistake on my little finger and it hurt and there was a bruise. Mama looked at the finger and said, "*Nu,* what's wrong with you, another injury? Wasn't the last one enough? It will take at least three days for the swelling to go down so you can play. Is that normal?" That's how I had a rest from time to time. And in the meanwhile, I listened to concerts and felt good.

Chapter Sixteen

One day, Mama started work at a canteen. She bought a good suit and coat, new shoes, and a matching bag, gathered her hair in a small bun, put on lipstick, and went to work. I went to her at the end of the day at the Christian school. Yashu was with Grandma. The way to the canteen was near a busy road full of long, crowded convoys of military trucks and other cars. I waited at least half an hour to cross the road and in the meantime many people went past me, particularly loud youngsters, but the ones who really raised their voices were drunk Russians, those who lay on the sidewalk and looked disgusting and frightening. I stood as far to the side as I could, facing the road, so I wouldn't see them and vomit next to them, God forbid. They shouted *krasavitsa, krasavitsa,* holding out their arms to women, grabbing their hair, or crazily whistling. Some soldiers danced the *kazachok,* waving their guns upwards as if firing; some threw off their shirts, remaining half-naked. I was very frightened of them and every time I crossed the road, I tried to keep a safe distance from them, so they wouldn't hold out their arms to me and catch hold of my foot.

Mama didn't rest for a moment at the canteen, serving the Russians who sat at the broad counter drinking vodka, eating sandwiches, salted fish, and peanuts. I stood on the side, watching the door open and close, open and close, and every minute more large, strong people came in. I tried to understand what they were saying to one another. For instance, what was the tall one with a thick mustache roaring at a plump woman with red lacquered nails, his leg touching hers? And what was he saying to Mama, when he leaned towards her, raising his glass and Mama looked straight at him and nodded, yes, yes, yes?

Mama wasn't afraid of the Russians' noise or of the man with the shaved head and wooden leg.

I saw him at the canteen all the time. Every time he wanted to pay, he removed his wooden leg, took out his money and put the leg back. I couldn't stop looking at him. I was waiting for him to throw the wooden leg at my head just because I was standing there looking at him. And, one day, he looked in my direction. Silently he gazed, gazed without a word, finally saying in Polish, "Whose child is this?"

"That's my daughter," said Mama while chopping vegetables.

"Doesn't she speak?"

"She speaks when she has to."

"Can't hear."

"She speaks, she speaks."

"Pretty as a picture on the wall, your daughter," said the man smiling at me.

Mama stopped chopping the vegetables on the board, glanced quickly at me, and returned to the knife.

In an instant my cheeks burned like an oven. When the man paid Mama, I was no longer afraid of him.

One day, I heard an acquaintance of Mama's called Tzasha suggesting she buy sugar more cheaply from two Russians.

Mama put some money from the canteen till in her bag and told me to hurry, "They're waiting for us," and we went with two Russians to the sugar place to close the deal. On the way we passed the cemetery. The two Russians walked in front and we walked a few steps behind. Suddenly, the two turned around to us, grabbed Mama's bag, and disappeared among the headstones.

"Mamushu, mamushu, mamushu!" I screamed, seizing Mama's hand.

Pale, Mama stood there, the bag handles in her hand. She looked sadly at them, saying, "I had the broken piano keys in there; I was taking them to be fixed."

I didn't know what Mama regretted most, the money or the piano keys. Finally, I realized that she was only sorry about the keys because the money was in her bra, as everyone did during the war.

"We must leave Poland," said Mama, two days later.

Yashu and I were with her in the small room. "We'll go to Palestine," she said.

"Palestine?" I said. "Where is that?"

"Ciocia Palemira, remember?" smiled Mama.

"Yes, yes," Yashu jumped up and down, "I remember Aunt Palemira."

"And that's Palestine," she said, "where we have a home, children. But first we'll go to Germany to get ready."

I didn't understand why Germany, but what instantly interested me was the house we'd have and the pink room I'd arranged in my mind every time Mama spoke about our home in Palestine. I arranged a blue room for my brother. I was glad to leave Kraków. I was happy to leave the Christian school and the priest with the hat who mourned our Lord Jesus every day, because of what the Jews did to him.

I was happy to leave the small room next to the kitchen and slam the door so the Polish landlords would hear me. I was glad to leave the piano behind; we went to Germany without it.

I said to myself, maybe we'll be happy in Germany like we were with Helmutt and Toni, without drunk Russians on every street corner and without Madame Jenia who loved our Bechstein. "Well, Danusha, have you practiced?"

All I wanted was to be near Mama. To sit on a chair at the side and watch, it didn't matter what.

We took the night train to Berlin. Yashu immediately fell asleep, and I followed. Waking for a moment, I heard the name Schtetin —Mama said it was a border station—and I went back to sleep. We arrived in Berlin in daylight.

Mama told the conductor that we were going to Hanover, after the Berlin station.

People at the train station gave us chocolates. Mama spoke to them. I sucked on each square for an hour, an hour. Like the rolls Toni brought us, or the almond sponge cake that Helmutt Sopp brought us. I wanted more. I looked at the people who had given us the chocolate, and smiled at them. They had boxes full of chocolates. Mama saw me and gestured to me, enough. Regretfully, I backed away from the chocolate they held in their hands, wanting only to give and give.

In Berlin we met Stella, Mama's fourth sister.

Grandma and Grandpa had sent her to study opera in Berlin in the days before the war. The sisters said she had an Aryan appearance and the voice of an angel. Her teachers predicted a great future for her. They said she had enormous talent, and admired her. They talked about her participating in an important concert and that her name was Stella Martini. They said that Mama and Papa traveled from Tarnopol specially to see Stella Martini sing at a concert in Berlin. I remember Mama saying that Stella appeared in a pink dress with a pale-blue belt. And then war broke out.

Stella remained in Berlin throughout and following the war. The sisters knew she was living with two older Russian women, Regina and Paulina, one of whom was a doctor. The Russian women treated her as their daughter.

In our family they called her orphan Stella, because she didn't marry and had never had children. Orphan Stella. In her stories, Mama never mentioned meeting Stella in Berlin. I don't know why and I didn't ask. I have a photograph of Stella. She's eighteen years old in the photograph, with long blonde hair falling to her shoulders. She has a beautiful, delicate face, and long, slender fingers with a ring and bracelets placed gently on her face.

I like looking at the photograph of Stella. When I saw her in Berlin, I looked hard at her and said to myself, when I'm grown up, I want to be a famous singer like Stella. I knew that one day I, too, would appear on some important stage. The most important thing was that I'd invite Mama to sit in the middle of the first row. In the recurring dream I had for many years, a man dressed in a dark suit sits down at the black piano, arranges his chair and opens the sheet music. I enter the stage with confident steps, wearing a long, tight dress with a low neckline, a transparent scarf over my shoulders. I am wearing pearl earrings, a matching bracelet and chain, like Maria Callas who sang *Tosca*. I saw her at the cinema years later. The audience claps, and then silence in the hall. The pianist plays the first notes. I look at the floor, take a breath, fill my chest; the pianist looks at me, motioning with his head to begin. I sing a famous aria. My voice is strong, clear, and beautiful; everyone in the audience is looking at me. During the sad moments, Mama puts a handkerchief on her cheek. The pianist is very focused, we exchange glances, I feel good on stage, right to the end of the concert, and then boom. A storm of applause, and bravo, bravo, bravo, they shout in the hall, for me. I'm excited and bow to the audience. A young woman dressed in a dark suit and stilettos brings me red roses. I hug the roses and look at Mama in the first row. Mama is very pleased. She turns to the woman sitting next to her and I read her lips: "What a wonderful girl my daughter is. From the day she was born she was special, beautiful, unbelievably talented. I am so proud of my daughter,"

Ah, a sweet dream…

Mama told the guests in the living room that one day, her cousins, Shmuel and Henia, appeared at the house in Kraków. In the family Henia was known as Hanchka. They said that Shlomo, a family friend, had been given a prestigious position on the

Jewish Committee established in Hanover, Germany, after the war. Shlomo had told them that if they'd come to Hanover, he'd help them to manage. Mama decided to leave Poland and go to Hanover with Shmuel and Hanchka.

She hoped to stand on her feet with the help of this family friend before reaching Palestine.

Stories about the horrors of the Nazis at the camps in Poland that relatives brought back when they returned to Kraków were unbearable. I didn't want to hear it all. I moved away and hummed a tune so I wouldn't hear.

Before leaving Kraków, Mama wanted to part from her dead father and ask him to intercede for her before God for their safe journey.

She reached the site of the huge Kraków cemetery and was horrified by the destruction and ruin. Crushed headstones, missing stones, parts of Jewish names and memorial words engraved with great love were scattered everywhere. She stooped to see some pieces and couldn't get up. It affected her badly. She couldn't find the graves of those dear to her. Her heart stopped and she sent up a prayer to God. That's what she said every time she spoke about the shameful destruction caused by those Christians. "That very night, I left Kraków with the children," she said.

"They took the headstones to build roads and sidewalks," said Bernard Cohen.

"Walls, too," added Izzy Rappaport.

"They even trod on the dead, damn them," recalled Bernard Cohen.

"They crushed headstones for gravel," raged Jacob Ketzelboim.

"Oy, oy, oy," sighed Klara Cohen, "what was left of a person's name, ah?"

And this is what Mama related about Berlin:

"I decided to walk around the city I knew before the war. I put the children to bed and went out into the streets of Berlin. *Berlin war in ruinen;* Berlin was in ruins. I was shocked by the destruction and devastation I saw everywhere. It's difficult to grasp how many destroyed buildings there were, one after another, hundreds and thousands, in streets on which nothing was left standing. All the huge department stores were rubble.

"The *Kurfürstendamm,* the most fashionable avenue in Berlin, was a place of ghosts one was afraid to pass through.

"I walked along shattered sidewalks, saw twisted steel bars, ceilings where I couldn't see what kept them up, steps climbing nowhere, and pillars supporting nothing. I saw a broken piano, the keyboard crushed on the wooden frame, ripped strings falling like spiders' webs. There was the stench of burning and rot in the air. Wretched men and women wandered the streets filling bags and blankets with junk they pulled out of the ruins, a gramophone, warped cooking pots, chairs with three legs, they carried it all away. To heat their homes, they even took broken window and door frames. They put it all on wheelbarrows and broken-down wagons and even on their backs.

"I looked at the famous cafés where I used to sit when visiting Berlin with my father before I married. I loved that joyful city. Now it was ruin upon ruin upon ruin. Cafés were destroyed. I recalled the romantic light of the streets, even cigarette smoke was chic, and how lovely the women once were in their bohemian fashions, accompanied by tall men, surrounded by the smell of alcohol and excellent tobacco; beauties with baskets of flowers, violets, red roses, and camellias passed us, and beautiful piano-playing in the cafés, accompanied by a violin, or a cello, and the sounds of an accordion; how interesting it was to hear conversations about literature and philosophy around tables until midnight, with healthy laughter and the smell of good coffee.

"Nothing was left of that scintillating, lively city. Sadness and depression dominated everything."

Mama paused as if she were carrying a sack on her back. I got up to fetch her water and a sugar cube. I saw the faint tremor of her raised little finger and knew she needed a sugar cube to go on. Mama raised her chin and I knew it was her way of saying thank you very much, Danusha. I looked down and returned to my seat.

"That was the same Berlin that was once an important cultural center in Europe, yes," Mr. Bogusławski cried out sadly. "Thirteen years previously, Marlene Dietrich sang 'Blue Angel' there. And Thomas Mann was awarded the Nobel Prize for literature, can you believe it?"

"But don't pity them," cried Bernard Cohen. "Who destroyed Europe, who?"

"Who finished my family, who?" said Klara Cohen.

"Who sent Jews to the gas chambers?" grumbled Bertha Ketzelboim, standing up. "And I don't want any valerian, Jacob; sit down and be quiet. I can also have a glass of water. Is there another sugar cube, Danusha?"

"Very well," said Jacob, "just don't get excited."

"I do want to get excited. They deserve it, those Nazis, damn them and their memory," and she waved her hand like the heroes.

"Very well, sit down," begged Jacob.

"What luck it was that the Nazis didn't manage to destroy

Kraków," said Bernard Cohen. "The Russians surprised them and the Nazis fled."

Mr. Meltzer turned blazing eyes to Mr. Bogusławski. As if to say, *nu*, say the calming words.

"Courage, Anna, courage, it isn't easy," whispered Mr. Bogusławski. "You're already setting out on a new path."

Mama put down the glass and looked first at him and then at me—at once I realized that I'd forgotten to bring Bertha Ketzelboim a sugar cube and she'd remained standing.

"Please bring a saucer of sugar cubes," said Mama. "Maybe others will want one, too. Bring them," and on her face was the devastation she'd seen in Berlin from which she hadn't yet calmed down. Then I remembered that Mama had someone mysterious in Berlin. Yes. He was called Doctor Fischer. She knew him from her travels with Grandpa to Berlin, and it was before she married Papa. I heard her sisters whispering and giggling about him during the war, "Doktor Fischer, Doktor Fischer," they'd say among themselves and Mama of course had blushed. They reminded her, what letters he'd sent her to Kraków, ah? They spoke of the letters and the words he'd written her. Wordlessly, I asked where the letters were; maybe Mama had kept them, and was there a photograph? Was he good-looking? I decided I had to search. Maybe when she was walking round ruined Berlin, Mama had remembered her suitor, Dr. Fischer, and the café where they'd sat together, with Grandpa Mordechai, of course, and maybe, deep in her heart, she'd hoped to meet him in Berlin after the war?

I didn't have an answer, but I made a note on a small piece of paper to look for the letters with those special words. I loved stories about love in books and films; I also made up stories when I was alone for a long time.

"We continued to Hanover," said Mama, "which was also destroyed. Hanover was bombed to the ground by the Allies. Shlomo, our family friend, arranged temporary lodging for us in a refugee camp called Vinnhorst, which had been a military hospital during the war. There were no children in the camp. I met a girl called Helinka who was also from Kraków. When talking to each other, we discovered that we were distantly related.

"In the displaced persons' camp were also my cousins Hanchka and Shmuel, with whom we came from Kraków. We were quite well organized.

"After a few days, I was informed that we had to move to Bergen Belsen near Hanover because a special camp had been established there for children who'd survived. I didn't want to move there. The name Bergen Belsen made me flinch. I'd heard terrible stories, and I decided to take action to prevent the move there.

"I left Danusha and Yashu at the camp with Helinka and went to UNWRA headquarters on Lindenberg Street, a place I'd heard of because it was responsible for so many things, including food packages for refugees.

"I dressed well and prayed to heaven that it would be all right.

"When I reached the place, I asked to speak to the director of UNWRA, and indeed was able to meet him face to face. I told him that I'd been left alone with two children and no means of earning a living, and asked him to intervene on our behalf. He was impressed by my German and asked about English.

"I looked directly at him and said in English: 'I know very good English as well.'

"I remember that the rolling r that came out of my mouth with the word 'very' impressed him. He looked at me and was impressed. He was even more impressed when he heard that I knew four languages, English, French, German and Polish, and I knew them very well. He immediately informed me that I had a job as an official at UNWRA. He explained to me that I would have to receive refugees from various countries and register them properly.

"I was given a small room in Vinnhorst, a suburb of Hanover. The room was in a complex divided into many rooms in which refugees were living. The building belonged to the displaced persons' camp. To tell the truth, great joy filled my heart when the director gave me a letter ordering double food rations for me and my children because I was an UNWRA employee. And I had a good salary. The future in Germany looked good."

Chapter Seventeen

At the Vinnhorst Refugee camp, we lived in a small, smelly room with a lot of mess and without a toilet or dining room. We had three beds, a small table, three chairs, and one shelf on the wall. Our clothes were scattered over the beds. We used a pot to relieve ourselves, which we had to empty every morning, while suffering the awful smell.

Mama went out to work at UNWRA every morning. Helinka was with us. She was a war refugee. That's how Mama referred to her. She was engaged to a good man. There wasn't much to do in the refugee camp. There were only adults, maybe two other children apart from me and Yashu, and there were many poor people whose clothing put them to shame—let's say a coat that was too short, sleeves that reached the elbow, or a coat that was too long, sweeping the dirt of the street. I saw people with a wool hat or cap who had bulging eyes and who rushed about from one side to another as if in never-ending terror, and many, many skin problems, and all the problems looked bad, really bad. There were people without hair on their heads and swollen bellies, or who made strange gestures with their hands, as if turning wheels in the air. Sometimes they made sounds I didn't understand, or knocked their heads against the wall. Mama said they were unfortunate people who had lost family during the war. What good luck we had to be able to stay with Helmutt and Toni Sopp.

We ate our meals in the Vinnhorst camp dining room, sitting aside, at a distance from all the poor refugees, and there was always a lot of noise there. People pushed and stepped on each other. I saw people hiding pieces of bread in pockets or a hat, and frenziedly grabbing food from the main dish, grabbing all the time. At night we also heard shouting. There were many rooms in the building; sometimes we heard weeping, like a river that got longer and longer, and then more and more weeping, like streams clinging to the river, becoming noisier, tumultuous, and then someone would come, light a candle and say soothingly, "Shhh. Shhh. Enough, enough."

Some evenings, Mama went to the cinema. From the moment her heels left the room I clung to the window, longing for her to return. Yashu put on his pajamas and got into bed with a book. I scratched the glass, scratched my palm, stared into the darkness, maybe she'd changed her mind, but nothing. There was only one streetlight that illuminated passersby on the street below—was that her? No. Was that her figure approaching now? No. It was another woman. Was that the sound of her heels? No. Had five minutes passed? No. An hour? Two hours? Yes, yes. Something bad, bad had happened to her. "Yashu, Mama's not coming back. Mama's gone. We're alone. Mama'leh, where is she? Do you hear me or not?"

I turned to the bed. Yashu was asleep. I returned to the window and the street. I pushed my head against the glass, scratched my hand, which was already bleeding, I scratched the other hand, and who was that crossing the street, Mama? Mama! "Yashu, Mama has come back, look." I jumped into bed and closed my eyes; finally I could fall asleep without worrying.

During the hours when Mama was working at UNWRA, my brother and I played at selling and buying, like they do in the market. We also played outside, digging in the snow outside the building we lived in, looking for treasure to buy and sell to adults in the camp. Once we found a ball and played with two UNWRA employees' children. Yashu went over to them, said something, and from then on, they'd look for him to play with them.

People in the camp called us *Jaś i Małgosia,* which means "Hansel and Gretel" in Polish. And we really were as alike as twins and we didn't budge from one another because of the adults that were everywhere. Sometimes my brother would disappear for a while, maybe to find himself some treasure, or because he'd heard of another new friend who'd arrived in the camp, and I was afraid. I didn't move until Yashu returned, with or without treasure. I stopped worrying only when he returned from his business and we continued playing.

If the adults asked me something, I'd smile but wouldn't answer any of them.

Mama came back from work in the afternoon. The minute we saw her we started fighting.

"Mama, he started it," I complained.

"You're older, give in."

"He grabbed it from me. It's mine…"

"You're smart, give in."

"I'm smart, I'm smart," Yashu interrupted.

"Yes, you're the smartest, my sweetheart."

I could find nothing to say to that. But when I was about nine, I no longer remained silent.

It started with the table. I sit on one side of the table. Mama sits opposite. We look at each other without looking away and then I say: "Mama loves Yashu more than me."

"Nonsense." She sits up straight and waves her fingers against the light. "Can you love one finger more than another?" she asks loudly. "I love you both just the same."

And she gives me a half-glance as if there's something in her eye. After her eyes were all right, she looks for Yashu who is playing on the side. She finds him, looks hard at him, purses her lips, and returns to me. I see she's having difficulty, and that makes me feel good. I think to myself, when shall I sit opposite her again and say that she loves Yashu more than me? Soon, I answer myself, very soon.

Mama didn't say, *I love you, Danusha. I love you, my darling daughter*. In front of guests and admirers in the living room she'd say, *My darling daughter*, but Yashu heard her say it and she'd hug him even without guests. "I love you, my Yashu," she'd say simply and often.

In the Vinnhorst refugee camp, I realized I'd found a way to hurt Mama, and was surprised to find that it made me feel good. From that day on, every time she started with her "Give in", I'd look at her directly and say, "Mama loves Yashu more than me," and then she'd wave her fingers with that *Nonsense* of hers, *can you love one finger more than another?* At the time, she waved her fingers without a ring, but in time there were rings, with or without a stone, and a bracelet and wedding ring were added. Mama had beautiful fingers.

Years later, my brother said to me: "I also felt that Mama loved me more than you."

My brother's words seared my heart, although I already knew it was true.

One day, in the middle of regular Vinnhorst life, just before Mama went to work at UNWRA, she stated that our lives needed some culture; good food wasn't enough. That day she asked us to play nicely, without fighting, and she came back with a piano. Four men carried the piano into the room, and I felt my heart sink. I knew that she'd soon find an excellent teacher for me.

Once again, we were crowded into a small room, this time in the displaced persons' camp, but our experience with the Bechstein in Kraków helped us get organized more quickly. Mama also bought a coffee set and porcelain dinnerware, special bed linen, a mirror inset with crystal and glass angels, a small round table with colored glasses, silver cutlery, and an oval porcelain serving dish with a maroon stripe around the edge. I noticed *sanatorium* written on the dish; I don't know where she got all these things.

Engraved on the silver cutlery were the letters WH. When we turned the cutlery over, the letters appeared as MH, the letters of Mama's Jewish name. Hanna only appeared on documents; the family called Mama Anna.

I think she bought the cutlery because of the German letters.

At Vinnhorst, Mama suffered from toothache. She had a severe gum infection. A dentist removed all her teeth and gave her dentures that looked completely natural. She had many admirers who wanted to take her out. And why not? She dressed well and looked special, with matching hat and gloves. I liked looking at her, the way she matched a blouse and skirt, shoes and bag. It was when she spoke on the telephone with people that I didn't want to hear her. We had a telephone in the room because of Mama's work. So it was by chance that I heard her invite a friend to dinner with us.

"How could you invite someone to dinner?" I said, approaching her. "How can we eat here? There's nothing here."

"Don't worry," smiled Mama. "I knew he wouldn't come."

If she was talking on the phone to her dentist or to his wife, she'd look bored, irritated, as if she didn't feel like listening to them. She'd put the receiver on the bed, comb her hair, put on stockings in the meantime, and the doctor or his wife would talk and talk into the air. She'd pick up the receiver just to say "Goodbye, goodbye," and then, "Surprise me, Danusha, and tidy the room, please," and go to work or to do errands.

I'd planned on surprising her—I wanted to do it alone, without Mama telling me, but she always got in first with do this and do that, "And never correct me in front of people, understand?"

I couldn't tell Mama, "I don't want to learn to play the piano", "I don't want to finish the food on my plate", "I don't want to go to the sanatorium alone, only with you."

She never shared her plans for us. She decided, we did it; we didn't know any other arrangement.

One day we moved from Vinnhorst to the city of Hanover itself. On the way we saw lots of destroyed buildings. Mama said that going from the camp at Vinnhorst to her work took too long, and apart from that, in the new apartment we'd finally have a kitchen and a bathroom. I heard her telling Helinka that the director of UNWRA helped her to get permission from the housing authority for a large room in the apartment of Germans on Podbeilski Street, no. 113.

The apartment belonged to the Zegers family, an elderly German couple. We were given a living room and one other room; the kitchen and bathroom were shared. Herr Zegers wore a wool hat at home. Frau Zegers walked around in gloves and a net scarf over her narrow shoulders. Those two would steal food Mama brought us from UNWRA, hiding it in the bathroom. Every time I went into the toilet one of them would knock on the door and call out, *"schnell schnell,"* hurry, hurry. I got used to relieving myself while hearing *"schnell, schnell,"* which annoyed me.

When we met Herr Zegers for the first time, he caught Mama's hand and said: "We didn't know what was happening. We didn't know."

Mama shook her head from side to side and was silent. I'd already heard lots of Germans say, "We didn't know what was happening, we didn't know anything." I didn't understand what they didn't know, but by theirs and Mama's faces I knew that something very bad had happened that nobody talked about out loud and better they not know about it.

One morning, we heard on the Zegers family radio that Stella

Martini would be singing at a special concert to be broadcast the following evening.

"Stella Martini?" cried Mama and looked at the old man sitting beside the radio. "Herr Zegers, did the announcer say Stella Martini?"

"Yes, she'll be singing on the radio tomorrow," said Herr Zegers and went back to his newspaper.

"Stella Martini is my sister," cried Mama, almost jumping.

"Yashu, Danusha, did you hear? Aunt Stella will be singing tomorrow on the radio, with an orchestra. She's performing at a concert."

"Your sister on the radio?" asked Herr Zegers, putting down the newspaper and taking off his glasses. "She studied singing?"

"Studied opera in Berlin, before the war."

"In Berlin?"

"Yes, yes, in Berlin, with the finest teachers."

"Forgive me, your sister is also Jewish, yes?"

"Of course," said Mama. "She's like me, born after me, do you understand?"

"Well, well, she'll be singing on the radio, and we will listen together, yes?"

On the day of the concert, Mama came home from work earlier than usual. She made sure we ate dinner before seven, took showers, and dressed in our Shabbat clothes. In the end, we combed our hair nicely and were seated in the living room maybe an hour before the concert. Mama was also nicely dressed and sat next to us. Herr and Frau Zegers were ready before us and kept us places close to the radio.

"First the musicians of the orchestra come on stage," explained Mama. "Now the pianist," she added. "Danusha, pay attention, after him the violinists come on, the cello, clarinet, and the drum. I wonder how many musicians are accompanying Stella; if it's an important concert, probably fifty. And there's the conductor, of course. He wears a frock coat, a special conductor's coat, and a bow tie, a small tie in the shape of a bow tied round the neck. And what will Stella wear? Maybe the pink dress with the pale-blue belt that she wore to the concert I went to… that we went to… in Berlin?" she said, and her shoulders sagged as if the chair had no back to it.

I asked Yashu, "Stop kicking the chair, stop it."

Mama looked at me and didn't say a word.

I returned her look and then she straightened and leaned back.

The concert hadn't yet begun, and Herr Zegers picked up the newspaper and made a noise.

Frau Zegers stirred the sugar in her tea while knocking on the saucer of the cup. I looked at her like Mama, when she asks us to stop making a noise, but Frau Zegers ignored me.

Stella sang operatic arias on the radio. She had a perfect voice; I mainly remember the Lehár operetta, which made my heart jolt. At the end of the concert we looked at one another, open-mouthed, huge eyes and with all the excitement of a festivity.

"Wunderbar, wunderbar," said the Zegerses admiringly, clapping their hands, and we joined in. Mama wiped away her tears with a handkerchief, and Frau Zegers handed out cubes of the chocolate that Mama used to bring from UNWRA and would occasionally give them a slab. What was annoying was that the Zegerses would help themselves without permission, as Mama explained. I sniffed the wrapping and that chocolate had clearly lain in the bathroom for a long time, in the usual hiding place. Even if it smelled like the bathroom, we enjoyed leaving the cube on our tongues for as long as possible. We all wanted to listen to

another concert, and Herr Zegers wanted to know if Stella's career was developing well after the war.

"With God's help," responded Mama, "*von Gott begnadet*, she is graced by God, so our Stella will succeed, I know it," and Mama's face was good, without tension or worry. This was exactly how her face was when she sang the aria of the "Queen of the Night" from *The Magic Flute* by Mozart:

Come my love, don't let me wait any longer
Come my love, so I may adorn your beloved head with roses
Your beloved head with roses.

I, too, would be willing to bring down the stars and the moon for Mama, as she used to say to us, just to hear her sing the "Queen of the Night" aria. It held a special magic for me, and if she stopped singing, I badgered her, "Mama, go on singing, please don't stop."

Mama would look at me and say, "But the song is finished, Danusha, that's the end."

I didn't believe her, I thought she was just saying that. Only when I grew up did I realize that there was an ending to that aria. Mama was asked to sing in Hebrew, "My God, my God, why hast thou forsaken me" before the refugees at Vinnhorst. There was a large hall there, and she sang in Hebrew and received an ovation. In that hall they held weddings, films, and blessings for the holidays. I learned to say the blessings in Hebrew, and on Hanukah I lit candles.

One day, in Hanover, we were taken to see a play in German, *Utz li Gutz li*.

We traveled to the play in a real car, like the cars that

belonged to some of the Nazis during the war. Mama sat beside the UNWRA driver looking out of the window and we sat in the back without saying a word. I felt like a baby in a pram. I liked the rocking, and I didn't want to get out of the car when we arrived. It always happened to me—I loved the journey and hated arriving in a strange place.

Life in the apartment at 113 Podbeilski Street in Hanover could have been rather good if it hadn't been for Hanchka.

Mama invited her to come and live with us. Hanchka, Mama's cousin, was short and limped because she had one leg shorter than the other. She came to us from a small town in Poland and told us things I didn't want to hear. She slept with me in the room. Mama and Yashu slept in the living room.

Hanchka prayed all the time, ch, ch, ch, and she talked about what had happened to her in the concentration camp. According to her stories, I understood that the concentration camp was a good thing and the camp commander was someone who did her favors.

Hanchka was completely different from us. She was dark, spoke in a loud whisper, which we weren't allowed to do, and she didn't know how to smile. She could scream like an animal with her mouth almost closed.

I barely looked at her face because of what I saw there, and that wasn't good. If someone told me I looked like a *shiksa*, a gentile, which was a compliment, Hanchka's face would become like a long, bent pencil and then I'd be punished for something, no matter what.

"What do you think, that you're a princess now? No, you aren't. Make the bed immediately," she'd scold me.

"First be a princess, then you can have others tidy up after you, do you hear?"

"Close your mouth or you'll never get a husband."

She'd stop near me when I was reading in German, a language she didn't know. I believed her with regard to a husband because of her confident, whispery voice.

She and Mama would walk behind me and say that I was messy. That I'd need a lot of rooms because I was a princess even before someone wanted to take me. That I was irresponsible. That my head was too big. That I walked like a duck, why? Because I was flat-footed.

I believed every word the two said about me. I felt like a dry leaf that was stepped on in the street. Ever after, whenever people looked at me, I got alarmed, telling myself, they can probably see my head is too big, that I walk crooked, that my mouth is open and not closed.

I have a photograph from those days. In the photograph you see me, my brother, and four other children, all of us Hebrew students in the Jewish community. Mama sent us to learn Hebrew from Yehuda, a teacher from Eretz Israel. The Hebrew teacher had thick, tall hair like a tower with steps.

On the back of the picture was written:

For eternal memory!
This picture was taken in Hanover, Germany, 1.5.47
Hebrew School, Department A
Yehuda Miriam

I like looking at the eternal memory photograph. In it is a girl with ringlets. Another without ringlets, just a ribbon, and another girl with brown eyes, and then me in a delicate wool blouse with bright embroidery and lace with a sweet pompom that Mama bought me. Even though I've grown up since then, I remember the blouse with the pompom. In the picture, my brother is standing next to me.

On the other side of the picture stands a tall boy, with straight hair and light eyes. His name is Peter, another Peter, and this Peter wanted to get close to me, and I didn't know what to do with Peter wanting to sit next to me and give me a candy. I looked at him with my mouth closed, and walked next to him as little as possible so he wouldn't see I was flatfooted and walked like a duck.

Peter smiled only at me, then immediately lowered his head and so did I. He kept a place for me in class. Sometimes I saw that he was waiting especially for me before we went into class, as well as when we finished studying.

One day, Mama, Hanchka, Yashu, and I went to a place called Blanke Neze, a small town near Bergen Belsen. A festivity was prepared in the town. We traveled in the car of someone from the Jewish Committee. I had a wreath of white marguerites on my head and wore a white dress. When I looked in the mirror, I saw that the wreath and dress suited me. I felt special. I so enjoyed sitting in the back of the car that with all the joy, I didn't know what to do with my hands, head, or feet. Everyone was in a good mood, not just me. We sang in German and with every song the joy increased. When they started singing, "There's a hole in the bucket…" everyone burst out laughing and I did too. Then I heard Hanchka's loud whisper in my ear: "Fool, why are you laughing? You don't understand anything."

I instantly stopped singing, looked at Mama in the front seat, and sank back into the back seat. What was bad about the car was that it was impossible to move, get away, go into another room, and close the door. I had to stay pressed against Hanchka, who got more enthusiastic and laughed aloud until the end of the song. I was sorry I couldn't throw up and stop the journey. I was sorry I didn't have a fever and have to return home at once. My eyes stung. The fever didn't reach my forehead and I wept in my heart. I knew how to weep without anyone seeing. The most painful tears were those that stayed inside.

Chapter Eighteen

It happened in the Bad district of Germany. Mama brought us, said, "Goodbye, Danusha, goodbye, Yashu," and left. For weeks we were left alone without Mama. It was like cutting off a leg or an arm. The body vanished, only the arm was left. The pain was unbearable, and it began in the summer, in Bad Harzburg.

First, we went on holiday without Hanchka—in itself a good start for me. We rented an apartment in Bad Harzburg, near a large forest. We went on a trip in the fresh air with Mama's friends, and sang songs in German. They'd raise one foot high, and boom, stamp with the foot on the first word of the song. I remember a line from the German song. Boom. "How good it is to marry but you have to know how to behave with women…" Boom. "How good it is to marry but you have to know how to behave with women…"

It was a pleasure to wander about the forest of Bad Harzburg and, most pleasurable of all, to listen to birds chirping. I didn't try and understand what they were saying, as I did in Brzeżany, wandering in the field with fire shooting down from the sky. Don't want to think about it, don't want to remember Brzeżany.

In the Bad Harzburg forest, I had a closer look at the rough trunks filled with soft, green padding, the smell of cool moss. The tall trees hid the sun; there was an evil darkness in the depths of the forest.

We walked in a line; her friends didn't really let me see Mama. They walked ahead and around, hiding her. The man walking ahead of me whistled like a bird, and Yashu, who was walking beside me, tried to copy him. Yashu exhaled and exhaled. Phoo. Phoo. Phoo. And another long phooo, without success. He put his fingers in his mouth, exhaled with all his strength, and then a hoooo came out of him. Yashu was thrilled, and practiced all the way. I looked for Mama among her friends. Every time I saw the scarf on her head, I relaxed.

At one of the junctions in the forest, I saw a sign pointing to a dirt road which read: "The Philosophers Way."

I thought it was a lovely, mysterious, and noble name. I said to Yashu, "Listen, what a lovely name," but he wanted to whistle and compete with all the walkers. I wanted to know where the road led; inside the forest, could there be mysterious houses where philosophers lived who had long beards and thick glasses and an enormous pile of books? Then we sat down to rest. My brother and I took blankets that Mama's friends had brought on the trip, wrapped them round our hips, and walked along the path, telling each other: "We're philosophers, we're philosophers." We felt important and that felt good to me.

One day, Mama and I went to a café in Bad Harzburg. Mama met a friend, we drank coffee, and ate cake. Mama's friend looked at me and said that her children always had a craving for baked potatoes.

"Really?" marveled Mama. "My children don't want to eat anything special."

And I didn't understand what she meant. Could children want something? Ask Mama for cake or candy? In the meantime, I slowly and quietly ate my cake. In my heart, I wished Mama would take me to a café again, that she'd buy me another cake, but she took me and Yashu to a house in Bad Harzburg. Two German women we didn't know lived there, Gertrude and Trude, and they had thin braids around their heads and freckles on their noses.

We entered the house and shook hands with Gertrude and Trude. We introduced ourselves, Yashu, Danusha, and they nodded with half-closed eyes.

"I'm going away, children," said Mama, setting down our suitcase next to the door. "Give Mama a kiss," and she bent down. We each kissed her cheek.

"Goodbye, Danusha, goodbye, Yashu," she said and went back to the path. And went away.

Aaah?

I was about nine and a half. Mama said, "You're big, give in." But nonetheless I couldn't breathe. I felt as if my heart had left with Mama, only my legs stayed in place.

Is that what happens when you die?

Gertrude and Trude said something. I didn't understand what they said. Yashu looked at me. I returned his look out of eyes that stared without understanding what was happening to us. Trude, or was it Gertrude, caught my arm, and walked me to a room with two beds. She put the suitcase down next to one of the beds and left the room. My brother followed her. Someone opened the door. A minute later, I heard Yashu playing outside.

Not knowing what to do, I stood at the door. The blankets on the beds were stretched under a white pillow. The other side was tucked under the mattress. The rugs on the floor were small. I looked at the colorful curtain at the window; it reached the floor. I approached it, lifted the edge and, raising it carefully, I moved into its folds.

I held out my arms to the sides, grasped the edges, pulled them towards me and turned on the spot. The curtain completely enveloped me. For an hour I stood close to the window without moving. My mouth was dry from the smell of moth balls in the room.

Gertrude or Trude came to call me to eat. I didn't want anything.

Gertrude or Trude stood at the door. Her clean apron looked like plywood.

"I'm waiting," she said.

I wanted to pee and pressed my legs together so it couldn't escape.

"I'm waiting for you, Danusha, do you hear me or not?" She approached the curtain and raised her voice.

Then she began to whistle a cheerful tune I didn't know. I couldn't bear it.

"Not coming out," I said in German.

"Come out of that curtain at once," she shouted, smacking her hand against the apron. Pam. Pam.

"Not coming out. I have to stay."

"We don't have to do anything; the only thing we have to do is die." Breathing out the sharp smell of garlic onto me, she moved away and continued whistling.

I came out of the curtain and followed her, found the toilet, and went inside.

That night in bed I couldn't sleep. I closed my eyes and asked myself, where is Mama, where is my Mama? Come, Mama, come, Mama, Mama, Mama.

The figure of a woman stood before me, transparent, blurred, I couldn't see a face, just a shadow. The woman approached my bed. My heart jumped in my chest. Mama? Mama?

I opened my eyes; the woman vanished. I looked around me. Yashu was asleep in his bed. We were alone.

Cautiously, I closed my eyes and shrank into the bed, waiting motionlessly. The woman returned. Dark and quiet, she stood beside my bed; a pleasant warmth spread through my body. I felt myself sinking into the bed, breathed quietly, and fell asleep.

In the morning, I looked for Mama. I didn't find her. My whole body ached; it was unbearable.

I hid behind the curtain, refusing to come out even when Gertrude or Trude called me to come out. And my nose was wet. I touched it with a finger; there was blood there. Pressing a handkerchief to my nose, I wept quietly. Mama, where was my Mama? Night returned. The minute I closed my eyes, the dark woman stood beside me. I breathed quietly and managed to fall asleep.

A few days later I got whooping cough. I couldn't sleep at

night because of the cough. My throat felt scratchy and my ribs ached in my chest. During the day I coughed behind the curtain. I coughed when I stood straight, or when I leaned against the wall and crossed my legs. I coughed the most when I sat on the floor with my head between my knees. The curtain trembled with the coughing and my forehead burned. I tried unsuccessfully to find a pulse.

I begged God, "Please make Mama come, make Mama take me away."

One night I turned over in bed and suddenly bumped into a leg. A warm leg. I got such a fright. What was it? Who was it? Mama? I felt an electric shock in the soles of my feet. I began to tremble. Was Mama lying next to me in bed?

No, I was dreaming. I closed and opened my eyes. The leg was there. I pinched the fingers on my right hand—it hurt. I carefully pushed my leg downward; the leg beside me was long, like Mama's.

I leaned on my elbow, sitting up a little. I laughed soundlessly and wept, *Mama, my Mama.*

Mama was sleeping. I put my palms on my cheeks and pressed hard. Shhh. Shhh. Shhh. The cough calmed down.

The next day Mama took us back to Hanover.

Mama told the guests in the living room about the good change in Hanover. She received food stamps, cigarettes, and coffee from UNWRA. In those days there was great hunger in Germany. Anyone who had coffee beans, which they called *Kaffeebohnen,* was well off. The Germans were mad for real coffee and cigarettes. She exchanged cigarettes and coffee for other products, and I realized she also had a good salary. For the first time in many years, she felt hopeful, for the day was coming when she'd travel with her children to Palestine, the country of her forebears, and in the meantime, she bought things for the home that would help her manage.

Then her dear relative, Henia, whom they called Hanchka, came to join us. Shmuel remained in the displaced persons' camp, and she helped with the children, helped during the hours when Mama was working hard at UNWRA with the poor refugees. The minute I heard Mama say the name Henia, I started to itch.

The good change Mama referred to made no such impression on me. I in fact suffered from all kinds of illnesses.

"Because of the lack of vitamins," explained Mama to the guests, "and the stress of having to move during the war also greatly affected us."

She related that the doctors in Hanover recommended she take the children on holiday to the health town of Bad Pyrmont, in order to breathe fresh air. She was given a two-week holiday, and traveled there with the children.

"We traveled to Bad Pyrmont in the spring," said Mama. "I rented a villa with a round balcony. There was good air, a little sun, more clouds, a promenade, and a pretty garden with plants.

"We stayed at a pension run by a German family. I tried to get hold of more vegetables and fruit to strengthen the children. I walked with them in a large park every day so they'd have as much fresh air as possible. In the park I encountered people disabled during the war, Germans missing a leg or an arm, sometimes both legs, and only half a face. Some had bandaged bodies, or casts, they walked on crutches and looked like demons. Some of the disabled would bend to the ground to pick up cigarette butts and then they'd try to light them in order to smoke. They didn't always succeed. They'd sit beside me on the bench without knowing I was a Jewess.

"I often heard them boasting that not long ago they could kill a thousand people a day, and now they can barely hold a cigarette butt, or a bit of a sandwich. They said that once they were high-ranking officers and now they're victims of war, ah?"

The moment Mama said the words *victims of war*, the living room began to rumble and mumble; it was the same with every new group of visitors. People cried out together, "Who started the war, who, and they're the victims? Walking about in bandages, on crutches, and what about us, eh?"

I could see by Mama's face that she disliked this indignation, and so did Mr. Bogusławski. He'd stand at the window, open it, and look out, winter or summer, the same.

"Close it, it's cold."

"Close it, it's hot, can't you see the thermometer?"

"Why play with the window in the middle of an event?"

And Mama? She'd look down without moving and Mr. Meltzer didn't take his eyes off her. He'd lean forwards and slide to the edge of the chair as if riding a horse, and approach her so he could hold out a hand to her and take her as far away as possible. This was how it was with the Bad Pyrmont story. Mama never mentioned Bad Harzburg, as if she'd never left us alone with Gertrude and Trude.

"In Bad Pyrmont I found a piano teacher for my daughter," said Mama. "Her name was Frau von Dorf. She was an educated woman, tall and very thin."

The minute Mama said the name Frau von Dorf, I saw the

tiny bald patch on her skull with the thin fringe. She asked me to play a small piece I knew, and I was shy. I spread trembling fingers on the keyboard, played something, and then she played a piece or two, changed the beat, and asked me to repeat it. I repeated it effortlessly.

Frau von Dorf concentrated while I was playing, and she had the deep furrows of a philosopher on her forehead. I saw Mama looking at her in shock. Mama always said, don't frown, look after the skin. Then Frau von Dorf turned to Mama and said frostily: "The child has a musical ear; I'll be glad to teach her piano."

I remember my face growing warm in a flash. I felt as if joy and sadness were arguing in my head.

Mama and Frau von Dorf decided between them that from then until the end of the holiday in Bad Pyrmont I'd have a piano lesson every day, and that's what happened.

In the afternoon, a masseuse came to the villa. Mama had a massage and sometimes she'd go for a walk. On her own. She'd just leave the villa, and I'd follow. She'd walk along the path, and I'd be at a distance, on the same path. She'd turn in the direction of an avenue of trees, I'd turn too, she'd look back, see me and stop, turn to me and say: "Yashu is on his own. Go back to the room. I'll be along soon."

I'd stop without a word. She'd turn her head and I'd be behind her.

"Stop chasing me, do you hear?"

I'd stop, wait for her to turn her head, and continue to follow her at a greater distance.

She would sometimes go out without my knowing, and it hurt me.

Once she gestured to me to approach and we walked

together. Sometimes she'd give up the walk and we'd go back to the room.

One day Helinka arrived in Bad Pyrmont. She was married and pregnant. The next day, just after we woke up, Mama said: "I'm going to Hanover. Helinka will stay with you. Goodbye, Danusha, goodbye, Yashu."

Picking up a small suitcase, she went away.

I don't remember feeling the same pain when Mama left Bad Pyrmont. I felt safer in the villa where we lived. We celebrated Passover night with Mama's friends, and she also promised to come and visit.

I do remember Helinka forcing me to eat. She wouldn't let me get up from the table before I'd finished eating everything on my plate. I threw the food on the floor. She picked it up and returned it to the plate. I screamed, "Leave me alone! You aren't my mother! Go away, go!"

Helinka remained, and my body grew stronger. My brother also got stronger. My piano playing with Frau von Dorf also got stronger, and two or three months later, we returned to Hanover. It was after this that we went to Bad Harzburg where I hid behind the curtain and got whooping cough, and Mama came to take us back to Hanover.

An UNWRA doctor examined us. An X-ray revealed that I had acute pneumonia. Yashu had mild pneumonia. The doctor sent us to a sanatorium for lung patients in Bad Rehburg, a few hours away from Hanover. We went there in the fall.

Mama and her friend took us in a car to the sanatorium in Bad Rehburg. We sat in the back like two sweet parcels. They set us down near the door, the handle went down, and the door opened. Mama said, "Goodbye, Danusha, goodbye, Yashu," and they went back to Hanover in the car.

We were left alone at the sanatorium. I didn't stamp my feet or look for a curtain to hide behind. I learned I had to manage alone.

Chapter Nineteen

One evening, on a summer's day in August when the guests expected a light breeze, or a cold winter's day with the wind whistling through the shutters, or in the fall when the sea was as smooth as glass, Mama told the guests in the living room about a man from Warsaw called Shiyeh. She said he worked for the Jewish Community Committee in Hanover, an honest man who was talented and had good relations with the British Mandate Authorities.

"*Er gab mir freie hand,* he gave me a free hand. Shiyeh promised to help me when I told him that I couldn't leave Germany before meeting the generous employers with whom the children and I lived during the war. I knew Helmutt Sopp's elderly father was a doctor in the city of Bielefeld, and I had his address. My friend Shiyeh's German driver knew the way very well.

"We arrived at the old doctor's house in the city of Bielefeld before noon on Sunday. We rang the bell.

"An elderly woman, whom Helmutt greatly resembled, opened the door without moving her lips or her eyes. Naturally I introduced myself by my Polish name, Anna *Kwiatkowski,* the name that Helmutt Sopp, his wife Toni, and the children Peter and Ammon all knew.

"'I'm Helmutt's older sister,' said the woman, a broad smile spreading over her face. 'Please come in.'

"She offered us a glass of tea and cookies, and said she'd heard about her brother's good housekeeper in Kraków and was very glad to meet me."

"An excellent housekeeper," said Mr. Bogusławski.

"Brave, too," said Klara Cohen.

"And beautiful," added her husband, Bernard.

"Thank you," she whispered in his direction. "Naturally I asked how Toni and Helmutt were.

"I told her how generous they'd been to me. Did she know that Helmutt left the house, leaving us everything in the pantry as well as a pile of coal? And as we know, times were very difficult. She knew nothing about all that.

"I told her I'd like to thank Helmutt and Toni personally, and did she know where I could find their address? She said that Toni and the children were with her sister in the town of Creußen. She added that Toni was very well, the children were well, but her eyes looked down and she barely looked up again and I could see there was some problem. And then she crossed her arms on her chest. Some nerve jumped in her cheek when she said: 'Unfortunately, Helmutt is in prison, in the city of Fürth in Bayern. He was accused of sterilizing thirty thousand mentally ill men in Poland during the war when he was the Director of the Hospital.'

"I asked her how long he'd be in prison, and tried to remain calm about what I heard.

"She told me faintly that he'd been given ten years in jail, ten years… and then she leaned towards me on the sofa, caught hold of my hand, begging me to intervene with the prison authorities on Helmutt's behalf. After all, I knew he was a good man."

"Thirty thousand. He sterilized thirty thousand men, oy vey," said Efraim Sonnenfeld, running his fingers from the chair to his knee.

"Mentally ill," corrected Mama gently, arranging her collar, "and he sterilized them; he didn't kill them."

"I wished we'd had a Helmutt like that in Auschwitz," said Izzy Rappaport, rolling his eyes to the ceiling. "There, everyone went to the gas chambers."

"He wouldn't have helped you, Mr. Rappaport," said Bernard Cohen. "He was a very small cog in the machine."

Mr. Bogusławski looked at Mama and called out, "Please go on, Anna. It takes courage."

"Well, I decided to travel to the jail in the city of Fürth in Bayern," said Mama. "I hoped I could get some information about the day my husband died so I could observe Memorial Day with the children."

I raised my eyes from the floor and immediately found Mama's eyes fixed on me. I stared back at her, wondering, Memorial Day for Papa? When have we ever had such a day? I'd never heard of it before. We finished staring at each other when Mama turned to the guests with a sad smile of *That's life; it isn't easy for us.* At that moment I preferred to get up from my chair and look for candy in the kitchen. I didn't find any. I dug about the conserves cupboard and found a paper packet of toffees wrapped in colored paper. I put one in my mouth and returned to my chair. The candy spread over my teeth, which was annoying. In the meantime, I heard Mama say that Shiyeh from the Community Committee took her to the prison in his car. At the gate, they refused to let her in to visit Helmutt Sopp because he was accused of severe crimes against humanity.

"You can send letters and parcels, but you can't visit," the guard told her and agreed to pass on the cigarettes and chocolate she'd brought especially for him. Disappointed, she returned to Hanover and decided to send a letter to the prison for him.

Helmutt Sopp answered her and so they began to correspond.

Helmutt's letters were short but feeling, she told the guests. He wrote how much he respected her as a woman of virtue and he thanked her warmly for the cigarettes and candies she'd sent him.

"That's not love," pounced Bertha Ketzelboim.

"Then it isn't," responded Mr. Bogusławski, gesturing to her to hush…

I looked at them and again got up from my chair.

Where? asked Mama with her eyes.

To have a drink, I gestured.

Again? Shaking her head and raising her eyebrows.

As much as I like. I stuck out my chin and went to the kitchen. I put another toffee in my mouth and sat down again. I heard the word *love* bouncing among the guests at least five times, but I wasn't sure that Mama heard. Maybe because nothing moved in her face and, in any case, we never mentioned words like that.

"I found Helmutt's letters very moving," she said. "He knew how to match the precise word to each situation, and he was sensitive and wise."

"What virtues did he write to you about?" Klara Cohen suddenly wanted to know.

Mama smiled indulgently at her, but Mr. Bogusławski was first. "The best virtues in a woman, Klara."

I smiled and Mama caught me before I could put a hand over my mouth. Nonetheless, I put two fingers in and showed her how I tugged the toffee from my upper teeth and how it stuck there. I removed my fingers and began making that sucking sound tzz, tzz, with my tongue between my teeth, which distorted my whole face. Again I pushed in two fingers, which Mama forbids, then my head fell back and when it straightened, I saw this confused her. She didn't make any warning sign, leaving me alone with the toffee and my fingers in my teeth.

"So he really did show Anna great respect," concluded Henia Sonnenfeld, and Mama smiled at her with shining eyes the color of her gown. Again I realized that everything related to Mama was special or superior, or worthy of admiration, respectful or virtuous.

And this is what Mama related:

"One Sunday, I went with my Varsovian friend to the town of Creußen. I wanted to meet with Toni Sopp.

"I rang the doorbell. Toni opened the door. She began to smile at me and stopped. She looked at Shiyeh who was standing behind me. He was wearing a hat and also had a *techka,* a briefcase. She must have been alarmed, maybe she thought he was from the police, or something like that. She drew close to me and whispered, *'Sie kommen zu mir als freund oder alles feind?'* Are you coming to me as a friend or an enemy?

"I embraced her, saying, 'I've come as a friend, Toni, and I have not forgotten how good you were to us.' Toni calmed down and invited us in.

"I was very happy to meet the children, Peter and Ammon. They'd grown since we parted and were glad to see me. Toni naturally wanted to know how Danusha and Yashu were, and I told her that they had pneumonia and were now at a special sanatorium recommended by UNWRA doctors. I explained about the organization and my work there.

"Suddenly a tall, handsome man in uniform entered the room. According to his insignia he was an officer.

"'Mrs. Kwiatkowski, please meet Major Oyette', said Toni. 'He's an American.'

"I didn't understand what an American officer was doing in the company of German Toni, and I didn't ask. I shook his hand, we exchanged several words in English, and I asked to speak with Toni in private.

"We went into an adjoining room. We sat opposite each other on a sofa. I took a deep breath, looked directly into her eyes and said: 'I have to tell you something most important. I'm a Jewess.'

"Toni burst into tears, hugged and kissed me. 'Oh, poor Frau Anna, having to hide with the children. How much you've suffered. How fortunate that Helmutt didn't know that you're a Jewess. He was a Nazi officer, as you know. Didn't you see all the Nazi officers walking around our house? Oh, dear Anna, if Helmutt had discovered you were Jewish he'd have handed you over to the Gestapo. Now he himself is in jail because of all the terrible things he did during the war.'

"I looked at Toni. I must admit I was shocked by the things she said about her husband. I felt she was talking about Helmutt as if he were a wicked stranger and not the father of her children. I naturally didn't tell her I'd gone especially to visit him in prison.

"And then Toni caught both my hands, smiled a sweet smile, and said: 'I also have a surprising story to tell you. I'm engaged to Major Oyette. Yes. To the American major. And he wants to marry me and take me and the children to America.'"

Mama blew a phoo phoo into her décolleté, moving her head as if saying oy, oy, oy, and said:

"What can I say, my friends, *außer sich,* I was amazed. I thought that Toni was imagining things, or exaggerating. She was a good woman, but *frivol,* frivolous, as you already know. Nonetheless, I parted from her warmly, promising each other we'd meet in the future."

"Engaged? How could she be engaged?" people cried out excitedly in the living room. "She wasn't divorced; her husband was in jail, wasn't he?"

"Ladies and gentlemen, you're forgetting what happened after the war," said Bernard Cohen. "Life wasn't normal anywhere throughout Europe."

"It was all a great mess," said Efraim Sonnenfeld, shaking his half-finger.

"Ten years in prison, *nu,* what did she have to wait for?" nodded Klara Cohen.

"And she was young, and still beautiful," said Bertha Ketzelboim, taking out her lipstick and putting it on her lips.

"So what? She could have visited, brought parcels, something?" grumbled Jacob Ketzelboim. "Running off to America, she can go to hell."

"What are you on about?" Bertha said angrily. "She's smart."

"She isn't, and that's that," said Bernard in a commanding voice and everyone fell silent.

"I left Toni and got into the car. Shiyeh's driver was waiting for us, and I couldn't calm down the entire journey," said Mama, and then, at last, my teeth were free of the toffee. Quietly, I got up, went directly to the kitchen, directly to the toffee and took two more. I opened one in the kitchen and kept the other in my hand.

Mama was saying, "I didn't understand when she'd had time to get engaged to her major. Her husband was barely distant and she'd already found herself a new patron? And now, thinking about it, even during the war Toni was surrounded by male friends who gave her presents, and if she didn't receive beautiful presents, she didn't stay in touch, yes. Nonetheless, I wondered at how quickly she'd arranged a new husband for herself, a new house, and another country, and the more I discussed it with Shiyeh, the more I began to think that maybe Toni wasn't really frivolous. Maybe she was smarter than I thought because of all the men around her, she'd chosen an American so she could leave behind the shame that awaited her and her children in post-war Germany. She knew how to think ahead, Toni. She really did.

"It was no less of a surprise to receive a letter from Toni shortly after my visit to her with Shiyeh—naturally I'd left my address with her. In her letter, she asked if she could visit me in Hanover."

The first time I heard Mama tell the story of Toni Sopp's visit to us in Hanover, I asked myself, did Toni Sopp visit us?

The German lady who gave me hot rolls and chocolates during the war came especially to visit us? I immediately made myself comfortable in my chair and, holding the toffee in my hand, I listened to every word.

Mama related, "One day, Toni arrived, accompanied by the

American officer who'd fallen in love with her. I knew about the visit in advance, and cleaned and tidied the room in her honor.

"At the appointed hour, Toni stood at the door, looked at the children, clasped her hands to her chest and cried: 'Dear children, how you've grown,' and she hugged and kissed them with great excitement. Then she took a paper bag of chocolates from her bag, saying, 'This is for you, darlings,' and gave them the bag. They ate the chocolates with great enjoyment."

I had no memory of either a hug or chocolate. I think we were at the sanatorium with other children recovering without their families. Maybe we were with Gertrude and Trude in Bad Harzburg. But Mama specifically said that Toni was enthusiastic about us—could I have forgotten that visit?

In the meantime, I heard Mama saying that Major Oyette, Toni's American suitor, had an impressive tuft of hair and a cleft in his chin like the American actor we see at the cinema, the one whose name she forgets, but I know it's Kirk Douglas. According to Mama, the major formally told her that he and Toni were engaged and he wanted to marry her, but the law forbade him to marry a German woman unless she could prove that she wasn't a Nazi. The fact that Helmutt Sopp, Toni's husband, was in jail and considered a war criminal was causing difficulties with the marriage and other hardships.

Mama cleared her throat, saying: "I was very surprised, and wondered whether Toni had divorced Helmutt. I was even more surprised when Toni turned to me with a self-indulgent smile and said: 'You know, Frau Anna, that I took you and both your children into my home although I knew you were a Jewess.'"

Mama fell silent.

I saw that the shock on people's faces seemed threatening.

"What do you mean, she knew? What did she know?" And they rounded on Mama.

"Evil woman."

"How egocentric."

"Those two have no shame."

"They deserve to be punished, that's what should happen."

"As I've told you all, I presented myself as the wife of a Polish officer lost in battle, and that is what Toni knew," said Mama, her voice barely heard in the shouting. She looked at Mr. Bogusławski, hoping he'd get up and help. He stood up, raised his arms in the air and flapped them, like an eagle that wants to fly and gives up, wants to fly and gives up. I'd seen an eagle like that at the cinema. Finally, when he said, "Anna, go on, we're with you," the guests quietened.

"Toni and Major Oyette asked me to make a short statement to a notary saying that Toni knew I was a Jewess from the day I arrived in their home. Yes, they explicitly asked that of me, or they wouldn't be able to marry. I must admit that at first I refused. I explained to them that it wouldn't be fair to Helmutt, who was in prison, for me to make a statement that would help his wife and children to leave him for an American. But I remembered that Toni had told me more than once that she didn't love her husband, he was unfaithful to her, but she was also unfaithful to him—I told you about the festivities going on in their home. I deliberated a lot and came to the conclusion that if I agreed to help her, maybe she'd start a new life, a better life for her and the children."

Mama lowered her voice, as if the coming sentences were difficult for her to speak.

"I remembered that Toni was always good to me; I trusted that in times of trouble she would help us, I really believed that.

And so, after much hard deliberation, I gave her the statement, but was left with a bad and bitter taste in my mouth."

Mama was silent.

"You aren't to blame," called out Bertha Ketzelboim. "You aren't to blame. What could you do when faced by those two?"

"Very true," said Izzy Rappaport, "we have to remember that Toni was the wife of a Nazi officer. We don't know what her position was. You've told us, Anna, that she was a high-school student when she married him."

I looked at Mama, saw that her eyes were bright and her neck slightly flushed, and I said to myself, ah, that's probably excitement, yes. Mama was excited when she spoke about Helmutt and Toni, and that's what I saw on her face every time she told the story, while I was thrusting toffee into my mouth.

The guests approached the refreshments table. I went to the window above my bed and looked at the sky. A dark cloud rose, the moon shone like an actor on stage illuminated by the circle of light just before the curtain comes down. I asked myself why Mama looked for Helmutt and Toni after the war—after all, she knew they were Nazis and she was a Jewess; after all, she'd lied to them when presenting herself as a Polish woman, so why was it important to her to find them after the war? Memorial Day for Papa? I'm not sure. The more I thought about it at the window, the more I understood that Mama wanted Helmutt and Toni to know that she had an important job at UNWRA, an international organization everyone knew about, that she had a good salary, plenty of food, and a driver with a briefcase at a time when the situation in Germany was very hard. How times change.

Toni had seen Mama. Helmutt hadn't as yet. He'd been tried and imprisoned for war crimes, so Mama told her guests, but she still continued to send him letters and chocolates. And maybe, maybe Mama missed Helmutt's good words in the past, and he probably continued to write beautiful words in the letters he sent her. That's what I told myself while standing at the window.

The moon vanished. The stars too. I wanted to sleep, and once again I was glad to be alone in my bed.

Chapter Twenty

A cold wind scattered reddish leaves on the sidewalks; overnight, the trees took on a fiery hue. That morning, I walked with Mama and Yashu to the little car. We wore warm clothing, a three-quarter-length coat, wool hat, gloves, and boots. Mama wore a long coat with fur in the collar, and a hat and gloves that matched her gray coat. She held two small suitcases that she gave to Shiyeh, who came to meet us. His strides were short and quick, and he had brown hair and a bulbous nose.

Shiyeh helped us into the car. A driver with a thin mustache and a military-like hat said good morning in German. Shiyeh said gaily in Polish, "We're off to the Sanatorium for Lung Disease at Bad Rehburg where you will get well, children."

"With God's help," said Mama, helping me off with my coat. She also helped Yashu, then gave him a kiss on his sweet head.

"Ready?" asked Shiyeh, turning around, and I saw in his eyes that he, too, was waiting for a good word from Mama.

"Ready," said Mama, giving him a lovely smile.

"Thank you," I said quietly to him and started coughing. I covered my mouth with my hand and stayed close to the window.

"Cough quietly," she whispered.

I couldn't.

I looked up at her and we gazed at one another. Mama sat on one side of the window. Yashu sat in the middle. I was behind the driver next to the window. I lowered my head and coughed in the direction of the floor. I looked up and Mama smiled at me. I went back to the window and if a cough came it didn't bother me. I enjoyed the car journey, even the prickling cold in my face. It was like pins dancing on my skin. More than anything I enjoyed the rocking and small jolts of the car.

Rows of trees began racing along the sides, climbing and descending the mountains, and a fine rain began to fall. I closed the window and counted the drops making paths down the glass.

After half an hour I'd had enough. I looked at Shiyeh. He had a broad neck and he wanted Mama to like him. He smiled kindly at her, trying to make interesting conversation. Mama responded politely but her face showed that she wanted to be left in peace. I saw it in her eyes that were on the road. Shiyeh didn't stop talking or asking questions, some of which he answered himself.

In my heart, I knew that there was no chance Mama would choose him, no chance at all. He was a good, generous man, but he was short, ugly, and without chic, as Mama would tell me when I chose or ate something. "Danusha, remember the notion of chic?" she'd ask, even before I knew how to read.

"Danusha, a pity there's no chic," she said when talking about the allocation of clothing to refugees. "There are actually a lot of good things, but they allocate them to people without choosing what suits them, or what's ugly, as if they're handing out food, everyone the same. D'you understand, Danusha?"

Honestly? Mama had a lot of chic and received many compliments as well as male friends. Shiyeh, for example, took her everywhere in the car with his private driver. She knew how to talk nicely to everyone, each one in his own language.

I said to myself, when I grow up I want to be like Mama, yes.

We drove for four to five hours and arrived at the sanatorium in Bad Rehburg.

Shiyeh removed the suitcases. Two nuns greeted us. The older nun noted down our names in a small notebook she'd taken out of her pocket. The younger nun took the two suitcases and smiled at us.

I kissed Mama. Yashu gave Mama a kiss. We shook hands with Shiyeh and thanked him. Mama thanked the nuns, said, "Goodbye, Danusha, goodbye, Yashu," got into the back seat, and the car immediately drove away.

The young nun took Yashu's suitcase, telling him to follow her. He looked at me, as if to say, what does she want? Off he went, both of us accustomed to obeying.

I remained with the older nun. I didn't cry. I was used to being handed over like a suitcase. Do they ask a suitcase if it wants to go away, or where it wants to go? No. Mama said go, I went. Sit, I sat. Eat, I ate. Play the piano, I played. Stand on a chair and recite Adam Asnyk, I recited. Goodbye, I'm going away, I stayed. The fierce pain would appear after the first day, the second day, and much more after the third day.

After resting on her feet, the older nun picked up the suitcase and motioned with her head for me to follow her. I walked fast at her pace. We entered a room with a white bed and a white table on which there were items covered with a white cloth. She sat me down on a chair beside the window, sat opposite me and said: "In a while we'll check your head, Danusha, to see if you have lice."

I knew what lice were. Mama had told me that the refugees at Vinnhorst brought lice to the camp. UNWRA doctors treated lice, but it was wise to stay away from people who scratched their heads, so as not to be infected, God forbid.

Two nuns entered the room. They wore white aprons over their dark habits, and held magnifying glasses. The nuns looked at my thick, clean hair and one said to the other that I'd probably come from a better place than the others. Afterwards, I realized that at the Bad Rehburg Sanatorium for Lung Patients there were poor refugees from all sorts of places, and there were two wings: the boys' wing and the girls' wing.

My brother was sent to the boys' wing on the day we arrived at the sanatorium and I didn't see him again. Just the one time.

I was walking along the corridor, approaching the door to the boys' wing that was always closed, and the door opened. Yashu stood there. His face was a lemon-yellow color. And as he saw me, he jumped, crying out, "Danusha, Danusha," and he bit his lips and held his face, and I saw how hard he was trying not to cry. He understood that crying was no use. I'd already learned that a long time ago. I looked at the floor. I couldn't bear to see my brother's beseeching eyes, I just couldn't. I felt I didn't have a speck of space for his suffering. Not one. Not one. I was filled with my own sorrow, do you understand Yashu, that's how I felt. "Go away, Yashu, go away," I cried out, turning back. "Go back to your room, Yashu, do you hear?"

He went.

The door closed behind him. I was left alone in the corridor.

In the girls' wing, I shared a room with two other girls. Vera was fair, Paula was dark-skinned.

Vera asked me to help her write a letter in German to her boyfriend. I wrote the boyfriend's name with a small letter. One day, he arrived at the sanatorium and shouted at Vera: "How dare you write my name with a small letter?"

Vera was alarmed. She hid behind the bed, pointed at me and shouted, "It wasn't me. It was her, it was her." I wasn't unnerved by him.

The daily schedule at the sanatorium upset me. There were two parts to the treatment of pneumonia: The first was that from morning until noon we lay in easy-chairs on the open veranda with thick blankets over our whole bodies. We lay like dolls, without moving.

"Absolute rest, children," said the nuns. "You are forbidden to get up or talk. Now open your mouths wide, wide, drink fish oil for your health."

I wanted to vomit. I sat huddled in my chair, looking at the sky. There was a cloud that looked like the blurred face of an old man or woman. The cloud twisted and vanished.

I heard two girls whispering on the side. The fat nun with hairs in her chin sat at the end of the row, and constantly motioned with her finger to be quiet.

I started translating words from Polish to German: hand, leg, head, nose, mouth, ears, eyes. Yashu's sad face jumps out at me. I close my eyes and add words: door, window, floor, curtain, corridor. I stop. Don't remember how to say corridor in German.

Yashu standing in the corridor, holding out his hand to me.

I begin to whisper: "Tree. Path. Earth. Sky. Bird."

I hear Yashu crying out, "Danusha, Danusha."

I whisper faster: "Bird. Fly. Away. Vanish. Don't want to be here. No. No. No."

Boom. I hear a bang in my ear. Like the closing of the door to the boys' wing.

I tried to fall asleep. Ants crept under the skin of my feet, climbed to the knee, spreading out to the sides; in the meantime another group of ants pricked my back. I banged my heels on the floor. Once, twice, three times, the ants went away. The fat nun gestured to me to stop.

I lay like a corpse. The ants came back and I'd had enough. I wanted to throw off the blanket, jump out of the easy-chair, and run to the forest. No, no, it was cold in there. I wanted to run to the room, get under the blanket on my bed, and stay there in the dark. Alone. Leave me alone, all of you.

Out of the corner of my eye I saw the fat nun watching me. Her eyebrows drew close together as if in a fight. The nun who sat at the other end had bulging eyes like the carp I saw in the Sopp's kitchen. She shut the book she had on her lap and stood up.

I looked to the side. The girl beside me had cheeks wet with tears and snot.

I closed my eyes and began to count backward in German: a hundred, ninety-nine, ninety-eight, ninety-seven… six, five…

When it was time for lunch I was the first to jump up.

And then they sent us to the room to sleep. There was no organized activity in the afternoon. Sometimes the nuns took us for a walk in the woods. We walked in a long line in absolute silence. I remembered the walks we took in the forest with Mama's friends, and how they sang beautifully, stamping their feet in time with the first word of the song. I started stamping my foot without singing. Four steps and stamp. Four and stamp. One of the nuns caught hold of my hand and from the pain I understood I had to stop.

After the walk we had supper. And then good night, good night, lights out, no stories, and no Mama.

The next day again without Mama. And again the easy-chair on the veranda with the prickly blanket and rows of ants walking on my body. I scratched. I couldn't bear it any longer. In my heart, I prayed something would happen to me and they'd take away the easy-chair. I wished my legs would be paralyzed.

If only I could vomit with a bad smell. If only I'd get a rash on my hands. If only I'd get a special illness. I was worried about Yashu because of the ants and the prickly blanket on the easy-chair; I was worried about him because he was little and he kept being left alone. Once because of the danger during the war. Once because of danger with his lungs. Once because Mama thought that a healing holiday for two children with Gertrude and Trude was good for the health.

I got diphtheria. An infectious disease. The nuns said I had to be isolated from the other children. Oh, what a joy! I lay in bed, alone from morning till evening in the isolation room, sure that this was the best way for me to get better. I read Mama's letters a hundred times. I especially loved reading the opening she invented with each letter. Mama wrote us:

Moja słodka Danoshaleh, My sweet Danusha…

*Moja Droga i cudowna mami i drogi Yashu…*my dearest, wonderful mami, and dear Yashu…

The words in Mama's letters tasted of sugar. I hugged the letters and decided that when I grew up I wanted to be like Mama and I'd also have friends.

In the meantime the diphtheria became worse. The nuns

decided to send me to hospital, which was the best decision they could have thought of for me. Life in the hospital was like a sweet dream, like honey.

"Look, what a sweet child we've received, look, look."

"She is so sweet, this little one, lovely as an angel."

"Oh, how charming, what's your name?"

"Danusha," I said quietly and looked around. Were they talking to me, me? I also looked behind me; I was alone. Again I heard, "Little doll, where have you come from? Do you want a sugar cube?"

I did. I sucked it slowly. For me, hospital was like a never-ending sugar cube on the tongue. I, Danusha, Yashu's sister, am not only a charming doll on Mama's writing paper. With my own ears, I hear the sweet words almost every hour. With my own eyes I see the worry about diphtheria; that I should feel good. The smell of urine and medication in that place didn't bother me. The patients started with their kind words early in the morning, until late at night, day after day, tirelessly, "Do you want me to make you a paper airplane?"

"Want a bird from a tree branch?"

"Want a drawing of a cat as a souvenir?"

Some patients looked at me without saying a word. Maybe they had a severe illness, or they'd forgotten how to talk. Sometimes, I saw that their cheeks were fallen into their mouths, they had no lips, just a hole was left, or they had bright eyes that looked at me, unwaveringly. Sometimes I didn't understand why they wept, especially near me. If they wept I instantly wanted to move far away from them, but then a doctor or nurse or nun would put a hand on my shoulder, whisper a secret in my ear, "Don't be afraid, Danusha. They aren't crying because of you—you're good for them."

The next day I'd return to the patients I was good for; in some cases I found an empty bed. A few hours later a new patient arrived, and again I'd see those big eyes looking at me as if I was something wonderful, and then I remembered the song "How Wonderful, How Wonderful" that I'd learned in Brzeżany, and I immediately went away.

After a while, Mama came to visit.

I remember one visit. She said Shiyeh was waiting outside and she brought a good smell into the corridor. She was wearing a good suit, a delicate scarf, and a leather bag that matched her shoes; in her hand she carried an embroidered handkerchief that she occasionally brought to her nose. Mama asked the nuns if she could meet with the director and head nurse. And then she gave me a slice of bread spread with a thick layer of butter. I almost choked on that butter, I wanted to vomit. Naturally I ate it all. When Mama returned to Hanover, the tension vanished and I left my room and went to the patients. I wanted to remain in the hospital with the diphtheria; it didn't bother me and neither did its severity, which they discussed next to me.

I stayed in Bad Rehburg for two months. I don't remember what happened to my brother. I saw him only that day when he stood at the door to the boys' wing, calling, "Danusha. Danusha." That picture of Yashu alone at the door haunted my dreams for many years.

When we grew up, Yashu told me that one of the nuns at the sanatorium wanted to undress him so he could bathe. He resisted, holding forcefully onto his pants. Another nun came to assist. She vigorously pulled his little hands away. He kicked, threw his head back and shrieked, leave me alone, leave me alone.

From the moment Yashu stood on his little legs, he'd been

taught that no one must see him without pants. Forbidden. Forbidden. It was life-threatening.

The two nuns didn't give in; they were large and strong and they managed to remove his pants.

He stood there alone, naked and trembling with fear.

Maybe he feared disaster. Maybe he thought he'd die.

I see my little brother standing alone and I weep.

Even more so because while my brother was telling me about it, he looked as if he were talking about another boy.

"*Meine teure kinder*," my dear children, said Mama to the guests in the living room, "they got pneumonia; my daughter's infection was particularly severe. I was very worried about my children's health and regretted having to leave them in a place they didn't know. It was a sanatorium for lung disease. And at this particular hard time, we had a savior in Shiyeh. He was born in Warsaw and lost his entire family—everyone—in the war, and yet he remained a good person.

"Shiyeh took an interest in me and the children, offering to take us to Bad Rehburg in the car the Jewish Committee put at his disposal; his German driver knew the way. So, every Sunday, I went with Shiyeh to visit the children. You must remember that it was very hard to get hold of food products at that time. Twice a day, the patients at the sanatorium received a plate of cereal with milk and a slice of bread spread with margarine, that's it. I bought fresh fruit and vegetables for the children and during the week, I called the sanatorium management to ask about the children and also made sure they received the fresh fruit and vegetables.

"After two months the children recovered and we returned to Hanover. I finally breathed a sigh of relief."

I heard Mama take a breath. And me?

I was sorry to leave the patients. Some left before me. They gave me little presents—a small wooden box in which they'd collected dry leaves, a beautiful stone, pictures. I was also sorry to part from the nurses and doctors.

Waiting in Hanover for me was ugly Hanchka who slept beside me in the bed.

"Duckfoot, big-head, scatterbrained." She was happy to see me, and Mama agreed with her.

Hanchka and Mama didn't know that I'd returned healthier and stronger from the sanatorium. I already felt this when sitting with Yashu in the back of Shiyeh's car.

Chapter Twenty-One

Slightly stooped, thin, a faded color to his eyes, Helmutt Sopp appeared at our home in Vinnhorst. It happened on a Sunday, Mama's day off. He held out both hands to her, holding hers in his, and was silent. Mama's face immediately reddened and she said in a trembling voice, "Please come in," and he didn't move.

Still holding onto her hand, he finally said, "I'm glad to see you, Frau Anna. You look wonderful," and came inside.

Mama moved her head slightly and we understood we had to approach him.

"Hello, Danusha," said Helmutt, shaking my hand. "How are you?"

I looked at Mama. She nodded. "Well, thank you," I said quietly. I saw great sadness in his eyes, even when he smiled.

"Hello, Yashu." Helmutt shook my brother's hand. "How are you?"

"Well, thank you," answered Yashu in German, clinging to Mama.

Mama stroked Yashu's head, glanced at the little table at the side of the room on which were notebooks and pencils, and both of us went and sat down. Then, inviting Helmutt to sit down in the armchair in the corner of the room, she sat down opposite him and they began talking in low voices so we wouldn't hear.

Helmutt's face was grave. I realized that the issue they were discussing was either very important or very secret. He didn't take his eyes off Mama, leaning towards her and speaking rather a lot. Then he straightened in his chair and was silent. Yashu was drawing in his notebook. I looked at Mama's face; she was leaning erect against the back of the chair. I noticed a conspicuous line along her neck. She folded her arms on her chest, dropped them, and raised them again. Glancing over, she saw that I'd seen almost everything. My neck hurt but I couldn't hear what Mama and Helmutt were saying. I understood a little of it, maybe because of the way she was sitting, or the shining blue color of her eyes, the red lipstick she put on her lips, or by his effort to draw close to her, how he talked and talked, and straightened up, as if he were an important director waiting for an answer.

It was also the way Mama talked little but looked directly at him, how he moved his head slightly and frowned meanwhile, swallowed, and again leaned towards her as if remembering something important he had to say to her. He was clearly speaking in a deep voice, even raising his hand to touch his head as if in disbelief, but Mama didn't budge; only her neck stiffened and, finally, she shook her head, saying gently, no, no, no. When she looked at the floor and then at him, I saw that her lips were trembling, and he took a deep, deep breath. His cheeks fell; there was a white color in his eyes as he rolled them upward, and then they were both silent.

I felt great tension in the air. I felt as if drops of cold water were coming in under my blouse and I knew that the world I'd known was changing.

Helmutt Sopp, that important Nazi officer, had come to us especially to visit Mama and he already knew from their exchange of letters that Mama was not Mrs. Kwiatkowski, as she'd introduced herself in Kraków. He knew that Mama was an observant Jewess—I heard her tell Shiyeh about the letters she'd written to Helmutt—but he'd still come to Hanover, to a camp for the displaced?

I was sure he needed something important from her, to which Mama had responded, no, no. When I looked at Mama, I was no longer sure about anything. Not even that she was breathing; nothing had shifted in her face from the moment he'd fallen silent and leaned back. It was the end, I realized, the end of their story. Could that be?

It wasn't only Helmutt who needed something from Mama. From her quiet conversations with Shiyeh, I realized that Toni, too, had sought Mama out; she had very important business with her. Their talks about Toni were very, very quiet. Sometimes I heard a few things. There were times I could barely hear a word.

The world I knew, then, had indeed changed.

After all, ever since I could remember, we'd needed things from others. From the Russians who'd allow us to finish the winter in our home in Tarnopol, from the Poles who'd agree to give us a room for the night, from the Germans who'd given Mama a job and agreed to take us in. How did this happen?

And here was Helmutt Sopp himself, coming to ask, I don't know what, of my Mama. Helmutt Sopp! The same one who, during the war, had hosted the most respected people in Kraków, who had had a long line of shining cars parked outside his house with drivers who incessantly polished the cars inside and out—I'd seen them from the window. For hours I'd listened to them in the living room, singing their songs to the beat. Papam. Papam. Papam. Pam-pam-pam, and every few minutes there was a pak, pak, like an explosion. Mama said it was the corks of champagne bottles: "That's what it sounds like when they open champagne, shhh."

Nights and days, weeks and months and years we were closed up alone in a tiny room off the kitchen, and we didn't say a word, not even when we couldn't fall sleep. And Mama, in a white apron, would come and go, come and go, come into the room, her finger on her mouth, shhh… shhh… go out, carrying heavy trays loaded with good food and drink, and again the wild laughter of the important guests and the tralalah, la, la, la about the beautiful Wisła.

Many times, she'd get into bed, sighing worriedly, not knowing how Helmutt's party would end; every week or two it was the same. And all that time I knew Mama barely slept. Sometimes she'd mention that some drunk could come in randomly and throw us into the street in the middle of the night, or punch us, a fist in the face. That's what she told her sisters, thinking I couldn't hear what she was saying when I was standing at the window.

Yes, I said to myself, Helmutt Sopp has some urgent business with Mama, and I saw this instantly that Sunday noon. Even now, in our living room in Haifa, I can see the picture very clearly:

Helmutt Sopp sitting in our little room in Vinnhorst, or Hanover as Mama tells it—doesn't matter. He has sweat on his forehead when he says, *Bitte, Frau Anna, entschuldigung Frau Anna,* and again *Entschuldigen zie bitte,* forgive me, please, Frau Anna, and Mama using the beautiful, delicate china service to serve him a cup of tea and nice cookies.

The tired, stooping Helmutt Sopp taking a silver cigarette box from his pocket, saying, May I smoke, Frau Anna? and offering her a cigarette.

"No thank you," she says, and he taps the end of the cigarette on the silver box, three or four times, and lights it, inhaling deeply, and exhaling the smoke to the side, not at Mama, as he used to. Then he takes a sip of tea and his hand is trembling. He smiles at her and again *bitte,* and *entschuldigung,* and repeats it… and she is silent.

Finally, she presses her hands to her chest, as if to say, forgive me, I'm sorry, and he looks directly at her and is silent. In the meantime, I'm getting on well in my notebook; the pencil trembles slightly, almost invisibly. I already have a long row of words in Hebrew that we learned from Yehuda, the Community Committee teacher, who made sure we could read properly:

Home
Family
Jew
Father
Mother
Children
Synagogue
Plant
Tree
Earth
Promised Land

And I also add below the German word *bitte,* which Helmutt says again and again. Actually, I like the word *bitte,* and what's the Promised Land? I have no idea how to say Promised Land in German or Polish.

"Yashu, what's the Promised Land?" I ask quietly, but Yashu is asleep, his head on his notebook. I make a note at the end of the page: *Ask Yehuda, the Community Committee Hebrew teacher, the meaning of the words Promised Land,* and Mama? Again she is shaking her head from side to side, slowly, her décolleté reddening. Helmutt doesn't take his eyes off her. He is silent; his cigarette is smoking, taking all the air out of the room. I cough into my elbow as Mama had taught us. Mama raises her head, looks, moves her head in the direction of the beds, and I understand everything at once. I put the notebooks and colors in the corner, straight as a ruler, tap on Yashu's leg, and we get up from the chairs and go to bed.

Mama makes up the small bed in the corner of the room with fine linen. Helmutt takes pajamas out of his bag, goes out briefly, and returns in gray pajamas.

He looks smaller in his pajamas. He arranges his clothes on the chair, gets into bed, says goodnight and turns to the wall.

Mama turns off the light.

Mama doesn't fall asleep.

Neither do I.

I think Helmutt and Yashu fall asleep immediately. Or am I imagining it?

Helmutt left early the next morning. That morning, Mama dressed very, very slowly. She brushed her hair with heavy movements, as if she had no strength left in her hands. She didn't talk to us until she left for work and we didn't ask or say anything. I felt we had to make an effort to be as good as possible.

When she returned in the evening, she heard us quarreling over the scissors. Instead of raising her voice, "Danusha, give in, give in," she turned on the tap and wordlessly had a drink of water.

My brother and I stopped quarreling. Yashu leaned his head against Mama and I folded clothes that were scattered over the beds. Then I put the towels back in place and looked at her.

Mama gazed back but I saw she didn't have the strength to talk. In the following days as well, Mama was quieter than usual. She spent a long time staring at the wall, thinking very serious thoughts, that much was clear.

In the meantime, I asked Yehuda the Community Committee teacher about the Promised Land and what it meant. He caressed my head and said that the Promised Land of our forefathers was Eretz Israel, and his eyes and nose were moist. He had a chill even when it stopped being cold.

"One day, I received a long letter from the prison," Mama told the guests in the living room, and then she took an envelope out of her bag with lots of stamps on it, waving it in the air and saying, "This is the letter."

"I've never seen an envelope like that," said Bernard Cohen and leaned forward. "It's clearly been touched by many hands. May I see it?"

Mama returned the letter to her bag, and straightened her jacket, saying:

"Helmutt Sopp wrote me a letter from the prison telling me that he was waiting for a retrial because the Polish doctors who worked with him in Kraków had testified in his favor. They said he was a good and friendly doctor. He carried out sterilization procedures on mentally ill patients in the hospital only because his commanding officers forced him to; this was the policy of the Nazi regime. They also said that there were places where the mentally ill were killed.

"A few weeks later I received another letter from Helmutt which, to my surprise, came from his father's house in Bielefeld. Did I tell you that I visited there and met his sister? Well, Helmutt wrote that he'd been released from prison and asked me to invite him to visit because he wanted to offer me something *très important*.

"A very important offer from Helmutt Sopp, *nu*. You can probably imagine that it was very hard for me to fall asleep that night."

"In war, people do terrible things to themselves," said Bernard Cohen. "We can make peace with God but not with ourselves."

Mama half turned her back on Bernard Cohen, straightening her jacket on her hips. She had on a fine concert suit that night, a black jacket that fitted on her hips, a narrow skirt, a red silk blouse, black heels, and nylon stockings, and I thought she was very elegant.

Mr. Bogusławski and Yozek Meltzer's eyes opened wide when they entered the living room, and Klara Cohen called out, "Anna, you're especially festive today," and Henia asked, "Where did you buy it?"

And then I remembered:

That's exactly what Mama wore for Helmutt. We also wore clean clothes and cut our nails, polished our shoes, and combed our hair nicely. It was very important to her to receive Helmutt Sopp properly, Mama told her guests. She didn't forget that she owed him her life and her children's lives. Naturally she cooked things he particularly liked and, with Hanchka's help, she set the table with beautiful dishes.

I listened to Mama and wondered whether Helmutt could have saved Papa or not, and didn't remember. I wondered, where could we have put a dining table in our small room at Vinnhorst? Next to the window? Or the bed? And let's say we were at Podbeilski Street in Hanover, as Mama tells it, in what order did we sit around the table? And where did ugly Hanchka sit? Next to Helmutt? Between me and my brother? Or did she stay in the kitchen? And what did Mama prepare especially for Helmutt, salt fish? Schnitzel or meatballs?

"Helmutt appeared," said Mama, arranging her hair as if he were about to appear in the living room in Haifa. I saw that Klara Cohen was also arranging her hair, and Bertha Ketzelboim took out her lipstick and put it on her lips.

"I saw a very thin, tall man. The time he'd spent in prison showed on him. We were both moved."

Mama stopped and looked at me. I nodded slightly in the direction of a glass of water on the side table next to her. She raised the glass and drank a little water.

"In prison there's none of Anna's gourmet food," whispered Bernard Cohen to Jacob Ketzelboim.

"There are '*mandabushkes*'—lice", replied Jacob, hiding a bitter smile behind his hand.

"I wonder what he wanted," remarked Klara Cohen.

"He wanted what men want," sighed Bernard Cohen. "Do you know what it's like being in prison alone?"

Mr. Bogusławski looked frowningly at Bernard. "Shhh…"

"Helmutt was glad to see me and the children," said Mama. "He didn't mention Toni and neither did I. I felt I'd done the right thing and there was no point in saying more about it. We sat down to eat. During the meal, Helmutt asked what happened to us after he left the house in Kraków. I told him what had happened; he listened and asked questions. Naturally I was very curious to know what proposition he had for me and though I thought about it a lot, I had no idea what he wanted."

Bernard Cohen turned his head towards Klara. She trod on his foot.

"After the meal, the children and Hanchka left the room," said Mama, "and we remained alone to talk. Helmutt said that although he'd been released from prison, his sentence banned him from practicing medicine for ten years. This of course distressed him greatly, particularly since after the war, many people required treatment. He knew that there was a great demand for private clinics. As a psychiatrist and the son of a doctor, he was of course willing to open a clinic, but was forbidden to run such an institution."

"That's really a pity for someone with all the experience he'd gained from the thousands who'd passed through his hands," remarked Efraim Sonnenfeld, wanting to see if Mama agreed.

By Mama's eyes I understood it would have been better if he'd remained quiet.

I also understood this from the elbow he received from his wife.

"He should have spent a few more years in prison," retorted Efraim Sonnenfeld.

"And how many of them actually went to prison?" mused Bernard Cohen.

"They walk about freely in Germany," answered Jacob Ketzelboim.

"Or in Argentina," added Efraim. "They were received with open arms."

"*Nu,* they had a lot of money," explained Bernard.

"Money they took from Jews," emphasized Klara in a whisper.

Mama gently touched her forehead, saying:

"As I was saying, Helmutt said he was actually forbidden to practice medicine during those difficult times for citizens after the war. He wanted to help patients. He badly wanted to help them. And then he took a deep breath, looked at me gravely, and said excitedly: 'Frau Anna, would you take it upon yourself to officially manage the institution I'm going to open? You know how much I respect and rely on you. I'm sure you will easily be able to get a license to open a clinic after the suffering you endured during the war.'"

Mama paused.

Intense, absolute silence fell on the living room. Not a single person moved in his chair. At the front of the building a car hooted. I heard a woman calling from one of the verandas: "Abraham, where are you? Come on home, Abraham, come home."

Mama rose from her armchair, walked towards the refreshments table, turned, and went back to her chair.

"Shall I make you a glass of tea?" I asked quietly.

"In a while," she said and turned to the guests. "Naturally I refused the offer. I was planning to emigrate to Eretz Israel. Helmutt was very surprised. He said, 'Frau Anna, why would you take two small children to a poor country? What is waiting for you there? How will you provide for yourself? If you agree to my proposal, I will share the profits with you fairly. You will be able to travel after a few years, if you really want to, and you'll be financially stable. Wouldn't that be preferable?'

"I regretted having to refuse him. The Promised Land was more important to me and the children, and that's what settled the matter for me. My whole body trembled when I told him that money certainly couldn't keep me in Germany. This land and this country will always remind me of the heaviest tragedy to befall my people. And he understood.

"*'Sie zeind eine edle natur'*, you are a naturally noble soul, Helmutt told me when he parted from me and went away."

The first time I heard Mama relate the story of Helmutt's proposal, I heard my heart beat. And maybe it was Mama's beating heart that reached my heart? I looked at her. She appeared very elegant and tall in her armchair. Her chin protruded and her chest rose and fell like a theater actress I'd seen at the Armon Cinema matinee before the film. Her name was Robina, Hanna Robina. It was several seconds after the curtain fell. Robina stood before the audience and made an effort to smile, and yet I could see how much she enjoyed standing before an audience that loved her so much. People in the hall were shouting bravo, bravo. Ah, what great moments.

It was a great moment for us in Haifa as well. I saw how people's eyebrows were raised and how their eyes darted hither and thither, as if looking for words. Mama was a queen at such great moments, larger than life. Ordinary life, as I learned from the moment we arrived in the Promised Land, made her yawn. She was a heroine in life-threatening situations, and acted promptly and with extraordinary resourcefulness. The war days were her finest hours, as I heard one of the actors say at the cinema. The urgent need to practice normal life was another story, for her and for me, even though we dreamed about it during the long nights of the war.

At last the guests left the house.

Mama put on a Mozart record, maybe Symphony no. 40, sat down in her armchair, and gazed at the wall opposite, as if there were a beautiful picture there. Tears fell on her cheeks as she said: "*Von Gottes begnadet*—may God grace anyone who writes such beautiful music. Goodnight, children."

I pulled the blanket over my head, and didn't know that Mama's relationship with Helmutt continued even after he rose that morning and quietly left.

Chapter Twenty-Two

"Danusha, do you remember where we got to?" asked Mr. Bogusławski quietly, helping me to take glasses off the wooden tray and put them on the table.

"You can say Eretz Israel, because I think we're finished with Hanover," I answered, going to the kitchen.

"That's what I thought," he said and straightened the glasses on the table into rows.

In my heart I said, maybe not, Mama might want to go back to Helmutt's visit to Vinnhorst, because two or three days after telling the guests in the living room in Haifa about his offer, she complained about how hard it was to find work in the country, and how could she support two children on her own, how? In Europe it was far easier to receive work offers. Who would have believed that while she was working for UNWRA, Mama was asked to run a clinic?

"Today we're talking about Eretz Israel," cried Mr. Bogusławski gaily, thrusting peanuts into his mouth.

"At long last she's come home," said Bernard Cohen, holding out a hand to Mr. Bogusławski. "Give me some," he whispered, and Mr. Bogusławski did so.

"She looked for a home for six years. Six years!" said Klara Cohen, holding out a hand to her husband: "Me too."

"None left," said Bernard Cohen, opening an empty hand.

"I often think about Helmutt Sopp's generous offer," Mama began. "Naturally I have no regrets about refusing him. I've always dreamed of returning to the sacred land of my forefathers and my people. Thoughts of my beloved country strengthened me during the terrible days of the war."

"All of us," said Bernard Cohen, licking his fingers.

"Not me," said Bertha Ketzelboim. "I knew what was waiting for us: more wars."

"I often thought," said Mama, "that Helmutt's dream was probably to establish a clinic for the mentally ill in his name. Maybe he dreamed of it during his imprisonment, and maybe he regretted sterilizing all those people who were mentally ill. Helmutt was an expert on the human psyche. I'm certain he wanted to help those poor patients; there were so many after the war. Sometimes I'm sorry I couldn't help him manifest his dream, because there was definitely a humanitarian aspect to it, right, together with the profit."

Mama sighed. "Who knows? Maybe Helmutt did manifest his dream later on and maybe he didn't."

I heard Mama talking about Helmutt's possible dream, and in my heart I asked, and what was her dream? What dream did Mama have that the war in Europe destroyed?

Bronka called Mama the first lady of Tarnopol. Yes, she was considered the first lady of Tarnopol in Eastern Galicia where she arrived from Kraków; and maybe Mama dreamed that her rich husband would earn a great deal of money and she'd return to her birthplace one day where she could host the Kraków aristocracy in her own hotel or the elegant living room in her home. Brocade and velvet, antique furniture carved by an artist. Silver dishes, porcelain, brass candlesticks, and goblets scattered on embroidered cloths on the sideboard and table, like Helmutt Sopp and Josef Wirth's houses, which she turned into luxury hotels in honor of especially famous guests. Ah, and the portrait, to this day she longs for the portrait painted of her as a girl. It would have fitted beautifully in a spacious living room or the lobby of a hotel, visited by ladies and gentlemen wearing haute couture of the finest designers… naturally, in a world without war.

"In the spring of 1947, we boarded a French ship called *Providence* on our way to Eretz Israel," Mama told the guests. "We set sail from the port of Marseille, the destination of many refugees. During the voyage, I learned that these were the days of the Shavuot festival. On the ship they held prayers in honor of the festival and, of course, we remembered the souls of our dear ones lost in the war. There was great excitement and it touched each and every traveler.

"The ship stopped in Alexandria, in Egypt, where for the first time in my life, I witnessed the highly developed business sense of the Arab merchants. Although they stood on the quay at a distance from the ship, they presented their wares to the passengers, bags, suitcases, purses, and if a passenger pointed at the pattern of a particular bag, the merchant wrote the price on cardboard and showed it to the passenger. Then they began to haggle with their fingers, higher, lower and so on. When they agreed on a price, the merchant threw the bag to the passenger, receiving the money in the same way, wrapped in paper. I was amazed to see how many bags and suitcases the merchants managed to sell, right up to the moment we set sail."

"Shrewd merchants, the Arabs," said Izzy Rappaport. "Here in Haifa, too."

"Haifa," said Mama, stressing the "fa". She took a deep breath, threw up her hands, and cried festively: "Congratulations, we've arrived at the Port of Haifa. I must admit I was surprised to see British soldiers standing with rifles and supervising activities at the Port.

"The British had tight faces as if we'd brought a bad smell with us. Now that I think of it, there really was a bad smell on the deck. The strong smell of sweat and dirt, as well as the sour smell of vomit, medication, and disinfectant. Maybe it came from the clothes of travelers who slept in the general area; where it was hot and crowded, the sanitary conditions were bad.

"When most of the people left the port, the smell also left, but the look remained on the faces of the British. They didn't have the patience to answer questions. It was as if they wanted us to get out from under their noses, even when I spoke to them politely in English."

Mama also spoke about a relative who was waiting for us at the port, Papa's nephew. His family had reached Eretz Israel before the war. She'd written to them about our arrival from Germany. The nephew took us to his home, and a few days later she met with the lawyer who had taken care of the apartment in a building her husband had bought for our family before the war.

"All the apartments in that building had been rented out for years," said Mama. "I expected to get some money that would help me to manage in the first days, but great disappointment and outrage awaited me. The same lawyer told me that barely any rental money was left; the man who took care of maintenance in the building and payment of taxes wasted the money and died from a heart attack. Ultimately I received very little money, barely enough to buy furniture.

"One of the tenants agreed to return the apartment he'd rented in our building. He kept one room for himself and we moved into an apartment on the third floor. In those days it was hard to find work in the country. However, I was filled with hope for the future."

I wasn't. I couldn't think about hope as I wandered about sunburned all summer and Mama was out busy with errands and assimilation or problems that had to be solved.

We arrived in Haifa a few days after the festival of Shavuot. Never in my whole life had I seen so much sun. My eyes hurt from the blinding light that came in the early morning and remained until evening. People told us the sun was good for our health and turned the skin a lovely color. Mama was impressed by what she was told and immediately took us to bathe at the Bat Galim pool. I was a little more than ten, with skin as white as milk; I burned like a fried fish at the pool. My body was covered in blisters, and so was my brother's. I didn't know the sun could burn like that. This beauty wasn't to Mama's taste or style and after the event at the pool she began to leave the house with a thin silk scarf covering her face.

"What's that?" I asked Mama in the heat of August.

"A scarf against sunburn," she said.

"Do I also need a scarf?" I asked.

"No," said Mama. "I'm being careful. Wear a hat," said Mama.

I didn't wear a hat or a scarf, even if my head hurt. I wanted to be like all the children in Haifa.

Mama's skin remained as white and beautiful as it had been in Poland.

"It's only in the beginning. In the end you'll get used to it," people told us.

"See how nice our children's color is," they repeated. "It's the color of health."

Mama gave in and made sure to stay in the shade.

We continued to go to the pool. I didn't get used to it. I walked around burned and hurting all summer. The noise in my ears was very painful. I'd never before heard children shrieking like that at a pool.

"People here scream in the street," I told Mama.

"In every place," sighed Mama, "in buses and in line at the clinic as well."

"In our building, too," I told Mama fearfully one day. "The woman on the second floor shouted like a mad woman at her child and slapped his face. The child cried and cried and she dragged him to the stairwell, screaming, 'You sit here, here, don't move, you hear me or not?' And then she went into the apartment and slammed the door."

"You don't have to listen to everything," Mama taught me, hurrying out again on errands.

I wanted to tell her about the boy who scratched at the door, wailing, "Mama, Mama, Mama, let me in, Mama let me…" But Mama didn't like hearing stories like that, and the sobbing of the child in the stairwell burned in my throat and in my eyes, more than the harsh sun of the first summer in the Promised Land.

After being alone for a while, I went out to the stairwell. I was worried about the child who was sobbing Mama, Mama. Slowly, I went down from the third floor to the second floor and saw him, and he stopped crying. He had sweat on his forehead, *shleikes* on his trousers, and on his cheek was a red swollen mark. I passed him carefully, and then I ran down the stairs as if someone was waiting for me outside. I walked out of the stairwell and leaned against the wall next to the sidewalk. After a few seconds I heard quiet knocks at the door, and it opened.

I went back to our apartment on the third floor; the boy wasn't there. A week or two went by and again shouts, a blow, the door slamming, and "Mama, open the door, Mama…"

In Haifa I saw people walking in the street and talking to themselves, sometimes shouting. Mama told me that it wasn't German. "You speak German; they speak Yiddish."

The people who talked liked that would wave their arms to the sides, in front, behind, as if arguing with the whole world and the heavens together. Next to our building was someone with a black beard and long hair held with a clothes peg. He held a rag doll on his hip and spoke to her very kindly and politely. I saw him several times near the building. Once I saw him walking along the street and speaking quietly to the doll, and then children approached him, laughing and throwing stones at him. "Madman!" they yelled at him. "Abnormal! Crazy!" I couldn't bear to watch or listen.

"Those are people who come from there," explained Mama.

"From there?"

"Yes, from there."

I didn't ask anymore.

Overseas, people mainly spoke quietly near me, or in sign language. One look from Mama in the direction of the piano and I immediately sat down to practice. A brief glance at bonbons or candies and I knew I could take one, or not. I understood everything alone. But at the Bat Galim swimming pool, Moshe and Tsipora didn't understand a thing, not a thing. Even when their mother stood with a towel next to the water and shouted, "Moshe, Tsipora, get out of the water, *nu*, get out."

She shouted at least five times in their direction before they listened and got out. Baruch's mother also stood there, waving a sandwich, calling to Baruch to come at once. Baruch didn't hear and didn't come. Said he was diving under water, "Look, look," and she didn't look. Wanted him to come at once and he didn't come. Only later did I understand what it was like to have your head underwater. I tried and actually liked it.

I noticed that the shouting in Eretz Israel didn't bother anyone. I said to myself, you'll get used to it, but I didn't.

The hardest was going to school every day, without a break, sitting in the same classroom, at the end in the corner. Sitting at the end was the most comfortable. I was tall and erect like Mama and could see what was written on the board, but the teacher was blind to what was happening next to me.

Mama registered me at a *Haredi,* an orthodox girls' school called *Beit Ya'akov,* and she registered my brother at a boys' school called *Yavne.*

Before the beginning of the school year, Mama wanted me and my brother to make progress in the subjects of Hebrew and Bible so we'd be as strong in class as the *Sabras,* those born in the country. She invited Doctor Plesner, a teacher from *Yavne* School, to give us private lessons.

Ginger-haired Doctor Plesner would arrive at our house at a few minutes to four; I saw him from the window. At exactly four o'clock he'd ring the bell. During his lessons I breathed well. But not at *Beit Ya'akov* School. It was a cold, dark stone building. The warm sun that accompanied me on my way to the classroom remained outside. I was ten and went straight into fourth grade. I felt like a refugee child, different from everybody. The only child in the class with many written mistakes and difficulty reading aloud in Hebrew. They all heard how I looked for words in which to answer and couldn't find them, stopping in the middle of a sentence. The words I'd learned to read in Polish and German were of no help to me, and I didn't have the patience to learn Hebrew with a teacher. Miriam, the class teacher, a plump young woman, taught us the meaning of prayers, like reading the *Shema,* which is read before going to sleep, and the blessings said during lightning and thunder.

Apart from prayers, I barely learned anything at all in school. At lunch time I returned to an empty house. Mama was out doing errands, and Yashu was already outside in the street. The moment I came in, I washed the floor. Mama didn't wash floors. She taught me when it was shining and when it wasn't. I was responsible for cleaning the apartment, not keeping it tidy, and then there was homework and supper. I barely had time to read a book, goodnight, sleep. Morning. School again, hours on the same chair in front of the same teacher who wore the same clothes, and "Listen, listen. You don't understand? So stop dreaming, where are you?" I thought I was going mad. "Where is Mama?" asked the teacher. "Tell her to come."

I told her to come, but not to wear the scarf against sunburn in front of the children, and not to call me Danusha, only Nechama, the name I was given in Eretz Israel, and not to speak Polish. I don't want you to, just Hebrew. English is all right, the teachers understand English, yes?

Mama would come to school, and it would be even more maddening because everything would be all right for two days.

She knew how to smile and speak nicely to the teacher and how to drive me mad on the way home with talking that made me even more deaf and dumb. Although they didn't mention Our Lord Jesus or the wicked Jews at the school in Haifa, the teachers were really boring. They'd talk and talk, saying the same things a hundred times. The moment the teacher entered the classroom, I'd start yawning, wanting to go to bed and sleep. The break was hardest because of the girls' shouts when jumping rope or playing hopscotch. Where was I? On the side, as close as possible to the gate. Standing and waiting to go home. Raising my head and wanting to catch a thread to a cloud that would take me to the cool forests of Bad Pyrmont. To the mysterious Philosophers Way.

I wanted to pack a small suitcase, put on a coat, hat, and gloves—don't even need a coat, hat, and gloves, maybe just a silk scarf on my head—and travel in a car with Mama and Yashu. Where? Doesn't matter.

I wanted to feel the smell of upholstery in the car, feel my soles tickle with the jolting of the car on the road, and see Shiyeh from the Community Committee, and a uniformed private driver. I saw nothing of that; we didn't even have a car in Haifa.

I missed Mama and life in the war with her sisters, the secrets and noisy parties with important people and polished cars at the window. I missed cousins and trains, for by the time I was ten I'd moved three countries, seven cities, and at least ten or twenty apartments. At every new place I came to, I learned very quickly: I had to sleep when I was awake, or pray like a Christian; show that I didn't understand anything, even when I understood very well indeed, or watch over Mama because she was weak.

At the school in Haifa, all I wanted was to sleep and to eat my sandwich and fruit.

"I understood, we understood, you understood," said the teacher, and I gazed at the hand with the chalk racing along the board, large words with punctuation, and she was already beginning a new line: "I traveled, you traveled, he traveled, we traveled..." In a flash the train journey from Hanover to Marseille returned to me.

First Mama said: "Danusha, Yashu, do you remember Ciocia Palemira?"

"I remember." Yashu jumped up and down.

"I also remember," I said quietly. "Eretz Israel." I gazed at the great darkness in the train window; it was warm and pleasant in the carriage. And how good it was to hear the choo, choo, choo, choo, choo, choo the train was making, I wanted that sound to go on all night.

We arrived at Marseille in the morning. It was hot and we changed our clothes before getting off the train. Mama wore a light suit and matching hat.

An enormous ship the size of ten buildings in Haifa was anchored in the port. I looked at the ship and worried about what would happen if it broke in two. Sank. I didn't know how to swim.

On the train I'd heard people talking about the problem of swimming in the sea. Alas for anyone who didn't know how to stay afloat in deep water. Oho, kaput, all of them.

Yashu was terrified, almost started to cry. Then he pointed at the ship and said excitedly, "Look, Danusha, there are boats on the ship, lots of little boats, do you see?" I wasn't reassured.

At the port there were many people with suitcases. They looked more or less like the people at the displaced persons' camp at Vinnhorst. Some wore a beret, or a hat; women wore scarves or shawls on their heads.

Children clung to adults and pushed in order to board the ship first. We didn't push. Mama said we'd wait quietly on the side, until there was less pressure. Our heavy suitcase stood next to us. Mama stayed erect, confident, the prettiest on the way to the deck.

Two sailors approached us. One sailor picked up the suitcase, the other gave a hand to Yashu and to me, and we finally boarded the ship. We were given a minute room called a cabin. In the cabin we each had a separate bed. Later on I understood that Mama had arranged a private cabin for us on the voyage to the Promised Land, so that we all had a comfortable place to lay our heads. Others slept in a wide, enormous, crowded, and noisy hall without windows. I heard people arguing about my-bed-his-bed-our beds, finally yelling from one corner to another, "Who's in charge here, who's in charge?!"

The ship sailed from the port with a fearful, nervous noise, and fortunately didn't fall over. Mama spoke a lot of French with the officers and those in charge and the captain. She told me that he was an educated man who spoke several languages. Yashu found a friend and a ball and that was enough for him, and I enjoyed sailing on the big sea, which was a great deal for me. I could walk along the deck and gaze at the sea as much as I wanted to. When it was cold on deck I peeped out of the round window in our cabin. The waves looked like mountains coming towards us, closer, closer, closer then disappearing. Behind them another row of waves formed, and another, and then another, for hours on end. Sometimes the waves leapt without any fixed order and that sight was also interesting and new to me. There were times when I felt bad in our cabin and went out for some fresh air and then saw too many people vomiting, yuck, yuck. When the sea was calm and the sun shining or setting, the colors of the sea were as beautiful as any of the cities, forests, and waterfalls I'd seen before from Shiyeh's car. Mama smiled at me and said, "I hope we'll see it again," and she meant the snow.

One day we stopped at the Port of Alexandria.

I was alone in the cabin. Close to the window, I peered out. A black man with a large whiteness in his eyes approached the window and peered into the cabin. I'd never ever seen someone like that.

"Mamushu, Mamushu!" I screamed in alarm and jumped back.

The man disappeared. I had time to notice that he had black hair like steel wool and something yellow on his back.

I ran on deck to find Mama. She was standing next to the black man and paying him. He gave her some of the yellow stuff he had on his back and said *banana*. Banana. The banana tasted very good.

We arrived in the Port of Haifa. Again there were many people in a small place, much noise and pushing, and piles of suitcases, and heat. Heat. I saw rings of perspiration on Mama's blouse, as well as on her forehead under her hat. She approached uniformed officers in French; she kept asking someone a lot of questions, but nobody listened to her, only gesturing to her and others to advance, advance. Mama looked at me, and I immediately grabbed a bit of her dress, holding onto Yashu with my other hand, and we started to go forwards until she found some soldiers standing on the side. She arranged her hat and approached them; we followed. I heard her address them politely in English. "Please, please," she repeated but the soldiers didn't respond.

She wiped away the moisture running down from her forehead. I didn't know how to help her and remembered Bronka. She knew better than all of us. I was worried about her and all of us. Finally Mama said as if to herself, "I must be patient. In any case, all the apartments in our building are taken."

I didn't understand her although we were talking as usual in Polish. Even Yashu spoke only Polish on ordinary days, and I didn't understand anything of what she said.

"There are tenants in our apartment," said Mama.

"So where will we live?" asked Yashu.

"Can we go back to sea?" I asked Mama.

"We'll be living with relatives until we manage," she said.

And that's what happened.

And then Mama found a villa for rent on the Carmel. The owners had gone abroad for a holiday, and we entered a house with a round veranda and plants with several kinds of cactus. The bookshelves in the living room were filled with books in German. I read some, understood little, and soon realized that they weren't for me. Yashu played chess with himself. Once he won when playing against the whites and once when playing against the blacks.

At the villa on the Carmel, Mama received a message from her sisters that Grandmother Rosa had died in Kraków. The message arrived late and so she sat with herself for a few hours, saying, "Children, quiet now, I'm in mourning." We sat beside her for several hours, I brought her water.

One day, Mama said: "Danusha, I've found a wonderful day center for girls not far from here. Let's go and see the place."

I didn't know what a day center was or what they do there, but I went with Mama to a large wood where there was a pleasant scent of pine, and swings.

Mama looked at the place and said, "An excellent day center, very suitable for you. You'll start tomorrow."

"With Mama and Yashu?" I asked quietly.

"No, no, no," said Mama. "I've found an excellent boys' center for Yashu. Just you."

"Me?" In my heart I felt like a girl without hands and feet. I didn't understand how I was suitable for this excellent day center. We left and I said to myself, I don't want to go to a day center. I don't want a day center. Don't want a day center.

I didn't stop saying the words until evening fell. Not even in my bed, at night; I continued until I fell asleep. In the morning I woke with pain in my foot. I looked at the place and saw a red swollen boil.

I said to myself, Oh, what an important boil, and called Mama.

Leaning on the pillow with my elbow, I raised my foot in the air, pointed at the boil, and said, "Mama must come and see what's happened to me. My foot is very swollen."

Mama sat panting on the bed beside me and said: "How did that happen to you?"

"I don't know, it just came and it hurts a lot."

"But you didn't have anything at all yesterday. Where did you get it from?"

I heard the anger in her voice and said quietly, "Don't know. I woke up and found it this morning. Ouch, ouch, don't touch me, it hurts."

Mama examined the bed and surrounding walls. "Maybe something stung you? There's nothing here. Get out of bed—try and walk. Maybe the swelling will go down, *nu*, get up."

I got out of bed and tried to take a step. "Ouch, ouch, ouch, it hurts. I can't." I hopped three steps on my healthy leg and returned to bed.

Over the following days I lay in bed with a bandaged foot, turning the pages of books in German that I didn't understand. Mama brought me a glass of tea in bed, breakfast, lunch, another glass of tea with a slice of cake, and supper. Sometimes she sat next to me and said, "Danusha, an apartment on the third floor of our building will become vacant soon and we'll move in. On the second floor, are you listening, there's a resident who's a dyed blonde. I of course know natural blonde, and she seems like a great gossip. Twice she's caught me on the stairs, 'Where are you from? Do you have a husband, children? What a very elegant dress, where did you buy it?' You know. I said to her, 'In Germany, Madame. And that's quite far, right?' Her husband peered out from behind the door; something was obviously wrong with him. Stay away from him. Do you want more tea?"

And then Mama imitated the voice of the woman from the second floor. Mama had a talent for imitating people. Sometimes she'd talk like a family member or acquaintance and I would immediately guess who she was talking about and we'd both laugh. Mama enjoyed preparing me food, and laughing with me. Her face looked like the face of a woman looking at a baby—sort of tender. I thought, maybe Mama likes my boil a little?

When I started treading on that foot, I said to myself, the Promised Land won't separate Mama and me either, not Haifa with its big sea and not the Carmel forests with the special day center. No one will separate Mama and me; I'll make sure of that. And I didn't know that Mama would also get used to being with me, and that when I grew up it would drive me mad, oh, how it would drive me mad, yes.

Chapter Twenty-Three

"How long does it take to cook a pot of soup on a burner? I don't understand!" Mama shouted at Bronia in Polish. I bent down to pass underneath the shouts and went to sit at my desk.

"And what's that smell stuck to the curtain? What are we, a market here?" Mama didn't leave Bronia alone, and, using the place next to the bathroom door, Yashu opened it quietly and disappeared inside.

"You talk about smell, and what was going on yesterday and the day before, ah, Madam Anna?" shouted Bronia in Hebrew, smacking the rollers in her hair. "This our time in kitchen and you not come in, yes." She bared her teeth, and again her upper gold tooth came out and she thrust it back in place with her tongue.

"Make sure you clean the kitchen, Bronia," warned Mama in Polish. "Clean it really well. Make sure you clean the sink," she said and went into the living room.

I got up from the desk and without a word followed her into the living room.

"Clean up, *khorosho*, good girl washes floor and she talk about cleanliness, cleanliness, ay, ya ya, *Bozhe moi*, Oh my God," I heard her grumbling and shifting into Russian.

The arguments didn't bother me. I managed in the little hall opposite the entrance. I had a bed under the window, a little desk with drawers, a closet with two doors, and this was in the apartment that finally became vacant on the third floor.

What actually fell vacant in our apartment was the living room and the hall: One room was still rented out to a young bachelor, who had a separate entrance; another room was rented to two sisters, Sonia and Bronia. The kitchen, toilet, and bathroom were shared—the same arrangement we had with the Sopp family in Kraków, except that in Haifa there were arguments and shouting with regard to the burners in the kitchen.

Mama slept in the living room, and the only place left for Yashu was next to Mama in the living room. There was a door there that led onto a large veranda. In the living room there was a sideboard with lovely porcelain plates, colorful glass dishes, and a carved mirror that Mama had brought from Germany. There was also a round table with chairs, a sofa, an armchair, a Grundig radio, and, of course, the piano Mama bought in Hanover. It came with us on the ship like a member of the family.

Attached to the sides of the piano were two brass candlesticks. I gazed at them from a distance for a long time. They reminded me of films I saw at the Armon Cinema about the homes of the wealthy nobility. Sometimes they reminded me of the life of our Stella, who sang at the opera or on the Zagerses's radio in Hanover.

I liked listening to concerts or excerpts from operas on our Grundig radio. I easily solved the musical quizzes, which pleased Mama and gave Bronia a headache. "That music doesn't move," she'd fume at the radio. Mama would smile at me when I knew the answer to the quiz, and I'd touch the pleat of her skirt as I did when I was little and needed to cling to her.

Once, I won a prize and my name was mentioned on the radio. The prize was in relation to *La Bohème*. Oh, I was so happy. Mama wasn't home, which upset me. While I waited for her to come back, I tidied up the living room, almost running from one side to the other with joy. When everything was in place I went to the mirror in the hall and saw that my face looked like a moon halfway through the month. There were stars in my eyes, unlike the girl I saw in the little black and white photograph I kept in a nylon packet. I have a nylon packet of many photographs from Poland and Germany, and a packet for photographs from Israel.

In the photograph from Germany, I'm sitting at the piano with notes in front of me. I'm wearing a dark dress with a round collar, my hands are touching the keyboard, and I'm looking at the camera. The sadness in my eyes seems as huge as the Mediterranean Sea. Even if I were doing it deliberately I couldn't have produced such sadness in front of the mirror.

The building in Haifa with its three floors was on Hanevi'im Street, not far from Herzl Street. I learned from the class teacher that these streets were named after people who had a dream.

I also started dreaming in Haifa. Maybe because of the sea, maybe because of the sky, but for the first time in my life I saw the sky from the edge of the west to the east, and from the edge of the north to the south, all a faded blue without the edge of a cloud. Is it any wonder that I began to dream?

In my mind, I saw exquisite palaces, turrets and curving stone steps, green gardens, and water fountains. Princes in royal robes strolled beside beautiful princesses holding parasols, their arms in long white gloves, and I had several good examples at the Armon Cinema near our house. The Armon Cinema was the most famous cinema in Haifa. It had a roof that opened up. In the summer, concerts with the Philharmonic Orchestra were held there; we heard the concerts from our veranda.

One evening I saw a film called *Carnegie Hall*. Pianist Arthur Rubinstein, cellist Gregor Piatigorsky, and violinist Jascha Heifetz appeared in the film, as well as a ballerina who danced the swan from the *Carnival of the Animals* by Saint-Saëns. I went to see that film maybe four or five times and wanted to see it again, just to make sure it came back to me in a dream.

At the Armon Cinema, I also saw a film about the life of Chopin. I couldn't stop crying. That always happens to me with Chopin. The sadness I hear in his music makes my heart ache.

In Haifa, Mama found a piano teacher for me and for herself she found a good seamstress, Mrs. Zelikowitz.

The piano nightmare returned to slash at me. I was sure Mama was already planning a list of people to invite to a concert. At long last we had a living room of our own. Mozart, Chopin, by candlelight, oh, what a successful evening it could have been. Everyone would talk about it, as they did in the Kraków living room. I didn't know, of course, that Mama would organize performances for herself instead, seated in the special armchair, wearing a blue gown, and I'd be saved from performing. However, unlike the performances, I was not saved from household chores. From the moment I returned from the great boredom of school, I'd lie on my bed and read Hebrew stories about travels around the world. Yehuda, the Hebrew teacher in Hanover, taught us to read and I also learned on my own, but it didn't help me with grammar and Bible lessons. How I loved reading about travels in exotic countries, seeing photographs of how people live in the wide world. I particularly remember the book about Mary, Queen of Scots. But then I'd hear Mama: "Danusha, wash the apartment. Why haven't you done it?"

I didn't always want to clean, and I didn't answer.

"Stop reading," she said.

"In a while."

"Do it now."

"Wait, I'm at the end of a chapter."

"Leave the chapter and get up to clean."

"At the end of the page."

"No, no, I'm waiting for a guest."

I got up to clean and saw that Mama had started a little argument with Bronia about the burners.

The guest who came to visit was talking with Mama. I heard him say that he didn't allow his daughter to help with the housework.

"I don't allow my daughter to help with the housework either," said Mama, looking at me, then returning to the guest. "Would you like a glass of tea?"

I went out to the stairwell at once. I went downstairs. I took a little walk in the street and returned to the yard. Mama should have told the guest good things about how her daughter helps in the house and is polite. I needed to hear good words. I hadn't heard any for a long time, and I missed the words I'd heard at the hospital in Germany. In the meanwhile, neither Yashu nor the crying child were downstairs.

Sometimes, a neighbor knocked on the door when I was ironing laundry. A moment before he came in, Mama would take the iron from me and continue ironing in my place. As soon as the neighbor left, she'd give the iron back to me; at first I was silent, but when I grew taller I began to shout, "Why does she take the iron away from me, so the neighbors won't see? Why does she pretend?"

"Why are you shouting? Look at your clothes scattered on the bed, and books all over the desk. Tidy this place up. This isn't a marketplace."

"She won't tell me how to arrange my books. That's my desk, mine." I stamped my foot.

"Stop shouting, do you hear me?" Mama approached and thwack, she slapped my face.

I fled to the toilet, locking the door behind me. It felt good to shout at Mama. I felt strong.

I was used to her slaps.

Once, when Mama slapped me, I ran to the toilet, grabbing a book on the way. I locked the door and sat down on the toilet to read. I came out of the toilet only after Mama said: "Goodbye, Danusha, goodbye, Yashu," and left the apartment.

After that, each time we had a fight and I saw Mama's hand rising, I escaped to the toilet or the bathroom. I locked the door and sat down on the toilet and read a book for half an hour, an hour—for as long as it took Mama to leave the apartment.

I enjoyed the quiet in the toilet. I made a habit of sitting there. If I wanted to read a Jules Verne book, I'd lock myself in the toilet or the bathroom, finishing a pile of books in this way.

Outside the toilet I barely read, as I was too busy cleaning. Mama didn't stoop to clean the house. She believed that a mother, any mother, shouldn't have to stoop in her own home, even if she dropped something on the floor. She told us that she'd heard her husband tell his mother, who had lived with us in Tarnopol: "Mama shouldn't stoop. I will pick it up for her." In those days it was the custom for men to stoop, not women, and if there were two men, the younger one stooped first.

Best of all was when I was ill. Like the case of the boil. The illnesses released me from quarrels and housework. The illnesses came one by one. A blocked nose, asthma, inhalations for sinusitis, tonsillitis, and laryngitis; every year had its laryngitis. There was also skin eczema, on my inner arms and elbows, but hardest of all was keratitis—a kind of eczema of the cornea of the eye, which started shortly after we arrived in Haifa.

This keratitis eczema was very painful and terribly itchy. I couldn't see in the light, neither sunlight nor electrical light. I'd walk in the street with my head bent, wearing dark glasses and supported by Mama.

I went with her to a job she had found in the meantime in a house for immigrants, where she cooked for the children. People in the immigrants' house asked, "Why is the child wearing dark glasses in the kitchen?"

What could I say?

Treatment for my eyes included a daily visit to the clinic. There were two doctors: Dr. Meshler, a specialist, and another doctor. They'd examine me and give me drops and ointments.

The treatment didn't help me to see. Sometimes Mama took me to a private doctor, and it didn't help. This drove Dr. Meshler crazy; he didn't like us getting advice from other doctors.

On the specialist's advice I began to receive an injection in the eyelid, the inner side, without an anesthetic. I remember the prick of a needle, and terrible pain climbing from the eyelid to the forehead, entering the skull, and a burning flame. My cheeks became wet but I didn't scream; I sat quietly on the doctor's chair as if they were giving me a candy. There were several injections of this kind—injections that didn't help.

One day I got a fever, even though the eye infection had calmed down a bit. The doctors thought the fever was healing the infection so they decided to give me milk injections in my backside to raise the fever. The milk injections were terribly painful. I wept and wept, my fever went up, and the keratitis eczema remained.

I lay in my bed in the hall most of the time. My sight was blurred; I couldn't read. I heard music and was bored for hours. Mama left for work in the immigrants' house every morning; she cooked, tidied, and returned home in the afternoon. Time stood still at home.

One day, I remember the letters Mama received from Dr. Fischer, her Berlin suitor, before she married. Her sisters had laughed at him during the war; his name only had to appear and there were small giggles. I waited for Mama to leave the house and I went through all the drawers. Finally, I found a pile of letters tied with a ribbon. She'd hidden them in the closet, underneath sheets and duvet covers. Ah, what excitement.

I opened the first letter with trembling hands; it was written in German. My sight was blurred—what could I do? What could I do? A magnifying glass. I found it in Mama's drawer. I went back to bed and tried to read one of the letters. I couldn't. I held the glass at a distance, closed my right eye, my left eye, I played with my head and the glass at the window. Finally I managed to make out some words, like *darling Anna, you're in my thoughts*. I was moved and wondered if anyone would write me letters: *Dearest Danusha, how I long for you*. I made up letters I'd receive, and time that stood still for hours and days began to be pleasant. I returned the letters Mama had received to their place and hoped for the day I could read letters from my love. I was tired. I lay in bed with closed eyes and a sore backside, telling myself, I'll have a suitor one day for sure, and this is what will happen:

...I'm sitting on a bench in an avenue of pine trees and looking at the opposite sidewalk. A tall, handsome man is crossing the street and approaching me. He is wearing a long coat, a scarf around his neck, and a hat on his head.

I rise to greet him. He holds out his hand to me and smiles. He has brown eyes, a straight nose, and a broad jaw.

We shake hands. Leaning towards me, he says, "I've bought tickets for the concert. There's still time, would you like to stroll along the avenue, or should we go to a café?"

The air is cool, pleasant. I want to stroll with him. He holds my arm, I rest my cheek on his shoulder, and he kisses my forehead, whispering, "Shall we go, my love?"

Oh, the sweetness of dreams. I also dreamed of being a famous actress. I dreamed of handsome men now waiting for me behind the scenes. I dreamed of being a great opera singer, invited to sing a duet with Maria Callas, yes. At the cinema, I saw her singing *Tosca* with the Philharmonic in Paris or Rome. She was so beautiful and majestic, with a transparent scarf on her bare shoulders, an elegant pearl necklace, and matching earrings and bracelet. I dreamed of her inviting me to come onstage, stand beside her, perform the "Flower Duet" from *Madame Butterfly* by Puccini, and Mama was wiping her eyes even before the conductor raised his baton.

How I loved watching films and hearing the English language. I understood everything without a translation. I remember the coronation ceremony of Elizabeth, Queen of England, which I saw at the cinema before I got the infection in my eyes. The film showed the Queen's travels all over the world. I wanted to sit like she did, her back erect, standing and walking with her head up, waving gently in greeting, a small, almost invisible gesture, just before the raising of the whip having time to send Mama that special smile that passed between us without anyone noticing, leaving in the carriage and horses just as the first tear reached her cheek.

I practiced a lot at home. Even though my vision was blurred I walked in front of the mirror with a book on my head, a long neck, straight shoulders. I progressed well with my practicing; it's a fact that to this day people think I'm tall because I walk like the Queen of England. I wanted to be like her when I grew up.

I continued to dream about princes even on days when the eye infection had calmed down a bit, mostly on my way to school, and even more on my way back. I was in no hurry to return home at noon. I walked slowly on purpose, but then the Arabs started firing on our home. The veranda of the living room faced Wadi Nisnas where Arabs were living.

Mama hugged me and Yashu, saying, "Children, war is starting again," and her voice trembled.

I immediately went to the closet. "Do we have to pack a suitcase?"

"No, no, no," said Mama, stamping her foot. "We aren't moving from here."

"And we're staying together," I told Yashu, pressing his hand.

Yashu peeped out of the window and called, "We've got guards, look, I can see them, and they have rifles."

"Come away from the window," said Mama, and boom, we heard firing from the other side of the street.

From that day on we began to run and hide behind buildings on the way to and from school, and this was our life until the end of the War of Independence.

Because of the shooting, we could no longer use the veranda or the living room. The young bachelor who lived in one of the rooms in our apartment left and Mama went to sleep in the inner room that fell vacant and Yashu went with her; I stayed in the hall—we just moved my bed to a wall away from the window. I wasn't afraid of that, only of the milk injections they continued to give me in my backside.

People from the Haganah came to us and put sandbags in the window facing the Wadi and also at the living room door facing the veranda. Nonetheless, a rifle bullet came in and stuck under Mama's armchair.

The main entrance to the building also faced the Wadi. Haganah people forbade us to pass there. They put a wooden ladder above the shops at the front of the building and told tenants to come and go by way of the ladder.

During these days I had to get daily treatment for keratitis eczema at the clinic. Mama and I went down from the third floor to the second, and then, "Turn around, Danusha, hold onto the window with both hands. Hold tight, don't let go, and put one foot out of the window. Yes, it's in the air, and now look for the rung of the ladder. I'm watching you, don't be afraid. Lower, straight, straight, found it? Step on it, good, and now the other foot. You can let go of the window, hold onto the ladder, hold tight… now go down slowly, slowly, foot, hand, foot hand, good, and you're on the sidewalk. I'm coming after you," and all this when both of us were wearing long skirts, Mama holding a bag in her hand, and I with dark glasses that mustn't fall, while barely seeing a meter in front of me.

People below guided us: "Right, left, straight, straight. Go back, go back," relating to the foot in the air, "now start putting it down, wait, stop. Put it down again. Why are you stopping now?"

"My glasses, wait…" I held my glasses in one hand and bullets whistled in my ears, boom, boom, boom. What could I do? I wasn't afraid, but I didn't know how to go down with one hand holding onto the ladder and one hand holding glasses.

"Don't be afraid. Let go of the glasses, we'll catch them. Put your foot down," they called up from below. "Don't be afraid," they encouraged me, and I really wasn't afraid. I was only afraid of the meeting with the doctors and the fact that they knew nothing about the illness and were experimenting with me. At the clinic I saw patients who were wounded in the war with bandages on their eyes; some were blind.

The ointments and drops they'd put in my eyes blurred my sight even more. I didn't want to stay blind. Without suitors. With all the sorrow and despair, I stopped dreaming about them. I held Mama's hand on the way home. And then that ladder again, in front of people, and I could hardly see. "Climb, Danusha," says Mama in Polish. "Shhh," I tell her quietly. "Hebrew, Hebrew," and I start to climb, while she looks for words, "Right, da, no, there… there… next, next, up, up. Bravo, a little more, up. One more," *nu* where is the window on the second floor, where is it?

One day, we came back from the clinic and it was hot and my head burned. I looked for air, approached the hall window, and heard a great silence outside. I rubbed my eyes. I bent over the sandbags and peeped out. A man in a beret lay face down on the road, motionless. Near his head was a pool of blood. The man looked completely dead. My heart sank. I wanted to shout, "Mama, come here quickly, quickly, there's a man lying on the road. He isn't moving. He's got blood on his head. He's dead. Hurry!"

I opened my mouth, but no voice came out. My eyes stung, my throat suffocated. I couldn't take my eyes off the poor man. Weeping pressed from inside me, and then a whole well poured out of me, and weeping came like a flooding river.

My shoulders heaved, my body trembled, my shirt got wet, and I felt as if I were drowning in my own tears.

Mama came up to me, glanced out of the window, and said: "Why are you crying so hard? What will his wife say? His children? Stop crying."

I couldn't stop.

"Stop it, stop it," she said, and went back to the burners in the kitchen.

I felt great pain in my heart for a person who leaves his home, and then boom. One bullet and he doesn't get up. Lies dead in the street. Like Papa. One moment he's hugging, the next he's disappeared. Where is my papa?

I wept and wept endlessly without Mama coming back and interfering with the tears. Finally, I sang in a whisper *how wonderful, how wonderful,* and wept harder. I wept my heart out, and the following day I recovered. No one understood how the miracle happened. They said, maybe it was from the antibiotics I'd received for the influenza, maybe from all that weeping that washed my eyes and took away my illness.

The doctors repeated, "Miracle, a miracle has taken place here."

Chapter Twenty-Four

One day there was a break in the War of Independence battles. It was before the Passover Festival. Loudspeakers in the street informed us that the Arabs had left and we could go out into the city without fear. I glanced into the street and I saw that the sacks on the roof of the building from which they'd fired at us had disappeared. The building opposite appeared to be empty.

"The loudspeaker is right," said the neighbor from the second floor.

"Yes, they've gone, they've gone," called the old man from the street. He wasn't afraid of anything after what had happened there, although he'd scream nervously every time he heard firing.

"Look, there's no post, no rifles, nothing," called a woman from the veranda on the first floor, pointing at the building in Wadi Nisnas.

I took a deep breath and called, "Mama, Yashu, come here,

look out of the window. They've gone; there's no more firing." Mama and Yashu peeped out through my window.

"Thank God," said Mama, "they really have gone."

"So we can put my bed back," I said excitedly, "and we can get rid of the ladder at the back."

"Why, let's leave it. It's fun climbing up the ladder," said Yashu.

"It's not fun at all."

"It is."

Mama hugged us both and sighed. "The war is over, children, another war." Tears rolled down her cheeks.

"Let's remove the bags from the window," said Yashu.

"Wait, first I want to talk to the neighbors," said Mama, without moving from her place.

I left the window and brought her a glass of water. She drank it. I took a handkerchief out of my pocket and gave it to her. She wiped her tears and smoothed her hair.

"All right?" she smiled at me.

"All right," I said and the two of us went out into the stairwell.

"Have you heard? Have you heard? The Arabs have gone, the loudspeakers said we can go out without fear," called out neighbors excitedly. "That's it, no more shooting at our building. We're done!"

Yashu went quickly downstairs. The neighbor, Mr. Bogusławski, had time to pat him on the shoulder. "At long last you can come and go through the main entrance. Are you going to try?"

"Of course," called Yashu, disappearing down the stairs.

I looked at Mama. She smiled a big smile and nodded. "With the help of God, all shall be well."

"With the help of God, all shall be well," I whispered after her, and went slowly downstairs. The door to the apartment on the second floor was partly open. The crying child was peeping out. He wasn't crying. His mother was holding onto his shoulders, and she looked at me with large brown eyes, her hair untidy around her face.

"Is it true that they've gone?" she asked me quietly. The boy nodded, yes, yes. His eyes begged me to agree.

"Yes, Madame, they even said so on the radio," I told her, glancing out the window of the stairwell. "Look, they've even taken the ladder away, which means that we can come and go through the usual entrance."

The crying child smiled at me, shrugged, hopped out through the door, and vanished in a second down the stairs.

I went downstairs to the street in front of the house. People were wandering about the stores and talking amongst themselves in several languages. I remembered the great joy I'd seen in the streets of Kraków three years earlier, at the end of the Great War in Europe. Church bells rang throughout the city, thousands of people thronged the streets, yelling, dancing, and embracing. In Haifa, people gazed worriedly at one another and frequently in the direction of the Wadi. I realized that maybe it wasn't the end, that there might be other wars.

I went home. Mr. Bogusławski and another man whom I didn't know had removed the sandbags from the hall window and the veranda door, dragging them down the stairs to the front of the building. We returned my bed to its place.

I felt good, and saw from Mama's face that we could worry less.

We celebrated the Passover Seder night with the Glatt family,

Mama's relatives who lived in Haifa. Mama thought they were good people for inviting us.

We wore festive clothes, polished our shoes, and Mama wore a special suit. I carried a bouquet of flowers and Yashu a wrapped gift.

"Surprise," said Mama, and the three of us set out on foot to the Glatt family.

Ah, how good it was to go down the stairs to the second floor, the first floor, without having to crawl out through the window onto the swaying wooden ladder. And the silence in the street—no whistling bullets and boom-boom-boom, no hiding in alleyways. How good it was to know that we wouldn't see a single dead body in the street. My heart filled with happiness to meet people who were walking in the street like us, wearing white shirts, saying "Happy Holiday, Happy Holiday," in Hebrew.

How good it was to sit around the festive table with family and read the *Haggadah*—the story of Passover—together. To sing all the songs loudly, even drum our hands on the table, and hear the same songs coming from the neighbors' verandas. Mama looked at me and Yashu, saying with moist eyes, "We are all Jews."

And, more than anything, it was good to walk in the street without itching eyes, without sunglasses, and without holding Mama's hand. I walked as upright as the Queen of England. I sat up straight in my chair at the Glatt family's house and felt as if I were sitting inside a cloud.

That night I couldn't fall asleep. Mama and Yashu fell asleep immediately—I heard their breathing. I thought about the woman with the lovely face I'd seen when I was lying with pain in my eyes. She looked at me and I saw in her face a promise for me, as if she were saying, "Don't worry, Danusha, you'll be all right, you'll get well." I knew then that she'd come to keep me safe, and I knew it would be all right. I also saw this special woman on the night I wept my heart out for the dead man in the street. And I felt as if I'd received a blow to the head. At Gertrude and Trude's house, in Bad Harzburg, a woman had appeared at my bedside at night. And it always happened on nights I couldn't fall asleep, and my whole body ached when Mama went away. And who was this beautiful woman? Had she come to comfort me?

Mama made sure I ate well. She went with me to doctors—not only one; she looked for specialists. Mama made sure I'd get the right medicine on time, and brought me a glass of tea in bed. But I felt that in her heart, she didn't really have a place for me. My brother did have a place. That's why I didn't budge from her; I so badly wanted comfort and didn't find it, even though in the Promised Land, they called me Nechama (the Hebrew word for comfort). I don't like the name Nechama. Nor Nachmush. I like Nellie; Mama called me Nellie when she brought me a glass of tea in bed, and that was nice for a minute or two, and afterwards? Again Nechama and Nechama and chchchch…

Once, a long time ago, I had a place. I had a big place in Papa's heart, and he left. And took with him the arms that hugged me and the heart that beat with joy, I'm sure because I remember the smile. He had a good smile, the best, and only for me. I could forget, I believed I'd erased it, but I couldn't really ever forget the laughter and the love I saw in his eyes when he looked at me. In all my life I have never seen eyes that looked at me like that. I longed for it. It hurt not to know and not to ask where he was, where was my father? He told me to go with Mama and he promised he'd come.

I pushed my head under the pillow and pressed it hard, where was he?

"The first days in the country were difficult, as you know," Mama told the guests in the living room.

"It was hard to obtain food. Meat, milk, fruit, and vegetables were rationed in small portions. I traveled to villages to buy eggs straight from the coop, and fresh vegetables, but the British police occasionally got on the bus and confiscated the produce that had been obtained illegally. I didn't have enough healthy food for my children.

"The shortage of vitamins mainly affected my daughter. She complained about prickling in her eyes, that the sun blinded her on her way to school so she couldn't see anything. I immediately took her to see a specialist who examined her and found strange marks on her pupils. He told me he'd never had a case like it, which of course greatly worried me.

"The child stopped going to school and we went instead to the clinic every day. The doctors tried various treatments, but nothing helped. I even took her to the famous Dr. Ticho in Jerusalem—you've heard of him, a world-famous eye specialist—and he also couldn't help us. The doctors said the illness was unknown in the country; in Europe they'd heard about it among people who lived in harsh conditions of scarcity, like dampness and no sun. They said they knew the illness developed after pneumonia. My daughter had pneumonia in Germany. I asked the doctors if there was any connection. I didn't get an answer.

"A short while before that, I'd found a half-day job at a daycare for immigrants' babies. I cooked for them and helped feed the little ones. Danusha used to come with me almost every morning because of her eye infection, naturally after the daily visit to the clinic. But the job didn't last and Danusha's infection didn't let up. The agency man informed me one day that because I had property, I had to give up my job for women who had neither property nor the means to make a living. I told the agency man that there was very little profit from the apartments and I had to support two children, one of whom had an eye infection that wasn't healing. It didn't help. So I was forced to leave my job, and in order not to waste time, I decided to learn Hebrew at an Ulpan."

Mama looked at me. I sat in my chair on the side, my eyes conveying to her that it was behind us, as she liked to say with a confident expression. On my knees was a notebook.

"How much suffering can one take?" asked Klara Cohen, looking at me. "She endured the Nazis and she endured the sanatorium, and again now?" She turned to Henia Sonnenfeld, but waited for an answer from me. I felt my face flame. I opened the notebook and wrote in large letters, *Bad girl, bad girl.*

"Anna must be made of steel, steel, poor woman," said Bertha Ketzelboim. "Can we open a window?"

"Courage, Danusha, courage," said Mr. Bogusławski, winking as he got up to open the window. When he sat down, he made a small gesture with his hand, whispering, "You aren't to blame, sweetheart."

"After the daily visit to the clinic," said Mama, waving a handkerchief before her face, "the child lay in her bed, listening for hours to classical music on the radio. She's a very musical child, like all my family. She listened to serious symphonic music, to operatic arias—she knew some of the arias before we emigrated here. I myself used to sing famous arias to the children. She loved musical quizzes and solved them very easily. I sent her answers to the radio, and her name was mentioned in the newspaper. She also learns the piano and has an excellent teacher."

"Nachas, nachas," true pride, called the men in agreement. "Congratulations," they said and Mama looked at me questioningly. I answered, No. No. I made a small motion with my head and so did she.

"Maybe the child would play something nice for us afterward?" asked Henia Sonnenfeld, taking out a fan from her bag and giving it to Mama.

Mama unfurled the fan and fanned herself with quick movements, from which I understood that an argument might start between the two of us. My heart beat in my chest. I quickly wrote in my notebook, *Lazy girl,* and at once slipped away to the toilet without a book.

Mama had warned me not to read in the toilet when there were guests in the apartment. I sat on the toilet seat slightly trembling with nervousness. I told myself, Mama won't ask you to play, calm down. She wants to get on with her story, the guests are curious. Didn't I see how their eyes were fixed on her? How Meltzer suffers, poor man, doesn't say a word, just looks at Mama. There are flames in his eye sockets. Meltzer also wants to get on with Mama's story, Bertha Ketzelboim too, they all want to get on.

One day, Meltzer arrived with socks that didn't match and he sat huddled all evening so that people wouldn't notice. Another day, he appeared with an unraveling seam in his pants, the thread dragged on the floor unraveling and unraveling, caught on a chair and brrrrrrr, the entire fold in his pants opened up. I wanted to tell him, Mr. Meltzer, what a pity, you don't stand a chance with my mama. You have no looks and no height, and neither do you have impressive prestige; you're wasting your efforts. In the meantime, I opened the toilet door slightly and peeped out. Mama was already talking about our great miracle, the penicillin treatment that supposedly helped. "The child received penicillin for the flu, which was a miracle from heaven."

I returned to my chair at the side and wrote in my notebook, *I was saved, we were saved, you were saved.*

Mama smiled at me, saying, "Just a few marks left in one eye, and thank God, they too disappeared in time. The child was saved from blindness.

"While the child was ill, riots began in the country. You already know that we had firing and casualties in Haifa. Our building was actually on the border between the Jewish and the Arab sides in Haifa. The British were positioned in the street adjacent to the stores at the front of our building. The living room of our apartment and the entrance to the building face Wadi Nisnas. One day, I was astounded to see from the veranda that on the roof of the Arab-owned building opposite, there were British soldiers who were helping several Arab men arrange sandbags on the roof. They formed a wall of sorts with narrow openings, which didn't look good. And then the Arabs began firing from there onto the street.

"The British who were still in control of the country were supposed to protect the inhabitants, all the inhabitants, but we were surprised to see British soldiers patrolling city streets in large tanks and doing nothing to prevent rioting in the streets. Ah? As if what happened in Europe wasn't enough.

"I was shocked one morning to find a bullet near my son's bed. The glass in the veranda door was shattered. The heavens had protected us. We at once moved to sleep in an inner room.

The young man who was renting the room had left. I went to the great synagogue on Herzl Street and asked them to say a prayer of gratitude in my name."

"Courage, Anna, it was the right thing to do." Mr. Bogusławski rose to his feet and Mama took the fan and fanned her face.

"As you know, the Jewish settlement did not give up the right to establish a Jewish State. Haganah people fought bravely. You can probably imagine what it meant to me to be in the country of my forefathers, knowing there were people here to protect us. Never again what happened to us in Germany, never again."

"Never again," declared Bernard Cohen.

"Never again," echoed everyone in unison.

"One day, the British left the Hadar Hacarmel boundaries," said Mama. "There was tension in the air. One announcement from the Commander of the British Army in the northern region hinted at what was about to happen. He said neither the police nor the army would intervene in clashes between Arabs and Jews. And then, you remember, the streets began to empty, the cafés as well. Stores and businesses were locked up. A great quiet fell on Haifa. That very night we heard an announcement on Kol Israel radio; I remember it to this day." Mama laid the fan on her knees, tightened her lips, and called out in a trembling voice: "The battle for Hebrew Haifa has begun…" Her throat choked. She stopped, swallowed, and rubbed her arm.

Bernard Cohen put a hand on her shoulder, saying quietly, "I'll go on, Anna." Pressing his heels into the floor, he cried: "Our roads for transportation will no longer be unprotected. Access to the port will no longer depend on rioters. The great hour we have spent weeks and months waiting for has arrived."

"I have the chills," said Henia Sonnenfeld, rubbing her arms.

"Me too, me too," whispered Klara and Bertha.

"Courage, ladies, courage," cried Mr. Bogusławski.

"Thank you," the three responded, and like the dancer Fred Astaire, he waved at them.

I looked at Mama. Her eyes were wet. I noticed that in Eretz Israel, her eyes were often wet. She gently pressed a scarf to her eyes.

"That very night loud explosions were heard," Bernard Cohen continued. "Haganah people broke through to downtown Haifa. Iraqi gangs who'd entrenched themselves in Arab houses returned heavy fire. I remember that the British police station was already in our hands the next day. Ah, it was wonderful. Finally our police could raise their heads high. Their Jewish pride and self-esteem were restored to them. They were no longer natives but real policemen. Within only twenty-four hours from the time the British left Haifa, the entire city was in Jewish hands, and this was on April 22nd, 1948, remember?"

"Hallelujah!" called out Mr. Bogusławski.

Mama returned her handkerchief to her pocket and said, "The city of Haifa was liberated, thank God. We breathed with relief. The two tenants in our apartment left, and another room was vacant. Yashu moved in. At long last, with God's help, we could begin a normal life in our city. And now, my friends, you are invited to drink tea and help yourselves to cake."

I looked at Mama, asking with my eyes, *A normal life? A normal life?*

Yes, she responded wordlessly.

I don't know a life like that, I signaled her with my head and wanted cake.

Chapter Twenty-Five

Mama wanted us to be children like the Sabras, children born in Eretz Israel, from the moment we reached the Port of Haifa. She spoke more loudly than usual on the subject, saying a hundred times, "The past is finished," ending with "What we have now is a normal life."

"Remember, a free people in our country means we are all Jews, understand?"

"No more favors from anyone, no more basements, and no running away to any other place, yes?"

"Our home is in the land of our forefathers. We're not moving from here. Yes?"

"We have a home of our own, yes?"

"We have no snow. There is sun and sky and the Mediterranean Sea, clear?"

Yashu and I would automatically say, "Yes", or "Fine".

However, every now and then she'd say, "Yes, Danusha? Do

you understand that what happened is over and we don't talk about it, and we have to be normal?"

"Did you hear me, Yashu? Did you hear that what happened is over and we don't talk about it because we have to be normal in the country of our forefathers?"

Yashu would say, "Yes, all right," so she'd leave him alone. Mama gave me some examples of normal life. The most compelling example was the swimming pool at Bat Galim. Every day, but every day, like the Sabras in the country of our forefathers, we went to the pool and got thoroughly burned, just as we should. At night she'd pour sour cream on us and freeze the burnt skin so that the next day we'd go sunburned to the pool and be just like Sabras. But it was no easy matter being like them. Every day we went like two fried meatballs—we could barely put on our swimsuits and we certainly couldn't speak like the Sabras because every part of our bodies hurt so much. And all this wasn't enough for Mama. At the end of our first summer in the country, even before the beginning of the school year, and even before the outbreak of the War of Independence, she managed to register us for summer camp at Kfar Yehoshua. Another summer camp. A month and a half after the excellent summer camp in the Carmel Forests from which I was saved by the boil on my foot.

There were woods there and a games field marked with white painted lines. At a central point of the summer camp was a notice board, a wooden table with several chairs, and two buckets of aster flowers. Sabras walked around shouting, "Hurray. Hurray. Hay. Hay. Hay."

I didn't understand this noise.

"Your children will get a lot of vitamins here, Anna," said Yoske, director of the summer camp. "That's why we're on a *moshav,* a farming collective. There's a chicken coop here, a vegetable garden, fresh milk from the cowshed, lots of vitamins, don't worry. At night, the children will sleep with well-established families on the *moshav*."

Yoske had a broad face and a large mustache. He wore a shirt and khaki-colored pants, a round hat on his head, and high work shoes. On his chest hung a metal whistle on a cord. When he talked about vitamins, he blew out his cheeks like a balloon.

"There will be a lot of activities here in the wood. Apart from that, in the large village hall the children will see performances, a choir will come, there'll be folk dancing, and more."

"Thank you, sir," smiled Mama, and I saw she was pleased.

"Yoske," he corrected her, and smiled as nicely as he could.

"Thank you very much… Yoske," Mama repeated in an irritating accent, leaning forwards to whisper things in his ear that we didn't need to hear.

Yoske nodded and it was alarming. Maybe she was talking about me and the piano in the hall for the choir and folk dancing?

I looked at Yashu. He already wanted to stay and play ball. Couldn't take his eyes off a group of children running after a ball in the playground. I wanted to go home, now.

"When do the children get up in the morning? When do they go to bed?" asked Mama, and then there was a shout. One of the children grabbed the ball from a girl leaning against a tree and ran off with it. The girl chased him but fell and started crying. Her girlfriends who were standing around her chased the boy, shouting and cursing his mother, and the boy's friends chased after the girls, shouting, "Throw us the ball, throw it, *nu,* throw it to us, you idiot."

Mama looked at them and then at Yoske, and finally at me

and Yashu. She gazed with her blue eyes at each of us in turn, as if everything here was just fine as far as she was concerned. I couldn't believe the changes in her. After all, according to how she raised us she should have said in Polish, "That's that, hold hands, children, come with me, we're going." But nothing happened apart from her waiting for Yoske to look up and see her. Yoske was busy with lists. She cleared her throat and touched her mouth with her fingers, and then completely surprised me by beckoning me to her. I kissed her cheek and Yashu did too. "Goodbye, Danusha, goodbye, Yashu," and off she went.

At the summer camp I quickly realized that the Hebrew I'd learned in Poland was different from what I heard around me. Polish and German didn't help me, and there were classes. I didn't want to participate in the game of dodgeball, or short-distance running. I didn't want to play at pulling rope, or paint, sculpt, embroider, folk dance, or play the recorder. They made me participate in social games. They had a game with chairs. The children ran around a row of chairs, one turning right, the other left, and when the counselor blew his whistle everyone had to sit down. I was out of the game in the first round. I sat on the side near a felled tree trunk and made sure that the whole line of ants safely reached their mound. I encouragingly pushed some of them with my little finger.

A counselor with two yellow braids approached me and invited me to come and paint with everyone. I sat down next to other girls at a long wooden board on a steel stand. I was given a sheet of paper. I painted a few smudges and wanted to go.

"Why do you paint only dark smudges?" asked the counselor.

I turned the paper over.

"Look at Avital's painting, see? She has a house, a yard with trees and flowers, and a nice butterfly, a sun in the sky. Maybe you could try too?"

"Excuse me, where is the toilet?" I asked quietly.

"At the edge of the wood, where the sacks are," she explained.

"May I go?"

"Sure, but come back to paint a house and sky, all right?"

Behind the sacks were planks of wood with a hole in the middle and a bad smell. I was afraid some animal would come out of the hole and bite my backside.

Toward evening, I was taken to sleep with a family who worked at a bakery. The smell of bread stuck to clothing and shoes, even blankets and sheets. For breakfast I was given two slices of thick, warm bread and a whole tomato, a hard-boiled egg, and a glass of fresh milk with a thick skin on top that made me nauseous.

And then again shouting in the woods and painful balls in the belly during dodgeball. When tugging rope I fell and grazed my knee. During the breaks I sat at the side. Yashu played with the boys—I barely saw him, even though there wasn't a door between us like the door between the girls' wing and the boys' wing at the sanatorium at Bad Rehburg.

I noticed that the children at the summer camp shouted all the time; they didn't speak but shouted what they wanted. I missed Mama and a bit of quiet. There were other girls who sat quietly. I didn't want to approach them, didn't want to hear; it was best to sit alone.

The counselors called me by the name I was given at the Port of Haifa. They said, "Come on, Nechama, come on over."

It took me an hour to realize that Nechama was me. And again, "Nechama, do this, dance, take a ball and practice." On the last day of the summer camp the counselors decided to do a play with us. I got the role of a lion. They put a heavy mask on my head and I had to prance on stage and say loudly how hard it was and what a responsibility it was to be the king of the animals.

I was embarrassed standing on stage in front of everyone. The mask suffocated me; my heart was beating in my ribs. I prayed for the nightmare to end. When it was my turn, I took a step forward, quickly said how hard it was, forgot about the responsibility, and immediately stepped back.

Mama was at the party. After the play I saw her talking to my counselor. I stood at the edge of the stage and gazed at them. Their brief glances at me, the counselor's gestures, and her cheerful ponytail that jumped from side to side, and Mama's pursed lips told me I'd given them cause to worry. They were clearly talking about the child who stood on the side, who had no friends, who didn't willingly participate in activities everyone enjoyed. And even when they gave her the important role of the lion, king of the animals, to strengthen her, she wasn't interested; it was a real pity.

Mama's lips looked like a line when she turned away from me and looked ahead. This showed me that I wasn't good enough for Mama, and I could have wept if they'd given me time to be alone during those moments.

We went home by bus. Mama didn't speak the whole way. Just once she turned to me and told me to keep my distance because I was crumpling her dress.

And then our first school year in Israel began, and normality shattered in our faces because the War of Independence broke out.

But, during that war Yashu didn't have to cry even once because he was circumcised. I didn't have to whisper even one Christian prayer. Mama didn't cover up with a country shawl to go out looking for a home for us, and she didn't hide her face from informers—only from the sun.

Haifa held fast and whole streets weren't destroyed as in Hanover; there were just holes in the walls of houses. We went down by ladder every morning to the clinic or to school, and we heard English from Jeeps driving near the building. "British soldiers," Mama told us, smiling at them, but the best sound I heard was the Hebrew spoken by Haganah people who kept us safe. About them, Mama said, "Oh, what men!"

And most importantly, I no longer heard: "You mustn't go out, mustn't talk to strangers, you don't know anything, smile, smile, and shhh, shhh."

Five months went by, and in Haifa the War of Independence came to an end. My eye infection passed, but other illnesses came. And then, one day, the teacher and some of the girls from my class came to visit me at home. I warned Mama not to call me Danusha, only Nechama. I told her not to say anything in Polish anywhere near the girls, and to take off her pretty gown—she had to wear ordinary clothes. Mama pretended to be busy creaming her eyes but a few minutes later she put on ordinary clothes and pinned a brooch to her blouse. When the girls came, I could find nothing to say to them and they talked among themselves and a bit with the teacher. Mama talked to my teacher all the time and I heard her say a few words in Yiddish and a bit in German. She stopped every now and then and they both looked at us. To this day I remember Mama's glance. It was as if she were saying, even when they enable the child to make connections, even when the teacher comes especially with nice girls, two of them very pretty, even then my daughter is silent. What will become of her, what?

On days when I was late or absent because I was ill, Mama wrote letters to the teacher in German. *Bitte es entschuldingen zu wollen,* which means, would the teacher please forgive…

The people and children around me didn't talk like that. I was sure that Mama was apologizing for me to the teacher for the unpleasantness caused by her daughter's frequent lateness and absence, how sorry she was that she had to request special treatment, and again she apologized and apologized, and so on.

Every time I brought a letter to the teacher with *Bitte es entschuldingen,* I was embarrassed, and there were many letters.

How angry I got at home; no one in class brought letters with words like that. They simply say, I confirm that my daughter had to go to the clinic today, and that's it. And my anger was of no use. I told her I wanted a simple, ordinary letter, like everyone else, without words in German and without appearances at the clinic in elegant suits. Honestly?

What I wanted most was to be all right, like Yashu, more or less.

One day, there was a party at school. We sat in the form of a U and sang an Israeli song. The children shouted and made a noise; the teacher couldn't stop the noise and I saw she was despairing. I also found the noise hard. I slammed my hand on the table and cried out: "Quiet!"

Everyone looked at me.

"Nechama, once more and you'll leave the classroom," shrieked the teacher, and there was quiet. At that moment I wanted to be ill with boils in my ears and on my back.

Teachers usually related well to me. Mrs. Daniel, the English teacher, put me in the first row because I knew English better than the other students. Mama had spoken English in Hanover, and I quickly absorbed the language. Mrs. Daniel knew I was bad at the Hebrew subjects and she decided that I was a lazy child. I felt it was an advantage to know English and that there was a chance I'd progress in Hebrew. The teacher looked at me with suspicious eyes; I was satisfied.

English didn't help me. My fourth grade report card was bad. Teachers said there was a big difference between my ability, which was obvious to everyone, and the grades on my report card. My brother who attended Yavne School managed well in his class.

At the end of fourth grade, Mama thought that the dark Beit Ya'akov wasn't suitable for me and transferred me to Leo Baeck School in Haifa. The head teacher tested me:

"Who was the first king?" he asked.

"King David," I said, and was held back a year. Another year in fourth grade. Mama was very ashamed, I less so.

Leo Baeck School was a Reform Jewish school, and boys and

girls studied together. The transition from an orthodox Jewish school was hard. At Leo Baeck boys wore a kippa only when studying Torah and when reading the Psalms every morning. The other lessons were as usual. At Leo Baeck, students and teachers said "Adonai"—my God—while at Beit Ya'akov we didn't say the specific name and prayed singing to "Adon Olam" —Master of the Universe. Worst of all was being put next to Efraim whose breath smelled. I felt it was wrong to sit next to a boy and even more so because his breath smelled. Every time Efraim opened his mouth, I at once turned my head away. Sometimes I didn't have time and wanted to vomit.

Mrs. Livne, my class teacher, discovered I had a pretty voice and suggested I sing in the choir. Maybe Mama told her I came from a very musical family. In literature lessons, when they read prose or poetry, I read well. At the end of the year I read in front of the whole school. My experience in Kraków where I stood on a chair and recited before Grandma Rosa didn't help me. They didn't ask me to read again. I was afraid that normal life was starting to evade me and that the Bat Galim pool and being sunburned like a fried meatball wouldn't help me for very long. Nor would sour cream before bedtime.

At Leo Baeck School, teachers took an interest in each and every child's order and cleanliness; they took most interest in me, maybe because of the clothes I wore, which were wrinkled and stained with sour cream and my peeling skin.

I wore the same underwear for a week and it had a smell; I didn't relate to it, and maybe the teachers sensed something. My schoolbag was messy and smelled of rotten apple or stale sausage.

One day, I tripped, fell on my knee, and bruised it. My schoolbag opened in front of the deputy head who was passing by at that very moment. Crumpled notebooks, blunt pencils, paper with scribbles and bits of dry sandwich fell out onto the ground. The deputy head remained standing, looked at the ground, at me, and again at the schoolbag, and asked me which class I was in, and my class teacher's name.

My cheeks flamed and I was ashamed. I looked down. I saw that several other children had stopped nearby. My knee hurt as I put everything back in the bag. I said to myself, now the deputy head knows what Mama and Hanchka said about me in Hanover, clumsy girl.

I went home. Did I tidy my schoolbag? No.

I felt that this schoolbag, with its scribbled papers and smelly remains of food, was appropriate for someone like me who wasn't worth anything; that's what I saw on Mama's face in relation to myself, that's all.

And I had no friends.

I returned to the mirror I knew in Brzeżany. I looked at myself and pretended that the girl in the mirror was my friend and she looked only at me. And what does she see? A head and bushy hair, eyebrows all right, a round face, ordinary nose, but that isn't important. What is important? Mouth, lips.

The girl in the mirror closely observes my lips and likes them. So I open my mouth a little, close it. Purse my lips, straighten them. Smile a small smile, closed mouth, stretch it a little, make it smaller, stretch it again, until I find a smile that is the right size, a smile like Mama's. And then I straighten my neck and shoulders and speak to the girl in the mirror, for instance, "You know you can find good clothes at Gabrielli's on Herzl Street."

"Really?" answers the girl in the mirror, "and how much do they cost?"

"Rather cheap. And you should know that the selection at Bata Shoes isn't bad at all."

And then I pause and say again, "There isn't a bad selection at Bata Shoes," but without moving my cheeks. I almost succeed, and I'm pleased. Mama made sure to speak with small motions. I never saw her laugh loudly and didn't see her frown, "Because facial expressions give you ugly wrinkles, Danusha, and you have to look after your skin, understood?"

Chapter Twenty-Six

I couldn't live a really normal life with the disappointment I brought Mama at every opportunity, and nor did Mama's stories in the living room add normality to my life.

I'd sit on my chair at the side, an arithmetic notebook on my lap, while Mama spoke. I couldn't always listen to her; I tried to find the common denominator between a third plus a ninth. *Nu,* how do you make a common denominator, and what do you do, and why is a common denominator actually necessary? I have no common denominator with Yashu and we get along fine. I don't share a common denominator with Mama either and we get along if there's no choice, and even if there is. Wait, maybe war is a common denominator for all of us, and you don't need numbers for that; there are enough words. In the meantime, I listen to how Mama tells about our leaving Brzeżany. I listen with half an ear, and again she makes no mention of her sister Bronka. Why is that?

I tap on my notebook with the pencil point. It breaks when I remember Bronka's face and the shawl on her head when she came from Kraków especially to take us away from Brzeżany. She accompanied us to the house of Mrs. Yuzchynska, in Lwów, and Mama says nothing about her, nothing?

I give up on common denominators and toss away the notebook. As far as I'm concerned, I won't finish my matriculation exams, just as Mama didn't finish, though Bronka did.

"Yashu also had trouble during the war and why are you the only one who stays back a year?" Mama asked me after the guests had left the house, and I didn't have a polite answer, only grief and rage because she'd hurt me and forgotten to speak about Bronka who had saved us in Brzeżany.

I spent two years in fourth grade and then I improved. Apart from arithmetic, I also did well in singing classes.

At the end of fifth grade, the head master suggested putting me straight into seventh grade if I studied all summer. He explained that I was tall for my age and stood out, even if I sat at the back of the class and leaned on the desk. I accepted his explanation, and only I knew that I frequently didn't go into the yard at break time because when I stood up, my height was only too obvious and I was embarrassed. I'd walk quietly along the wall and stand not far from the seventh grade girls. My height suited seventh grade.

All summer, I read the Book of Amos and at the end of the vacation they tested me. I knew that Amatzia was the High Priest of Beit El, and Jeroboam the King of Israel. I also knew that Amatzia told Amos, *"O seer, go, flee away to the land of Judah,"* and

I passed into seventh grade. At long last I looked as if I were more or less the height of children in the class.

One day, the supervisor came to our classroom during a Bible lesson.

He asked a question: "Was it appropriate to crown a king in Israel?"

I put up my hand to give my opinion, and before I'd finished explaining why royalty brought about a terrible rift among the people, the Bible teacher stopped me to ask another question. The following lesson, the teacher came up to me, smiled, and said: "Listen, Nechama, the Supervisor was sorry I didn't let you finish your answer. He thinks you're a deep thinker, that's what he said in the teachers' room."

I blushed immediately. A deep thinker? Me?

"Thank you, teacher," I said quietly. My heart filled with sugar.

I didn't tell Mama, but for the first time in the Promised Land, and after almost four years at school, I climbed onto the table at home. Mama was out and Yashu wasn't there either when I started walking up and down in front of the mirror and I saw stars in my eyes, even though it was the middle of the day.

Before the end-of-year teachers' meeting, I warned Mama not to wear heels, "And without a lot of color on her eyes; everyone dresses simply, you too," I asked. "Besides, I'm not happy in class anyway…"

Mama didn't say a word and an hour or two later asked, "No suit?"

"No suit. The blouse and skirt you wear to work."

When we went in to the teacher, she told Mama what the supervisor had said, emphasizing that the Bible teacher had asked to make it clear. I looked at Mama but she smiled at the teacher with her mouth closed. The teacher also said a few good words about my polite behavior and then we got up and left. Mama didn't say a word: not in Hebrew or French or German or English, not even in Polish, nothing. Shh. I thought, even when strangers were impressed by me she lost all the words in all the languages she knew.

By the time we got home without a single word, I didn't believe I'd ever lead a normal life in the Promised Land, or any other land. It was a fact: I felt nice with Mama's friends, and ignored Mama when she looked at me.

We sat in a café at least once a week; I sat quietly on the side. I drank a glass of tea and ate a slice of cake I chose from the display window, a *cremeshnitte*, or *Sabrina*. Mama's friends talked about someone who didn't have enough of it, and someone else who wanted this as well as that. They talked a lot about men, sharing who was worthy, who wasn't. They laughed amongst themselves and winked at me. Occasionally they looked for a good match for war widows in the city. They made a lot of matches at that table and the matchmakers would receive a little gift for every *Mitzvah*, good deed. Mama didn't receive little gifts for making matches. Years later she received big gifts for helping people get the compensation they deserved from Germany. That's what she called it, compensation for victims from Germany. But she seldom spoke about this with her friends or anyone else. "It's a very good deed," she'd tell me before going to Germany. "Goodbye, Danusha, goodbye, Yashu."

Mama said I was growing up, and I couldn't bear the preoccupation with bodily changes. "Oh, what a developed young girl," the shop lady would say, fixing her eyes on my chest. I felt as if I were burning inside. I'd immediately close the curtain of the changing cubicle tightly, pressing it up against the wall.

"Open the curtain, Nechama," said Mama.

"Not opening it."

"The shop lady has found an excellent bra for you."

"I don't need a bra."

"Stop playing games. Open the curtain and be done with it."

"Not opening it."

"We'll be late for the doctor, Nechama, do you hear me?"

"So make that shop lady stop looking."

"*Nu*?"

"Give it to me, I'll do it alone," I said, putting out my hand from behind the curtain to receive the bra.

I was ashamed of my chest that was developing fast and I was ashamed of my height that again stood out. At the time it was common to think that a woman who was too tall wasn't pretty enough. I only looked at my face in the mirror; I knew it was important for a woman to be beautiful. I had long dark-red hair. Mama's friend looked at me and said that the color titian suited blue eyes. I tied up my hair and boys in the class looked at me. If a boy knocked into me during break or pulled my hair, I'd run to the toilet and wait there until break was over. Even random glances from boys embarrassed me; it was as if they were touching me with their eyes. I couldn't bear it, not even when I grew up.

I was also embarrassed at the cinema. Every time a man and a woman came closer to kiss, I'd look down. I felt as if I were in the picture and the man on the screen wanted to touch me.

I felt bad in class. More than anything, I was ashamed of

wearing a bra. The boys would steal up behind me, pull the elastic of the bra and run off. I always tried to stand with my back to the wall.

I didn't want to grow up. Preoccupation with monthly menstruation tired me. I got my sex education from Mama—in a two-minute walk in the street.

"Tell me, Nechama, did the young man do anything to you?"

"What young man?"

"The one who lived in our apartment, did he do anything to you?" I understood she meant the young man who once lived in one of our rooms. He had a separate entrance and he'd left long ago. Why now?

"I asked you if he did something."

"Something?"

"You know by now," she said.

"No, I don't know what Mama's talking about," I said, lengthening my stride in the street. She caught up with me. "Did he put anything inside you down below?"

"No," I whispered, alarmed by her and what she was saying.

Mama made a disbelieving gesture with her head, and I received no further sex education—not from her or anyone else. That night I couldn't fall asleep with all the thoughts rushing about my mind. Could the young man have put something inside me without my feeling it? Could someone put something inside without my feeling it? Doesn't it hurt? I had no one to ask. I kept an even greater distance from boys.

Whenever a boy knocked into me by chance, even if he were tall and good-looking, I'd think he was disgusting, smelly, or that he had a large nose, dirty fingernails, and yellow in his ears, and I'd run away.

But I couldn't run away from Mama's guests. Not from Mr.

Bogusławski or from Mr. Cohen or Ketzelboim or Sonnenfeld. They were always sitting with us in the living room, and it was impossible to move them anywhere. Sometimes, they'd look at me when I rose from my chair and then someone would say, "Anna, how have you kept our princess hidden? What a child! Take her to a photographer and get some pictures taken," or "What's this, Anna, she needs a groom, at least a European prince. The child can go straight to your closet." Things like that.

Mama would respond half-angrily, sometimes really angrily, and I realized that the taller I got, the angrier she got.

"You're jealous of me," she threw at me at the end of an argument between us, let's say about tidying the room, which was harder than any random encounter with a boy at school. In my heart I felt she was angry about my appearance, even in a harangue about the mess in my desk drawers.

My room was a mess, but this was the situation in our home, and not only in the drawers. The clothes in closets were thrown on top of each other in a pile, newspapers and books were scattered on the beds and the table, and shoes were tossed in the middle of the room with socks here and there.

Mama used to say it was Bohemian disorder, like her parents' home in Kraków. She was rather proud of her Bohemian disorder, but we couldn't find socks and underwear. And then, one day, some random day, she'd decide to make order in one of the corners and take the opportunity to throw things that were mine straight into the garbage can. How I hated the days of order and organization.

"Why does she throw out my notebook without asking? I need that notebook. Why doesn't she ask me?" I yelled at her on one occasion when she'd thrown out an important notebook.

"Stop shouting, you monster. Stop it."

"I'll shout as much as I like, and she'd better not touch my things again."

"You're jealous of me," she said, and left the room.

"Ahhh?"

Her words were like sandpaper on skin, kchch and kchch and kchch. I had skin problems anyway; I got strange rashes on my arms and they itched.

Sometimes, we went to lie down at noon and I'd fall asleep. If there was a ring at the door, she'd shout from her room: "Danusha, get up and open the door. Danusha? Can't you hear there's someone at the door? *Nu*, get up and see who it is."

I got up. Opened it. Closed it. And I began to shout at her. I shouted in the evening, in the morning, at noon; it felt good. The moment I started shouting, Mama would turn her back on me and fall silent. It was as if she were telling me, talk to the wall, but I saw that the muscles in her back were listening hard, very hard, and I had a lot to say to her. Sometimes she'd close a door between us, the kitchen door, bathroom door, or the bedroom door. It felt bad standing with my nose to the door, but I didn't stop shouting.

When Mama complained about my room I shouted most of all. When she said to me, you're jealous of me, I shouted less, or fell silent. I could find no words to respond to that.

One evening, I went to the cinema alone. I saw a film about Marie Antoinette and they guillotined her. I couldn't stop crying. One moment she was a lovely, famous queen whom everyone respected, and then boom. A guillotine to the head and no Marie and no Antoinette.

I cried during the film and I cried on the way home. I hid my face when I got home, and then I cried into my pillow, and the next day. I wept for Marie Antoinette as if she were a beloved member of the family who was lost to me forever. I thought about my family. We had lived quietly in Tarnopol, Eastern Galicia. Mama had told us about the pretty three-story house we had there. The store with its many clients. I saw from the pictures I'd kept in the nylon packet that Papa was a tall, broad-shouldered, and handsome man. He was wearing a good three-piece suit, a tie, a long coat, and a hat with a broad band like Clark Gable, and he had a pipe in his hand.

In the picture, Mama was standing next to Papa. She was wearing a thick fur coat, an elegant hat, and a gold chain. She had a small bag and pointed high-heeled shoes. They were both looking at the camera as if they enjoyed their lives. I have another picture in the packet, from the time I was a baby—perhaps two or three months old. Mama was holding me in her arms, my head resting on a soft pillow embroidered just like the lace dress I was wearing. A long dress delicately gathered at the edge. I look like a sweet, special princess. And then boom! I feel Marie's guillotine on my head.

Is it any wonder I couldn't stop crying? Afterwards I felt better.

Chapter Twenty-Seven

One day, Mama went to Tel Aviv and I stayed with Yashu, as had happened before. It started off as an ordinary day that ended with a surprise for me. Mama was forty-five, and that night she walked near the telephone and waited for it to ring. She'd approach, wait, and again walk away, like the films at the Armon Cinema when the woman wanted someone very badly. When she returned from Tel Aviv she didn't sit down to drink or eat. She barely said a word to friends who called her on the phone.

"Don't worry," I said, "the phone will ring in a while."

"Why does it take him so long?" Mama wondered in a weak voice, and looked at me. I saw worry in her eyes and her fingers that pushed against each other. Yashu followed me into the kitchen, asking quietly, "Who takes so long? What's she talking about?"

"We'll hear soon," I answered, and he went back to his room.

I brought tea to the living room and two small cookies.

"No need," she said, waving it away. "You drink it," she added, stroking the telephone.

"Where did I put my lipstick? Have you seen it, Danusha?"

I brought her one I found in the bathroom.

Mama opened the lid and immediately frowned.

"I had a dark red one. Have you seen it?"

I went to look for it in her drawer. I wanted to encourage her, even though I knew you don't need lipstick when you pick up a phone, but I wanted her to calm down.

Finally, the phone rang and it was less than a minute after she'd put on the dark red lipstick. Mama laughed all the time, saying, "Yitzhak…" and laughing again, "Yitzhak… Yitzhak…"

Yashu came and sat down next to me in the living room. We raised eyebrows at one another. Yitzhak? And then we heard them deciding that Yitzhak would come to us in Haifa at the end of the week.

Mama bought new clothes for herself and for us. She bought flowers. She put a special embroidered table cloth on the table and set it beautifully for Shabbat.

Yitzhak came to us with roses, and from the moment he came in they couldn't leave each other alone. They embraced, laughed, whispered secrets in the living room, as if they were alone in the house. Right after the first coffee, they went into Mama's bedroom, closed the door and stayed there for hours. Yashu and I remained sitting alone in the living room. From the laughing we heard, I knew that Mama was happy and I felt miserable.

The thought of Yitzhak touching Mama drove me nuts. I said to Yashu, "Mama's in the room with Yitzhak. You're lucky to have a room to yourself."

Yashu looked at me as if this was nothing new, and went to open the refrigerator, took a peach, and went to his room.

I stood close to Mama's door, went away, back to my corner. My mind flew back to Mama's room and then to the desk. I couldn't concentrate on the book. Although Yitzhak was as handsome as a film star, tall, with a long face, straight nose, thick eyebrows, and full lips, I believed that games behind a closed door were something ugly and forbidden.

Mama had taught me that a woman should be clean and pure. She didn't say so openly, but that's what I understood from what she and her friends spoke about in the café or things she said to the seamstress, Mrs. Zelikowitz, who came to our house. Every time the two mentioned a woman men courted, I heard Mama say angrily: "She isn't a respectable woman and if anything happens to her, it's her fault because she's made herself a laughing-stock."

Mrs. Zelikowitz clicked her tongue and agreed with Mama.

I listened to every word Mama spoke, and vowed I'd never let a man make a laughing-stock out of me, and that's that.

Even in Kraków, in Franca's apartment, near Mama and her sisters, I heard how women sometimes made a laughing-stock of themselves. When Grandma Rosa said I had a Galician temperament, I understood this to be promiscuous behavior. Even then I thought to myself that men would not touch me, no matter what. Mama's conversations with Mrs. Zelikowitz reinforced my belief that a respectable woman shouldn't make a laughing-stock of herself.

I was certain that Mama, too, wouldn't allow a strange man to touch her. But then Yitzhak appeared, a broker at the diamond exchange, the son of a wealthy, privileged family from Kraków who'd lost his wife and little daughter in the war and had immigrated to the country with nothing.

I returned to the living room. I looked at the closed door of

Mama's room and said to myself: "She's betraying everything she taught me. She's a betrayer. I will never believe her again."

I felt like an orphan. From the day I remember myself, I haven't budged from Mama; we slept in the same bed, we were together in the same rooms, for two years I stood beside her in Helmut and Toni Sopp's kitchen and watched her. I went with her to meetings, waited for her until she finished work. I only parted from her at the Bad in Germany, and this was because it was important for health and recovery. In Haifa, we went to the clinic every day together, never a space between us. Mama also had a lot of errands, but from the moment she returned home, no door had ever closed between us, not even when the tenant left and Mama moved from the living room to the bedroom. I knew her breathing, I knew when she fell asleep, when she was pretending. I didn't get annoyed for no reason when she'd call me, "Get up and open the door," waking me up although she wasn't asleep.

And now a strange, tall man from Tel Aviv appears in our home. He makes no impression on me with his sad eyes. I have enough with my own heart and eyes. I hear secret sounds and they come out for a drink of water, maybe the toilet. I peep out: Mama is in the passage, smiling to herself, not even looking at me, and her cheeks are a burning red. Yitzhak also has a red mark on his neck. And then without a word they return to the room, closing the door again and laughing, hee, hee, hee, aay, shhh, shhh. Shhh, shhh.

Where am I? Alone in the living room.

The book is closed on my lap, the Grundig radio is turned off, neither the mirror nor the window interest me. In my ears I hear the waves of the Mediterranean Sea, wash, wash, wash. In the end, I'm tired of all the tension and go into the kitchen, and boom. I knock into the table and hit my knee; annoyed, I push the table, open the cupboard, take out a tin of biscuits, take a handful, bend down to put the tin back, and boom. I hit my head on the cupboard door, ouch. I shout and grab my head; the lid of the tin flies out of my hands and screeches along the floor.

I peep out of the kitchen. Mama doesn't come. The door between us remains closed.

I wanted to kill Yitzhak. And it didn't help to hear in the café what Mama's friends thought. According to what I heard, the time had come to live a normal life, which meant falling in love with a man from a good family and finding a friend for this life—what else was left?

I sat on the floor at a distance of four or five feet from the door to the room that seemed like a wall, and imagined how I'd kill him with a sword. Imagined him standing in the yard of the building, myself approaching from behind, and wham! I cleave him in two. There was also the possibility of leaping upon him and choking his neck with both hands, not stopping until he grunts and dies. No, no, better the hangman's rope. I'll throw a rope over the branch of a tree in the yard, make a loop around Yitzhak's neck, let's say while he's sitting on the grass and smoking a cigarette. Yitzhak smoked incessantly. If I pull hard on the rope, he'll remain hanging with a cigarette between his fingers.

I couldn't fall asleep at night for thoughts about Yitzhak's approaching death.

One night, Yitzhak came out of the room without his underwear. He thought I was asleep. I saw him walking naked to the bathroom and closing the door behind him.

I froze in my bed. It was the first time in my life I'd ever seen a man without underwear. I felt a terrible disgust; I wanted to vomit. That picture didn't leave me. For years I shrank from approaching a naked man. It nauseated me.

"How are you feeling?" asked Yitzhak on his and Mama's wedding day. I lay in bed with laryngitis, but Mama had decided we wouldn't go to the doctor.

I turned my head to the wall.

"Do you have a fever?" asked Yitzhak, bending over me.

I was silent.

"Would you like a glass of tea?"

I was silent.

"A slice of cake?"

I was silent.

"I'm sorry you're ill. Feel better, Danusha," said Yitzhak, gently patting my shoulder.

"Nechama," I told him.

"What?" he asked.

I was silent and he went to sit in the living room with Yashu.

I lay in the hall with a high fever and said to myself, nothing to do with me. As far as I'm concerned, let their party be ruined.

They were married by a rabbi and then came back to celebrate at home. Mama and several friends had prepared food in advance—sandwiches, apple compote, cakes, and cold tea.

And then came the time to celebrate my brother's bar-mitzvah. Like the wedding, several friends of Mama and a few relatives came to celebrate; Mama's sisters and my cousins hadn't yet immigrated to Israel.

I remember my brother standing in front of the ark in the synagogue. Yitzhak stood next to him while he said his speech. I was moved by the picture I saw, and saddened too. I was sorry my brother was doing the ceremony with a step-father.

After a while I got used to Yitzhak. I drove out the thoughts of the death I'd prepared for him.

In the meantime, Yitzhak moved to Haifa and looked for a job. He and Mama decided to build him a kiosk at the entrance to the building in which we lived. I told Mama that it wasn't a good idea to open a kiosk; there was already one nearby, and we heard that the owner was angry with Mama. My brother was in favor of opening it.

The kiosk opened. Yitzhak sat there and sold chocolate, wafer cookies, and cold drinks. I also sat there sometimes, Mama too, but I was ashamed to tell people we had a kiosk.

The work in the kiosk didn't appeal to Yitzhak. He said he was tired of waiting for clients.

Neither did he want to sit in the living room and listen to Mama's stories; he'd go into town in the evening and wander around. That's what I heard him say to Mama and she didn't ask any more questions.

One day, he decided to return to Tel Aviv, coming only on the weekends, always with a bunch of pink gladioli. For years I hated gladioli.

From the moment Yitzhak came in, quarrels started between him and Mama. I think she was angry with him for deciding to leave us and return to Tel Aviv.

Saturday meals became largely a nightmare. Yitzhak was angry, Mama cried, and I of course was on her side. If he thought

I was laughing at the blessing, he'd get up to slap me, and I'd immediately escape and run around the table, and he'd run after me with a broom. Yashu would look down at his shirt and I saw he could barely hold back his laughter.

I'd at once escape to the toilet with a book my brother received for his bar-mitzvah. They didn't give me a bat-mitzvah.

I read *The Human Comedy* by William Saroyan, *Quo Vadis* by Sienkiewicz, and *Shakespeare for Children*—plays written like stories.

Mama said that Yitzhak was agitated because of his great suffering during the war. Towards the end of the war in Europe, he'd gone with his brother to Romania on business. His wife and daughter remained behind in Kraków. When he returned, he discovered that the two had been sent with other relatives to an extermination camp. This tragedy haunted him for years. After the war, he and his brother immigrated to Eretz Israel. A short while after this, his brother died from heart disease. Mama said that this was the reason he chain-smoked, and why he sometimes needed a broom in his hand.

When we had guests, Yitzhak and Mama didn't fight—things were even pleasant. There were conversations, some laughter. We had quite a few guests and when they left, the anger returned to live with us. I'd hear how Yitzhak would flare up behind the locked door of Mama's room. Within minutes there was flaming fire in Polish.

I wanted to sit with Yashu but he went out with friends.

In time, I realized why Yashu was outside all the time. Why he couldn't stay home for an hour or two. He never spoke and I was ashamed to ask, but I thought that after being closed up in a cold, dark cellar with *Goyim*, gentiles, for two years, he had to have light and life outside—as much outside as possible. After two years with strangers, with the constant fear of being alone, he had to play every single day with friends he loved. Go on trips with them, come back and find them again the following day.

I also understood that Mama was disappointed in Yitzhak because he didn't say nice things to her and as she saw it, he didn't appreciate her. From him I understood that she got on his nerves with her complaints about his returning to Tel Aviv. He would yell at her furiously and she didn't stay silent; she got under his skin with sand paper, as she did to me.

I couldn't bear the nastiness between them. I'd cover my ears with a pillow and press hard, but I could still hear them getting tired of each other.

Every Sunday, Yitzhak left the house.

The door to Mama's room would open and stay that way all week. We went back to being together. Sometimes we lay in the living room, Mama on the sofa, I on the armchair that opened out —the story chair. We'd talk quietly about guests who'd been with us on Saturday.

"Danusha, did you see Mrs. Fischer's ornament, the one with the wig? That ornament isn't real; it's *echte matsia,* fake. And how she pretends to be rich." Or she'd tell me she met someone in the street and she'd imitate his voice mockingly; I'd quickly guess who it was and we'd both laugh.

And then, "I'll take you to a café on Nordau when I go to meet my friends," she promised me.

"But when?" I asked every time she promised.

"Tomorrow. No, the next day. Next week at the latest."

"Next week?"

"Maybe even before."

And she didn't take me. She went alone. In a bad mood, I

waited for her to return from the café. I glanced out of the window and listened at the door when I heard steps on the stairs —was it Mama?

"Wasn't that great? Just as well you didn't come with me," she said when she returned that evening, but in my disappointment, I didn't say a thing.

Once, to make it up to me for something, Mama went out, saying she had a surprise for me.

I waited and waited; I was very curious. I wanted to hope, maybe Mama had bought me a new blouse? Maybe a chain or a bracelet? I stuck to the window, looking out at passersby—was it her?

When I heard her coming up the stairs I waited at the door, jumping with excitement. Mama opened her bag, took out an envelope, and gave it to me. I sat on the sofa and carefully opened the envelope. It was a photograph of Mama.

"Look how photogenic I am. It's a good photograph, isn't it?" she asked, looking at me.

Mama. Mama. Mama. Mama. Mama.

Where am I?

I'm on my way to Sarah. Sarah saved my life.

Chapter Twenty-Eight

Sarah has kind eyes like enveloping velvet. Her hair is short, curly, and she's tall. Sarah wants to be my friend. She sits next to me in class, and she asks to be my friend. I ignore the offer. Sarah doesn't give up. We leave class together in the direction of home. We walk slowly so we have time to say everything in our hearts.

Sarah and I have known each other since ninth grade. She was born in Israel and is the only daughter of divorced parents. She lives with her mother, a handicrafts teacher, and their home is quiet—no guests. Sarah came to visit me at home, and one day she decided I should be tidier. She threw out papers from my drawer, old notebooks, torn wrappings, paper packets with bits of sandwiches, and fruit peels; she threw out piles, naturally after asking me about each thing. "Can I throw this out, Nechama, is it all right?"

"The teacher most certainly told her to tidy your drawers," said Mama, after seeing my spotless desk.

"She most certainly did not," I told Mama. "Sarah decided to do it on her own."

Mama didn't believe I had a friend; she thought she was my only friend. I also knew nothing about friends, apart from Mama's friends. Mama thought it was natural for Yashu to have many friends; he would go to Bnei Akiva—the Youth Movement —and everyone wanted to be close to him. She thought that it was natural that only she should want to be close to me, and my relationship with Sarah seemed strange to her.

In high school I was rather irritating because I was the righteous one in the class. During exams students would copy from one another, from me too—I was considered good in Humanities. The issue of copying angered me. I even argued with students about it, and they got really mad at me. I was almost the only one in class who thought like that, which amused Sarah.

The teacher called me the class conscience. I was chosen for the class committee by a majority of votes. I was head of the committee, which didn't change a thing during the breaks. Nobody wanted me to join their group. There was only Sarah. She tried to make me laugh, which made me feel good.

I remember the first time I visited Sarah.

"Where is the toilet?" I asked.

Sarah showed me and waited for me to finish. Then she asked, "Do you want something to eat or drink?"

"No, thank you," I hurriedly answered, and it was so good to hear, "Do you want to eat or drink something?" And all this without my even being sick in bed. I saw in her eyes that she really was interested in me and wanted me to feel good. In time I began to visit her after school and later on the Sabbath as well. I walked from Hadar to Bat Galim, and it was a long way. I left behind Mama and Yitzhak's crazy shouting, and Sarah's home became a place of healing for me.

Sarah and I had long talks. We spoke about girls' issues, friends, and clothes. She listened to me with her whole body, engaging her shoulders and hands to draw me near her. In my heart, I already knew, no matter what I did, Sarah would love me either way. Like Papa. Sarah was the only one I told about him. I spoke about him more softly than usual, and Sarah thought it came from a place that was sacred to his memory. I looked at her, and she nodded gravely. I told her about the walks we took together in the fields. About the songs he taught me. I sang, *How wonderful, how wonderful that there are nights like these,* and Sarah held my hand and felt how cold my fingers were and how they trembled, and then I told her that her kind heart reminded me of missing my father. Sarah was moved to tears and so was I. Something opened up in me. I wept and wept.

We sat on the sofa in the living room; we were alone. A record of the "Queen of the Night" aria from Mozart's *Magic Flute* was playing on the gramophone. I told Sarah how I killed Papa in my heart, and how I didn't realize I was killing a living nerve inside me. The Gestapo executed Papa, and I killed him at the railway station in Brzeżany and have never wept for him since. When I parted from Papa, a great darkness fell on me, without a single star, I told her. I couldn't find one reminder of him within me—no voice, no picture.

The record ended. Sarah asked if she could put it on again. I nodded and closed my eyes.

And then Papa came to me.

...There's a path, and there's snow. A house, surrounded by a yard. Papa is standing in the yard near the gate. Mama is standing at a distance; my brother and I are standing beside her.

We're preparing to leave. I'm very small, maybe five, and I'm crying.

And then I disengage from Mama, run to Papa screaming, *Tatusho, tatusho, tatusho...*

Papa holds out his arms to me; his cheeks are wet and he holds me tight, both of us weeping to the heavens. I can't see out of my eyes for weeping, and I hug Papa's neck tightly, shouting *Tatusho, tatusho, tatusho* ... where is my *tatusho*...?

That evening I asked Mama if Papa said nice words to her.

"Yes, he was a good man," answered Mama, holding onto the back of the chair.

Once, I had enough of Sarah and we were cross with each other. She put a pencil box between us so I wouldn't touch her half of the table. But then, unintentionally, I touched her side with my elbow. Sarah looked at the table, took a clothes brush out of her bag, cleaned the place and returned the brush to her bag. We both burst out laughing and the quarrel was erased.

Sarah knew how to imitate the film actress Betty Grable, who had long and beautiful legs. She'd raise her dress to the knees, swing her bent leg to the side, shake it in the air, put it down, and then the other leg, and I'd choke with laughter. Laughing with Sarah was so good—I didn't know this before. I always sat with adults who had gone through hell in their lives, each one a worse hell than another, and there was no end to their memories of sadness and suffering. Even in the photographs I have in the nylon packet you can see how nicely I'm sitting in the company of adults, my lips about to cry like theirs.

Sarah taught me to laugh with my mouth open. Ha. Ha. Ha. Hee. Hee. Hee. The wrinkles didn't matter. Once we were laughing so hard Mama came in, alarmed: "What's wrong? What's happened?"

She was astonished to find us laughing enthusiastically with all our hearts. I felt free even when Mama made a disappointed face, and I felt completely cheerful when she asked angrily, "Where are you going now?"

I said politely, "Why is Mama asking where I'm going? Did she ever ask Yashu where he was going?"

Mama opened a pair of large eyes and said, "I have no complaints about him; he's a good student." She turned on her heel and went into the kitchen. I held up my head, straightened my shoulders, waved goodbye like the Queen of England, and opened the door without Mama noticing that the princess had gone out into the street. The air I breathed outside was particularly sweet. Sarah called Mama "Vicky", after Victoria, Queen of England, and Yitzhak was "Vicker". When I'd appear at her house on the Sabbath, she'd guess, "Vicky and Vicker aren't getting along again?"

She told me how she'd once come to visit me at home, maybe on a Saturday evening, and I wasn't home. "I saw Vicky lying on the sofa in the living room with a damp cloth on her forehead. Her cheeks were wet. She was holding a handkerchief in one hand and wiping her tears. She was probably crying after a fight with Vicker. I wanted to comfort her. I said to her, 'You're too strong for your husband and maybe it's hard for you to accept that he has a mind of his own.'

"'How could I not be strong?' said Vicky. 'I alone saved two children in the war. For one night's sleep I gave away a solid gold bracelet, yes, that's what I did for them, and that's nothing,' and she continued to weep."

I also saw how much Mama wept. I pitied her and was angry with Yitzhak. I told Yashu that we needed to consider her, help with household chores, and not annoy her. I explained that our lives were still before us, we had a chance for something good. A few days later, Mama was standing in the kitchen cutting a cake she'd made for her guests—it was story night.

"Danusha, put the tea service on the table and fill the little dishes with nuts and cookies," she said, in a voice that had forgotten all her troubles.

I did as she asked, and she began to tell me about one of her friends who had gone traveling in Europe, "Just listen to what happened to her there—"

Suddenly we heard a knock at the door. Sarah stood on the threshold.

"Do you want to go walking with me?" asked Sarah.

I smiled at her and nodded.

"Mama, where's my sweater? I'm going out with Sarah, where is the sweater?"

Mama stopped cutting the cake and looked at me, then at the table that was set. Again she looked at me, and then glanced at the door, and by her eyes I realized she was saying, *What, you're leaving me alone again?*

In the meantime, we went into the eleventh grade and my difficulties with mathematics increased.

At the end of the year, they decided to keep me back a year.

Why? No idea, just because. Mama found a private teacher for me; she hoped the problems with mathematics would be quickly resolved, but this didn't happen.

Sarah went to the seminary. I could also have gone to the seminary, even with my difficulties with mathematics, but I didn't. Why? Because at the time, the seminary wasn't considered as good as high school, where, ultimately, you received a matriculation certificate.

I started eleventh grade again. I wanted to believe I'd get a matriculation certificate, and when I got to the end of the year for the second time, I realized I'd better leave. Deep in my heart I knew I was doing the right thing, and I also knew that I was better off learning alone, as I did in Kraków, when I taught myself to read, helped occasionally by my cousin, Adam. I dreamed of being free, and that's what I did. I left school at the end of tenth grade. But shame found its place under my skin. Didn't go away. Every form I filled in after that, I wrote ten in the column under the number of school years. Girls I knew had completed twelve. Shame followed me like a long shadow. And it hurt. My brother, who had gone to the Bnei Akiva youth movement more seriously than to school, and didn't know English, was hugely successful. Later on, he did his doctorate with ease in America.

Mama was furious with me. "I got you a private teacher, and you stayed back a year. I don't understand it. Why couldn't you study and succeed like Yashu?"

"Why couldn't I be like Yashu?" I yelled at her. "Because I had to take care of you. It wasn't only you taking care of me, and it took all my strength. Who stood by you with a sweet smile, facing people's evil eyes? Who stood by you when you were alone? Who listens to all your stories? Yashu? Do you think after all that I have the strength to study?"

Mama went into her bedroom and slammed the door. I stood there, continuing to shout. I didn't relent.

After I stayed back a year for the second time, Mama began to take action with regard to compensation from Germany. She went to Germany for a week or two and came back. Went for a month and came back. Went for two or three months and came back. Yitzhak was in Tel Aviv; we remained at home, and it was best for us to be together. We took care of each other and felt mature and responsible. We ate lunch with a relative; supper and breakfast we prepared for ourselves.

I enjoyed the quiet in the house. I didn't hear any complaints about the piles of books in my room, or about the clothes scattered on the bed. I could wash the floor whenever I liked, read long into the night in bed. My brother could make a sandwich and leave the crumbs on the counter, throw his shirt and pants on the floor, and bring friends over and make a noise. It didn't disturb me, as long as there was light in every room and cheerfulness.

I spent the money Mama left us on books and candies. Yashu would buy a travel card for the bus or train and go on trips. Particularly if there was a school holiday, Succoth or Passover, and definitely during the summer holidays. He'd go away with Bnei Akiva to get to know Jerusalem, or the Ramon Crater, but also with two friends, to some place they'd decide. Or, more accurately, Yashu would decide and his friends would agree. Mama would barely have left and he'd be poring over maps with friends, planning routes. "We have a beautiful country," he'd report when he came home. He'd throw down his backpack at the door or in the middle of the living room and sit down. It didn't bother me. Once he suggested I join them for a trip, but it wasn't for me. I was embarrassed in front of his friends, and I knew he didn't really want me to come with them.

We approved of Mama's arrangement with Germany. And Mama approved even more. She managed to arrange compensation for herself and for others. She resolved cases that were almost lost with her stubbornness and creativity, and gained many compliments and much respect. I heard a lot about it while doing errands or on the way back, when we met acquaintances who had heard of her miracles.

During one of Mama's trips, on the day she was supposed to return, I washed the floor, cleaning the dirt off the windows as well as under the beds, and then, tired, I lay on the bed in Mama's room. My head slipped off the pillow, I closed half an eye, and in front of me I saw her drawer in the chest of drawers. I was curious. What did Mama have in her drawer? In my drawer I had a mess of books and boring notebooks. What did she have in hers?

Leaning on my elbow, I opened the drawer. There was a book in there and papers. I went through the papers and then, almost at the bottom of the pile, I found a package of letters.

Carefully, I opened the first letter. At the top edge of the paper, on the left-hand side, were the words:

Dr. med. Helmutt Sopp

Underneath was an unfamiliar address and then:

Liebe gute sehr verehrte Frau Anna!

Ah? Beloved, good, dear Frau Anna. I immediately closed it. My heart fell. Mama was communicating with Sopp?

"Yashu?" I called aloud, and went into the living room. "Yashu, where are you?"

Yashu wasn't at home. I'd forgotten—he'd gone south to the Judean desert.

Putting a cube of chocolate in my mouth, I sat down on Mama's armchair and thought, Mama is in Germany. Helmutt Sopp is in Germany. Could they be meeting? Could she have looked for him as she did when we were in Hanover? Could he have found her? In the living room in Haifa, she'd told them about his generous offer to run a clinic with him in Germany. Could he have some new offer for her?

At once I returned to the letters. I opened the first letter and ran through the lines in German. From what I understood, Helmutt Sopp wrote to Mama about his work, took an interest in how she was, asked about us, the children. That's it.

I asked myself why Mama sought him out. Could she have wanted to know what happened to Papa before his death? I hadn't asked Mama if Helmutt Sopp could have saved Papa. Had Mama asked? I have no idea. Perhaps she hoped that Helmutt would tell her what had happened in the prison on the day she sent him to Papa on the pretext that he was her friend's Jewish husband, and she'd mistakenly given him her husband's Jewish name. And could Helmutt have seen Papa's papers with the name Kwiatkowski and understood what Mama was trying so hard to conceal?

Helmutt knew that all the guests in his house—doctors, officers, government officials, and people in various roles, even their wives—everyone knew Mama's name. After all, before his guests, he took pride in the famous Kwiat-cognac that Mama prepared and that he named after her. Could Helmutt have done something to prevent exposing the connection between Papa and Mama, for which she'd been grateful all these years?

Had he wanted to ensure his life after the war by saving a Jewess and her two children?

I wanted a drink of cold water and to talk about it with Sarah. I was ashamed. Better stay silent, I told myself, and heard a knock at the door. I immediately put the letters back in their place.

Sarah arrived, and then Yashu. That night, Mama returned and the following morning she said, "You've cleaned well, Danusha. Come and see the gift I've brought you."

At the café with her friends, I heard her describing her successes in Germany. Once, a friend asked, "And that doctor you told us about, did you meet him?"

Mama smiled with her mouth closed, saying, "It wasn't a time for meetings."

Mama also told us that she'd spent most of her time living in Bronka's family home in Bad Homburg. Franca lives in Belgium. Stella came from Berlin and stayed with Bronka; she was appearing at a concert in the spa town.

"You have no idea what it's like to meet sisters," Mama told her friends. "We were so close to one another, and when we met in Bad Homburg, and we wept at what we went through during the war. We also wept and sang quietly with Stella when she sang arias to a large audience."

Mama stopped, swallowed, and held her throat.

"It was like it used to be, once, a long time ago, when we'd sing in our home in Kraków and our parents were with us, my sister Lydia and our young brother Aharon, may God rest their souls." Mama's voice trembled. She wiped away a tear with her handkerchief and drank some water from the glass I handed her.

"At the end of the concert, the audience clapped Stella with enthusiasm," added Mama, "and of course there was an encore. And then Bronka and I went up on stage and hugged our sister. We wiped each other's tears with a handkerchief. After a day or two, Stella returned to Berlin and I went to Hanover to meet an important director about the issue of compensation."

On Mama's next trip to Germany, I didn't find Sopp's letters in the drawer. Maybe Mama had taken them with her to show her sisters. I remembered how they'd whisper secrets in Franca's kitchen in Kraków during the war.

Mama would bring me gifts that didn't suit me from her trips to Germany. Even when we lived in Hanover, she'd buy me earrings for ears with holes in them. I didn't have holes in my ears. I remember weeping over the gift we both knew wasn't right for me. She also brought me a sweater that was too small, or beautiful boots that were a size too big.

A week or two later, I saw Mama's friend wearing the sweater. "Look at the gift your mother brought me. Beautiful, huh?" said the friend, sticking out her chest.

I was silent. I wanted to yawn.

Yashu received gifts he didn't have to pass on, like a football or battledress suitable for his age.

In letters, however, there were plenty of good words, like the letter I received from Hanover:

Moja droga, cudowna, słodka mamo i droga Yashu…

My dear, wonderful, sweet Mami and dear Yashu,

Have you any idea of how happy I am to receive a letter from you or dear Yitzhak? When you're far from home, you see everything through different eyes and I frequently worry about you. I blame myself for leaving you alone for such long periods, and it makes me happy and calms me to know that you are getting along fine.

You see, my treasures, I've been diagnosed with a medical problem. A doctor found that my left kidney isn't functioning and recommends treatment here. Naturally I refused—there are good doctors in Israel, although Ciocia Bronka and the doctor said I must stay.

And she ended:

I kiss your dear faces and bless you, Mama.

I read the letter and thought, how far Mama has to travel to come closer.

She didn't know that in the meantime I'd learned to manage alone.

Epilogue

In Tel Aviv, once, I saw a German newspaper, *Frau*. It had a column of questions on psychological issues and Doctor Helmutt Sopp was signed under the answers to readers.

I often asked myself about the relationship between Mama and Helmutt, which was like a melody playing throughout her life. Love? Longing? Memories, or a secret?

Had Mama met Helmutt Sopp on her travels to Germany? I have no idea.

After her death, I read in one of the letters how happy Helmutt was to receive Mama's kind letter, which arrived as a very dear gift on his birthday. He was happy that Mama was fine and that the children had grown. And then he wrote that his wife Toni had come to visit from America and they'd talked a lot about Frau Anna, and the great fear of that time. The painful memories preyed on their hearts to this day. Now he and Toni are glad that everyone is healthy and living well. Their sons Peter and Ammon have married and each has two children. About himself, he wrote that he was alone. He'd chosen not to remarry. His work at the practice was very successful, helping him deal with many things. He worked as a psychotherapist, mainly treating cases of depression, which prevented him from leaving his patients. And indeed, he hadn't enjoyed a holiday in many years. But should Mama visit Europe again, she must come to see him. He was living in Nois, not far from the Rhine and the area was really very beautiful.

Later, he thanks Mama for her invitation to visit Israel. He writes that he's thinking about taking a few days off and flying to Israel. He hears from people that the country is very beautiful and he hopes to visit Mama in Tel Aviv.

Helmutt Sopp died aged seventy-one and didn't visit Mama in Israel. Perhaps common sense won.

When I reached the right age, Mama wanted to marry me off quickly, as if there was something wrong with me.

At the last living room in Haifa, before my wedding in front of thrilled guests, I understood that Mama felt best when she was busy saving lives. In the days of the Second World War she was at her best, which was how she felt when traveling to Germany and helping survivors.

That evening, I saw the light in her eyes and the fresh color in her cheeks. She returned to the days of that war in her stories and it occurred to me, could it be that more than anything Mama saved, she herself was saved from boredom, and the lives of others were a breath of fresh air for her?

And who was always nearby to listen?

I was her most loyal audience. I never took my eyes off her, for years. I heard her sing, tell stories, weep, laugh when she imitated acquaintances... Even when we quarreled I stayed near her and didn't leave. It seems I needed Mama's support. When I grew up and wanted to move away from her, she didn't allow it. Perhaps more than I did, she needed my eyes on her?

The last time I sat in the living room before my marriage, I finally realized at the end of the evening that Mama would never ever leave me. That she couldn't live without me, that even if I traveled across the sea, she'd find me. After the wedding, I understood something else: Even if I moved to Tel Aviv and shouted at the top of my voice at her, she wouldn't leave me alone but would make a pact with my husband. And this is what happened.

Only after many years an enormous rainbow opened over my life. With my brother's encouragement, I began to study at university. For the first time, I gave myself permission to go out toward a truly liberated life. To choose. To decide. To feel each moment. And then came a new experience: the sweet, great liberty I was deprived of for so long. I have a good photograph in a fine frame of the MA graduation ceremony at university.

In the picture, I am wearing an elegant white dress of shimmering silk, like a bride. I am wearing a delicate brooch, earrings, and a bracelet; my hair is gathered up with a clip behind and my cheeks are smooth and shining.

I'm holding a certificate on which is written in large letters, university undergraduate and graduate degrees. And I have a large, liberated smile on my face.

My friend Sarah says, "People in the picture are staring."

I am silent.

"Who are they staring at?" asks Sarah, and looks at me. "At whom, Nechama, at whom?"

I am silent.

"At the most beautiful of women," she says and my eyes fill up.

I gave birth to three children—two sons and a daughter, children who are loved. I was amazed to discover that it is natural and possible to love a daughter. Ah, what a wonderful discovery.

One day, I went to a synagogue in Jerusalem.

In the audience, I saw a sweet girl standing silently, wearing a white lace dress.

I looked at the girl and said to myself, look, the girl in the synagogue is you as you once used to be: a sweet, innocent little girl in a white dress with a wreath of flowers on her head.

Tears flowed down my cheeks. What did everyone want from the little girl I used to be? All I tried to do was straighten up, wake up, connect, and at once the blow fell, without my doing anything bad to anyone.

The girl in the synagogue in Jerusalem held her mother's hand. Her shoulder was pressed to her dress. I saw the girl enjoyed standing next to her mother. I saw that the mother enjoyed the girl standing next to her. So what did Mama, Grandma, and Hanchka want from me, ah? I couldn't stop crying.

I often go to concerts, and I weep sometimes, like at the "Rhapsody in Blue" by Gershwin, where the sounds bring a sort of longing, for love? For a dream? And perhaps more than anything, tears of the gratitude I feel for what I have long experienced, that people pay attention to me and accept me as I am, and if they criticize me, I've learned that it isn't the end of the world.

Have I lived? Perhaps too little, perhaps too late. I didn't allow myself to be happy. I said, survive Nechama, survive, that is what's important. All the rest is nonsense. Is it?

When I was a child I walked as closely as I could to Mama. I wanted protection and I got it—I stayed alive.

Mama was the sky above my head, sometimes bright, sometimes shining or twinkling, as well as darkening. She birthed in me a curiosity to know the great world, connecting me to it through languages and melodies.

Mama died at the age of ninety-three, without a single wrinkle in her face. At the funeral, my friend Sarah said: "It seemed as if that woman would live forever. She was larger than life."

Sometimes I look at the picture of Mama and her sisters taken at a relative's wedding. They are wearing stylish clothes with hairstyles and suitable ornaments. Franca, Bronka, and her daughter, and Stella, all smiling into the camera. Mama is also smiling, with her mouth closed.

I gaze intently at Mama's beautiful face. The profound sadness I see in her eyes breaks my heart.

Acknowledgments

I thank Nechama Tiechtel – Danusha – from the very bottom of my heart, for sharing with me her incredible and painful story of survival.

I thank Michal Heruti, my editor, for accompanying me on this fascinating journey, and Modan Publishing House for publishing the Hebrew edition.

I am thankful for Noel Canin for her wonderful and skillful translation of the book.

My special gratitude to Tali and Benny Carmi and the entire team at eBookPro Publishing House for their professional and empathetic guidance in publishing my book worldwide.

And finally, I thank the team at HarperCollins and particularly at One More Chapter for their kind companionship along the way.

The author and One More Chapter would like to thank everyone who contributed to the publication of this story...

Analytics
Emma Harvey
Connor Hayes
Maria Osa

Audio
Charlotte Brown

Contracts
Olivia Bignold-Jordan
Florence Shepherd

Design
Lucy Bennett
Fiona Greenway
Holly Macdonald
Liane Payne
Dean Russell
Caroline Young

Digital Sales
Hannah Lismore
Fliss Porter
Georgina Ugen
Kelly Webster

Editorial
Charlotte Ledger
Lydia Mason
Bethan Morgan
Jennie Rothwell
Tony Russell
Kimberley Young

Harper360
Emily Gerbner
Jean Marie Kelly
Juliette Pasquini
emma sullivan

HarperCollins Canada
Peter Borcsok

International Sales
Hannah Avery
Alice Gomer
Phillipa Walker

Marketing & Publicity
Emma Petfield
Sara Roberts
Helena Towers

Operations
Melissa Okusanya
Hannah Stamp

Production
Denis Manson
Simon Moore
Sophie Waeland

Rights
Lana Beckwith
Samuel Birkett
Aliona Ladus
Agnes Rigou
Zoe Shine
Aisling Smyth
Emily Yolland

The HarperCollins Distribution Team

The HarperCollins Finance & Royalties Team

The HarperCollins Legal Team

The HarperCollins Technology Team

Trade Marketing
Ben Hurd

UK Sales
Yazmeen Akhtar
Laura Carpenter
Isabel Coburn
Jay Cochrane
Sarah Munro
Gemma Rayner
Erin White
Leah Woods

And every other essential link in the chain from delivery drivers to booksellers to librarians and beyond!

Insights, Interviews & More . . .

About the author

Meet Malka Adler

© Malka Adler

Malka Adler was born in a small village near the Sea of Galilee in northern Israel. After taking a creative writing course, she fell in love with the art.

She has written six books, four of which are about the Holocaust. She obtained her undergraduate and graduate degrees in educational counselling at Bar Ilan University and is a family and couples' therapist, writer, and facilitator of several reading clubs.

Malka is married, has three sons and is a grandmother.

Author Q&A

Has your family history influenced your writing?

To this day, I have written four books about the Holocaust. I never quite knew why I was so drawn to the subject, until one year ago. I was staying with my ninety-five-year-old aunt, my father's sister, when I noticed a framed photograph of a young man and woman. When I asked her who they were, she told me they were my grandfather's brother and sister. "The woman was murdered in Treblinka with her three children and you, Malka, are named after her. Didn't you know?"

I didn't know. I'd known I was named after my father's aunt, who I had been told was from Bulgaria. My father had insisted on the name, but I never knew why.

When I asked my older brother whether he had known that our father's relatives had died in Treblinka, he replied that he had not.

He decided to look into the matter and within just a few days, in the wake of my aunt's revelation, traveled to

Author Q&A *(continued)*

Komotini in Greece, a small town near the border with Bulgaria, where our grandfather's family had lived for many years.

When my father was ten, his family relocated from Komotini to Bulgaria in search of better income, and later my father decided to immigrate to the land of Israel as a pioneer. In 1936 he participated in the establishment of a small agricultural settlement—Kfar Hittim, near the Sea of Galilee, together with a group of young Bulgarian pioneers. Two years later, he brought his parents, brother, and sister to Israel.

Then, World War II broke out. In 1943, all the Jews who lived in Komotini in Greece were transported to Treblinka, my grandfather's family among them.

My father knew of the terrible tragedy that had befallen his family, but he and his father chose never to speak of it with us.

And so, my brother traveled to Komotini where he found documents confirming our aunt's

© Malka Adler

The fields of Kfar-Hittim, The Arbel cliff and the Lake of Galilee. Malka Adler's birthplace and childhood views.

story. I was named after my great aunt, who died young with her children. As I said, I had not consciously known, but as a child I went through some strange and extraordinary experiences. My mother used to tell me how there were nights when I would scream, "as though you were being slaughtered, Malka. What were you dreaming?" The entire household would be startled awake in the middle of the night. I never awoke during these episodes and remembered nothing of them come morning. Some nights I would sit up straight at the foot of the bed, shouting angrily in gibberish as though I were speaking in front of an auditorium filled with people. I remembered nothing in the morning, nor did I recall sleepwalking, open-eyed, outside. I would go for a short walk and then return, my mother always in my wake. She took me to doctors who said there was nothing that could be done, that it would pass as I grew older, and warned her not to wake me during these walks, lest she startle me. Naturally, she never allowed me to go to sleepaway camp unless she herself was there, sleeping beside me.

As I grew older, the episodes did indeed pass.

When I started writing Holocaust stories, I couldn't help but feel like I was there. I am always fascinated by programs about the Holocaust. I never leave the house without something small to eat in my purse, and I don't throw food away. It's always in the back of my mind that whatever food remains could go to someone, and if not to a person then at least an animal.

Was the name I was given the cause of these eccentricities? I have no idea. I have a friend who is an astrologist and a psychic, and she claims that giving a person someone else's name can have a great influence on them.

What was your inspiration for writing this book?

This book is based on a true story. I met the heroine at a couples and family therapy convention. We are both therapists and had been invited to watch a comedy show. We sat beside one another by chance—we were not acquainted. At the end of the show, the woman, who introduced herself as Nechama, told me she liked my laugh and would be happy to get to know me. We arranged to meet.

Nechama told me about her childhood in the Holocaust. The topic was of great interest to me, as by that point I had already written three Holocaust books.

A year later, Nechama asked me if I would be willing to write a book detailing her story, as she remembered it. I told her I would be happy to do it, on the condition that it would not be written as a biography, where I would be forced to stick closely to the details and include photographs and documents and publish through a private publisher. Rather, I told her I wished to write a book based on the story of her life, giving me the liberty to include parts of my own imagination, expand on things as I see fit, and write a book that would catch the eye of a known publisher. She agreed.

Nechama is

Malka Adler. In the background – her little village, Kfar Hittim, on the hill overlooking the Lake of Galilee.

Danusha in the book. When World War II broke out she was just over two years old, and she was eight when it ended.

We got to work.

For many long months she came to my house and slowly told me her story. Our sessions were not easy. We touched on painful subjects, including some that had never been touched on by Nechama before. We progressed slowly, carefully, and sensitively, and she touched my heart. More than once we shed some tears, and the further we got the clearer it became to me: my motivation for writing this book was to allow Danusha, for once, to be at the front of the stage. For once, I wanted the spotlight on her. I was pained while listening to her story to hear how she was always behind. Pushed to the side. Quiet. Silenced.

I wanted her to be the heroine.

When the book was published, I was approached for an interview by the weekend column of a big newspaper.

I told the journalist to interview Nechama; to take her photo. And indeed, she was honored with a long and fascinating article and a beautiful picture. I only asked to briefly address the process we'd been through and to relay my important message: Nechama is a true hero. After fighting both an external war and the internal one for her mother's heart, she raised children, studied, became a therapist, and now she helps people. That is true heroism.

The Polish Girl was highly praised in Israel and is recommended by the Israeli Ministry of Education for middle-school and high-school reading.

Reading Group Guide: Discussion Questions for *The Polish Girl*

1. WHAT DO YOU THINK THE CORE themes of this story are?
2. HOW EFFECTIVE IS THE PROLOGUE in establishing these themes?
3. THE BOOK IS SET BETWEEN TWO interweaving timelines – Danusha and her family's ordeal during the war and their struggle to come to terms with it in the narrative present years later – how does this frame shape the reading experience?
4. HOW DOES THE LENS OF THE fraught mother-daughter relationship at the heart of the book affect the overall image of the war and their journey to survive it?
5. THE NARRATIVE VISITS MANY locations in modern-day Poland and Ukraine – how have the events of the story informed your understanding of the complex history of this region?

6. Danusha relishes how she can now look out at huge skies stretching all around her like the sea. She also vividly remembers the lilac tree from Helmutt Sopp's garden and often compares her mother to storm and starlight. What role do nature motifs play in the story and how do they contrast with the brutal realities of the war?

7. The book deals with several complex relationships set against the backdrop of one of the darkest periods in recorded history – what effect does this have on any sense of objective morality?

8. Do you have a favourite scene or description?

9. If there was one more chapter, what do you think would happen?

10. What did you enjoy most about the story? Is "enjoy" the right word?

Don't miss *The Brothers of Auschwitz*, another unforgettable historical novel by Malka Adler following the story of a family separated by the Holocaust and their harrowing journey back to each other.

Dov and Yitzhak live in a small village in the mountains of Hungary, isolated both from the world and from the horrors of the war. But one day in 1944, everything changes. The Nazis storm the homes of the Jewish villagers and inform them they have one hour. One hour before the train will take them to Auschwitz.

Six decades later, from the safety of their living rooms at home in Israel, the brothers finally break their silence to a friend who will never let their stories be forgotten…